KINDLING

MICK FARREN

KINDLING

A TOM DOHERTY ASSOCIATES
BOOK
NEW YORK

KINDLING

A Tor Book
Published by Tom Doherty Associates, LLC
175 Fifth Avenue
New York, NY 10010

www.tor.com

Tor® is a registered trademark of Tom Doherty Associates, LLC.

Library of Congress Cataloging-in-Publication Data

Farren, Mick.
     Kindling / Mick Farren.—1st ed.
          p.   cm.
     "A Tom Doherty Associates book."
     ISBN 0-765-30656-5 (alk. paper)
     EAN 978-0765-30656-2
     1. International relations—Fiction.   2. Imperialism—Fiction.
3. Friendship—Fiction.   4. Youth—Fiction.   I. Title.

PS3556.A7727K56 2004
813'.54—dc22

                                                             2003071142

First Edition: August 2004

Printed in the United States of America

0   9   8   7   6   5   4   3   2   1

KINDLING

ONE

❧

ARGO

Argo Weaver stood in the doorway of the bedroom and pointed the pistol at his stepfather. The two-shot horse pistol, with its long twin barrels and two hammers, was heavy, but his hand was steady and his aim did not falter. Argo Weaver's stepfather snored softly. To say that his mother slept next to the man was an exaggeration. She slept in the same bed, as she had done since Argo's father had been confirmed killed, but she was turned away from the man, as far from him as was physically possible to be and still remain under the same covers. When Argo fired, she would wake screaming. She would be terrified. She might even be spattered by her loveless husband's blood. The effect on his mother, as Argo could picture all too clearly, would be devastating. He had imagined the scene he was now acting out a hundred times since the man called Herman Kretch had come to their house. He would cock both of the pistol's hammers. He would slowly squeeze the first of the triggers, and, in the flash and report, payback would be exacted for all the cruelties large and small that Kretch had inflicted on Argo, his mother, and his sisters. Over and above the personal, to murder Kretch while he slept would also serve as a just punishment for the crime of being a collaborator.

With his left hand, Argo eased back the first of the hammers. The double click-click was loud in the night, and the tone of his stepfather's breathing changed for a moment. He shifted position slightly, but did not wake. Argo waited for a few moments, just to make sure, and then slowly cocked the second hammer. The pistol had been made by George and James Bolton of Jamestown. That information was engraved on the left-hand barrel, and it was dated according to the old Mother Goddess calendar, the use of which had been forbidden since the Mosul occupation and the coming of the men from the Ministry of Virtue. According to his step-father, it was a type of small-bore, double-barreled pistol known as a "cuckold's special." Although, as far as Argo knew, Kretch had never used the gun since he came to their house, he liked ostentatiously to clean it, sipping 'shine and acting the big man. As he ran a strip of oiled rag down one of the barrels and tightened the dual spring mechanisms with a small screwdriver, he had explained to Argo why the weapon had been given such a name. *"You shoot her, and then you shoot him, and then, if you feel like it, you reload and shoot yourself."* But Herman Kretch was not the kind to shoot himself. He held his miserable life in far too high regard.

With the pistol cocked, Argo again took aim, but his finger did not immediately go to a trigger. This was the point beyond which his imagination was increasingly less clear. After the shot, he knew he would run, but what of his mother and two sisters? Herman Kretch was their sole support. The large, raw-boned man with the pot belly, red face, and muttonchop side-whiskers might be a bully, a braggart, and an occasional drunkard, but, for the three women Argo would have to leave behind, life would become close to impossible without him. The Mosul, the Ministry men, and the collaborators who ran things in the occupied territories showed no kindness to the widows and orphans of their defeated enemies and had scant tolerance for those who did. Herman Kretch might be a swine as far as Argo was concerned, but he was not a liar. He had made it very clear when he had proposed marriage to Argo's mother that it was not to be a union of love or even affection. He wanted a strong woman to cook and clean for him, to fetch and carry, and to warm his bed. That she was good-looking only made it an added plus, and that she came to him with three children presented no real problem. Argo, Mathilde, and Gwennie were of an age to be useful, and it made them a source of unpaid labor in these dark times when the conquered worked from morning to night and, even so, barely survived. They were three pairs of extra hands to be exploited in the fields, to help with the livestock, and clean up in the workshop where Herman Kretch repaired boots, shoes, and other leather goods for the Army of Occupation. Argo's stepfather not only kissed the boots of the Mosul, but he mended and shined them, too, along with their saddles and harnesses. He was equally pragmatic and open about his collaboration. *"Hassan IX and his Mosul will take it all in the end. Carolina has gone, and the Virginia Freestate, too. Albany can't hold for long on its own. We may not like it, but Hassan is the future, and we better buckle down and get used to it."*

Without even Kretch to protect them, his mother and sisters could all too easily become three more refugees in the woods and wild places, wandering aimlessly without papers until they starved or worse. Although the worst of the atrocities that had occurred in the direct wake of defeat had been mitigated, the woods were still full of deserters, fugitives, the displaced, and the migrant crazy, as well as the regular Mosul patrols (who fired first and rarely bothered to ask questions), the Indians, who moved like ghosts, and the ghosts themselves. Under Mosul rule, women on their own were vulnerable from every side. Without even the meager rights accorded to the males among subject peoples in the Empire of Hassan IX, carpetbaggers and scallywags could seize their homes and property. The young and comely might simply disappear to serve as an officer's concubine or in the bordellos, cribs, and joyhouses of Savannah and Newport. The old would find themselves driven out to die in the rain. Rape was still a popular pastime among the Mogul grunts, the Mamaluke troopers, and Teuton *uhlans,* although they were now restrained by their captains from the pillage and razing of all but the occasional village or small town. Worst of all, any woman could be fingered as a witch on the most flimsy pretext and hanged if they were lucky, or put to torture and then burned alive if they were not.

The entire chain of events that had led to Argo Weaver standing over his stepfather with a loaded gun and a murderous if wavering resolve had started when, earlier that day, the Ministry men and priests of the Zhaithan had burned Gaila Ford for heresy. The execution by fire of Gaila Ford was by no means the first witch-burning in the village of Thakenham. Even with a population of less than three hundred, the place had still apparently harbored a major complement of women who were deemed by the Zhaithan Ministry of Virtue to constitute a threat and abomination to the Twin

Deities, Ignir and Aksura. The burning of Gaila Ford, however, had been invested with a certain significance. The villagers had talked of nothing else for the two weeks since she had been taken, denounced with full ritual by the Masked Informer, and arrested by the Ministry men backed by a squad of Mosul soldiers from the garrison at Bridgehampton. The collaborators expressed a general opinion that it was a miracle she had survived for so long. Those, like Argo, who had as little to do with the Mosul as they could, held their silence and contained their anger. Argo had known Gaila Ford well. How could he not? Her husband, Henry, and Argo's father, Jackvance Weaver, had gone to the war together. They had enlisted in the same company of the 9th Virginia Freestate Volunteers and had by all accounts died together in the final doomed attempt to hold the Mosul horde at Richmond. Ford had been what was called a handsome woman. She was too mature to be taken as brothel fodder to Savannah, but even Argo, at just fourteen, was well aware that she turned the heads of many men and set them to wondering what she did in her cottage of an evening, all alone, widowed and childless but still obviously in her prime. That alone might have been enough to get her denounced, but worse still, she made it clear to all, in deed if not in word, that she still considered herself a freewoman of the Americas and not a second-class subject of the Mosul Empire.

A number of men had proposed marriage to her just as Herman Kretch had made his overtures to Argo's mother. Without children to consider, she had dismissed these offers out of hand. Apparently she wanted nothing to do with the cowards, gimps, and snivelers who, for their own reasons, had avoided the call to serve. Argo suspected that she might have wed either Jed Pett or Struther Broad, the only two men to return to the village alive, but seemingly neither of the shattered survivors had asked her to take them. Gaila Ford had been well liked by most. She rarely complained, seemed capable of remaining cheerful in impossible situations, and had proved a tower of strength during the winter sickness a year and some earlier. Any one of these qualities would have brought her to the attention of the Ministry of Virtue, and the entire list was more than enough to bring her finally to the flame. Argo loathed to agree with the collaborators, but it really was a miracle she had remained alive and free, at least in her own mind, for as long as she had.

The wood of her pyre had been piled at the north end of the village square, in front of where the church of the Mother Goddess had once stood, and where the Mosul now had their fire tower. The priests of Zhaithan were great believers in lessons taught by example, and the entire village would be assembled in the square, by force if necessary, to witness the prolonged and agonizing death. The only exceptions would be the children and teenagers under fifteen. This was not because the priests or the Ministry men sought to preserve any childhood innocence. They had simply learned by experience in their two centuries of conquest that children were too unpredictable and could be a potential for disruption of the solemnity of the ritual putting-to-death. The younger teenagers were excluded for similar if slightly different reasons. The priests also knew that the boys and girls already passing through the confused rage of puberty were one of the deepest repositories of resentment against the occupation, and if any futile protest was to occur, it would be the young who triggered it. Too full of life fully to grasp the true and absolute reality of death, they were less easily deterred by the muskets and bayonets of the soldiers.

Not that the young of the village could really be prevented from watching the burning of Gaila Ford. It was just that they would not be standing with the adults. Instead, they would be peering through gaps in the shuttered upper-floor windows of the houses around the square. They would be squatting precariously on the thatch or tile of the higher roofs or wedged between trunk and bough of the taller trees. Argo was among the latter. He had hidden himself, along with Will Steed and Jason Halfacre, in the big oak at the other end of the village street from where the flame would be lit. The three of them were in place well before the villagers began to gather and the collaborators checked the parish rolls and the lists of residents to see that none were deliberately staying away. The checking was hardly needed, however, since the morbid attraction of the brutal spectacle was more than enough to overcome any principled and dangerous boycott of the execution. Even those whom Gaila Ford had nursed through the two great bouts of winter sickness would stare transfixed as she died.

Argo's stepfather had specifically forbidden him to go anywhere near the square or the burning. *"The rules are the rules, boy, and, while I personally think it might be an education to you to see the Ford woman get what's coming to her, the rules come first."* Accordingly, Argo had been dispatched with a shovel and a rake to clear the dead leaves that were clogging the ditch at the north end of the top field. In a charade of obedience, Argo had headed for the top field with the designated implements, but only remained by the neglected ditch long enough to hide the tools in the long grass before heading for the village to where he had arranged to meet Will and Jason. He took the long way round so he would not accidentally meet his father along the shorter route. He considered going to watch the burning as an act of open rebellion, but he was still doing all he could not to be caught. Under normal circumstances, Herman Kretch would not have given a damn whether Argo watched the execution or not, but ever since Gaila Ford had been denounced, his behavior had been tense and strange. He had seemed more angry and impatient than usual, and Argo had wondered about this. Herman Kretch was not one to be unduly upset by anything like a witchburning that did not affect him directly, and Argo could only suppose it was nothing more than coincidence. Then, just two days earlier, he had overheard two women gossiping as they waited on the interminable line for their weekly flour ration. A story was apparently circulating that his stepfather had been the Masked Informer who had denounced Gaila Ford, and he had done it because she had rebuffed his advances when he had gone to Ford's cottage one 'shine-drunk night, looking for an alternative bed partner to Argo's mother. Argo hated his stepfather but still found this hard to believe. And how could these women know? The identity of the Masked Informer, with hidden face and in the shapeless robe that dragged along the ground and disguised physical build and even gender, was supposed to be known only to the priests. Argo tried to listen longer, but the women had seen him and lowered their voices.

The tree that the three boys had selected was a tall and venerable oak on which village lovers had, in happier times, made it a practice to carve their linked initials. It was at the opposite end of the square from where the execution would take place, and it afforded them a better view than that of many of the adults on the ground. Argo, Will, and Jason had arranged to be in position early, well before the majority of the villagers had arrived, so they would not be spotted clambering into the high branches. They had lain and stared through the late summer foliage as the square rapidly filled with drab and ragged people who seemed to carry their air of defeat around with them like a collective shroud. As the crowd entered the square, the men went to the right and the women to the left. He saw his mother and stepfather dividing and going their separate ways. The onlookers were strictly divided by sex, and even couples had to separate until the burning was over. This segregation was enforced at all Zhaithan gatherings and assemblies. Argo had never understood why this had to happen, and no one older had ever been able to give him a reason, but many things ordered by the Mosul conquerors had no discernable reason except maybe to degrade and humiliate those under their rule. The women in the square far outnumbered the men, but that was the way of it in the wake of the terrible slaughter that had come with the Mosul invaders. The Mosul also tended to take their time where subject peoples were concerned, and, by Argo's estimate, the crowd had been kept standing in silence for at least a half hour before Gaila Ford was finally brought out from the two-storey building on the northwest corner of the square that, in the old days, had been the constable's station and the village lock-up but was now draped with the black flags and the red flame insignia of Hassan IX and served the local office of the Ministry of Virtue.

Many who had been held by the Ministry men for a full two weeks had to be carried to their deaths, but Gaila Ford emerged walking, wearing the paper shift and headdress of the condemned heretic. She had undoubtedly been repeatedly tortured during her imprisonment, but, although plainly weak and unsteady, she seemed determined to go out standing tall. A red-robed priest kept pace on either side of her, and two lines of soldiers flanked her as she was led to where the wood was stacked around the base of the iron A-frame and the metal ramp that led up to it.

Abomination!
Abomination!
Abomination!
Abomination!
Abomination!
Abomination!

For a moment she faltered. One of the priests gripped her arm to steady her, but she shook free. With what had to be the very last of her strength, Gaila Ford was plainly demonstrating to them all, including her anonymous betrayer, that she had not been broken, even by the Ministry torturers. Argo could feel tears welling up in his eyes, but he quickly wiped them away before either Jason or Will noticed. She mounted the ramp that led to the hideous scaffold of blackened metal, and then stood in front of the instrument of her destruction, motionless, with her back to the chanting crowd. The two priests followed Gaila Ford up the ramp. One quickly turned her around while the other beckoned to a pair of already-designated Mosul soldiers to come and secure the chains at her wrists, waist, and ankles that would hold her in place for the consuming fire. Her arms were stretched above her head and her legs pulled apart so her body conformed to the up-pointing triangle of the scaffold. Gaila Ford neither resisted nor made any further protest. She had gone to her end with all the dignity that she could summon, and now she seemed resigned. Once her chains were locked, a third soldier moved forward with a red-painted can of kerosene. He thoroughly doused the wood at Gaila's feet and then splashed the last of the flammable liquid down the front of her body. As it soaked into the heretic's shift, the paper became close to transparent. She was plainly naked beneath the ritual garment, and the crowd fell silent at the sight until the Ministry man signaled curtly for the second phase of the death chant as the priests and soldiers moved back from the pyre and left Gaila Ford alone with her fate.

Burn the witch!
Burn the witch!

The chant was hesitant at first, but, under the grim gaze of the priests and soldiers, it grew in baleful intensity, as though the villagers were being forced to beg for their own oppression.

Burn the witch!
Burn the witch!
Burn the witch!
Burn the witch!
Burn the witch!

The first fire was taken directly from the Zhaithan sacred flame. While a prayer was offered up to Ignir and Aksura, a bundle of oil-soaked rags on the end of a Mosul pike was thrust into the hemispherical bowl mounted on the tall, tapering pylon. When the rags were thoroughly ignited, the pike was carried to the pyre and applied to the wood. Rumor had it that, now and again, a merciful executioner would rapidly strangle the victim before they burned. Either that was a lie, or no mercy had been shown in Gaila's case. The kerosene caught with an explosive sigh and a first eager fireball, and then, as it took a fuller hold, Argo had his last glimpse of Gaila contorting against the chains that held her, before her helpless figure was hidden by the conflagration. The flames burned orange, and the black smoke rose to stain the already-grey sky. A capricious wind suddenly swirled a loose smoke vortex down and directly into the square, filling the village with the stench of kerosene and burned flesh. The assembled villagers coughed, and some actually gagged, but the Ministry men refused to dismiss them. At that moment, Argo Weaver knew he could no longer stay in this place. He knew he had to run, he had to go north, he had to try and make it across the now-stalled-and-static battle lines where Carlyle of Albany was still managing to hold back the Mosul advance. Argo was as aware as any fourteen-year-old could be aware that the odds were probably against him making it. More likely he would be picked up by a patrol or lose himself in the wilderness, but at fourteen he didn't play the odds, and even if he did, what did he really have to lose? With a teenager's optimism he pictured himself finding one of the secret ways through the Mosul lines which, according to rumor and hearsay, would bring him to the free territory of the Kingdom of Albany. He saw himself, brave and dashing in the uniform of the Albany Royal Guard, in the vanguard of the long-awaited advance that would put Hassan IX to total rout and push him and his unholy legions back into the Northern Ocean, or perhaps, somewhere in the woods or wilderness, he would make contact with the partisans, the guerrillas of the resistance, the ones whom the Mosul called bandits. On a sudden impulse, he began swinging down out of the branches of the old oak. He did not care if he was seen; he just wanted to be away from the smoke and the stench, the cringing villagers. Will called after him in surprise. "Hey, Argo, where you going?"

Argo looked up and realized that he was never going to see Will Steed again. "I'm going north, Will. I'm going north."

Will wanted to know what he meant, but Argo was already on the ground and slipping away between two buildings. Once clear of the village, he hurried, heading for home, but when the house and barn were in sight, he remembered that his stepfather would not be back from the village, and Argo did not want to be there when Herman Kretch returned from the burning. If he had not been drinking already, he would undoubtedly start. Argo changed direction and began walking more slowly in the direction of what the boys called Hunchback Hill. The high ground provided him with a view of both the village and his home, and as he squatted down on the short grass, settling himself to wait, an unbidden but very clear and absolute feeling came over him. He was looking at the two places, really the only two places that he had ever known, aside from the journeys in the old days to market at Bridgehampton, and he was looking at them for the last time in this prelude to his departure.

The Ministry men must have finally dismissed the villagers, because Argo saw a small swarm of dark figures moving away from the cluster of houses and other buildings that constituted the center of Thakenham. With the strange insight that seemed to have overtaken him, Argo realized that he truly hated the people among whom he had been born and raised. He hated their submission and their willingness to surrender, and the way they could watch, so ragged, drab, and unmoving, a horror like the burning of Gaila Ford without doing or saying anything except coughing and grimacing when the smoke billowed too thick or the stench of death became too gaggingly unbearable. With the natural intolerance of youth, he could feel nothing but contempt for the way that the villagers would endure anything, even slavery in all but the name, in order to survive, and how they lacked the courage to stand up to their oppressors and die with some degree of dignity and while shreds of honor still remained.

The Mosul had come soon after Argo's eleventh birthday. The invasion force had landed near Savannah on July 5th '96 by the old and now-forbidden Mother Goddess calendar, and, on that hot summer day, the world had changed forever. The Mosul had immediately established multiple beachheads and then fanned out to cut through the courageous but disorganized forces of the Southland Alliance in a matter of days. Within a month, Atlanta had fallen, and, with Florida cut off and the infamous treaty concluded with George Jebb and his gang of traitors in St. Petersburg,

Hassan IX had turned his attention and his armed might to the north, in the direction of the rich lands between the Appalachians and the ocean. The Southland Alliance, although doomed, had bought time for the Republic of the Carolinas and the Virginia Freestate to marshal their troops and to mount a more concerted defense. For seven bloody months, battle after battle had raged, and at the height of the terrible Winter Campaign of '97 it had actually seemed as though the Mosul would be pushed back, but an armada of troopships, under steam and sail, continued to bring what appeared to be limitless divisions of battle-hardened men and inexhaustible supplies of munitions. The ships of the Flame Banner shuttled back and forth across the Northern Ocean from Cadiz and Lisbon and other ports in conquered Hispania, protected from the privateers of the Norse Union, the small but effective Royal Albany Navy, and the pirates up from the Caribbean by formidable escorts of ironclads. It appeared that all of Southern Europe, if not North Africa and Asia Minor, was being stripped of men and machines to feed Hassan IX's megalomaniac conquest of the Americas.

The outcome was probably inevitable. Volunteer farmers, miners, and merchants, a few mountain men, hunters, and traders, and their mostly amateur and inexperienced officers, were no match for Hassan's highly disciplined and religiously motivated blitzkrieg. The men of Virginia might be brave and strong, they might be crack shots, and, one on one, as they had so often and proudly boasted in the early days of the conflict, worth any ten Mosul, but they had gone to war with a fatally imprecise idea of what manner of foe they faced. Two hundred years of carnage might have come and gone since the Mosul, originally tribal nomads from an area to the east of the Black Sea, had advanced into Europe with fire and sword and formed their unassailable alliance with the Teutons of Germany and the Mamaluke warlords in North Africa to subjugate the land of the Franks, the city states of Italia, and all of the Hispanic Peninsula. Somehow the people of the Americas had felt immune to the danger. They had become too safe in their supposed isolation and too confident of the broad protection of the ocean. Many of the American settlers' parents, grandparents, and great-grandparents might have crossed the seas as a direct result of the Mosul terror, but even that had not equipped them to face down the most murderous and implacable war machine the world had ever had the misfortune to see, or to defeat the Mosul's iron discipline, fanatic religious motivation, and honed battle tactics. Through the spring of '98, the tide of conflict had turned against the defenders, until, fighting little more than desperate rearguard actions, and constantly regrouping as their numbers were decimated, they had fallen back on Richmond for the last battle of a war that seemed to have taken on the towering melancholy of a grand and tragic opera. On May 10th, all hope for Virginia and the Carolinas had gone with the wind as the last stand had collapsed to relentless shot and shell followed by butchery and fire.

In Thakenham, the war had seemed to happen in a number of phases. At first, life had seemed strangely routine and eerily close to normal. The majority of the men might have gone off to the September start of the war, boasting that they would be home well before Solsticetide, but the cows still had to be milked, the eggs collected, the hogs slopped, the bread baked, and the beer brewed. Dogs still barked, babies still cried, roofs leaked when it rained, and eleven-year-old boys roamed the woods and fields playing soldier and wishing they were men already, so they could go off gloriously campaigning like their fathers. In the beginning all had been optimism. The headlines of the broadsheets and the wireless broadcasts had always trumpeted imminent victory and continued to promote the happy certainty that the Mosul would be driven into the sea by the end of the year, but some of the volunteers' letters home were less sure. They had hinted that the fighting was far more grim and a lot less decisive than the official reports wanted it to be. By October, the first casualty lists had been posted on the public notice board in the village square, but, since none of those listed were Thakenham men, no one paid them too much mind. As the days grew shorter, and the lists of the dead and missing grew longer, however, the atmosphere changed. The official reports now stressed the heroic rather than the victorious, and those, like Argo's mother, who were capable of reading between the lines of the propaganda, knew that which was already bad was rapidly turning worse.

Even blind optimism had to cease when the casualty lists were no longer posted, the broadsheets were no longer distributed beyond the confines of Richmond and Lynchburg, and the wireless played music more than the repetitively grim war news. Although the fighting never passed through their village, the residents of Thakenham had heard the sound of the guns in the distance, at first from the south, but then moving up and past them, and finally booming from the north. Exhausted soldiers, in small groups, squads, and companies, had trudged up the Bridgehampton Road on their way to whatever place had been selected for their next attempt to contain the invaders. Argo had stood beside his mother with a hand on her shoulder as the ragged lines of retreating men had tramped through the village. He had looked for his father among the walking wounded, but his father had never come. At the start of the retreat, the columns were still organized by regiment. Argo could tell that by their uniforms and collar tabs, but, as the enemy front rolled deeper and deeper into Virginia, and company after company, and battalion after battalion, were wiped out by the iron Teuton land-crawlers, the savage Mamaluke cavalry, the jogging columns of implacable Mosul foot soldiers, and the Dark Things that no one dared name, the squads became cobbled together from all the survivors who could be rounded up and sent back to the lines. Now old men and boys only a couple of years older than Argo were being sent to face the foreign invaders.

One late afternoon, a group of about forty men had passed through town, and Argo had recognized that some were wearing the patches of the 9th Virginia. He ran up and grabbed one of them by the torn sleeve of his tunic. "Hey Mister, do you know Jackvance Weaver?"

The soldier had looked at him with a blank, ghost-haunted stare. "I don't know no one no more, kid."

"He was in the 9th Virginia."

The soldier quickened his pace, wanting to get away from Argo and his questions. "I told you, kid. I don't know no one."

"He's my father."

The man halted and looked down at Argo. He sighed and shook his head. "Kid, we've got good men scattered all the way from here to hell, and most of them are either dead or on their way to Richmond, which is the next best thing. My best advice to you is to stop hoping. It's maybe the dead who should be grateful."

Around the time of this encounter, the people of Virginia had started looking for a miracle. To the north was the Kingdom of Albany, with supposedly large and quite formidable forces massed on the banks of the Potomac River. In the snug and smokey inns, in parish meeting rooms, and around the home fires the same question was asked over and over. *"Why doesn't Albany come?"* It was asked the loudest by the cowards and slackers, the ones like Herman Kretch, who had remained safe at home while others like Jackvance Weaver did the fighting and the dying. *"Why doesn't Albany come?"* What Herman Kretch did not know, or anyone else in Thakenham, and only a very few in all of the lands that were under threat or had already fallen, was that Albany was not going to come. General James Dean, known simply as the Old Man, who, after a long and distinguished career exploring and mapping the interior, had taken command of the Army of Richmond, had met in secret with King Carlyle II and his staff and had come to a logical if desperate decision. Even with a fresh army from Albany added to Dean's battle-weary troops, Richmond could not stand. *"Why doesn't Albany come?"* Because at best they might turn a futile final battle into a few more weeks of equally futile final siege. In the long run, such a move could only increase the numbers of the dead. Richmond could not be rescued, and Carlyle would save his strength for an attempt to stop Hassan at the Potomac.

The night that Richmond fell, church bells all through Virginia had rung for an hour, in an eerie peal, and then stopped. It was like a signal. *No more.* All motion ceased for about five days, as though the world was holding its breath. In that last terrible month, the last time they were allowed to call it May, even spring itself seemed to pause and wait while a steady and unrelenting late-winter rain had fallen. And then the first Mamaluke column had ridden into the village. Thakenham had been lucky. The previous night they had sacked and burned Coster's Mill, indulging to the full in all the rape and murder for which they had become notorious. Swarthy and stone-faced, the hard horsemen with their spiked helmets and eagle-beak noses were seemingly sated and too hungover to engage in yet another orgy, and they had simply posted the orders of occupation and moved on. A few days later the priests had come, along with their retinue of Mosul soldiers and the men from the Zhaithan Ministry of Virtue, to begin setting up the frightening network of spies and informers that maintained the political and philosophical Mosul armlock on their subject peoples.

Suddenly more columns of men were on the move, details of chained prisoners, guarded by detachments of armed and whip-wielding troops, going in both directions, some headed north to perform slave labor under the direction of Teuton engineers digging trenches and bunkers on the Mosul side of the Potomac, while others were driven south to Savannah to work on the construction of the citadel that would be Hassan IX's capital in the new world. And it was from one of these starved and wretched prisoners that the first word had come that both Jackvance Weaver and Hank Ford had been blown to pieces by Mosul cannon as they had taken part in the final stand before the gates of Richmond. Then and only then had his mother cried, and only in private, away from the spying eyes of the other villagers.

As Argo sat on Hunchback Hill, reflecting on all that had gone before, a half-formed vision came to him, unbidden, for no reason he could fathom. The face of a girl appeared to his inner sight, a girl with red hair and the kind of skin that freckled when it was too long in the sun. Argo did not know the girl, but she was not exactly a stranger. She had the familiarity of a dream dreamed more than once, or some glimpse of encounters and adventures to come. Argo set no store by stuff like prescience and prophecy, but he simply recognized, with the most certain and matter-of-fact intuition, that he would see the red-haired girl again, either in dream or reality. Kretch and his mother had now been home for some time, and smoke was rising from the chimney of the house, but Argo continued to sit, clasping his knees and thinking. He decided it would be better to wait until well after dark before he went back inside. If his stepfather was drinking 'shine, the possibility existed that he would have drunk himself unconscious if Argo delayed his return. Thus Argo continued to sit until the moon rose, and only then did he slowly descend the hill. Unfortunately, he had failed to delay long enough. The moment his weight caused the porch to creak, his stepfather was snarling in the doorway. "Defy me, would you, you little bastard? Get in here."

The razor strop lay in full view on the kitchen table, right beside the lamp. The message was plain. Somehow Herman Kretch had found out that Argo had been to the execution instead of cleaning out the ditch by the top field, and now a beating was inevitable. The razor strop was his stepfather's favorite instrument of discipline, and when he swung it at Argo's bared buttocks it hurt like hell and left welts like the mark of a brand. Argo inhaled deeply and took comfort in the fact that it would be the last thrashing that Kretch ever inflicted on him. Without a word, he turned on his heel and started back for the door, but his stepfather immediately wanted to know what he was doing. "Where are you going?"

Argo looked back, slack-faced and sullen, failing to understand. Surely it was obvious? "To the root cellar, sir."

Usually his stepfather conducted this kind of punishment down in the root cellar in comparative privacy, but it appeared that tonight he had a greater humiliation in mind. Maybe unpleasantly inflamed by the execution and the 'shine he had put away in the aftermath, he had added cruelty on his mind. "Right here, boy. You'll take your medicine right here."

Argo could hardly believe what he was hearing. The beating was going to be carried out right there in the family kitchen, in front of the big stone hearth and in full view of his mother and sisters? "No!"

"What did you say, boy?"

Argo saw the looks of horror on the faces of the women and shook his head. "Not here."

"Right here."

Argo's mother got to her feet. "I'm taking the girls outside."

Kretch glared at her. "The hell you are. You sit right back down there, or it'll go worse for the boy."

His mother summoned a nervous defiance. "You can make me sit here, but the girls don't need to watch this."

"They'll learn what to expect when they're bigger and maybe decide they can defy me."

Argo's mother gestured to Mathilde and Gwennie. "Outside, girls."

"You want me to have his papers revoked? You want them to see their precious brother marched off in chains to a labor camp?" Kretch's threat was no idle one. Argo only remained in the comparative safety of Thakenham because Kretch had used his collaborator's clout with the Ministry of Virtue to ensure that Argo was not sent off to forced labor in Savannah or set to digging trenches beside the Potomac. Argo's mother sat back down again with a face like stone and gathered the girls to her. Content with his victory, Kretch turned his attention to Argo. "Shuck those britches, boy, and grab your ankles."

Argo did as he was told, trying to think of nothing, trying to forget that his mother and sisters were right there to witness his exposed humiliation. He stared straight into the fire as Kretch slapped the strop into his palm as though testing it, even though, after all the other times he had used it, no testing was needed. Argo was determined to give the man as little satisfaction as possible, even if it prolonged the punishment, but he could not help but gasp as the first blow seared his taut skin. As blow followed blow, to Argo's blurred and tear-distorted vision, the flames of the log fire leapt with each searing cut of the leather and each wide-burning stripe. The flames danced before him just as they had danced around the chained form of Gaila Ford before they had consumed her. After what seemed like an eternity, his stepfather finally tossed the strop onto the table. "Pull up your pants, boy. That's your medicine for tonight. Remember it the next time you get an urge to ignore what I tell you."

The fabric was rough on his throbbing flesh, but Argo again tried to hide the hurt. His mother was on her feet, bustling the girls out of the room. As Argo buckled his belt, Kretch jerked a dismissive thumb. "Now thank me and get out of here."

Argo stared at the floor, unable to look his stepfather in the face, but he stubbornly shook his head. "No."

Kretch actually laughed and poured himself a drink. "Well, you've got some stones and no mistake. You want the same all over again?"

"No, sir."

"So thank me and get to your bed."

"I knew Gaila Ford."

"We all knew Gaila Ford, boy. We knew her, and now she's scattered ashes, and good riddance as far as I'm concerned. She wasn't the first, and she won't be the last. Now thank me for your beating or get those breeks down for a double dose. It's your choice."

Argo wished he had the strength to endure a second thrashing just to show the bastard he couldn't be intimidated. But he knew a second time around, Kretch would whip him bloody. With the taste of gall in his mouth, he spoke to the wood of the floor in a monotone. "Thank you, sir. Thank you for my beating."

As he fled from the room, Kretch crowed after him. "You can't win, boy. You know that, don't you? You can't win."

Argo lay for the longest time in his narrow bed, blanket thrown back despite an early autumn chill, his flesh throbbing but a cold resolve hardening to the point that it couldn't be denied. This was the night that he would not only run from Thakenham, but kill Herman Kretch in his bed while he slept. He only slipped from his bed when the house was silent, and Argo was certain the rest of the family slumbered. He took the big canvas satchel that he had used for his schoolbooks before the Mosul had come and closed the school, and moved silently through the house, gathering what he thought he needed to survive in the wild: spare shirts and socks, beef jerky and hard crackers, a slab of cheese, the old water bottle that had belonged to his father, a lighter and spare flints. Finally he had taken the pistol and all of Kretch's ammunition from the hiding place in back of the linen press. Leaving his boots and bundle by the door, and moving silently in his stockinged feet, he had slowly climbed the stairs and gone to the bedroom where Kretch and his mother slept.

From the doorway he pointed the pistol. He cocked both hammers, but before pulling either trigger he had paused. In theory it had all seemed so easy. A hundred times, Argo had pictured himself standing over his stepfather with the twin barrels pointed true and unwavering as he slowly squeezed the trigger. Except he simply could not pull even the first of the twin triggers. So many factors crowded in: the womenfolk alone, the hue and cry that would follow him as a murderer rather than just a boy runaway, the very fact that perhaps he was not ready to take the life of another human being. He knew he was not, in the end, going to shoot Herman Ketch. He might feel like a traitor to his own anger, but he knew he could run but not yet kill. He lowered the pistol and carefully released one hammer and then the second. He hurried down the stairs, stepped into his boots, shrugged into his jacket, hooked the satchel over his shoulder. His last move was to stick the pistol in his belt. He might not be able to kill Kretch, but he would steal his gun, the gun that meant so much to the drunken bastard. Argo Weaver opened the door and stepped out into the night. A dog barked in the distance.

CORDELIA

Lady Cordelia Blakeney had paid a seamstress a full forty shillings for the alterations to her new uniform. If judged according to the most stringent interpretation of the dress regulations of the Royal Women's Auxiliary, it fitted a little too snugly to the most crucial parts of her body, but RWA officers like Cordelia, assigned to permanent posts in the capital, either at the War Office or the Headquarters of the General Staff, were permitted some considerable laxity in matters like dress regulations and overnight passes. The Kingdom of Albany might be at war, but that did not mean the social waltz and romantic entanglements in and around Albany Castle and the court of Carlyle II had been completely discontinued. Indeed, they had actually taken on an increased sense of immediate urgency. In wartime, the sense of living for and in the moment was a kind of heightened reality that came with the knowledge that, without reason or warning, death might snatch the moment away and leave nothing but grief on one side of the affair and oblivion on the other. The young men came and went with dizzying if delicious rapidity, moving on a five-stage circuit between the royal castle at Albany, to the field headquarters at Frederick, the great port of Manhattan, the equally crucial base at Baltimore, and the front itself. Only a week earlier she had been consoling her cousin Daphne, who was devastated to the point of hysteria after her current lover, a captain in the Intelligence Corps, had been lost on a mission across the Potomac. This week, Daphne was sufficiently recovered to be pursuing a major in one of the newly formed tank regiments.

Cordelia checked herself in the full-length mirror in the ladies room on the second floor of the War Office building. The delegation from the Norse Union had arrived, and First Lieutenant the Lady Cordelia Blakeney wanted to look her best. Although field green was not the most flattering of colors, it was the best that could be done in wartime, and it did not do a total disservice to her red hair and pale skin. Unfortunately, her stint as driver for Colonel Blackwood had put her a little too much in the late-summer sun, and, even now that her duties put her back inside the castle and the War Office, a dusting of freckles still covered her nose. She knew some men found freckles cute, but she would have preferred her complexion to be a flawless porcelain. That, however, was not possible. The rules of the RWA might be fairly lax, but the use of excess makeup was frowned upon among junior officers, no matter how highborn. All in all, though, Cordelia was fairly pleased with herself. Her buttons and insignia gleamed, her epaulets hung just right, her tunic nipped in her waist to perfection, and the tighter-than-regulation pencil skirt left only a minimum to the imagination of any Norse naval commander or Air Corps major. She twisted around for a glimpse of the backs of her legs. Silk stockings were scarce, and she wanted to be assured that the seams of the ones she had were straight. She hoped that at least one of the Norse officers had enough unscrupulous practicality to bring a supply with him, along with the good Scotch whiskey they usually handed out as gifts. The Norse were rapidly emerging as the possible saviors of Albany, perhaps of all the Americas, in much more than just Scotch and silk stockings. Although in Europe they maintained an uneasy peace with the Mosul Empire, with the English Channel as the dividing line between their conflicting spheres of influence, the Norse were moving closer and closer to an open alliance with Albany to halt Hassan IX's invasion of the New World.

The Norse were far fewer in number than the Mosul, and controlled a great deal less territory, but they had technology and heavy industry, and that gave them an increasing edge. The Mosul, strangled by the constraining coils of their disgusting religion, failed to progress. The Zhaithan priests were hard-pressed to tell a scientist from a heretic, and that completely stifled all research and innovation. The foundries of Damascus and the Ruhr turned out cannon and musket twenty-four hours a day, but they produced only crude quantity, and nothing to compare with the sophistication of the repeating rifles being developed in Birmingham and Stockholm or the keels of the submarines being laid in the shipyards along the Clyde. The courtship between Albany and the Norse was a slow one, but progress was definitely being made. Already the prefabricated parts of Norse gasoline-powered tanks were being delivered to the port of Manhattan by cargo ship and assembled in a huge, roaring factory complex in the city of Brooklyn. Norse Air Corps instructors were training the crews of Albany's first small squadron of airships, and cadres of officers from Albany were attending advanced command schools in London and Stockholm, learning to apply the use of these new weapons on the battlefield and in naval tactics on the high seas. The wedding of Albany and the NU was inevitable. Their people came from the same stock, and shared culture and customs. Many spoke an approximation of the same language, and the two nations could only move closer together in the face of the common threat. On a personal level, Cordelia only hoped the process would be considerably faster.

She emerged from the ladies' room into a busy second-floor corridor and ran straight into Coral Metcalfe. Cordelia and Coral had been friends since they had been little girls. The two had gone to different schools and been separated, except at holiday times, through their teen years, but now their war work caused them once again to move in the same circles. Metcalfe was a chronic gossip and something of a ladylike slut, although Cordelia, with her record of conquests, was hardly one to judge. On this particular morning, Coral seemed especially excited. "Have you seen them yet?"

Cordelia did not have to ask whom. She was well aware that Coral was talking about the newly arrived Norse delegation. Coral was very taken with everything Norse, particularly young English-speaking officers. "No, not yet. Have you?"

Coral Metcalfe nodded enthusiastically. "I managed to tag along with the reception committee, and, oh, my dear, there are a couple of real dolls among their number."

"Really?"

"Really."

Cordelia smiled. "I'll be there later when they meet with the king and Jack Kennedy."

"Lucky you, you'll get to speak to them."

Cordelia nodded. "Or die trying."

Coral looked at her watch. "Got to go, darling. I'm in trouble already."

With that, Coral Metcalfe hurried away. The girl always seemed to be late for something. She had been late all her life. She also reminded Cordelia that she, too, was supposed to be somewhere and had better not linger. The morning promised to be deary. It would be spent filling manpower reports and approving supply requisitions, but by noon she would be on her way to the castle for the start of the vital conference between the Norse Union delegates led by Vice President Ingmar Ericksen and the king and his ministers. Cordelia had wangled things so she was one of the squad of RWA girls who'd be there to fetch things, organize the distribution of papers and the spreading of maps, but, above all, to look decorative and put the Norse officers in the most pleasant of moods. The king wanted a consignment of the highly secret Norse rocket bombs, while the girls of the RWA, with the possible exception of that little prig and professional virgin Pamela Stanley, simply wanted the Norse.

Leaving nothing to chance, Cordelia signed out of her office at eleven forty-five and took the public tram the five blocks to the castle. The war had brought a considerable social leveling to the Kingdom of Albany. In the old days she would rather have walked than take the trolley, but now she grabbed one of the brass rails and swung herself onto the rattling, clanging, slow-moving conveyance as though she'd been doing it all her life. With their backs to the wall, the people of Albany faced a grim reality, and no room remained for the putting on of airs. As the trolley car rattled up Mason Street, the sky was overcast and promised rain. Cordelia had neglected to bring a raincoat, but she did not let that dampen her spirits. Even if the skies opened, some officer would undoubtedly be gallant enough to drape his trench coat over her shoulders to protect her from the weather. Nothing was more attractive than a damsel distressed by a downpour. As she rode the trolley and anticipated the afternoon and evening to come, Cordelia stared at the passing streets and reflected on how one could never mistake Albany for anything but a city at war. The high percentage of uniforms on the sidewalks, the army trucks and the drab green military steamers that jammed the streets, the recruiting posters and patriotic billboards that had replaced most commercial advertising, all told of a people in a high order of military readiness. But Albany was also a city with a certain optimism. In the dark days after the Battle of Richmond and the fall of Virginia and the Carolinas, a desperation had been in the air, a sense that it was only a matter of time before the Mosul rolled on over Albany. But then the enemy had been halted at the Potomac, and everyone had breathed again. Two years of stalemate had not been easy. Albany threw everything it had into the war effort, galvanized by the knowledge that the Mosul attack could come at any time, but with the domestic military buildup and the tacit support of the NU, a feeling had spread that, when the Mosul came, as, without doubt, they sooner or later would, Albany would be in a position to repulse their assault, and the essential spine of their invasion could be broken. If that happened, it would only be a matter of effort and resolution to push the invaders back the way they had come, down through Virginia and the Carolinas and ultimately into the sea.

Cordelia dropped off the trolley in front of the Calder Street gate of the castle and showed her pass and identity card to one of the military policemen standing guard. Before the invasion, before the war, she, her family, and the other highborn of Albany, had thought of Calder Street, with its iron portcullis guarding the dark and narrow tunnel through the high stone wall, as the tradesmen's and servants' entrance, its use somewhat beneath their aristocratic dignity. But that was definitely no longer the case. During the panic over the possibility of Mosul suicide attacks that had swept the capital in the first months after the landings in Savannah, it had been decided that the Grand Gate, flanked by its statues and carved lions, was too open and vulnerable, and it had been closed and sealed for the duration. All who had business in the castle, even visiting dignitaries and the king himself, had, from then on, come and gone through Calder Street.

Like so many of the dire imaginings in those early days, the anticipated suicide attacks had never materialized, but the custom of using the tunnel had remained, as had the squads of MPs, the hastily erected sandbagged gun emplacements, and the twin multibarreled Bergman guns that were capable of sweeping the entire length of Calder Street with a deadly and sustained hail of one-inch cannister shot. Rumor also insisted that land mines had been laid beneath the flagstones that could seal this single public access in a chain of massive explosions, and each and every time Cordelia passed though the dark space, she could not help wondering if she really was walking over a ton or more of explosives, nor recalling that the fact that she, just like everyone else, was now using the same route to enter and leave a Castle that was foremost among the last solid symbols of freedom and equality in the Americas.

Before the war, Cordelia had been little more than a child, a spoiled aristocrat brat with a title and a self-centered petulance who believed she had a right to anything and everything she might demand. Before the danger had brought its sobering dose of hard reality, she had lived on whim, caprice, and an overbearing belief in the complete and unquestionable superiority of her class. The horrors of those early days, especially the fall of Atlanta and the example of the hideous fate that had befallen that unfortunate city's ruling class, had been a lesson in survival that had mercifully been quickly learned by lady and servant alike. The Mosul atrocities had made it painfully clear to Lady Cordelia Blakeney, her friends, relatives, and all of those like her, that their airs, graces, and hereditary lineage would not save them from the shot and shell, nor from the rape, pillage, and fire that would inevitably follow. As the tales of the hanged, the burned, and the gruesomely impaled were carried north to Albany, the whole of the nation's social structure saw, with a terrible clarity, that to continue as they were would be to court as sure and certain a doom as had destroyed all the lands to the south.

With a weird irony, the arrival of the Mosul hordes had saved the Kingdom of Albany from itself. Without the external threat of foreign invasion to unite them, the country had been tottering closer and closer to the edge of revolution with the reeling determination of a self-destructive drunkard, and Carlyle I, the father of their present king, was perhaps the self-destructive drunkard in question. In the early part of his reign, he had been sufficiently dashing that his self-indulgent extravagance and narrow autocratic perspectives had been dismissed as nothing more than youthful swagger, but as he grew to full maturity, it had become clear that neither his attitudes nor his behavior were going to change. Even the aristocracy knew in their hearts that the elder Carlyle was a stupid man, only concerned with the maintenance of his own power and position, although to voice such knowledge was to court charges of treason and sedition. Queen Diana, with her good works, worthy causes, and apparent consideration and compassion for the poor and needy, had, for a long time, been able to mitigate the spreading dislike of her husband, but, after her death, after the well-liked Diana had been one of the hundreds of victims of the influenza epidemic of '84, nothing remained to prevent the inevitable head-on clash between Carlyle I and his subjects. The elder Carlyle had been a strange combination of stubbornness and fear. On one hand, he believed that his place on the throne was a divine gift from the Goddess, and that none had the right to question his actions or to challenge or question his decisions, but, on the other, he lived in constant terror that his own people would force him into exile or worse, in the same way the people of Virginia had overthrown their monarchy more than half a century earlier. He was never able to see that, at best, he held power by an unwritten compromise and unspoken transaction that a king could only lead, and the people would only follow, if all were assured that the direction taken was ultimately for the good of the country as a whole.

When in '88 he had attempted to dissolve the Common Parliament after his call for and their rejection of a massive increase in the general taxation, it had seemed that the only way out would be open revolution. In that crisis, moderation had managed to prevail, but only by a near miracle, and the country had staggered on for another four years with Parliament and the king at loggerheads. In the winter of '93, the poor had marched in the streets, and only the cool resolve of then-Colonel Virgil Dunbar had prevented bloodshed on Regent Square. The traditional but rapidly waning loyalty of the army had kept Carlyle I in power, but even then it had looked like little more than a matter of time before Albany became a republic or a military dictatorship. Through '94 and '95, the situation had continued to deteriorate, and Cordelia could clearly remember how she had overheard her father admit to her mother, late one night when Cordelia should have been asleep, how he had made discreet enquiries as to what kind of reception the Blakeney family might expect in either London or Oslo should they decided to abandon Albany and relocate in the Norse Union. Then Dunbar and a number of other popular army officers had been arrested. Whether they had in fact been planning a move against the king, or whether it had been the product of the elder Carlyle's fevered imagination, was still a subject of debate. Either way, everyone was aware that the moment of truth had come, and for days the capital had seemed to wait, strangely quiet, hanging in the balance, as though to see where and when the first crack would expand into an irreparable fissure and the first move of open revolt would be made. Would the die of change and upheaval be cast by the revolutionary workers on the streets, the rank and file of the army, or some conspiracy of the Commons and the officer corps? But then Hassan IX's troops had hit the beaches, and everything had changed.

Everyone in Albany knew the outcome of what had come to be known as the Midnight Meeting, although few who had not actually been present were sure of the exact details, beyond that the historic encounter between the king, the leaders of the Commons, and the army had taken place very late at night, and the end result had been that Carlyle I had abdicated in favor of his son, Carlyle II, who was perceived by the vast majority of the nation to have inherited the popularity, wit, and intelligence of his mother and only the bold good looks of his father. Virgil Dunbar was promoted to full general and placed in command of the projected Army of the Potomac that would attempt the halt the Mosul northern advance at that already formidable natural barrier. A war cabinet headed by Prime Minister Jack Kennedy was formed that not only included members of the already elected Common Parliament, but also the radicals, seditionaries, and revolutionaries who had previously been considered enemies of the state. By the end of the extraordinary and singularly uncompromising meeting, Albany had entered a new, dangerous, but thoroughly modern world and was as ready as it would ever be to steel itself for the conflict to come. In the fearful but also headily energetic days that followed, the older Carlyle had departed for exile in a country house outside Stockholm, and men and women from the entire spectrum of political beliefs had rallied to the colors, and even the previously privileged and titled young, like Cordelia and her friends, had abandoned much of their former frivolity and put on the admittedly fashionable new uniforms. A king was still in the castle, but now all, him included, entered by the dark, arched tunnel from Calder Street that had once been the servants' access, and all were well aware that this new Carlyle would only remain in the castle as long as the Mosul were held at bay.

Cordelia emerged from the dark into the light of the Quadrangle, the wide central courtyard that was the architectural heart around which the rest of the walls, blocks, and towers of Albany Castle were constructed. The leaves of the two great and spreading oak trees in the center of the Quadrangle were rapidly turning on brown and gold on the sides of the trees most exposed to the prevailing chill winds from the north. Winter was already beginning to make itself felt in Albany, and everyone to whom Cordelia spoke seemed certain that the winter would also bring the first Mosul assault on the Potomac line. High and low, throughout the city, everyone was certain the two-year stalemate would come to an end before the first snow, and the defenses of Albany, so far to the south, would be put to the test. The Great Oaks in the Quadrangle were a definite symbol of Albany and its freedom. Their roots extended deep into the foundations, into the earth that surrounded the masonry of cellars and dungeons and the secret tunnels that were supposed to honeycomb the subterranean depths of Albany Castle, and their passive presence in all the historic events of the kingdom, both good and bad, was a given factor in the nation's folklore. Out in the countryside, other trees were showing even greater signs of the coming of winter. Leaves were already turning rust red, and all too soon a strong wind would strip branches to the lacy skeletons of autumn.

Cordelia's destination was the West Tower. The meeting with the delegates from the Norse Union was to be held in the impressive circular reception room on the second floor. Before the war, the Round Room had been the scene of balls, banquets, and, earlier still, prior to the death of Queen Diana, lavish masques. The unique domed ceiling with its radiating beams that had once rung to the sound of music and laughter now only felt the terrible tension of statesmanship and the grim debate of war councils. Cordelia's orders were to report to Colonel Grace Patton, a stocky career soldier who had been in the peacetime RWA and was rumored to be a discreet but determined lesbian under her ramrod-stiff professional exterior. Patton was the price that the young RWA officers had to pay for being close to the center of events, proximity to the king, his ministers, and, last but far from least, the stunning array of young officers who passed through the castle as part of their duties. As Cordelia started up the steps that led to the arched entrance of the West Tower, Lacy Davenport, another lieutenant with approximately the same duties, and definitely the same desires, as Cordelia, hurried to catch up with her. "Are we late?"

Cordelia half turned but did not stop. "Not quite."

"With Patton, not quite doesn't make it."

Cordelia raised both eyebrows in acknowledgment of the fact. "I'm well aware of that. She arrives early and expects you to be there before her."

"Have you seen any of these young men from the NU?"

"Not yet, but I ran into Coral Metcalfe at the War Office. She was with the welcoming committee, and she said" —Cordelia thought for a moment—"there were a couple of 'real dolls.' "

" 'Real dolls'? She said that?"

"Don't be a snob, Davenport. There's a war on, and we're all equal now. Coral has very good taste, even though she might express it in a somewhat shopgirl vernacular."

At the top of the steps the two women had to pass through a second security check. Normally, these internal checkpoints were fairly perfunctory for anyone already in uniform, but this one was of an intensity that made it clear the Guards of the Household Regiment were taking no chances that a bomber or assassin might slip into a meeting at which not only the king, the prime minister, and most of the War Cabinet would be present, but also the party from the NU and that nation's vice president. Should a Mosul suicide squad manage to kill only half of those present, the Albany military machine would be headless and effectively crippled. Cordelia raised her arms and allowed herself to be patted down by a Household Guard corporal who at least had the good grace not to openly show how much he was enjoying this part of his homefront duty assignment. In the old days, the Household Regiment had been dressed up like toy soldiers or the cast of a bad operetta in red coats and white buckskin breeches and festooned with more gold braid than a Solstice tree. On ceremonial occasions they had added mirror-polished breastplates and plumed helmets and clanked around rattling their sabers in a way that had looked quite formidable to the little Cordelia and her schoolfriends, but now seemed patently absurd. The outbreak of real hostilities had swept away all the pomp and foolishness. Now the Household Regiment wore the same olive drab and matte black insignia as every other Albany squaddie, and the sabers had been replaced by coveted Norse repeating rifles acquired under the lease-lend deal between Albany and the NU that everyone hoped would be extended and expanded at the upcoming meeting, and perhaps even broadened into a full alliance, with the Norse openly joining with Albany and formally declaring war on the empire of Hassan IX.

The corporal took a final look at Cordelia's and Lacy's passes and checked one more time that their faces matched the sepia photographs on their identity cards before he waved them through. Now Cordelia really was late. She hadn't factored in the time consumed by the increased security, and, as she and Lacy hurriedly climbed the regal and sweeping staircase that spiraled up the outside wall of the West Tower to the Round Room, she hoped to the Goddess that Patton was not her usual extrapunctual and ultrapunctilious self. As they entered one of the antechambers that led to the Round Room, she saw to her dismay that not only had Patton arrived, but she had a dozen other young RWA officers already formed up for inspection, standing in a dressed line at full attention. The colonel turned and looked bleakly at Cordelia and Lacy. "I'm delighted that you ladies could join us. You are too generous with your time."

"I'm sorry, ma'am. Getting past the security took longer than we anticipated."

Colonel Patton gestured to the inspection line. "These officers seem to have managed the calculation."

Both Cordelia and Lacy nodded, looking suitably chastened. "Yes, Colonel."

"It is incumbent on all officers to expect the unexpected and plan accordingly."

"Yes, ma'am."

"I suggest you reflect on that during the week you spend confined to your quarters."

Cordelia cursed silently. Damn Patton. There went all hope of close and private fraternization with the Norse officers. "Yes, ma'am. Thank you, ma'am." And damn you to hell.

"Now get in line, and don't waste any more of my time."

Cordelia and Lacy quickly joined the others. Patton turned and walked down the line, looking hard at each junior officer in turn, apparently assuring herself that each met her exacting standards of dress and decorum and was suitably turned out to be present at such a vital and august assembly. Finally she halted and nodded as though marginally satisfied. "I suppose you'll do. Stand at ease."

The lieutenants relaxed from attention, but not by much. Patton flicked an invisible piece of lint from her immaculate uniform and addressed them as a group. "Now that Blakeney and Davenport have graced the party, I have a reminder for you all. I'm well aware that you have basically been assigned here as decorative adjuncts at what will still be, despite the gender enlightenment of the times, a predominately male gathering, but I'm warning you now. Don't get carried away. You also have a job to do, and I expect you to do it with speed and efficiency. If one of the delegates wants something, you get it for them, and you get it for them quickly. If you are needed to take notes or provide any other assistance, you do it. There will be points when the meeting breaks for refreshments, and you may make conversation during those breaks, but you don't speak unless spoken to." The Colonel paused to let all this sink in. "And let me warn you in no uncertain terms that any girl trying to become the center of attention will find herself winding bandages in the mud beside the Potomac so fast she won't believe it. War is neither a dinner party nor a society ball, and I don't want to see it being treated as such." She paused again, looking sternly from face to face. "Do you ladies have any questions? Is there any part of what I've said that anyone doesn't understand?"

When Patton delivered a speech of this kind, it was her habit to finish by asking for questions, but that did not mean she actually wanted any, and the rank of girls knew better than to ask unless they truly foresaw a problem. Seemingly no one did, because no one spoke. Again the colonel nodded. "Very well. Dismissed. Proceed into the Round Room and try not to make bloody fools of yourselves."

As the women turned to leave the anteroom, Patton's hard blue eyes fixed on Cordelia. "Blakeney."

Cordelia halted and stiffened to attention. More trouble? "Yes, Colonel?"

"If that uniform of yours was a little less formfitting, you might be able to move a little faster."

"Yes, Colonel."

"I would suggest you have your dressmaker let out a little."

Cordelia did her best to keep her expression formally blank, but her jaw stiffened at the contempt that Patton put into the word "dressmaker." "Yes, Colonel."

"You're coming perilously close to the limits of what is acceptable, Blakeney."

"Yes, Colonel."

"And I think you might go a little lighter on the lipstick."

"Yes, Colonel."

Furious at being confined to quarters when the NU boys were in town, and convinced that Patton had it in for her and the other aristocrats who had received their commissions through family contacts at court while the Colonel had come up the hard way and faced all the tribulations and frustrations of a lowborn woman attempting to succeed as a career soldier under the former peacetime regime, Cordelia entered the Round Room fuming. But she was quickly distracted by the changes that had been made in the huge interior space since the last time she had been there. The centerpiece was a wide, circular table. Although gleaming and immaculately finished, it was obviously of recent construction and perhaps purpose-built for the conference. A clear symbolism of the equality of all those attending

the conference must have been part of the design, and it reminded Cordelia
of the childhood tales of the mythic court of Utha the Dragon King and his
knights, where no one hero was elevated above another. She didn't think
this nod to ancient fable was any accident. Utha the Dragon King was a
piece of folklore common to both Albany and the Norse. According to
legend, it had been Utha who had forged the thousand-year alliance between the Scandinavian Vikings and the English of the islands that had, in
turn, led to the very first seafaring settlements in the Americas. The room
was already fairly crowded, even though the primary participants had
yet to make their entrances. Beneath the flags and banners that streamed
from the rafters, decorated with the heraldic symbols of both nations, the
Crowned Bear of Albany and the North Star of the NU hanging side by
side, a large and well-armed contingent of the Household Regiment was
positioned round the walls, while parliamentary private secretaries, civil
servants, and aides from the War Office and the General Staff shuffled papers and held low-voiced conversations. Castle servants were laying out a
bar and buffet that would come into play when the conference decided to
adjourn for refreshments, and the smell of percolating coffee—quite a rar-
ity now that the enemy occupied the lands to the south—and the sight of
food and drink reminded Cordelia that in her hurry to reach the War Office and then the castle, she had neglected to eat yet that day.

The level of conversation suddenly dropped away as the principals began to file into the room. They made their entrances in what some, Cordelia
included, might have described as a reverse pecking order. The politicians
came first: seated members of the Common Parliament and representatives
of the labor unions and trade guilds, including Vincent Corleone, the leader
of the United Workers Party, whose dark Sicilian eyes and melancholy good
looks had always caused a stir in Cordelia's otherwise aristocratic heart.
They were followed by the religious leaders of the kingdom, Archbishop
Belfast, Rabbi Stern, the Shaman Grey Wolf, and the Lady Gretchen, High
Priestess of the Mother Goddess. In tune with the tenor of both the meeting and the times, the religious leaders wore no ceremonial robes. The men
were in dark frock coats, and the Lady Gretchen wore a floor-length bur-
gundy robe with a pushed-back cowl that allowed her thick grey hair to fall
free, almost to her waist. The Reverend Bearclaw Manson was not a religious leader, but he walked in just behind them. "Reverend" was little more

than a nickname, but the small man with his buckskins and unkempt hair tied back in a ponytail exercised a similar mystic sway over many in the kingdom. Often vanishing, sometimes for a year or more at a time, he was credited with knowing more about the uncharted interior of the continent than any other individual in Albany, and also with being in closer touch with the world of the invisible than perhaps any living man, except for possibly the mysterious Yancey Slide, who some said was actually not human at all, and who would undoubtedly have been invited to attend the meeting had he and his Ranger band of scouts and marauders not been somewhere south of the Potomac wreaking covert havoc behind enemy lines.

Cordelia found it somewhat fitting that the strange little Manson was followed by the representatives of Albany's remaining free American allies, Earl Long III from Grand Louisiana, Chanchootok of the Ohio, and Naxat of the Montreal Nations. Grand Louisiana was not yet formally at war with Hassan IX, but with the Mosul already in Atlanta, and with a large proportion of the population of the Earldom being the second and third generation descendants of Frank and Hispanian refugees from the Mosul horror, or those from the former city states of Roma, Venezia, Tuscany, Naples, and Milan, plus all the others that now made up what was known as the Province of Italia, the lands down on the Gulf and along the Mississippi knew their time of trial would not be long in coming. The Ohio and Montreal Nations covered Albany's right flank in the north. In times past, both aboriginal confederacies had fought wars with Albany, but in the face of the Mosul invasion, urgent and enduring treaties had been made. The Ohio and the Montreal recognized Hassan IX as a far greater foe and a more fundamental danger to their lands. They had held back the settlers from across the Ocean from penetrating too deeply into the interior since the Vikings had first settled, and now they would do everything in their power to stay the advance of the Mosul.

Long, Chanchootok, and Naxat walked in together, side by side, and acted as heralds for the people that everyone there had really come to see. The Norse delegation was some twenty strong. Apart from Vice President Ingmar Ericksen, whose craggy face Cordelia recognized from pictures in the Albany newspapers, she didn't know any of their names, but except for the Vice President, who was somber in a formal morning coat, they all sported somewhat dashing military uniforms, long, belted coats with decorations and shoulder boards, that were a mixture of the field grey of the Norse Army, the dark blue of its formidable Navy, and the lighter blue of the small but growing Air Corps. Cordelia observed that Coral Metcalfe was quite correct. Some of the younger officers were "real dolls," and her appraisal was already being reciprocated if Cordelia was any judge of men. A blond Air Corps captain was looking directly at her with the hungry expression of one who has traveled a long way without the company of women. It was not, however, the moment for even the most mild and silent flirtation. All other eyes were now on the arched entrance of the Round Room as the final three men walked in. To the left was Prime Minister Jack Kennedy, to the right Field Marshal Virgil Dunbar, and, in the center, the king.

The three most powerful men in the room constituted an odd contrast one from the other, both visually, right there and then, and also in terms of their respective but completely different backgrounds. The venerable Kennedy, with his broad shoulders and carefully shaped mane of white hair, had fought tooth and nail with the king's father to preserve Albany as a parliamentary democracy. Although he now walked with a silver-topped cane, a truculent cigar jutted from the corner of his mouth and he radiated dogged and unrelenting energy. Dunbar, who had been imprisoned by the old king for much the same reasons that Kennedy had fought him, had a similar energy, but was cooler and more introverted. He walked with a limp after a Mosul sniper had nicked him in the leg during an overly exposed surveillance of the enemy lines. The king himself walked straight and with a reserved formality. He had the whole weight of the war thrust on his shoulders at the age of just twenty-seven, but, in his simple, unadorned, but immaculate uniform, his high, polished riding boots, and with his light brown hair neatly combed to one side, he carried the burden with a quiet dignity and determination never to reveal what the responsibility might be costing him, except for a certain strained pallor he could do nothing to disguise. Carlyle II led by example and seemed outwardly confident that, if he held himself intact, his people would follow him to either victory or an honorable defeat.

By the time the three had reached the round table, the others designated to sit there had found their respective places and stood beside their high-backed leather chairs. The king seated himself without any theatrical display and indicated with an unassuming gesture that the others should do the same. "Mr. Vice President, my lords, ladies and gentlemen, shall we all be seated and see what can be done to extinguish once and for all this flame of evil that has burned its way to our borders?"

RAPHAEL

"Fire!"

Thirty hammers of thirty unloaded muskets clicked in unison.

"Reload!"

Powder—wadding—ball—wadding—use the ramrod—replace.

"Take aim!"

The hard butts of thirty muskets were raised in unison to the shoulders of thirty conscript trainees.

"Fire!"

This time only twenty-nine hammers came down together. One was a fraction of a second late, and every one of the thirty trainees knew it was Pascal, one of the three Franks in the company, who had fallen behind. As the squad stood rigid and motionless, muskets still in the firing position, Gunnery Instructor Y'assir advanced on Pascal, stood in front of him, and looked the boy up and down. "You fired late, maggot."

Pascal responded with the training school bellow that he knew was expected of him; no point in compounding the crime of firing late with the equal offense of a faltering reply. "Yes, Gunnery Instructor! I fired late, Gunnery Instructor!"

"And what do you do when you fire late, maggot?"

The response was again a familiar bellowed ritual. "I become a traitor to the Deities and the Emperor, Gunnery Instructor!"

"And what is the only fitting fate for a traitor, maggot?"

"Death, Gunnery Instructor! Death is the only fitting fate for a traitor, Gunnery Instructor!"

"I can't hear you, maggot!"

"Death, Gunnery Instructor! Death is the only fitting fate for a traitor, Gunnery Instructor!"

The one thing that the company of conscript trainees knew was that Pascal would not die. Although executions were hardly a rare occurrence on the training camp that lay outside the ruins of Madrid, the boy would not be killed for a moment's hesitation in one of the most routine and fundamental of drills. If that was the punishment for every such infraction, Hassan IX would have no army left to fight.

"Company, lower arms!"

In a snap, three-part motion, the trainees brought their muskets down to their sides and stood at attention, stiff as their own ramrods. Y'assir walked slowly along the line of young men, some of them little more than boys, then turned and walked back again until he was once more standing in front of the unfortunate Pascal. Without warning, his good right arm shot out and a clublike clenched fist struck the conscript just above and exactly between his eyes. Pascal went down like a felled tree. One moment he had been standing, and the next he was laid out on the parade ground at right angles to the line formed by his companions, blinking, looking stunned, but making no sound.

"On your feet, maggot!"

Pascal blinked once more, shook his head, scrambled to his feet, and rejoined the line. A newcomer might have expected that the drill would have continued, but the conscripts knew that, with Gunnery Instructor Y'assir, nothing should be taken for granted. Y'assir was the hardest of hard men, full Mamaluke, cold and unbending, once upon a time one of the Mu-Kadar, the Immortals, the pampered elite. He had only been brought back across the ocean and assigned to the post of gunnery instructor after a saber cut from a Virginia cavalryman, received at the Battle of Richmond, had severed the tendons in his left arm, rendering it useless. No longer able to fight or even ride, the Mamaluke compensated for what he saw as his fall from grace, his loss of glory, and his failure to die in the service of Emperor by an unrelenting and specific brutality. Although he was too much of a professional to ever voice his bitterness, it was plainly expressed each time he disciplined a recruit. He punched Pascal a second time, in exactly the same spot on his forehead, but Pascal must have had just enough warning to brace himself for the second blow. He merely staggered back and then quickly rejoined the line, but blood now flowed from a cut above his nose. Without comment from Y'assir, the drill continued.

"Reload!"

Powder—wadding—ball—wadding—use the ramrod—replace.

"Take aim!"

The muskets leveled as one.

"Fire!"

This time thirty hammers again clicked in unison.

"Reload!"

Powder—wadding—ball—wadding—use the ramrod—replace.

"Take aim!"

Y'assir could keep this up until the shoulders of the trainees were black and blue.

"Fire!"

The trick was to make the moves without thinking. If you thought about it, you fumbled. Raphael Vega let his hands go through the drill while he thought about the drawings in the hidden notebook concealed beneath his mattress in the barracks. Although forbidden by both military regulations and the dictates of the Zhaithan, Raphael Vega drew because, in the training camp, the officers and the instructors like Y'assir did everything they could to break the will and destroy the minds of the conscript trainees. Once upon a time, Raphael Vega had been an attractive fourteen-year-old with olive skin, fine features, and straight black hair that, no matter how much he combed it back, fell into his dark brown eyes like a raven curtain. The young girls had started treating him to hot, dramatic glances, and many had predicted that he would be a handsome man. All that had changed, though, when the Mosul had taken him for a conscript. No more girls, no more hot looks, and, with his head shaved, his eyes seemed to harden and his features take on a uniform coarseness. Whether he would ever be a man, handsome or otherwise, was also extremely debatable. The Mosul did not want men; they wanted automatons who would advance when ordered into the fire of whatever enemy confronted them, without hesitation, fear, or question. Raphael Vega would let himself be turned into a Mosul soldier. With Hispania long conquered and decimated, he could do nothing about that, but he was not going to allow himself to be transformed into a thing without a brain. The drawings were where he hid his individuality and concealed his freedom of mind. His art was his medium of rebellion, a means of maintaining his identity under the harsh discipline meted out by Y'assir and his other superiors, and the constant Zhaithan religious indoctrination. When he had first come to the camp, he had drawn more openly and even circulated scrawls of naked women and mythic beasts among his barrack mates. Then he had been caught, and ten savage strokes of the formal cane that left him striped and bloody had cured him of that, and also taught him that the Zhaithan Ministry of Virtue even had its spies and snitches, known as zed-hunters, in among the raw recruits. After the caning, he drew strictly in secret, and trusted no one.

"Reload!"

Powder—wadding—ball—wadding—use the ramrod—replace.

"Take aim!"

The muskets leveled as one.

"Fire!"

Pascal was again slightly slower than the rest, but this time Y'assir chose to ignore it. Blood had run down into the Frankish trainee's eyes from the cut on his forehead. Maybe the gunnery instructor wanted the company to become accustomed to the sight of blood on their companions.

"Reload!"

Powder—wadding—ball—wadding—use the ramrod—replace.

"Take aim!"

Raphael aimed at an imaginary target.

"Fire!"

The drill was a pantomime, conducted without ammunition, for one simple reason, and everybody knew it. The training camp was presently suffering from a shortage of powder. Even the fact that they were using the old-fashioned muzzle-loading muskets was the result of yet another supply problem. Hassan IX might rule an empire that stretched from the Indus to Hispania and the Northern Ocean, but it was an empire that was far from efficient in anything but the practice of terror and oppression. The movement of supplies was a constant and labyrinthine foul-up. The Mosul were conquerors but hardly organizers, and such organizational skills that might be found among the defeated and subject peoples were either ignored or severely hampered by the hidebound distrust of the Zhaithan priests, who viewed science, technology, and even the simple art of logistics as hell-spawned abominations and only tolerated them on the most grudging and material sufferance. Like the old saying went in the subject nations that had boasted railroad systems before the coming of the Mosul, the trains now never ran on time, if they ran at all. The grand alliance with the Teutons should, in theory, have put some of this to rights. The Teutons were skilled engineers, and, within the Mosul domain, they were the masters of heavy industry, but it was common knowledge that the Teutons' fatal weakness was that they were far too fond of power and authority. They could be seduced by strength. That was why they had voluntarily allied themselves with the Mosul in the first place and made their rape of Europe possible. It was also why they had allowed the Zhaithan to infiltrate their society, bringing as it did the chaos of distrust and holy repression under the guise of order and religious uniformity.

Despite the Zhaithan spies and zed-hunters, the conscript trainees in Raphael's company had heard a wide-enough selection of horror stories about Mosul foul-ups. Not even the Ministry of Virtue could keep soldiers from complaining and spreading rumors. They had heard the whispers in the night and grouching on the forced marches about how entire regiments had starved on the Asian Front while perfectly good food had rotted less than a hundred kilometers away, awaiting transportation that never came because it had been ordered to the wrong place. Y'assir himself had made it clear that maps were not to be trusted unless they were of Teuton or even enemy origin. The worst stories, however, were those of the human-wave assaults, employed extensively in the invasion of the Americas, in which the front ranks were not issued with weapons at all because the inevitability of their deaths was so absolute. The trainees all prayed that they would be furnished with modern Krupp breechloaders before they shipped out for the Americas. A modern weapon was a fairly definite guarantee that they would not immediately be placed in the front lines of a "forlorn hope" suicide squad the moment they arrived at the front. Y'assir had come as close to promising them as he came to promising anything except punishment and death that they were supposed to be so armed, and thus they had some chance of surviving at least their first encounter with the enemy. On the other hand, he made it clear that, in the Provincial Levies, what was supposed to be, and what was, were two very different things. "It could well be that the guns intended for you boys will be left standing on some loading dock between here and the Ruhr for the next three months. Or, even if they do arrive, you'll find you've been issued with the wrong ammunition."

When Y'assir finally dismissed them, the trainees stumbled to their barracks, too tired to do anything but fall into their bunks. The sun had set and the interior of the barrack room was quite dark. Some lit the stubs of candles that were the only light permitted to them after sunset, while others just flopped on their mattresses with exhausted sighs and groans. Some sat hunched on their bunks and blindly turned the pages of their pocket-sized copies of the Yasma, the holy book of Zhaithan, that were issued to all recruits when they came to the training camp, and, as Raphael knew well, was the only book they could own on penalty of dire punishment. Indeed, the Yasma would have been the only book permitted in all of the empire if the priests completely had their way, but that was something beyond even the cruel and fanatic capabilities of the worshipers of Ignir and Aksura. Raphael hated the Yasma, with its rules and its ancient tales of hideousness and carnage, the deities and the demons, the interminable lists of rules and regulations and the equally endless genealogies. He would have simply lost the book had it not been one of the items regularly checked during the gunnery instructor's routine inspections, and woe to any trainee who could not produce his copy of the Yasma. He even had to regularly fan through the pages to make it look as though he was actually reading the accursed texts.

The short interval between dismissal and lights-out was the only time that the trainees showed any kind of personality. Through the rest of their waking hours they moved as one, and with their shorn heads and rough cotton uniforms, they looked as alike as it was possible to make them. In their preparations for bed, they showed small idiosyncrasies. Renaldo obsessively inspected his hair and toenails. Pablo stared at his lit candle stub as though looking for some kind of answer or inner reason, or maybe trying to hypnotize himself away to someplace out of the training camp. The four trainees from the Lowlands gambled compulsively. The quartet stuck to each other like glue, and in every available moment they pitched copper coins or rolled dice, and had an elaborate system of memorized credit and debit, so nothing was ever put on paper. Pascal was usually talkative, but on this night he simply lay facedown on his bunk after bearing the brunt of Y'assir's practiced ire for the whole of the long, hot day. Raphael would have liked to have vanished into the latrine and drawn for a while. A portrait of an imaginary girl with caramel skin, huge eyes, and dark hair had lodged in his mind, and he wanted to get it down on paper, in this case the blank back of a supply requisition form he had filched while no one was looking. He had no idea where the pictures in his head came from, and he never knew when they might vanish. The girl's face was somehow, in some mysterious way, important, but, since he had been caught and caned, he had become extremely circumspect with his drawing. He had no desire to feel the burning cuts of the formal cane ever again if he could in any way help it.

"Lights out!" All too soon, Underofficer Beg, Y'assir's immediate deputy, had screamed from the barrack room door, and the trainees snuffed out their candles. After that the only light came from a small iron brazier on the top of a tall tripod: not a heating device, but a reminder of the presence of the gods. Even in the darkness the Zhaithan refused to release their grip. Raphael had no recall of falling asleep. The next thing he knew was a violent hammering that he thought at first was inside his head but then realized was being created by a squad of underofficers led by Beg who were rousing the trainees with their batons, tipping them out of their bunks, upending the rough straw mattresses, and screaming.

"Out! Out! Out! Quit your snoring and start roaring!"

Outside, the dawn had yet to break. One of the Lowlanders had the temerity to ask what was going on, and, amazingly, he received an answer. "You're all shipping out, maggot. Out of here, across the ocean, and off to the front to be blown to pieces. And are we glad to be rid of you little bastards."

Raphael wanted to protest. How could the training be over? He did not feel trained. He did not feel like a soldier, but in the Mosul legions, no one protested.

JESAMINE

Jesamine woke to the sound of the call to prayer and the subsequent bustle of the waking camp that was just outside the blackened ruins of the Virginia town that had been called Alexandria. She had only slept fitfully that night. The flesh of her bottom still smarted from the colonel's late night ministrations. Drunk on schnapps and lager after early-evening hours spent in the Teuton officers' mess, Colonel Helmut Phaall of the 4th Engineers, the man who owned her body, if not her soul, had taken a mind to thrash her soundly with the same quirt he used on his charger Wotan, inflicting some fifteen slow and lingering stripes with the plaited leather before forcing her to her knees to finish him in the manner that had, for some time, been his preferred method of consummation. The colonel had gone to some lengths to explain that the beating in no way constituted a punishment. She had neither transgressed nor displeased him, and the pain he was so liberally meting out was purely for his own amusement, and, in keeping with her abject and lowly station, she should willingly suffer the chastisement with good grace and in the eternal hope of finding favor in not only his eyes but in those of the All-seeing Twin Deities. Colonel Phaall had, at the same time, however, made it quite clear that she was free to moan, gasp, whimper, or sob, just as long as she didn't "wake up the whole damned camp." He had absolutely no objection to hearing her suffer. Indeed, it was the perfect complement to the visual spectacle of her bare body twisting and her muscles clenching and contracting with each cut of the whip.

Her normal practice was to slip from her cot in the officers' slave pavilion and remain as invisible as possible until Phaall had departed for his duties of the day, but on this particular morning that was not possible. On a final alcoholic whim, Phaall had ordered his manservant Reinhardt to escort her to her cot and chain her as regulations dictated. Normally the rules concerning the chaining of concubines were not scrupulously observed. It created too many problems and too much work for the orderlies and the menservants who had to see to their enforcement. None of the slave girls in this Teuton camp were captured Virginians, or even Americans. They had all made the long ocean voyage with their officers from Cadiz or Lisbon, so if they attempted to escape, where exactly were they going to go? A few concubines had tried to run, just as a percentage of soldiers, especially the Provincial Levies, tried to desert, but most were caught and brought back to either be hanged or burned, while the others either perished in the swamps to the north, among the snakes and mosquitos, or wandered until they starved in the forests to the south or were eaten by wolves, foraging pigs, or wild dogs. Why Phaall had suddenly decided that Jesamine was a flight risk was a mystery, but she could only take his final order to Reinhardt at face value.

"Better hook her up tonight. Don't want her fleeing the coop in a snit because I decided to freshen her up a little. I've put in too much fucking time training the bitch. I don't need all the bother of breaking in a new one."

Thus she greeted the morning wearing a padlocked leather collar attached to a meter and a half of light steel chain that was, in turn, fastened to the iron frame of her folding cot. Reinhardt had the responsibility of keeping collar and chain polished and gleaming, and it was also the manservant's duty to free her at the start of the day. Unfortunately, releasing Jesamine was only one of the demands on his time as the new day got underway. Phaall needed his breakfast; he would have to be shaved and might also require a bath. Papers and maps had to be located, and although Reinhardt would have polished the colonel's boots and filled his flask with schnapps the night before, a Teuton colonel of Engineers could find a dozen or more tasks for his manservant before he went about his duties. Jesamine might wait, hungry and confined to her cot, until close to lunchtime before Reinhardt came to unlock her restraining collar unless Phaall wanted to fuck her during or after his breakfast, and that was rarely on his menu of morning desires. In the minimal way that reasonable kindness might be defined in any camp of the Mosul, the manservant Reinhardt treated Jesamine with reasonable kindness. He did not slap her around, subject her to intimate indignities behind Phaall's back, or otherwise abuse her the way some of the servants did. He rarely carried tales about her to the colonel, and, now and then, he would slip her small treats like unfinished bottles of schnapps, chocolate, candied fruit, and pastries from the officers' mess. In the hard world of the Mosul, however, kindness was always a matter of transaction. A manservant did not merit his own concubine and had to be content with the small selection of ugly native whores who were sent to the front to be used by the rank and file. In return for the titbits and the blind eye he turned to her indiscretions, she would allow him to touch her body and sometimes pleasure him with hand or mouth. She would never, however, permit Reinhardt full penetration, since discovery of such a violation would certainly slow-hang the both of them.

The officers' concubines were housed in a large, pavilion-style tent of camouflaged canvas where some two dozen women slept in cots identical to Jesamine's. Beside each cot was a steel locker in which each woman kept her cosmetics, folded clothes, small personal vanities, and the inevitable copy of the Yasma. When not in use, each concubine's chain and collar hung from a hook at the side of the locker. A tiny measure of privacy was afforded each cot by the tent of mosquito netting that protected it from the troublesome insects that seemed to thrive in the constantly flooded wetlands beside the wide river the Americans called the Potomac. As on any other morning, the slave pavilion was a chaos of sleepy women preparing for another day in their particular kind of servitude. It smelled of bodies and bad perfume, stale cooking, fear, and the pervading damp of the bottomlands beside the river that, according the current rumors, the army would soon cross in what promised to be a bloody and final assault on the kingdom of Albany. Women's voices surrounded Jesamine, some sleepy and complaining, others bickering and petulant.

One of the problems that beset the officers' concubines was that they had far too little with which occupy their time or their minds while the men who owned their lives were away about their duties. It had once been suggested, probably by a priest or an agent of the Ministry of Virtue, that, here in the Americas, the concubines on the campaign should be put to work just like any other collection of servants or slaves. To the religious mindset, this made perfect sense. Idle hands did the devil's work, and food needed to be prepared and laundry to be done. Clothes required mending, and a hundred things had to be fetched and carried on any given day in the camp. They might be the playthings of the military elite, but they were also slaves, and slaves were supposed to work. This idea, however, was unanimously vetoed by the officers. They didn't want their women with rough red hands and dirt under their fingernails. It spoiled the illusion. And thus the concubines at the front succumbed to the chronic and narcissistic boredom that had beset seraglios, harems, and whorehouses all down the centuries. They retreated into an almost mindless pettiness of gossip, intrigue, jealousy, backbiting, and fantasy. One of the favorite illusions was for women to imagine that they would make their officers fall in love with them and thus gain their freedom. Maybe for one in a hundred the dream came true, but for the great majority it was a chimeric escape into a refuge of impossible hope. Jesamine had seen this romantic absurdity happen for real a few times on the other side of the ocean, in the permanent garrisons where the men also had little to do and time on their hands. Here at the front, though, in the New World, she doubted that it was possible when the officers had an entire campaign of conquest to keep them occupied and amused. Jesamine's desire for a way out was as strong as any woman's in the tent, but she refused to attach any kind of hope to the hard and professionally cruel men who controlled their lives. Jesamine prided herself on being a complete realist.

Kahlfa, the concubine of a cavalry major called Urman, approached Jesamine's cot. She nursed a cup of hard Mosul coffee, probably sweetened with honey if she had any. Kahlfa and Jesamine were both from the mountains to the southeast of the Mamaluke homelands, and both had the caramel complexion, large dark eyes, straight noses, and black hair for which the mountain women were famous. They had been blessed with similar smooth and muscular bodies, and it was the combination of those faces and bodies that had saved them the hard labor and ceaseless toil of the common working slaves. The women of the mountains were accustomed to the idea of slavery, if, indeed, anyone could become accustomed to slavery. The Mamalukes had been raiding their lands and carrying off their people apparently since the beginning of history. Jesamine and Kahlfa weren't alike enough to be taken for sisters, but perhaps cousins, and they had one other thing in common. The mountain women were also famous for their voices, and they both sang. It was a talent both Kahlfa and Jesamine put to good use in the officers' mess, and, as performers rather than objects, it gave them moments when they were more public property than merely the toys of Urman and Phaall, respectively. Kahlfa had confided in Jesamine how she hoped that her singing might lead to a betterment of her situation, but while humoring her, Jesamine had inwardly dismissed the idea as one more wistful but ultimately forlorn hope. All that Jesamine expected from her singing was that maybe, if Phaall abused her too badly, some other officer, more appreciative of her worth, might buy her from the colonel or win her by making her an object of a wager. In this, though, she was little better than a thoroughbred horse that was being overridden and beaten by its owner in a way that caused another to step in and stop the wanton waste of good flesh.

Kahlfa pulled back the mosquito netting, thinking that Jesamine had overslept. "You'd better wake up, girl, or you'll be in trouble." Then she saw that Jesamine was chained. "He had you hooked up? What did he do that for? What did you do?"

Jesamine threw back her blanket and rolled over to display her welts. "He freshened me with the quirt, didn't he?"

"You'd displeased him?"

Jesamine shook her head. "He made it clear it was just for his amusement."

"And did you like it, too?"

"No, of course not."

"There are some who do, girl."

"I know that."

"By all accounts, Ravenna can't get enough of her colonel's cane."

Jesamine nodded. "So I've heard."

They both glanced at a tall, dark, full-bodied woman cooking eggs for herself on one of the three communal hotplates while talking to the pale blond twins, Mai and Leah, who performed a different kind of act for the officers in the mess. "I heard she provokes him to get him to beat her."

"I heard that, too."

"It might be guilt."

Jesamine eased herself up, letting the chain fall between her breasts. "Guilt?"

Kahlfa sat down on the end of the cot and lowered her voice. "She's suspected of being our Virtue girl."

"She's a zed-hunter?"

"Our very own."

"What makes you say that?"

"You remember when they arrested Yvonne, a month or so back?"

Jesamine looked surprised that Kahlfa even asked. "Of course I do."

"I was standing next to that Ravenna. Everyone else looked terrified, but she seemed like she was expecting it."

"It took me completely by surprise."

"And there was something else, too."

"What else?"

"She looked pleased, smug almost, as if she'd just won some kind of victory or scored points."

"Maybe she was just pleased it wasn't her. I mean, she's been in the cage more than once."

In a corner of the pavilion, near the row of hot plates and the common washing facilities, was a low steel cage, three feet deep by three feet high and a little over four feet long. It was used as an alternative punishment to the routine beatings, both formal and informal, and also as a lockdown for new arrivals who were deemed to need time to acclimate to their status and surroundings.

Kahlfa shrugged. "Believe what you like. I'm going to be watching her."

Jesamine trusted Kahlfa as much as she trusted anyone in the camp, but she was far from sure that Ravenna was their current snitch. Identifying who might be a spy for the Ministry of Virtue was another of the more popular pastimes in the concubines' pavilion, second only to the constant discussions of the means and machinations by which the woman who believed they could win their freedom by impossible romance might achieve their desired objective. "Look at her now. Even when she's doing something, she also seems to be watching. See the way she's looking at the twins?"

Jesamine turned over and again lay on her stomach, regarding the blond twins. Mai and Leah were unique among the concubines in that they were the only ones who did not belong to any particular officer. They had been brought to the camp by the celebrated—although some said insane—Mamaluke cavalry colonel Hussa Kastar, the leader of a troop of Mu-Kadar, one of the Immortals, who was reputed to have had no less than a half-dozen horses shot out from under him in the advance through the Carolinas and Virginia. Unfortunately, he had apparently begun to assume that he really was immortal in more than just title, and that his invincibility was absolute. The errors of these assumptions had been proved just three months earlier, when, on an ill-considered and foolhardy intelligence gathering raid into enemy territory, Kastar had been shot dead by an Albany lookout. According to normal custom and protocol, that would have been the end for the twins, but some of the other officers had intervened to save them from the quick deaths that would have followed after the demise of their owner. This was no act of compassion, though, merely Kastar's brother officers realizing that Mai and Leah were simply too rare an item to be wastefully strangled or to have their identical white throats cut. A consortium of officers had worked out a deal whereby Mai and Leah had become the collective property of all the members of the mess, acting as a syndicate. If any officer wanted them for his private use, he had to make a sizable donation to mess funds. The twins had seemingly taken the dubious step up from slavery to a form of controlled prostitution. Only the Teutons could have worked out such an unprecedented arrangement, and how it was reconciled with the complexities of Zhaithan law, even in the more relaxed form of the combat zone, that allowed a certain leeway in personal behavior, was a mystery to the other women in the pavilion.

Jesamine had seen the twins act a dozen or more times, either on evenings when she and Kahlfa were required to sing, or on what were euphemistically called "lady's nights," when the officers brought their concubines with them and the girls found themselves passed around like schnapps, beer, and the cigars that had become so popular since the conquest of the tobacco-growing lands of the Americas. Their performances were gymnastic, innovative, highly pornographic, and, of course, incestuous, and the officers' mess could not get enough of them. Men en masse were both fascinated and aroused beyond reason by two women having ornate and flamboyant lesbian sex one with the other, and the sight of twins so publically engaged was treated as even more of an erotic charge. Jesamine knew this from firsthand experience. She had seen and felt the effect that the twins had on Phaall, and suffered his engorged excitement in the aftermath. The twins' popularity, and the perquisites and small measure of freedom it allowed them, had set them apart from the rest of the concubines. Jesamine personally considered them a little stupid and felt the airs that they put on were probably not a good idea in the long run. Right at that moment, the two were dressed in matching, pale blue, hooded jellabas that would have been fairly modest garments had the outer seams not been slit from hem almost to armpit and the neckline not plunged nearly to their navels, revealing a considerable area of white and intimate, naked flesh. Jesamine was of the opinion that to walk around like that, first thing in the Mosul morning, was courting an eventual disaster. To be too noticeable was to risk coming to the attention of the Ministry of Virtue, or, at the other extreme, to court the bitter envy of the other women. Indeed, a few whispered threats had been made against Mai and Leah, but no woman was going to follow through while they were such a hit with the officers. Others, on the other hand, actively sought their friendship in the hope of making use of their supposed influence with the officers in the camp, just as Ravenna seemed to be doing right then. The woman who Kahlfa suspected of being a Zhaithan spy was actually cooking up another batch of eggs for the twins, who seemed to accept the gesture as no more than they deserved.

As Jesamine stared thoughtfully at the twins, Kahlfa traced the curved stripe of one of Jesamine's welts with a cool finger. "I could probably find some salve for that."

"It's okay. I'll live. I just wish Reinhardt would get here soon and unlock this damned collar."

"I'd kiss your bruises better if there weren't so many to see."

Jesamine laughed. She had no shame that Kahlfa and she had now and again taken comfort from each other's touch. Before she could do more than laugh, though, a cry went up. "Male in the tent!"

It was a routine warning, but, always fearful of trouble and a sudden visit from the Ministry of Virtue, the women all stopped whatever they were doing and warily looked to the entrance. When it turned out to only be the manservant Reinhardt, they made noises of relief and went back to what they had previously been doing. Presumably he had arrived to free Jesamine from her collar and chain, and that was no cause for alarm or comment, but Jesamine noticed that he was carrying a small napkin-wrapped bundle. Treats? Jesamine could use a treat right there and then, although obviously Reinhardt would expect her favors in return.

She smiled jokingly as he approached. "About time. I thought you were going to leave me like this all day."

A certain familiarity existed between Jesamine and Reinhardt that went beyond private and public manners of address between servant and slave of the same master. Jesamine could hardly see how it might be otherwise. She had taken him in her hand and mouth too often, and listened to his moans of forbidden pleasure, for him to pretend they were strangers. Like everything else in the camp, however, the familiarity was a calculated transaction. He could hardly betray her, since she would immediately betray him, and they would slowly and painfully hang together. Most times Reinhardt would have laughed at her bantering complaint, but instead he scowled. "I am in no mood for jokes. Our colonel has one full and foul hangover. I fully expected him to take the quirt to me as well."

"Is he about his business?"

Reinhardt nodded. "Thank the Deities he'll be away until late. Something to do with barges." He looked down at the welts on Jesamine's buttocks as he unlocked the collar. "He really laid it on you good, didn't he, girl?"

"Good isn't the word I'd choose."

Kahlfa rose from the bed. "I think I'll make myself scarce."

Jesamine quicky grasped her by the hand. "No, stay." She looked up at Reinhardt. "Do you have something there for me?"

"I thought you might need a little something after the whipping you took."

Jesamine reached up and quickly patted his cheek, but only after checking that Ravenna or any of the other women were not looking. "You're so sweet and thoughtful."

She quickly unwrapped the bundle, revealing that it contained two pockets of pita bread, with lamb kebab chunks and salad, a clay oven—cooked half chicken, a honey cake, and two thin, dark cheroots. At the sight of the food, Jesamine flashed the servant a dazzling smile, and Kahlfa made no more moves to leave. "Thank you, Reinhardt. You are my bene-factor and my only true friend. I will share these with Kahlfa."

Reinhardt lowered his voice. "Then I'll expect the two of you to meet me later."

Jesamine held her smile fixed. It was a chore, but she had been with him for much less. "You know we will."

Reinhardt looked quickly around. "So, the usual place?"

"Down in the willows where no one can see us."

"At sunset."

"We'll be there."

He nodded, then turned and hurried out of the tent. Kahlfa was al-ready tearing off a piece of chicken. "So, we have to do him later?"

Jesamine picked up one of the petas. "Isn't it worth it not to have to eat slave slop?"

Kahlfa chewed and nodded, speaking with her mouth full. "I guess so."

"You can kiss him and tickle his asshole while I suck him off. Isn't it worth it? You know how fast he is."

"One day we'll be caught."

"One day we'll be caught doing something."

"I'd rather it was later than sooner, though."

"Then leave that damned chicken alone."

Kahlfa continued to chew. "Don't worry. I'll be there, kissing and tickling."

They ate quickly and in silence. When they were finished, Jesamine stretched. "I've been having these dreams."

"Again?"

"Almost every night."

Kahlfa, who had been sniffing one of the cheroots, looked around, apparently more worried by Jesamine's dreams being overheard than by the coming illegal assignation with Reinhardt. "About the young men again?"

"The same ones."

Kahlfa gestured to the entrance to the tent. "Let's go and smoke these outside. I don't want to talk dreams in here."

T W O

ARGO

Argo Weaver had no experience of freedom. He had often roamed the woods with Will and Jason, but they had always returned to their homes to sleep and eat. To be out on his own with no place of shelter to which to return was something else entirely. He had fled with a bag of food, a blanket, his stepfather's pistol and ammunition, but only the most nebulous of plans. Argo had been out for three days, and no matter how he tried to husband his scant stolen rations, they were rapidly dwindling to nothing. He had also learned that a wool blanket was of little use for sleeping in the woods, and now the thing was little more than a large damp rag, and he was sorely tempted to discard it as a useless sodden burden. His boots, though, were proving sound and watertight, something he did not like to admit since they were the handiwork of his stepfather, although, after just the first three days and nights, the significance of Herman Kretch, his mother, and his sisters was rapidly diminishing and taking on a shadowy quality. Where once the four of them had dominated his life, they were fast becoming a part of a past to which there was no possible return. Argo was also learning just how abysmally ignorant he was about anything beyond the narrow confines of Thakenham. In some respects, it was just as well that he had made no concrete plans because, if he had, he would have been forced to radically revise them.

He had imagined that he would find the woods to be an uninhabited wasteland once he was beyond the familiar tracks and trails a day's walk out from the village where he had grown up. Almost immediately he discovered this to be a long way from the truth. Although he had yet to encounter any living people, either friend, foe, or impartial, something for which, so far, he was profoundly glad, the signs of human traffic were plain to see beside the main trails and even along more hidden paths and the sheltered banks of streams and gullies. The ashes and charred wood of campfires, the bones, rinds, and paper packaging left where food had been eaten, items of discarded clothing, old and yellowing broadsheets, a single, cast-off boot, all combined with footprints, blazes on the trunks of trees, and broken branches to bear testimony that the woods were neither empty nor untraveled. Argo's most disturbing find had come in an otherwise pretty glade where the animal-scattered bones of two corpses with ominous bullet holes in the back of each skull lay amid the sunlit ferns. Argo had no idea of who the dead might have been, or why they had been shot, and he did not especially want to guess, but the remains were enough to set him hurrying on, watchful and ready to jump at the slightest sound or movement.

Constant vigilance, when coupled with what was little more than an endless trudging boredom, all too easy slipped away. The woods, of course, offered an infinite variety of sights, but after days on his lone march, Argo started to see it as an infinite variety of the same thing, and his prevalent emotion became one of nagging worry. He worried about his food, now all but gone. He worried about his navigation, rudimentary in the extreme. He was fairly confident that he was going roughly north, and he presumed he would see some advance warning signs before he actually reached the Mosul lines, but, beyond that, his best direction-finding technique was to point his right shoulder towards the rising sun, and if, when the sun set, it was to his left, assume he was doing approximately okay. He knew the geography of Virginia would not allow him to go too far wrong. If he veered too far to the west, he would see the mountains, and if he strayed to the east, he would ultimately run into the sea. He was not pressed for time, so detours did not bother him. Food was his major concern. He might have been raised in the country, but he placed little reliance on his trapping skills. He might, with some trial and error, trap a bird or rabbit, but that would require staying in one place, and Argo definitely didn't want to do that. The other alternative was to risk approaching human habitation to beg, steal, or, since he had his pistol, commit armed robbery if sufficiently driven to desperation. Images of village stores packed with goodies, and hot apple pies cooling on cottage window ledges, floated into his mind, but he realized these were fantasies of a lost past. Precious few pies cooled on window ledges under the Mosul occupation, and the stores were empty of their peacetime goods. He supposed it might be possible to bring down a deer with his pistol, but so far he had not seen anything like a deer, and even if he did, to fire a shot would be a long-range advertisement of his presence.

Every so often, a panic of birds would clatter into the air from the overhead canopy of leaves and branches, maybe spooked by a predator or by Argo himself. These eruptions of noise served as regular reminders to keep watching his back and not fall into the negligence of a trudging, introspective, hungry daydream. On the afternoon of the fourth day, he had his first contact with anything except the birds and the trees and the constant uneven ground under his feet. He was crossing a shallow ravine when a pack of wild dogs appeared out of nowhere, above and behind him. The dogs stopped and Argo stopped, and the canines and the boy stared silently at each other. The pack was made up of eight or nine mutts of assorted shapes and sizes, and their leader, the alpha male, seemed to be a black-and-white, wall-eyed, half-breed collie. They might once have been domesticated pets, but their lolling tongues and watchful eyes told how they had long since reverted to the wild. Argo's hand went slowly to the butt of his gun. He had plenty of ammunition, but, as with his earlier deer-hunting fantasy, he was aware that to fire a shot would be foolhardy, guaranteed to attract the attention of any Mosul patrol that might be in the vicinity. On the other hand, the dogs could be as hungry as he was, and a shot might turn out to be the only way to save his life. Perhaps just a single bullet would work. To kill or even wound one dog, preferably the big collie, might be enough to scare off the others. Despite the tension of the confrontation, he also wondered if he could eat a dog. Could he cook the carcass in such a way that he would not betray himself by the smoke of his fire, or would he have to eat it raw? Before he could make a decision, however, the dogs turned and loped away, perhaps deciding he was not worth their trouble. They were gone as suddenly and silently as they had appeared, but, for the rest of the afternoon, he could not shake the feeling that he was being followed, and that possibly the dogs were trailing him at a distance, waiting for a moment when he could be taken unawares. As it turned out, though, it was something else entirely that took him by surprise.

The sun was setting, making it almost as dark as night where the trees grew most thickly, while, in other spots, the last red rays were almost blinding as they lanced through gaps in the foliage. Argo was glumly contemplating another restless, uneasy night on the hard ground, huddled in his damp blanket, when a voice seemed to come out of nowhere. "You're no woodsman, Argo Weaver. I've been following you for maybe three hours, and you never even suspected."

The voice was that of a woman, a young woman, and she seemed to know him. Something was familiar about her voice, but Argo could not put a name to it. At first he simply froze in his tracks, uncertain of the direction from which the words had come.

"You look like you're hungry. Do you want an apple?"

Now he spun round, pulling his pistol from his belt. The speaker seemed to be behind him. He cocked one of the hammers. "Don't make any sudden moves."

"Is that all the thanks I get? I offer you an apple, and you pull a gun on me?"

"Why don't you show yourself?"

"You're really not up to this, Argo. If I was a Mosul, you'd have been dead meat five minutes ago. You know that some of those devils are cannibals?"

"Just show yourself, damn it."

"Are you saying you don't recognize me?"

Branches moved in a shadowy thicket, and a figure ducked from cover, emerging into the open. But whoever she was, she stood between Argo and the fading light and was only an indistinct silhouette. Argo cocked the hammer on the second barrel of his pistol. For all he knew there might be more than one of them. "Just come ahead slow and easy. I could still shoot you."

"You really are a babe in the woods. You ought to get yourself back to Thakenham."

The woman came slowly towards him, and, as she approached, he was able to make out more details. She was dressed in a ragtag collection of bits of uniform, mostly covered in a long, dirty duster coat. On her head she sported the kind of officer's kepi that had been favored by the men of the Southland Alliance, with a square of fabric in back that protected the wearer's neck from the sun. Argo was not sure what you called the thing. "Who are you?"

"You really don't know me? It hasn't been that long."

She reached up and pulled off the cap. A shock of unkempt blond hair tumbled out. Argo was suddenly looking at a face that had once been familiar. "Bonnie? Bonnie Appleford?"

"Finally, he remembers me."

The Appleford family had farmed a modest spread just outside of Thakenham, mainly raising dairy cattle and sturdy plough horses that Old Tom Appleford had traded at the market in Bridgehampton. Argo hadn't known Bonnie well, but he had known her. She had been two, maybe three years older than Argo, a wide gulf when the boy is ten or eleven years old and the girl fourteen or fifteen. Her father had been killed when he had attempted to prevent the Mosul from confiscating his horses, and Bonnie had disappeared shortly after that. She had been a shapely, good-looking girl, what the older boys had called "a piece of ass." Even before the Mosul conquest, she had gained herself a reputation for wildness and going to parties in the deep woods beyond the Bridgehampton Road with the other almost-grown kids, the rowdy and rebellious ones who scandalized Christians and Wiccans alike, drinking wine and 'shine and dancing round a fire to the dirty four-four.

"We thought you'd been taken by the Mosul."

"Those devils will never take me."

"You ran?"

"Fucking right I ran."

"And you've been out here ever since?"

"I've been a lot of places, kid. I've been a whole lot of places. There are more people in the bush than you know, Argo. Partisans, refugees, moonshiners, and aborigines; the strange ones that have gone feral, and the ones we don't even talk about. The Mosul try hard, but the bastards can't catch all of us."

She was close to him now, and he could see that her duster and the jacket under it were festooned with badges. It seemed like she was wearing the insignia of half the regiments that had fought in the war. He could also see that, despite her strange and ragged clothes and generally unkempt appearance, she had grown into an extremely attractive young woman. He felt a certain stirring that caused him to completely forget that he was still pointing his gun at her. Bonnie, on the other hand, was very well aware of it. "Will you put that piece away? It's hardly the way to show you're pleased to see me."

"I'm sorry."

He turned away and carefully uncocked the hammers. Bonnie nodded. "That's better."

Argo was about to stuff the gun back in the waistband of his pants, but Bonnie stopped him. "Let me see that thing."

Argo passed the pistol to her without a word. Bonnie examined it for a moment. "Made by George and James Bolton of Jamestown?"

"That's what it says."

"A cuckold's piece?"

"That what my stepfather used to call it."

Bonnie Appleford raised an eyebrow. "Your stepfather?"

"My mother married Herman Kretch."

"She must have been desperate. Herman Kretch was a pig, and I can only assume he still is."

"He still is."

"Then you're well away from him."

Argo grimaced. "You don't have to tell me."

"So are you running from the Mosul, or are you running from him?"

"I'm going north to Albany."

"It took you long enough."

"I was just a kid."

Bonnie looked Argo up and down. "But now you're a man?"

"I'm fourteen."

Bonnie's expression was dismissive. "You're still a kid."

Argo tried to look older than his age. "You think so?"

She suddenly raised the gun and pointed it at Argo's head. She cocked both hammers with a deft ease that indicated she had handled a lot of weapons since Argo had last seen her. "You gave up your gun, didn't you? All I had to do was ask."

"I trusted you."

"That's the first lesson you learn out here. Don't trust anyone unless you know them really well."

"I know you."

Bonnie corrected him. "You *used* to know me. You have no idea what I might have become."

"You want to shoot me?"

Bonnie suddenly looked sad. "No, kid, I'm just showing you the way things are out here. You never give up your weapon just because someone asks, and you don't trust anyone just because you knew them before the war." She uncocked the pistol and handed it back to him. "And you definitely don't trust a woman just because she looks like me. There are sluts who'll slit your throat for the price of meal, or because some Teuton pimp told them to."

Argo had nothing to say. His humiliation was close to complete. He avoided Bonnie Appleford's eyes as he replaced the gun in his belt. The light was now almost gone, and Bonnie looked around. "We had better find ourselves a sheltered place to bed down for the night. There was a niche between some big tree roots back a-ways that could suit us."

She turned and walked back the way that Argo had come as though completely confident that he would follow her. Wherever Bonnie Appleford had been, and whatever she had done since she had left Thakenham, she had acquired a definite natural authority. They walked for about twenty yards, and then she indicated a space between the exposed roots of an old oak. "That will do us just fine. It'll be a comfortable fit, with some protection from the wind, and we'll be all but invisible if anyone should happen by. Start gathering some dry leaves, okay?"

She slipped out of her duster, and Argo saw that a wide belt was strapped about her hips, supporting the weight of a heavy holstered six-shooter and large sheathed Jones knife. The mystery deepened regarding what Bonnie had been up to since her escape from Thakenham. Argo did not think it was appropriate to comment on the weapons after all his other blunders, so he simply did as he was told, respecting that Bonnie seemed to know infinitely more about life in the wild than he did. Argo started piling leaves into the niche between the roots and packing them down until they were thick enough to provide a layer of insulation between their two bodies and the ground. When was finished, Bonnie covered them with her coat and his blanket and then stood back and inspected the makeshift creation. "That should do."

Argo was suddenly afflicted with a severe awkwardness. Their makeshift bed might have been out in the great wide open, and fashioned from leaves and old clothes, but it was still a bed, and he was about to share it with a grown and good-looking woman; indeed, a grown and good-looking woman who appeared to know much more than Argo did about practically everything. She noticed his hesitation and looked at him questioningly. "Is there a problem?"

Argo shook his head. "No."

"So? Are you just going to stand there?"

She unbuckled the belt with its gun and knife, then knelt down and placed them on a level part of the nearest tree root so they were in easy reach. "Is it okay if I take this side?"

"Sure. I don't mind."

"So, lay yourself down. There's nothing else to do."

Argo lowered himself down onto the bed of leaves, but remained sitting. Bonnie gestured to his gun. "You'd better do something with that if you don't want to blow your balls off in the night."

As he slipped the pistol into the top of the bag, leaving it within reach just as Bonnie had done with hers, his stomach growled. He let hunger override his more complex emotions. "You said something about an apple?"

"You think I'm Eve in the Bible?"

"No, but you offered me an apple earlier."

"That's right. I did." She produced a slightly bruised Golden Delicious. "Here, kid, knock yourself out."

Argo bit into the apple, pleased to be eating, and also pleased to have something to do. "I wish we had a fire."

"Are you cold?"

Argo shook his head. "No, not really. Not yet. I just like to look into a fire."

This was only partially true. He remembered the fire that had burned Gaila Ford, and he remembered the fire that last night in what had been his home, when his stepfather had been beating him. Some fires he liked, but there were others that he hated. Fire could be both a friend and an enemy. But that had been so since the dawn of time.

Bonnie sighed. "I know what you mean, but a fire would tell everyone for miles around that we were here."

"I know that. I was just wishing."

Bonnie pulled a metal flask from her jacket and offered it to him. "Take a hit on this. It's almost as good as a fire, both for the body and the mind."

Argo uncapped the flask and took a tentative hit. It was not what he had expected. "This isn't 'shine."

"You've drunk 'shine?"

"Enough to know that this isn't it."

"That, kid, is old-fashioned sipping whiskey from before the war. It was made by a Mr. John Daniels, who used to ply his trade in Lynchburg before the Mosul ruined everything. He called it Old Number Seven, and there isn't too much of it left anymore, so go easy."

Argo took a second sip and gave the flask back to Bonnie. The liquor made his head momentarily spin. Bonnie drank herself and then replaced the cap on the flask and placed it down beside her. "Lay back, Argo Weaver. We should get our rest when and where we can."

Argo finally lay back, but he was careful not to make any kind of physical contact with Bonnie. She smiled and then laughed. "Don't be shy, Argo. Cuddle up close. The nights are getting cold, and we should share the heat. Believe me, you don't have to be a gentleman with me."

He moved a little closer. Bonnie raised herself up on one elbow and looked down at him. A shiver ran through Argo that wasn't from the chill of the night. Bonnie smiled again, and her face softened. She brushed his hair out of his eyes. A half-moon was showing through the trees, and he realized that Bonnie was beautiful when she was not acting tough. "Have you ever done it with a girl, Argo Weaver?"

He tried to sound nonchalant. "Sure, lots of times."

He knew he had failed miserably when she immediately disbelieved him. "Oh, yeah? Who with?"

"I can't tell you that."

"Always the gentleman?"

"That's right."

Bonnie was suddenly a teasing teenage girl again. "You've never done it."

"I have, too."

"You're a bloody liar."

"I am not."

"Oh, yes, you are."

"You promise not to laugh at me?"

"I won't laugh."

Argo turned his head away. "I am a liar. I'm a liar and a virgin."

Bonnie reached for the flask. "With that combination going for you, we'd better both have another drink."

"I thought good whiskey was hard to find?"

"This may turn out to be an occasion."

They both drank from the flask, and then Bonnie leaned close to Argo and gently kissed him. Their lips lingered, and gentleness was replaced by a pressing insistence. Their tongues intertwined, their mouths pressed harder, with a primal hunger, and Argo's hands were on Bonnie's body. She helped him by slipping out of her uniform jacket and unbuttoned her undershirt. Her breasts were pale in the light of the rising moon as he fondled and kissed them. Unbidden, her hands were inside his pants, stroking and fondling in return. Her breathing was quickening, and Argo realized that Bonnie was not only doing him the supreme favor, she was also satisfying her own needs and apparently becoming as aroused as he was. In some respects this revelation frightened him more than his first idea that she was merely taking pity on his callow inadequacy. He was suddenly responsible for ensuring her pleasure, and he had no idea how to accomplish this and only knew what to do in the broadest sense. He felt her hips rise slightly as she eased down her buckskin pants. He knew that this was going to be it, that novice first experience that he was going to remember for all of the rest of his life. Free of the confining leathers, her thighs, as pale under the moon as her breasts, spread beneath him, and she used her hands to ease him inside her, at the same time breathing hoarse words of endearment into his ear, coupled with a certain passionate instruction. "That's right. That feels so good. That really feels good."

At first the movements of his hips were slow and tentative, as he told himself in elated amazement that, after all the imagining, this was it, this was how it really felt. How much better to be doing this with someone like Bonnie, rather than an ignorant Thakenham farm girl who might be just as clumsy and ignorant as he was, and to be guided to all the right moves and responses by a voice that came from deep in her throat. "That's right, sweetness. So nice. So nice and so easy."

But an urgency inside Argo could not be content with nice and easy. As one of Bonnie's legs circled his waist, his thrusts came harder and faster. Rational thought and sensitive intentions deserted him. He was nothing but a selfish and driving animal. Bonnie was panting and making small mewing sounds, and, when she now spoke, the words came in breathless fits and starts. "Oh, Argo . . . baby . . . that feels . . . wonderful. Oh . . . yes! But please . . . slow down. Please slow . . . down so I . . . can enjoy it . . . too."

But Argo could not listen, even when her voice became less husky and more insistent. "Slow down, boy."

"I'm not . . . a boy."

"Oh, yes . . . you are, and you need . . . to slow down."

But Argo could only cry out. "I think I'm going to . . ."

His climax came well before he would have desired, even before he could speak its name, and, in the seconds after, as his breath came in harsh bursts and his senses reeled, he feared that Bonnie would treat his failure to sustain with both disappointment and contempt. He could only babble excuses. "I'm sorry. I fucked up, didn't I? I just couldn't hold it back."

Instead of pulling back from him as Argo would have expected, she held him even tighter, cradling him in her arms and kissing him to stem his guilt. "My dear, sweet Argo. It was your first time. Did you think you could be a great lover with no experience and no knowledge of the game? It's lucky for you I have the wise-woman's protection."

"Protection?"

"Against me getting knocked up, stupid."

For a time, they lay side by side until the chill of the night on their damp bodies caused them to pull the blanket and coat over themselves, but it wasn't too long before Argo felt desire stirring again. Bonnie felt his rekindled excitement and laughed. "That's the great thing about you young men. You recover so very quickly."

This time, Bonnie took him by surprise and slid down his body to take him in her mouth. She brought him to a state of gasping, undulating excitement and then straddled him so, this time, she could control the speed of his response. The moon had risen almost to its zenith, and Argo gazed up at her in awe as her marble body rhythmically rode him, her spine alternately arching and relaxing, her eyes closed and face fixed in ecstatic and transported, loose-lipped concentration. When it was over, they seemed to have exhausted both themselves and all possible conversation. They fell asleep quickly, and the next sound that Argo heard was the faint crunch of boots on dry leaves and the snap of a twig in the mid-distance.

CORDELIA

The conference in the Round Room of the West Tower had adjourned for refreshments and, as far as Cordelia was concerned, not before time. She was well aware that politics were important, but so much politics had flowed back and forth in the last few hours that her head was starting to spin. The high point of all the talk, as far as she was concerned, had been when Field Marshal Virgil Dunbar had risen to speak. His address to the delegates seated at the round table and all the other onlookers, aides, and guards, like Cordelia herself, crowded around the walls, had begun as a simple report from the Potomac front. He had described the extensive preparations that had been made. The huge earthworks that had been raised, reinforced with steel and stone, all along the north bank of the river. He had thanked the delegates from the Norse Union at length for the breechloading field guns, the airships, the improved wireless communications, all of which would give the kingdom of Albany a fighting chance when the Mosul assault finally came. But then, with an increasingly grim demeanor, he had warned the assembly that despite their high morale, more advanced technology, and superior weapons, the army of Albany could in no way match the sheer, overwhelming numbers that the Mosul could put into the field.

"We could go on killing them day after day, night after night, until the river is so choked with corpses that Hassan could advance over his own dead, and they would still keep coming."

Having delivered both the good and bad news, Dunbar then waxed unexpectedly eloquent for a normally taciturn and practical military man.

"As the day of confrontation approaches, it is not only Albany that stands at the crossroads of its destiny. What we do here may shape the fate of the entire world and dictate the path of history for the next thousand years. We live in terrible times, and a terrible task faces us. If we cannot rise to this desperate moment, if we cannot hold the line and, once and for all, turn back the tide of this horror that already holds one entire continent in its monstrous grip, we may see all of humanity fall to the powers of evil. We may see liberty itself consumed in the flames and the light of hope extinguished for centuries to come."

A spontaneous round of applause had followed this impassioned conclusion to Dunbar's address, but then the delegates had fallen silent as Vice President Ingmar Ericksen had risen to his feet to speak on behalf of the Norse Union. From the start, his tone had been regretful. The NU would not take the final step and declare war on the Mosul Empire, despite all the hopes on the part of the king and Jack Kennedy that, in so doing, a second front would be created. Without either the passion of Dunbar or the wit and urbane reason of Jack Kennedy, he methodically explained how, while technologically advanced and unarguably having the advantage in both sea and air power, the Norse Union had neither the numerical advantages nor the command of landmass enjoyed by the Mosul Empire. To openly declare war would be to court disaster. The Norse Union could put up a costly fight, but, in the long run, there was very little that they could do in a state of declared war to prevent the Mosul from crossing the English Channel. The clipper port of Bristol, and the naval bases at Portsmouth and Plymouth, would certainly be taken, and the great provincial capital of London would be placed in dire peril. He went on to explain how his generals had made it clear that, if the NU went to war with the Mosul, far from establishing a second front that would lighten the pressure on the conflict on the Potomac, it could in fact prove, in the long run, to be to Albany's fatal detriment, since much-needed supplies and munitions would have to be diverted from the Americas to this new theatre of combat in Northern Europe.

Oddly, as Ericksen rejected Albany's ultimate goal for the conference, Cordelia sensed very little disappointment among the representatives of Albany. Kennedy, Dunbar, and the king sat poker-faced and solemn, but hardly crushed by disappointment. She suspected that this meeting was primarily for show and that all the major decisions had been thrashed out in private much earlier. This seemed even more likely as Ericksen went on to outline what the Norse would do as an alternative to a head-on declaration of war. The right of passage on the high seas would be rigorously enforced, and, where the Mosul convoy routes between Cadiz, Lisbon, and Savannah crossed the sea lanes used by Norse Union clipper ships bound for Cape Horn and the Far East, any obstruction of their merchant shipping would be treated as an act of hostility and be met with overwhelming retaliatory force. To ensure that the Mosul would fully understand this, the great Norse battleships the *Odin,* the *Drake,* and the *Covenant,* supported by the cruisers *Victory, Bjorn,* and *Freida,* plus a free-roaming wolf pack of submarines and their attendant supply ships, would be deployed in the Northern Ocean, while a fourth cruiser, the *Cromwell,* supplied from Manhattan and Baltimore, would be stationed in international waters off the Chesapeake Bay to keep the Mosul from establishing a second supply base almost on the front line at Norfolk Harbor. Perhaps more important, the Norse would increase the volume and expand the scope of the materiel they were supplying to Albany under the lend-lease deal, and it would include more submarines and airships, and, in the future, the previously denied rocket bombs, along with Norse advisors to train Albany crews, would be made available. Cordelia knew that all this, especially the rocket bombs and the submarines, was probably what Kennedy and the king had really wanted in the first place.

As Cordelia took her turn at the buffet, helping herself to a glass of cranberry juice that she spiked with a fairly powerful shot of gin after assuring herself that Colonel Patton was otherwise occupied and would not immediately bust her for drinking on duty, she found that, quite by accident, she was standing next to the prime minister, a discovery that caused her to attempt to salute and curtsy at the same time and almost spill her drink in the process, something that would never do for a titled lady and commissioned officer in a very public place. Jack Kennedy had merely smiled. Maybe young women becoming confused and undone was something that happened to him all the time. Even in his late seventies, and leaning on his cane, the man still had an overwhelming aura of power and potency.

"Do I know you?"

Cordelia shook her head. "No, sir. Not really."

"You remind me a lot of an old friend."

"An old friend, sir?"

"A lady called Dulcimer Blakeney."

"My mother, sir."

"Then you must be the Lady Cordelia."

"That's right."

"You were just a child the last time I saw you."

"I'm not a child any longer, sir."

"So I see."

Stories had been whispered about Kennedy and her mother for as long as Cordelia could remember. The Prime Minister's eyes twinkled, and Cordelia felt her heart flutter. Would she dare an affair with the formidable but equally notorious Jack Kennedy? He was more than old enough to be her father. Indeed, he might well be older than her father. To compound the sense of incest, he had, in all probability, if the venerable gossip was to be given credence, slept with her own mother.

"Can I assist you with anything, sir?"

"No, my dear, I am still able to help myself."

The flutter came again. I'll wager you are, you magnificent old goat.

"Perhaps another time."

"Yes, sir."

With a final twinkle, Kennedy turned away and was instantly engaged in conversation with Vincent Corleone of the United Workers. The moment of temptation was over, and Cordelia still did not know what she would have done, or what sins she might have agreed to, had it continued. She might have followed Kennedy and hovered on the fringe of the conversation looking demure and gorgeous, but that would have probably come under the heading of what Patton had called "trying to become the center of attention," and, without looking around, she knew that the RWA colonel was somewhere in the room waiting for one of her aristocratic underlings to commit some kind of transgression so she could fall on them like the wrath divine. Cordelia decided that she would content herself with her illicit, but fortunately undetected, drinking on duty and leave it at that. She looked around to see what else she could see during this social break in the conference and discovered that a very tall and very blond Norse Air Corps captain, the same one who had looked at her on his way in, was standing right behind her with the expression of a man who wanted to start a conversation but was not sure of exactly the right opening line. He could only be one of the ones that Coral Metcalfe had described as "real dolls," and Cordelia decided that she would give him all the encouragement he might require to get him started. "Do you have everything you need, sir?"

The captain blinked. He seemed a little surprised. "Everything I need?"

"Food? A drink? I'm not exactly a waitress, but part of my duty assignment is to see that you gentlemen are kept happy."

The captain raised a glass that looked like it contained Scotch and soda and smiled. "I have a drink, but I'm extremely happy to be talking to you."

Cordelia placed his accent as Irish and decided that he had a smooth line in charm, tempered by just the right degree of shyness. "So you don't need anything?"

The captain glanced in the direction of Kennedy and Corleone. "Are you part of the prime minister's staff?"

Cordelia shook her head. "No, I'm just a humble lieutenant attached to the War Office."

"You and Prime Minister Kennedy seemed to be on quite intimate terms."

"He knew my mother rather well."

"Your mother . . ."

"Before she was married. The prime minister seems to have known a lot of people's mothers, if the legends are to be believed."

"Prime Minister Kennedy is quite a hero in our country."

"He is in ours, but he also has something of a reputation as a ladies' man."

"Is that good or bad?"

"I always found it quite endearing." Cordelia was aware that the refreshment break would all too soon end and the conference return to the business at hand. She did not want to lose the tall blond captain just because his shyness was stopping him from getting to the point. "Do you have a name, or do I have to go on calling you sir?"

He smiled. "It's Phelan Mallory."

Cordelia offered her hand. "Cordelia Blakeney."

"Well, Miss Blakeney . . ."

"Actually, it's Lady Blakeney, but don't let that put you off."

"Well, Lady Blakeney, this may seem a little forward, but there is a war on, and time is at something of a premium . . ."

He hesitated, and Cordelia inwardly fumed. Ask the question, goddamn it. "Yes?"

"I was wondering if perhaps you would like to join me for a quieter drink after tonight's banquet."

Damn Patton to the most torturous circle of hell. "Unfortunately, I'm in trouble. I'm confined to my quarters."

Captain Phelan Mallory looked crestfallen. He clearly assumed she was rejecting him. "Oh, dear."

"Really, I wish I could, but we have this colonel, and this morning I was late, and she decided to make an issue of it."

Finally Mallory said something intelligent. "Perhaps if I made an official request that you be attached to our delegation as an aide?"

Cordelia looked at him with unbelievably innocent eyes. This one would be putty in her hands. "You could do that?"

"How could it be a problem? We need your help. Right now, no one from the Norse Union is going to be refused anything."

Delegates were already moving back to their places at the round table. Phelan caught the urgency. "Will you be at the banquet?"

"Of course."

"Then I'll be able to find you. I'll have a pass or whatever official papers you think we might need."

Cordelia beamed. "I'll make myself very easy to find."

The delegates resumed their seats, and a silence fell over the room. Jane Tennyson, the Norse ambassador to the Court of Albany, rose to speak. Her speech promised to be boring but important. It had fallen to Tennyson to outline the terms of what was to be called the Treaty of Military Exchange, the official instrument by which the supply of munitions from the NU to Albany would be increased. Cordelia, however, had no problem with what would be an hour or more of dry diplomatic details. She was already planning her evening and feeling triumphantly elated that she had not only snared her young officer but also outfoxed Colonel damn-her-eyes Grace Patton. With an official request from the NU delegation for her services, there was not a thing the awful woman could do about it.

Maybe later she would make Cordelia's life miserable, but that was later, and later was when Cordelia would deal with it.

RAPHAEL

Raphael had found a niche on the troopship were he could not only draw, but be away from seasick boys and the stench of vomit. This hiding place was on the deck, close to the stern, in a space between what looked like two grey-painted pieces of winding gear that was just large enough for him to squat out of sight. He had no idea of the two objects' function, but they suited his need for a sheltered spot where he would not be easily seen. His hiding place was less than comfortable. He was sitting on the cold steel plates of the deck and resting his back against an iron cogwheel some two feet in diameter, but he found that if he used his greatcoat as a backrest and sat on the blanket from his bunk, he could be reasonably comfortable. He also discovered that no one seemed to be particularly bothered about how he vanished every day that the troopship was not buffeted by rain and squalls, or what he might be up to. As long as he showed for morning and evening roll call to prove that he had neither been accidentally swept over the side nor deliberately drowned himself, no interest was expressed in what he did the rest of the time. The majority of the officers and the Zhaithan priests on their way to the Americas took passage on more comfortable vessels, positioned nearer to the safer center stations in the flotilla of ships that made up the convoy. The ones of the lesser elite, who had been given berths on the same ship as Raphael, a wallowing steam-driven tub called the MSS *Saracen* relegated to the comparatively exposed starboard side of the convoy, stayed strictly in their cabins and the officers' saloon and certainly did not prowl the decks seeking out transgressing conscripts.

The crew of the *Saracen,* and the ship's handful of officers, did not appear to have any problem with Raphael being up on deck. Most assumed, if they saw him at all, that he was doing exactly what he was doing: finding himself a very sensible refuge in the brisk, fresh ocean air, away from the overcrowded holds and their largely seasick human cargo. The majority of sailors ignored him, a few nodded, but one, a common seaman from the city of Naples who was not much older than Raphael himself, would stop for a brief conversation and even share his tea with him. His name was Placido, and he had crossed the ocean no less then seven times and seemed to know the ropes both figuratively and literally.

"It might seem bad below decks on this scow, but think yourself lucky we're not carrying horses."

"Horses?" The idea had not occurred to Raphael that the Mosul would transport horses across the ocean. "Don't they already have horses in the Americas?"

"Some, but apparently not enough. The poor bloody horses get killed at the same rate as the men, don't they? Although they know less about why they're here and what they're doing."

"From what I've seen, most of the men don't have a clue. I hardly know what I'm doing here."

Placido had responded with a sage nod. "You've got a point there, brother. But face it, you know a little more than a poor dumb horse, am I right?"

"I guess so."

"The horses can't sneak up on the deck and make themselves scarce."

Placido then lit a hand-rolled cigarette with a wood match that he struck in his thumbnail with the skill of a veteran. He puffed on it and offered Raphael a drag. "Smoke?"

Raphael took a drag and coughed. He did not really enjoy the new fad of smoking tobacco, but joined Placido to be sociable. He doubted he would live long enough to need to worry about lung disease. "Why is it so bad when the ship's carrying horses?"

"They scream, my friend. All the time they scream. And if the swell gets bad, they try and kick their way out of the stalls. A lot get injured and have to be butchered on the deck, and then it's 'Placido, clean up the blood,' and horsemeat stew on the menu all the way to Savannah." He glanced over his shoulder to see that no one was around to overhear. "Of course, the bastard officers' horses, that's a different matter. They have grooms with them twenty-four hours a day to make sure nothing happens to them, but ain't that always the way of it?"

Placido had also shown an interest in Raphael's drawings and had made complimentary noises as he leafed through his homemade sketchbook. "These are really good, man."

"Thanks."

"No, I mean it. You're a fucking artist. I'm from Italia, don't forget. We know all about art. You didn't ought to be in this shit."

Raphael had laughed bitterly. "You and me seem to be the only ones who think that way."

Placido had agreed. "Ain't that the truth, and no mistake? And you want to keep those out of sight of the priests and snitches. They don't take kindly to grunts who show any kind of talent except maybe for killing and dying."

Raphael looked rueful. "I already got ten with the formal cane because I got careless."

"Damn. I bet that hurt."

"You're not kidding."

"Here at sea they use the lash. I don't know which is worse, the cane or the lash, and, believe me, I really don't want to fucking find out."

Eventually Placido asked the inevitable question. "You think I could maybe have one of those? Maybe one of the naked girls? It'd look fucking fine over my bunk."

"I don't know. That's how I got into trouble before."

"You don't have to worry. The priests don't bother us here at sea. They stick to their own part of the ship, and the master-at-arms, he don't care what we stick up over our bunks. If anyone asks, I won't tell them where I got it, I swear. I'll say I bought it off a peddler while I was on shore leave, outside a Cadiz whorehouse or something."

"Your word on that?"

"My word. And I'm not looking for something for nothing. Next time I come by, I'll bring you a shot of whiskey and a cigar."

That was the best offer Raphael had ever had for his work. "Yeah?"

"Sure. That's the only things the fucking Americas are good for, tobacco and whiskey."

Still with some trepidation despite all of Placido's assurances, Raphael handed over one of his fantasy nudes, and the deckhand went about his business.

The ocean voyage was the first time that Raphael had been able to draw without constant interruption since he had been pressed into the service. Almost everyone else seemed to be living in constant fear of attack.

Indeed, fear and rumors were the twin coins of their floating realm among the ones who were well enough to speak or not so sick they wanted to die anyway. Although the Norse Union was not officially at war, its big battleships had, by all accounts, fired on a number of convoys under the pretext of keeping the sea lanes clear for the Norse clipper ships on course for Cape Horn and the Far East. The Albany navy also made regular hit-and-run attacks on the Mosul convoys, but these usually came when the transports and their escorts were close to sighting the Americas, just a day or so out of Savannah. Grim stories were also circulating of Albany having a number of submarines, and maybe more in the future. The idea of submarines had become the horror of everyone involved in the convoy traffic, from the ranking officer to the lowliest rating and the wretched human cargo of soldiers in the hold. That strange iron boats, like man-made sharks, could cruise invisibly beneath the surface of the waves and fire explosive torpedoes capable of sinking a ship in a single devastating surprise explosion was like some supernatural nightmare against which the Mosul ships had no defense.

Up to that point, the Mosul had, despite some fairly heavy losses, been reasonably successful at moving their convoys across the ocean and back comparatively intact. The key was to keep up and maintain a formation in which the transports were closely grouped, like a herd of cattle or a flock of sheep, and surrounded by a protective screen of well-armed ironclads. For a transport to fall behind, because of engine trouble or some other delaying problem, was almost certainly to court destruction and become the victim of scavenging Caribbean pirates or the privateers who were little better than pirates except that they sailed under a Norse Union flag of convenience. Much of the *Saracen*'s ability to keep up with the convoy and remain in comparative safety was due to the stokers who, hour after backbreaking hour, fed coal to the furnaces that heated the boilers. At regular intervals, two or three of them would stumble out onto the deck, gasping for air and leaning on the nearest available railing as though almost ready to pass out from their exertions in the heat and smoke. Stripped to the waist, and with their red faces and coal-blackened, sweat-streaked bodies, they looked like the damned on a brief remission from some terrible metal hell deep in the bowels of the ship, and, in many respects, they were exactly that.

Honing his skills, Raphael had sketched a number of these apparitions from the stokehold, along with the ever-present ocean waves and deckhands going about their duties. He sketched some soldiers rolling dice between the bunks in the hold, details of various parts of the ship visible from his hiding place, and, one time, a Mamaluke major leaning on the rail of the upper deck that was forbidden to the rank and file, staring loftily across the water at a setting sun, completely unaware that a humble conscript was observing him from below and recording his image. By far the majority of Raphael's time, however, was still spent putting the visions that crowded his head down on whatever paper he could beg, find, or steal. Raphael drew more of the naked women that Placido had liked so much, and also mythic beasts, unworldly landscapes, and memories of his home before the Mosul had come and sundered his family, but he kept returning to the likeness of a single face: the girl with caramel skin, huge eyes, and dark hair.

JESAMINE

He laid her down gently, and she held him tightly
On the banks 'neath the dog rose beside the wide river
In the willows, in the wonder, see the clear waters glide
His love buried deeply, her passion surrendered
For the lingering moment, no call or remembrance
No sound on the wind where so many had died

After the third or fourth round of schnapps, these conquering Teuton heroes liked it sentimental to the point of maudlin. In an hour or less they could be nasty or even fighting drunk, ready to call each other out with dueling sabers, but, right at that moment, as Jesamine sang, she had them in the palm of her hand, and a few were actually close to mawkish alcohol tears. Behind her, an Hispanic boy soldier played soft guitar, no doubt grateful that his talent had caused him to be plucked from some conscript suicide squad among the Provincial Levies. This was not to say that later in the night he might not be bent over a cushion, stripped of his britches, and sodomized by some hulking Mamaluke just because he was still there. In the empire of the Mosul, all took their chances, and lived by the whim of the warlord, one hour at a time.

Tender, so tender, so yielding the softness
So willing, so tender, so fragile, so young
For a future remembered in fragments so fleeting
In dreams and memories in tears and in grief
Tomorrows and tomorrows not owned by the lovers
And all that came after the joy of their meeting
Stolen by time in the cloak of a thief

The rhyme pattern was tricky, and shifted from verse to verse, but the kid with guitar, whose name was Garcia, proved more than able to follow the contours of the ballad, and, because he had done so well, Jesamine had whispered to him between songs, "When we're done, try and slip away while you can, brother. I know you want to see the twins do their thing, but it could turn ugly later. Believe me, boy, it could turn real ugly."

The boy had nodded his gratitude, and Jesamine wished she, too, could slip away unnoticed, but she was expected to join Phaall to look decorative and be available. Also, Garcia was only an adjunct while Jesamine was just too damned visible. When her performance was concluded, it had been met with a loud burst of applause. She had bowed politely and made her way to where Colonel Phaall lounged with his cronies—a major, a captain, and another colonel. Some sat on Mosul-style floor cushions, and others, like Phaall, on more Teutonic upright folding chairs. Phaall was drinking schnapps, chased by foaming steins of lager. As Jesamine draped herself at his feet, he patted her on the ass and then promptly proceeded to ignore her. A discussion seemed to be in progress regarding some kind of military problem.

"So the bastards are getting cheeky."

"So it would seem."

"So what exactly did the report say?"

The major in the group around Phaall was Urman, the cavalryman who owned Kahfla, and he seemed to have most of the pertinent information on the subject under discussion. "We just had confirmation. It's as we've suspected for a while. A small force of Albany Rangers, almost certainly in cahoots with the bandit groups in the Appalachians, is definitely operating here, south of the river, right under our noses, gathering intelligence and performing random acts of sabotage. It would seem that some of the attacks that we've been attributing to generalized native resistance are in fact their handiwork."

Usually Jesamine had little or no interest in the war talk of Phaall and his companions, except insomuch as it distracted the colonel's bleary mess-tent focus away from her, but mention of Albany Rangers in the area piqued her interest. For Jesamine, the idea of making contact with enemy guerrillas and maybe escaping across the river with them seemed like a much more attractive fantasy than the popular concubine's dream of having her master fall in love with her and grant her freedom. While Jesamine maintained her well-practiced expression of pliable vacancy, she listened and prepared to take mental notes.

Phaall shrugged. "Well, thank the Deities that I'm an engineer, and it's not my problem. Surely all that's needed is a search-and-destroy mission: winkle out the swine and kill them. Isn't that what the Mamalukes are for?"

The other colonel, whose name was Fragg, and who commanded an infantry regiment, looked round to make sure no one was paying undue attention, but like everyone else in the group, he did not think of Jesamine as a potential eavesdropper. "We all know the Mamalukes aren't exactly precise. They'll crash around the forest on their chargers, burn a couple of villages, and hang a few dozen of entirely the wrong people. These Rangers know their business. They'll know all about the Mamalukes while they're still miles away, and simply vanish."

Phaall stared at Urman. "So what about your boys? Can't they do the job? Aren't they capable of exercising a little precision? We need this nipped in the bud before some rear echelon shithead in Savannah decides this is an issue he can ride to a promotion, and we find ourselves up to our asses in Ministry of Virtue headhunters and Special Forces."

"We could, but there's one other problem."

"What's that?"

"There's a story going round that a demon is leading these Rangers and keeping them in telepathic touch with Albany and maybe the aborigines in the mountains."

Phaall quickly poured himself another schnapps and drank it down in one. "Shit. I hate all that other-side, weird woo-hoo. Wars should be fought man on man without resorting to all this night-crawling, black resources crap. It's bad enough that we have to have the Dark Things up here slipping out of their pens and eating the occasional private, but fucking demons? We don't need no fucking demons at this stage of the game. Does Savannah know about this supposed demon?"

Urman shook his head. "Not yet. We've so far managed to bury the reports as lacking confirmation, but we can't go on doing that for very long. Confirmation's getting harder and harder to avoid or plausibly deny. These bastards are a fact of life."

For once Jesamine found herself in agreement with Phaall. The human side of the Mosul war machine was sickeningly ugly, but that they also made use of ghostly and supernatural dark forces made something deep inside her being cringe with a very fundamental horror. She knew about the small paranormal army of Dark Things and their attendant Mothmen that were now quartered out on the perimeter of the camp. She had never seen them, and, indeed, they were extremely secret and extremely off-limits, but at night a strange glow radiated from the pens where they were confined that could not be hidden or explained away. Everyone on the south bank of the Potomac knew the unthinkable things were there, and, from the way Phaall was talking, even the officers feared and loathed them.

Phaall looked hard at Urman. "Could your men take out these Rangers?"

The major all but squirmed. "Normally I'd say yes, but with a demon involved, I really don't know. How the hell do you go about capturing or killing a demon?"

Fragg nodded. "He's right. None of us knows what we might be up against. We need to call in a few experts, but that means a request to Savannah, and that's the last damn thing we want."

The captain, a subordinate of Fragg whom Jesamine knew as an ineffectual bully called Munz, fresh from across the ocean, spoke for the first time. "Could we not bring in one of our own Zhaithan people to neutralize the demon? Still keep it in the family, so to speak, but get some help with the dark side?"

The others looked at him as though he was retarded, but Fragg was the first to put their contempt into words. "Are you out of your mind, young captain? You tell the Zhaithan any damned thing, and it goes straight back to Savannah. We don't have any bloody Zhaithan in the family. That's a contradiction in terms. Invite in the Zhaithan, any Zhaithan, and that's the fox in the fucking henhouse, boy."

Phaall finished his lager and signaled for another. "Even if they could be trusted, which they can't, they're fucking useless. They're really good at scaring old women and burning heretics, but confront them with a genuine tooth-and-claw enemy, and they'll sure as shit get directions from the Deities to be someplace else that's well out of the line of fire."

Phaall's beer was set in front of him, and he leaned back in his chair. Preparations were being made for the twins to perform. "My best advice to you, young Captain Munz, is to keep your mouth shut until you know what you're talking about. Right now you can watch Mai and Leah do what they do. Pay attention. You might learn something. And while you're watching, reflect how the twins are something else the Zhaithan would like stopped, except, if they tried it, they'd have a bloody mutiny in the Potomac Officer Corps." From Munz, he turned his attention to Flagg and Urman. "As for the rest of us, gentlemen, we might be best advised to let these Rangers and their alleged demon become someone else's problem. Maybe our first consideration should be to cover our own rear ends."

Almost on cue, the round of applause that greeted the appearance of the blond twins followed his words. Even though Jesamine had seen the performance dozens of times before, she dutifully turned her head to watch, reflecting with bored amazement how the men never tired of the same routine. The twins' hair was teased out, and their pink-white bodies were draped in the kind of diaphanous chiffon scarves, pale blue in this instance, that Jesamine and Kahfla privately and laughingly called "giftwrapping." The pair slowly unwrapped each other, undulating to the sound of beaten tablas. When the only remaining scarves were down around their hips, they embraced, and as they kissed, and each identical sister's hands fondled the other's breasts, every male eye in the mess was on them.

ARGO

Bonnie clapped a hand over Argo's mouth and hissed into his ear. "Freeze. Don't move so much as a muscle."

He had woken to a sound that had infiltrated his sleep like a warning, but that he had not consciously heard. At first he could not see anything except Bonnie's face close to his, but he knew from the urgency of both her tone and her breathing that something was seriously amiss, and this was no overture to fresh rapture. He also knew enough to do exactly as he was told, and as she slowly removed her hand, he made no sound and willed himself to sink, as low and invisible as possible, into their bed of leaves. Very slowly she wordlessly pointed, and for the first time he saw the moving shapes between the trees, some fifty or so yards away, although it was hard to judge the exact distance. Argo had no idea how long he had slept, but the moon was still bright, and he was able to make out the shapes of men moving in single file. He could see that they wore the round cooking-pot helmets and the baggy tunics of Mosul foot soldiers. Their rifles were slung over their shoulders, and they moved as though footsore and weary. Nothing about them indicated that they expected to encounter anything dangerous or even untoward in this part of the Virginia woods, especially a runaway boy and a strange, armed young woman. One by one, they passed in the distance and disappeared from sight, but for a long time, Bonnie remained prone and stock-still, and Argo did the same, although he was able to move his head enough to see that she held her pistol in her right hand. Finally, after what seemed to Argo like fifteen or twenty minutes had elapsed, Bonnie slowly got her feet. "I think they're gone." She sniffed the air. "Since they arrived in these parts, the Mosul have taken to smoking like ducks to water. You can smell the tobacco on them coming and going."

Argo also got up, and Bonnie grinned at him. "You did okay there, kid."

"I didn't do anything."

"And that was exactly the right thing to do. Most people only see movement in the dark."

"You think that was a Mosul patrol?"

"More like an infantry company on a night march. Those bastards looked shagged out and dragging. A patrol is usually a bit more alert."

Bonnie was holstering her pistol, and Argo had to ask the obvious question. "Would you have shot it out with them if they'd seen us?"

"How many of them do you figure there were?"

"I don't know. Maybe a dozen."

"I thought there were more, but, okay, say it was a dozen."

"Okay."

"And between us we had eight shots before we had to reload, so if we scored with every shot and they all missed, there would still be four left when we were done shooting. Right?"

"Right."

"So we'd be fucked."

"Right."

"And with the Mosul, it's a real good idea to keep one bullet for yourself, because you absolutely don't want to be taken alive by those fuckers."

Argo lowered his eyes, thinking of Gaila Ford, the fire, and the torture that must have gone before. "I know that much."

Bonnie stretched, looked up at the moon, and sighed. "It's hardly worth going back to sleep now. I figure we might as well move on."

She pulled out her flask, took a hit, and offered it to Argo. "Breakfast?"

He swallowed a slug of the John Daniels and returned the flask. "Can I ask you something?"

"Depends on what it is."

"What have you been doing since you left Thakenham?"

She laughed. "You mean how did I get like this?"

"Something like that."

"I've been fighting the bastards, kid. I've been fighting them every way I can."

Argo could hardly believe what he was hearing. "You've been up in Albany?"

Bonnie busied herself straightening her clothes and kicking away the leaves so the telltale signs of their bedding down were not quite so obvious. As he watched her, Argo felt a little odd, as though the most important night of his life so far was being erased like it never happened. Bonnie, on the other hand, didn't seem to notice. "You've been under Mosul occupation too long, kid. They want you to believe the only fight is along the Potomac. There's plenty more going on than that."

"There is?"

"Why do you think that the bastards don't go into the Appalachians or can't hold the Shenandoah Valley?"

"I never heard any of that."

"That's because the Mosul Information Ministry doesn't want you to hear about it."

"So there are really folks still fighting in Virginia?"

"More than you might suspect." She looked around as though calculating which direction to take. "Can you walk and talk at the same time?"

"Sure."

"So let's move."

As they walked through darkness and on into the dawn, Bonnie unfolded a picture of the world that was totally at odds with all that Argo had believed over the last two years and all he had heard through the filter of Mosul propaganda. He had been led to believe that the invaders had an iron grip on all the lands south of the Potomac, west of the ocean, and east of the Wilderness, but, according to Bonnie Appleford, much had slipped through the fingers of that iron grip, and the hills were alive with pockets of stubborn and sometimes formidable resistance. The core of this opposition was in the Appalachians, where well-organized partisans, with weapons supplied by Albany, but very much a law unto themselves, controlled the high ground and made hit-and-run forays on enemy positions, turning total Mosul occupation into a practical impossibility along the Blue Ridge and in large areas of the Shenandoah Valley.

"The Mosul don't like mountains, just like they don't like cold—that's why the Swiss maintain their neutrality. It's why the Mosul have never been able to run over the Saami and come down on the Norse from the far north, and that's why they had to fall back when they confronted the Russe under Joseph the Terrible."

Argo had frowned. "Russland doesn't have mountains."

"But it has plenty of cold."

Big things were planned for the coming winter. Hassan IX was fully expected to launch his assault across the Potomac at Albany, but the Appalachian partisans intended to come down in force and snap at his rear. The only problem was that they lacked a unified command structure. What had made them guerrillas also made them hard to coordinate. The bearded and buckskinned mountain men, and the trappers out of the interior with their flowing hair and necklaces of bear teeth, would chance unbelievable odds and fight like savages with gun and knife, tooth and nail if need be, but they were resolutely incapable of following any orders that did not fit in with their perceptions of how the fight should be fought. The war bands of the aboriginal nations had rigid internal discipline, but, without an encyclopedic knowledge of historic blood feuds and vendettas, no commander could ever really predict when two parties from different tribes might suddenly refuse to cooperate because of some long-held grudge that might go back a hundred years or more. Even the survivors from Virginia, the Carolinas, and the Southland Alliance, who had decided, when all was lost, to take the fight into the hills, came with their own set of problems. Although the partisans were nominally under the flag and the strategic control of Albany, many were still hearing the old cry of *"Why doesn't Albany come?"* No matter how many times they were told of General James Dean and the secret meeting before the fall of Richmond, where the terrible and pragmatic decision was made that Albany would hold the Potomac and not rush down into Virginia, they were distrustful of Carlyle, Kennedy, and anything that might emanate from the Albany General Staff.

"And then, of course, there are the bandits."

Argo had looked at Bonnie in surprise. "Bandits?"

"Sure, kid. Bandits."

"I thought bandits were just what the Mosul called the partisans."

"Hell, no. There are bandits. Country horse thieves like the Bush family, who suddenly became patriots, outlaws like the Blind Rebels or English John and his boys, who started to fight the Mosul because there was nothing left to steal. Displaced moonshiners, psycho barn burners, out-of-work bank robbers like the Presley Brothers and their mad old patriarch, weird-ass, cousin-marrying hillbillies who only hate the Mosul marginally more than they hate each other, city gangs like the Sicilian Bloods and the Richmond Shamrocks who found their cities burned around them. They'll all fight because that's all they know, but they're mainly in it for the looting, and you never want to turn your back on them if you can help it."

As Bonnie talked, she seemed to Argo to constantly vary in age. One moment she was a wild and wilful teenager who treated the entire war like one great adventure, and the next she was grave and thoughtful, experienced way beyond her years.

"Communication and coordination is the real problem. With so many different groups, each with their own agenda, and each with their own ideas of how to fuck with the Mosul, it can become close to impossible to mount any kind of concerted effort. In fact, it can be a full-time job just figuring out where everyone's at in the geography."

Argo found himself walking beside her in silence, partly listening as she described this swashbuckling and chaotic sector of the war, and partly just staring at her and the way the dappled sunlight through the overhead leaves touched her face. He could scarcely believe what had come to pass the previous night. Did he feel any different? So much was different, and events were moving at such a dizzying pace, that it impossible to tell. He wished that he could talk to her about it, tell her how he felt and try to explain his confusion, but she had said nothing, and he did not feel comfortable raising the subject when the stuff that she was telling him about was so much more important in the fullness of the world. Yet it had been his first time, and that had to mean something, if only to him.

"Yeah, kid, communication. That's the big headache. We have a few NU wireless sets from Albany, and, at the opposite end of the scale, windwalkers and wisewomen, but its really a mess. Thank the fucking Goddess for Yancey Slide."

"Who's Yancey Slide?"

"You never heard of Yancey Slide? No, I guess you wouldn't have. Not in Thakenham. Yancey Slide, Argo, is a walking miracle. He seems to have the ability to always turn up where he's wanted. He speaks a couple of dozen languages, including aboriginal dialects. And he can shoot the eye out of a pigeon with a pistol at a hundred fucking paces."

"You sound like you like him."

"You don't exactly like Yancey Slide. There's even those who say he's a demon. I don't know if that's true or not, but the story's good in that it seems to spook the Mosul and scare the Zhaithan, who are much more into that stuff, what with their Dark Things, their Mothmen, and their Seekers."

Argo stopped. They'd been walking almost nonstop since before dawn, and he was tired, but mainly he wanted a straight answer to his next question. "The one thing I don't understand in all this is what you're doing, Bonnie. I mean, you talk as though you're one of the partisans, but here you are wandering around the forest on your own."

Bonnie also halted, grinning as she turned to face Argo. "Having doubts about me?"

Argo avoided her eyes. "No, but you did tell me not to trust anyone."

"Very good, kid. You're starting to learn."

A sudden resentment flared inside Argo, rooted, as far as he could tell, in the fact that events of the previous night seemed to be being treated as though they had never happened. "I wish you'd stop calling me kid."

"Okay, Argo Weaver, I'll tell you what I'm doing wandering around the forest. I'm part of the partisan communications net. I guess you could call me a courier, and right now I'm on my way to rendezvous with Yancey Slide."

"You're saying you're actually on a mission for the partisans?"

"That's right, I'm on a mission."

Now the resentment threatened to consume him. "So why are you taking me along with you? Just because we knew each other once? Just because you found me wandering in the woods? If you're some important courier, won't I just slow you down? Or am I just a diversion that you'll dump when you get bored with me, or when you get closer to the action?"

A sudden look of sadness passed across Bonnie Appleford's face for the first time since they had met. "I was told to bring you, Argo."

Argo could not believe what he was hearing. "Told to bring me?"

"This is complicated."

"Why don't you try to explain? I'm not as stupid as I look. I may not know too much, but I have survived two years of the Mosul."

"My orders to meet up with Slide came telepathically, via a wise-woman. Can you accept that?"

Argo nodded. "I guess so. It's kind of weird, but I know such things exist. I know the Mosul use dark forces, so I guess you guys can, too. Yeah, I'll buy it."

"Well, she told me something else as well."

"About me?"

"She said I would meet a man-child who I would make into a man."

Argo was suddenly in the grip of complete and violent emotion. A part of him wanted to hit and hurt Bonnie, while another wanted to cry like a baby. The end result was that he blurted out the first thing that came into his head, and then felt like a total fool. "But I thought you liked me."

"I do like you, stupid."

"But you would have done the same whether you liked me or not. You would have fucked me because the wisewoman told you that you would."

Again the look of sadness. "Yes, Argo, that is absolutely true."

"So whether you liked me or not made no difference?"

"This is not the time to be thinking like that."

"No? You want to tell me how I should be thinking, because I'm fucked if I know."

"We're in a war, kid."

Argo's voice rose in both pitch and volume. "Stop calling me kid."

Bonnie's face hardened. "Then stop acting like one. What do you want? That we fall in love and live happily ever after? I'm sorry, but this is neither the time nor the place. There's a whole fucking invading army to get in the way of that. I did what the wisewoman predicted, and I really enjoyed it, and I think you're a hell of young man, but the wisewoman told me one other thing that rather overshadows everything else."

"What's that?"

"She told me that I should take you to Slide."

"Me? Why me?"

"She didn't seem to know exactly, but she recognized you as being somehow significant."

Argo is disbelief made him flounder. "Me? Significant?"

"I didn't think you were ready for that piece of information quite yet, but now you've forced it out of me, you're going to have to live with it, because it's the Goddess's own fucking truth."

CORDELIA

Phelan Mallory had a pleasant room all to himself in the Royal Taconic Hotel. The more senior officers had been given suites, but Cordelia could not see that he had anything to complain about. Neither was she complaining herself; indeed, the morning sun that streamed through the drapes had found her disheveled, a little bleary-eyed, but smiling at the new day with a decidedly smug satisfaction as she lay beside the young man from the Norse Union amid the ruined sheets of the hotel-room bed. If pleasure in wartime was a matter of gathering rosebuds where one might, she had certainly garnered a few in the dark of the night that had just passed. Air Corps Captain Phelan Mallory hadn't been a particularly inventive lover, but what he lacked in imagination he had made up for in stamina, endurance, and definite willingness to learn, and she could, without undue modesty, pride herself that she had shown him a thing or two without coming across as the total stereotype of the titled whore about whom everyone liked to gossip. She had noticed, though, that he seemed a little overly impressed by her title. At first he had used it jokingly, but later, in the throes of passion, he had became decidedly serious. *"Lady Cordelia! Lady Cordelia! Lady Cordelia! Lady . . . Cordelia!"* At the time, she had been having too much fun to take exception to the fact that he might in his own way be fucking her title as much as fucking her, and later, she had dismissed it as a minor aberration. What could she expect from a boy who had been raised in an egalitarian and somewhat socialist society? In the gathering of anything as fleeting as rosebuds, it paid to tolerate whatever proved exciting.

Cordelia disentangled herself from the top sheet that had somehow become wound around her body and sat up. She looked down at Phelan Mallory. He appeared so much younger when he was asleep, but that seemed to be the way of it with these newly minted heroes. So brave and upright, but like little boys when they slept. She slipped from the bed and padded across the room, feeling naked and delicious. Cordelia was not so jaded that it placed her beyond feeling both divine and decadent after a night of debauchery in the best hotel in town, a night that was wholly official and even part of the war effort. Phelan had seen to that when he had requested and been granted her temporary transfer to the Norse delegation. Maybe in a spare moment she should slip into the cathedral and offer a small prayer to the Goddess for this very excellent night she had just so thoroughly enjoyed. Using one of Phelan's uniform shirts as a robe, Cordelia went to the window and looked out. The overcast of the previous day had blown through, and the sun was shining. The day seemed in perfect accord with her mood. Below her, on Constitution Avenue, the city was already coming alive. A trolley carrying early morning workers clanged and rumbled away after leaving a stop in front of the hotel; a mail van and a drab green Army steamer drove past; a truck was dropping off copies of the *Albany Morning Post* to a newsstand on the corner that was just opening, while a group of children in dark red caps and blazers ambled past, meandering their way to school. A flock of city pigeons spiraled up into the clear morning air, and the smell of baking wafted from somewhere else in the hotel. A day like today made it hard to believe that a fierce and brutal enemy horde waited to the south, intent on turning all she could see into ash and rubble, and Cordelia resolved that, for a little while, she would steer clear of fear and general war thoughts. She would enjoy her temporary good mood and the sense of heavy satisfaction for as long as it lasted. The troubles of the world would still be there when the euphoria passed.

Unfortunately, the world insisted on coming to her sooner than she expected, in the form of a discreet but insistent rapping on the door. She glanced at Phelan, but, although he stirred in his sleep, he did not wake. She moved to the door and spoke just loud enough to be heard by whomever was on the other side. "Who is it?"

"Bellboy. Message for Captain Mallory."

Cordelia decided that, in Phelan's shirt, she was sufficiently dressed for a bellhop. She opened the door. The boy was thirteen or fourteen, with red hair and freckles very much like Cordelia's. He was dressed in blue hotel livery with a lot of gold buttons and a rather silly pillbox hat on the side of his head, and he carried a small but official-looking buff envelope on a silver tray. "Message for Captain Phelan Mallory, miss."

"Captain Mallory's asleep. I'll take it."

"You have to sign for it."

"That's okay."

"I don't know, miss. I'm really supposed to give this to Captain Mallory."

Cordelia looked stern, but smiled inwardly. The boy probably thought she was some expensive prostitute, and the idea amused her. At the same time, she used a voice of authority that defined her as Lady Cordelia with its aristocratic resonance. "I said you can leave it with me."

"Whatever you say, miss."

She scrawled something illegible on the delivery slip. "Wait just a minute."

The night before, Phelan had dumped out his loose change on the dresser along with all the other odds and ends that men insisted on carrying around with them. She found a half crown, returned to the door, and handed it to the bellhop. "Here."

He touched his cap. "Thank you very much, miss."

As he thanked her, he dropped his eyes to her bare legs. "You look very nice this morning, if I may say so."

"Don't be cheeky, boy, or you'll be in real trouble. If I report you to the manager, he'll skin you alive."

"Yes, miss. Sorry, miss."

Cordelia closed the door, smiling to herself. So the bellhop liked her legs, did he?

"What's going on?"

Cordelia sighed. Now Phelan was awake, the day seemed to be starting in earnest, and she was not exactly ready for that. She would have liked to continue her solitary savoring of the afterglow for a little while longer. "A bellboy just brought you a note. It looks official."

"Did he bring any coffee?"

"Bellboys don't bring coffee. They bring notes. It's room service that brings coffee."

"Could you order me some coffee?"

Cordelia fully subscribed to the concept that mornings-after were the true test of love or even lust. They might also be what separated the whores from the ladies. She decided that Phelan needed a reprimand. "Remember me, darling? Lady Cordelia? I don't order coffee, I have coffee ordered for me."

Phelan scratched his head and rubbed the sleep out of his eyes. "I'm sorry."

"So you should be."

"No, really. I am."

"So order some coffee, although you'll probably have to settle for tea or some nasty coffee substitute made from acorns or something. There's a major shortage, now the Mosul hold the south and all of the plantations."

Phelan rubbed his eyes one more time, picked up the telephone from the table beside the bed, and cranked the handle for an operator. He waited a few moments and then spoke. "This is Captain Mallory in room nine forty, could I please have some coffee sent up?"

A pause ensued. "That's right. I am part of the delegation from the Norse Union."

A second pause. "Very well. In that case, I'd like a pot of coffee for two."

Cordelia sat down on the bed. "You're probably being given the last coffee in Albany."

"Really?"

"No, I'm teasing you."

"Did you say something about a note?"

"You don't do mornings very well, do you?"

"Do I have to apologize again?"

"Yes."

"I'm sorry."

Cordelia leaned over and kissed him. "Then I forgive you, because you had more Scotch that I did, and you've found us coffee, and you're also a hell of a lovely fuck."

Phelan actually look shocked. "A hell of a lovely fuck."

"Read your note, and don't be such a bloody prude."

He slit open the envelope, unfolded the message, and cursed. "Damn."

"Bad news?"

"I have to fly a dirigible down to Manhattan to show the flag over some kind of parade."

"When?"

"Later today."

"Does that mean this is the end of the affair?"

Phelan shook his head. "No, it's just a quick day trip, a simple public relations job. I'll be back in Albany by tomorrow." He thought for a moment. "In fact . . ."

"In fact what?"

"In fact, you could come with me."

Cordelia's eyes widened. "I could?"

Phelan frowned. "Maybe it's not such a good idea. Maybe you wouldn't want to go up in an airship."

"The hell I wouldn't."

"You wouldn't be scared?"

"Do I strike you as the scared type? How do we square this with the regulations and such?"

Phelan shrugged. "I think we just keep quiet and don't advertise the fact. You're attached to me for the duration of the visit, but there's no specific definition of your duties in any of the paperwork."

"So far my duties have been to eat dinner, drink Scotch, and fuck your brains out. We would seem to have some not-inconsiderable latitude."

Again Phelan looked a little uncomfortable, and Cordelia regarded him curiously. "You get uncomfortable when I talk dirty, don't you?"

He looked away. "Maybe there's a time and a place."

"And if a hotel room, without our clothes, after a long and erotic night isn't the place, would you like to tell me what is?"

Before he could answer her question, the coffee arrived. He looked round so helplessly that Cordelia went and got it from the maid and even poured some for him. "So that's settled, I'm going?"

Phelan nodded. "Since it's only a public relations jaunt and not a combat mission, I don't see why not."

"What time do we have to leave?"

"We have to be at the landing field at Grover's Mill at noon."

"Well, that's only about forty minutes out of the city. We have hours to kill." Cordelia stood up and let Phelan's shirt fall from her shoulders. "I think it's time to do a little more to cure some of this innate prudery you keep exhibiting."

Phelan put down his coffee, eyes fixed on her proudly naked body. "Why, Lady Cordelia . . ."

She pursed her lips and crawled sinuously onto the bed. "Just Cordelia, please, Captain. I'm attached to the Air Corps now, and will soon go up in your flying machine."

RAPHAEL

"My name is Underofficer Melchior, and, until something occurs to change the situation, I am yours and you are mine and we are all together. I am your mother, father, holy mentor, and the wrath of the Twin Deities all rolled into one. Until you know better, you don't so much as take a shit without my express consent. You are the little lambs, and I am the slaughterer, and any of you callow youths who think I'm exaggerating will find himself in a world of hurt. Everything I'm going to say to you, I'm only going to say once, so listen up and pay real good attention. As you will observe, you have arrived in Savannah, jewel of the empire of Our Lord Hassan IX, may his name be blessed, here in the Americas. You have arrived, and yet you haven't arrived, because, as you have all probably observed, we are not snug in the harbor of Savannah but bobbing on the bloody water a full half mile from the shore. Never repeat this in front of an officer or the mighty Zhaithan, but this is because the harbor of Savannah is less well organized and more ass upside than a Turk whorehouse on a hot night with Teutons in town. Since our victorious armies first landed here, three harbor masters have been executed, and the fourth is presently on his way north to surrender to the enemy before he goes the same way. We, meanwhile, will be transported to dry land in a relay of open boats and will not be walking down any gangplank and onto the dock like civilized soldiers should."

The livid scar running down Underofficer Melchior's left cheek bore mute testimony to all he had been and seen and survived. He was a short and swarthy barrel-chested man, clearly full-blood Mosul but with an attitude unlike anything Raphael had ever encountered in his life before. On a few points he shared similarities with Gunnery Instructor Y'assir, but, in other ways, especially his loud and vocal cynicism and complete contempt for any authority other than his own, he was the total opposite. Raphael could only assume that much of this was because, where Y'assir's task had been to prepare them for the reality of combat, the ultimate outcome of that preparation was wholly theoretical, and when the trainees finally advanced into battle, Y'assir would be thousands of miles away, still in the training camp outside Madrid, feeding more young men into first stage of the never-ending meat grinder. Melchior, on the other hand, would be right there with them. And yet, Raphael wondered if he should be assuming so much so readily. The main gist of what the underofficer seemed to be trying to hammer home was that they should assume nothing.

"This is not to say that any of you are civilized soldiers. Far from it. You are rookies, you are replacements, you are the lowest of the low and the most expendable of the expendable. Once on land, you will be issued with proper uniforms, kit, and weapons which will go halfway to making you look like soldiers, but that will be no more than an illusion. You know nothing, and therefore you will do nothing except what I tell you. So far, you have survived your basic training camp where underofficers and gunnery instructors have attempted to make your life miserable from morning to night, and you have survived the crossing of the ocean without being drowned, torpedoed, or otherwise blown up, and no doubt your life on the high seas has been made equally miserable by seasickness, rotten food, rats, and boredom. You might think that the worst was behind you, and in that you would learn the inadvisability of thinking. You, my lads, are about to enter an even worse misery. In all respects the worst misery of all. The boredom will be more crushing, the fatigue more unbearable, the fear more crippling, the food more lousy, if there's food at all, the rats fatter, the mud deeper, and, on top of all that, you have the final possibility of slow and agonizing death, bleeding out your last hours, all alone, gutshot in some stinking shell hole. Welcome to the war, lads. Welcome to the war."

When the engines of the steamship *Saracen* had finally fallen silent, and the anchor had been dropped, the men in the holds had been ordered on deck, company by company, where, in parade formation, they had each been assigned one of a group of underofficers that had come out to the ship in a small boat. From that point on, until, as Melchior had put it at the commencement of his address, "something occurs to change the situation," the assigned underofficer would be their immediate superior and in charge of every aspect of their lives. Raphael had often wondered if, when he reached the front, he would remain in the company of the same group of conscripts with whom he had come through training and made the sea voyage. It would seem the logical way to organize the system, but he was already well aware that logic was not a strong criterion in the Mosul war machine.

Melchior took a moment to pace the line of his new band of charges before he continued. He did not seem particularly impressed. "The next thing that I am going to tell you is crucially important, so, if my voice has started to drone or lull you into some parade ground reverie, wake up and listen hard. When the boats eventually come to take you to the shore, stay together. I will repeat this just once. Stay together. The Ministry of Virtue and the Shore Patrol are totally unable to distinguish a deserter from a lost lamb and will happily hang any man separated from his unit and unable to give a plausible account of himself. Each unit is identified by a code of letters and numbers while in transit to the front. The transit code for this sorry bunch is HDF947. What is your transit code?"

The question took the company by surprise, and the response was ragged. "HDF947, Underofficer."

"Again!"

"HDF947, Underofficer."

"Over the next few days, your lives may depend on knowing your transit code."

"HDF947, Underofficer."

"I still can't hear you."

"HDF947, Underofficer!"

"Are you soldiers or blushing tarts?"

"HDF947, Underofficer!"

Melchior slowly nodded. "Very well. One final thing. No doubt you have all been secretly hoping for some rear-echelon sinecure which would allow you to visit knocking shops and lounge around smoking opium and never see a shot fired in anger. Do not be ashamed if you have. It is only reasonable. It shows a sense of the practical and a fine grasp of reality. Indeed, I applaud your pragmatism. The empire of Our Lord Hassan IX, may his name be blessed, does not require heroes. All it requires is cannon fodder. I also do not require heroes, because heroes tend to get those around them killed, and since I am included in that number, I loathe heroes, because it is my intention never to die. What is my intention?"

"Your intention is never to die, Underofficer!"

"Again."

"Your intention is never to die, Underofficer!"

"Unfortunately, such dreams of a safe and secure billet are not for the likes of us. You lads have paid no bribes and have no friends in high places, otherwise you wouldn't be here at all. You lads are going straight up the Continental Highway to the front. If you're lucky, you'll ride there in a truck. If you're unlucky, you walk. Either way, your destination, our destination, is the Potomac. The big push is coming, my lads, the big push is coming, and there's going to be a lot of dying to be done. And, by that token, you may find that your practical, hands-on military careers will be astonishingly short."

ARGO

Argo and Bonnie walked in silence for a long time and might have remained silent for even longer if the woods had not started to thin, the forest giving way to open country that would make any continued lack of conversation impossible. The noncommunication between them was not one of either anger or resentment. It was simultaneously simpler and more complex. Argo was completely overwhelmed by all the revelations that Bonnie had so suddenly dropped on him. He was not sure why Bonnie was so quiet; maybe he had offended her, or perhaps she was simply giving him time to digest all that had happened and all that he had learned. Before the Mosul had come, he had been nothing more than an ordinary kid. Not dumb exactly, but hardly anything special. Then the occupation had made his life as narrow and circumscribed as the ditch at the north end of the top field. The only contrasts to the drab round of grim deprivation and his stepfather's bullying were the moments of exceptional horror, as when the news had come that his father was dead or when Gaila Ford had been burned. Now, suddenly, in the space of just a few hours, doors to a wholly unknown world of both hope and danger had seemingly opened to him. He had not only lost his virginity, but he had discovered that he was being talked about by wisewomen and being deliberately brought to meet a being who was alleged by some to be an actual demon. The thoughts that raced through Argo's head had no starting place and certainly no conclusion. How? Why? What? He could not even frame the questions. He had no place among wisewomen and demons. He had known he would do it with a girl sooner or later, but he had never imagined that it would be anyone like the wild Bonnie Appleford in leather and buckskin with a knife and pistol at her hip and who knew all about the darkest workings of this world and maybe the next. Yet Bonnie had once been like him, maybe not exactly the same, but close enough, and she appeared to have made that transition. What Argo did not know was the cost she might have paid, and what it would cost him, and what would he use for the payment, when he was really nothing but a runaway kid from Thakenham.

He felt like he was about to go round again in the whole circle of thought when Bonnie spoke for the first time in maybe an hour. Her voice was soft and sympathetic, as though she understood his confusion. "Argo?"

"Yes?"

"Are you okay?"

He took a deep breath and nodded. "I guess so."

"I know I gave you a lot to chew on."

"You certainly did."

"You had to know sooner or later."

"I'm not blaming you."

"I know this is easier to say than do, but we're going to have to cross open country soon, and you're going to have to put all those thoughts to one side. You are going to have to be alert and ready for anything. You're also going to have to do exactly as I tell you without question or argument."

Now that Argo was looking at his surroundings rather than blindly taking his direction from Bonnie, he could see the change in light where the trees ended. For most of the morning they had been moving into an area of forest that seemed much less frequented by humans. The tracks and the pieces of debris had dwindled and vanished, and Bonnie seemed to be leading him into parts where not even the Mosul went, but open ground was another and more daunting matter. "Can we cross open country without being spotted?"

"We can follow hedgerows and use the natural lay of the land. We've got a good chance as long as we don't skyline ourselves or do anything too obvious. Of course, if we run into a troop of cavalry, or anything really bad, we're fucked, but, with foot patrols and the like, open country is kind of a two-edged sword. They may be able to spot us, but we can also see them coming a long way off."

The two of them kept going until they reached the edge of the trees, and then they paused, crouching in the shadows and staring out across the rolling fields. After a couple of minutes, Argo once again looked to Bonnie for a lead. "You think it's safe to make a move?"

"You see anything?"

Argo shook his head. "Not a damn thing."

"Me, neither."

"So?"

Bonnie stood up. "What the hell? We can't stay here all day. There's a fuck of a lot of country, and the even the Mosul don't have unlimited manpower. All we can do is play the odds." She pointed. "You see that hedgerow at the other end of this first field?"

Argo nodded. "I see it."

"We'll make for that, and then follow it for cover."

"Whatever you say."

"Just keep your eyes peeled and sing out if you see anything."

Moving in the open after being so long in the woods felt strange and exposed. The sky was suddenly very large, and the sun seemed dangerously bright and hard on the eyes. Argo wondered if this was how forest creatures felt when they had to move across open ground. After walking for about fifteen minutes, all the while expecting a Mosul patrol to appear out of nowhere, they reached the comparative cover of the overgrown and untended hedgerow that, as Bonnie had predicted, grew on either side of a man-made ditch with a sluggish stream of muddy water in the bottom. "It looks like no one has tended these fields since the invasion."

Bonnie nodded. "I think you're right. It feels like the Mosul may have run off the cattle or whatever might have been here and then just left it. Does it feel deserted to you?"

Argo again looked around, but this time he also listened. "No smoke. No sounds. Not even a dog barking."

She pulled a crumpled, hand-drawn map from her pocket and studied it. "I wish I had a proper, more detailed map, but according to my reckoning, if we keep going in this direction for a couple of hours, we should hit a stream, and then once we've crossed that, we'll be back into woodland after only another mile or so."

"And what then?"

"We'll be back under cover, and Slide should have left some kind of sign for us."

Argo frowned. "Sign? What kind of sign?"

"With Yancey, you never can tell, but we'll know it when we see it."

They started moving again. The sun was high and warm, and Argo slipped out of his jacket and slung it over his shoulder. The day was turning hot, one of those early autumn days that are a complete reprise of summer and could make one forget about the winter to come. He would almost have been able to enjoy the experience if it hadn't been for the constant sense of danger, which was reinforced yet again after they had been following the overgrown ditch for maybe twenty minutes. They came upon a rusting steel plough and the skeleton of a dead mule half hidden in the long grass. The mule's skull was pierced by a plainly visible bullet hole. Argo stared down at the remains and thought of all the farm folk who had vanished from around Thakenham. If he really was special, he had a responsibility to all of them. "It would seem that the Mosul were here a very long time ago."

"So maybe we're okay."

"I wonder what happened to the farmer." Argo spoke without thinking. He had failed to remember that Bonnie's father had been one of the farmers from Thakenham who had died at the hands of the Mosul.

A look of iron-hard bitterness crossed her face. "They probably took him away to hang or burn him in front of his family. The bastards had a real talent for dragging honest men from their work and murdering them."

Argo realized that he had stirred up a whole mess of bad memories, and felt like a bastard himself. Once again he didn't know what to say, and the discomfort of silence again descended on them as they left the legacy of Mosul murder and continued on their way. To make matters worse, Bonnie paced ahead as though she didn't want to look at him. As they walked, they still saw no sign of any human presence, although a considerable population of fat grey rabbits hopped and skittered for cover as they approached. Around Thakenham, the food shortages had caused all game to have long since been shot or trapped, and Argo took this abundance of wildlife as a further sign that the land across which they passed was devoid of people, hostile or otherwise. He would have mentioned this positive observation to Bonnie, except that to speak right there and then, in the wake of his previous blurted stupidity, seemed like an intrusion. He could see that her shoulders were hunched, as though she was hugging a weight of pain to her chest, and it was not until they found the stream almost exactly where Bonnie had predicted it would be that her mood changed and the pall of horror lifted.

Argo was not totally certain that it was a stream at all. He was uncertain where the divide came between what was a stream and what was a small river. The merely snaky line on Bonnie's rough map was a quick-flowing expanse of sparkling water that cut a deep gully between banks of sandy soil and exposed boulders and wound between tall overhanging trees and tangles of bulrushes and wild iris on the outside of curves where the flow was less strong. Bonnie found a spot where the bank was only a couple of feet high and sat down. She leaned forward, splashed water on her face, and then pulled two strips of beef jerky from her pocket. "You want one of these?"

Argo smiled, mainly from relief, although he was hungry and had been wondering for some time when someone was going to bring up the subject of food. "I certainly do."

She handed him one, and he took it and bit off a chunk. "Thanks."

Bonnie stood up and looked around. Still no indication of trouble presented itself. "How long is it since you took a bath?"

The question took Argo completely by surprise. "What?"

"I was wondering how long it's been since clean water touched your body."

Argo shrugged awkwardly. "I don't know."

"It's got to be at least four or five days, though. Right?"

"I suppose so."

Only a girl could see a stream and immediately think about bathing. She pointed to a tall oak with low branches stretching out over the stream. "Could you climb that?"

"Of course. Easy."

"So shinny up it and see what you can see. If there's nothing, you can keep watch while I get cleaned up, and then I'll do the same for you."

Argo dropped his coat, jacket, and bag, pulled his pistol, and swung himself into the lower branches of the tree, climbing until he reached a vantage point where leaves did not obscure his view and he could see all around. Bonnie called up to him. "Anything?"

"Not a damned thing."

"Okay, then."

Before Argo could even climb down, Bonnie was stripping off her clothes, dropping everything carelessly on the riverbank except for her knife and pistol, which she positioned with some care. Then she splashed out into the stream and let out a protracted gasp. "Oh, fuck."

"Is it cold?"

"A little, but it feels so fucking good."

At the midpoint, the water came up to her waist. Argo could only suppose that the depth was a result of the recent rains, although his mind was hardly engaged by the subject of the comparative depths of streams and rivers. Bonnie was only a few feet away, naked as a jaybird, splashing cold water on her full, firm breasts and apparently washing away the black cloud of memory that had descended on her after his tactless remark. He felt himself in the stiffening grip of excitement. He was, after all, only a teenager, who already knew how good sex can feel, with his first lover flaunting herself in front of him.

She squatted down so only her head showed above the surface and ducked under altogether, only to emerge a few seconds later, bubbling and gasping. "Damn!" She stood up, water streaming down her body, and when she raised both arms, elbows high, to push her wet hair out of her eyes, Argo all but groaned. Bonnie must have known the effect she was having on him, because she looked at him and laughed out loud. "You're not watching out, you're watching me."

"I can't help it."

Bonnie was the wild and wilful teenager again, the one who treated everything like a great adventure. "Oh, shit. Come on in. There's no one around. We can't be afraid all the time."

Argo marveled at how she could so precipitously shift her moods and personality, but he needed no second urging to dump all sense and responsibility and join her in the water. He stripped off his clothes as fast as he could, hopping on one leg as he fumbled to get his pants and boots off at the same time. Once naked, he jumped headlong into the water, sending up a wave of spray. The two of them sported together, gasping and giggling, grabbing each other and simultaneously splashing and frolicking like children, but also touching each other with the bold intimacy of recent sexual partners, delighting in the mindless sensation of their own heated bodies in the cold water. Bonnie slid an audacious, exploring hand between Argo's legs. "My, my."

"What?"

She put her mouth close to his ear. "You shrunk when you hit the water."

"That's what happens."

"If you say so."

Now she actually licked his ear. He could feel her nipples, hard from the cold, brush his arm. "So a little while in the sun will fix it?"

But as she said the word "sun," a shadow fell over the water. Argo felt it more than saw it, and spun round, almost losing his footing on the rocks and pebbles of the streambed. A tall stranger stood on the bank where they had left their scattered clothes. His black shirt and pants were covered by a long canvas duster that hung open to reveal a matched pair of strange bone-handled, flat-sided pistols like no weapons Argo had ever seen before, one in a shoulder holster and a second at his hip. The hilt of a sword protruded from behind his left shoulder, suspended from a shoulder strap, in easy reach of the stranger's right hand. It looked oriental to Argo, although he knew nothing about swords from the Far East. As the figure stared down at the naked couple, the thumbs of his gloved hands were hooked in the tooled leather of his gun belt, but his face was hidden by the broad, turned-down brim of his black hat. His very presence seemed to chill the air. From his position of disadvantage, all Argo could see was that the man smoked a thin cheroot, gripped in his teeth and jutting from the corner of his mouth. His invisible eyes looked Argo and Bonnie up and down as though he could see clear through to their hearts and minds, and then he slowly took the cheroot from his mouth and spat out flecks of tobacco before speaking in voice that sounded as though it came from the grave. "You should have both continued to be afraid. Now the two of you are quite dead. You know that, don't you?"

THREE

CORDELIA

The city was laid out beneath her like an intricate and fascinating model. The castle alone was a wonderment with its tiny towers and battlements and the green of the pygmy trees in the central courtyard. All round the structure, little matchbox vehicles moved along miniature streets, and the sun shimmered on the water of a scaled-down river. The airship, simply known as the NU98, had taken off from the army field at Grover's Mill, some forty minutes by fast automobile north of the city, near where the Taconic and Mohawk rivers had their confluence, and when it passed over Albany, enough time had elapsed for it to gain some considerable altitude before it reached the center of the capital. Phelan stood behind Cordelia as she peered delightedly out of the smooth mica windows that ran in a narrow strip along each side of the gondola, and it was not until the city had fallen away astern, and the NU98 was moving down the valley of the Taconic, that she looked back at him and spoke for the first time. Cordelia's voice, in the normal run of her life, rarely took on a tone of awe, but it did now, and she was not ashamed for Phelan to hear it. "You love this, don't you?"

He nodded, his face grave. "Yes, I do. I really love it. It's such a shame that it took the threat of war to put us in the air. Man has always dreamed of flying, but it's only come to pass because we want to use it as yet another means for killing each other."

"That's a strange statement for a military man."

"I'm not a military man, I'm a flier."

"But you wear the uniform."

"I have to. There's no other way that I'd be able to fly."

"But you'd be willing to drop bombs on the enemy, if that's what it took."

"I didn't say I was a pacifist. I know the Mosul have to be stopped. I am quite prepared to drop bombs on their armies, or even on their cities and factories, should it come to that. It's just that, having felt the freedom of the skies, I regret that our first ventures in air have to be acts of destruction."

Cordelia was seeing an entire other side to Phelan that she had previously not suspected, and she felt somehow touched. She had previously judged him to be a stiffly correct but probably somewhat shallow young officer. He did his job, and, off duty, might be a transitory source of fun, but, up to that point, she had considered him totally lacking in any real emotional depth. Apparently this was not the case when it came to riding the silver, cigar-shaped airship into the blue. Among the towering cloud-scapes, he had at least a part of the soul of a poet. She suddenly wanted to make love to Phelan Mallory right there in the gondola of the NU98, in his territory, high above the earth. For all she knew, it might have been the first time such a thing had ever been attempted, except she could see that it was totally impossible in the current context. The gondola was nothing more that a single long cabin constructed from wood and aluminum, approximately rectangular, but tapering to a point at each end like the bow of a ship to minimize wind resistance, and a full crew was aboard: a steersman, a navigator, an engineer, a radio operator, plus a bombardier and two gunners who were little more than passengers like Cordelia, since, on this short excursion to Manhattan, the NU98 carried neither mounted guns nor explosives. The only part of the gondola where a couple might find a certain degree of privacy was the small chemical toilet in the rear, and, if she and Phelan went in there together, the other men would be well aware exactly what they were up to. She knew that Phelan was far too upright to indulge in any such extreme outrageousness while his men grinned and nudged each other, no matter what delights she might offer him or what appeals she might make to his sense of erotic history. It was a shame, but she could do nothing, so she turned and again stared out of the window as the airship proceeded on down the Taconic Valley, with the Catskill Mountains on one side and Heights of Hudson on the other. She had to be content with watching the way that the flying machine cast its elongated, early-afternoon shadow across the tops of the trees and the open fields as it passed over them.

When Cordelia had first seen the NU98 in all its ribbed and silver splendor, a giant cigar-shaped creation with its code number and the North Star symbol of the Norse Air Corps emblazoned on the side of the rigid fuselage that protected the helium-filled gasbags, it had been moored with ground crew in attendance, and all ready for boarding. As she had climbed the steps that led to the gondola, a single thought had leapt into her mind. *It looks so exceedingly phallic.* At the time, she had thought of whispering this to Mallory as some airheaded sexy aside, but she had immediately thought better of it and kept quiet. Now, having seen more clearly his love for both flying and his flying machine, she was glad that she had restrained herself. She was also glad she had not played the idiot slut, because something a little strange had happened when she stepped aboard the dirigible. A very curious feeling had come over her, a sudden thrill of shock and fear. Obviously a girl might be expected to experience such emotions when confronting her first voyage through empty space, except the shock had seemed somehow external. She was not afraid for herself, more for the entire fate of the supposedly extremely safe and simple mission. She was too much of a snob to think in terms of prescience or visionary foresight. Lady Cordelia had always considered hints of things to come, channeled from the other side, to be the province of aborigines, Goddess fanatics, and the superstitious lower orders in general, even though, since the outbreak of war, the aristocracy were no longer supposed to think so condescendingly. She could not help but consider such things, however, particularly when the oddness of the fleeting experience was confirmed by the twinge of very normal anxiety she had felt when the two great engines, on either side of the gondola, were started up while the NU98 was still on the ground. For a few moments, the noise had been deafening, and the vibration had threatened to shake the fragile gondola to pieces, but then the dirigible had started to rise, and the noise had been washed behind them by the slipstream, and the vibration cushioned by the very act of flight.

As they headed south, the forests below looked more and more green, confirming how the onset of winter was a matter of latitude as well as the calendar, and Cordelia was reminded that, even farther south, down at the front, it was probably still late summer. Even Manhattan would be warmer than Albany, and she started to consider the prospects of a balmy night spent in the bustling, cosmopolitan, and altogether wide-open city. Phelan better damn well leave his Norse prudery along with his silver airship when they reached the island city, because Cordelia intended to sample the maximum possible fun. She wished she had brought some civilian clothes with her. In anticipation of her original tryst with Phelan, she had prepared a small overnight bag with a clean shirt and knickers, makeup and contraception, but nothing like the evening dress with which she would dearly have liked to show off. She would simply have to make do with her uniform and an attitude. In Albany, of course, uniforms had become high fashion, but she was not sure how war-obsessed they were in the more sophisticated port.

After about an hour and a half, the truth began to dawn on Cordelia that perhaps air travel was a little boring. Once one had moved past the novelty of looking down on the world from a few thousand feet in the sky and imagining the mere mortals on the ground staring up in amazement while domestic animals panicked as the shadow crossed their fields, there was really very little to do. Cordelia wished that she had anticipated the onset of boredom and brought a book, a magazine, or even a flask. A drink would certainly have helped, but how could she have known? The promoted impression was that to fly would be a headlong experience of breathless excitement. The crew did not share her problem, because they were fully occupied. The steersman watched the gauges and meters in front of him, all inexplicable to Cordelia, and made small but continuous adjustments to the trim levers and the big aluminum wheel. The engineer monitored his own gauges and advanced or retarded the running of the twin engines. The navigator sat at a small table with his maps spread in front of him, glancing down at regular intervals, checking the lay of the land and the physical features that passed beneath him and calling out regular course corrections. The wireless operator sat hunched over his set with headphones clamped to his ears, while Phelan seemed to be totally in his element coordinating the whole operation. For the passengers, though, aviation was little more than a dull spectator sport, with a pleasant view of the slowly passing landscape.

All this suddenly changed at about two hours into the flight, when the wireless operator sat up straight and the long and short pulses of the Standard Hamilton Wireless Code leaked from his headphones. He immediately began scribbling a translation onto a notepad, and, when the transmission was finished, he ripped off the top sheet and handed it to Phelan, who read it and then moved up beside the navigator. New maps were pulled out and spread on the table, and what looked to Cordelia like a new course was plotted with dividers, pencil, straightedge, and protractor. After a short discussion, Phelan made some notes and gave them to the steersman, who straightaway began spinning the wheel that controlled their horizontal direction. Cordelia did not like the look of this one bit and made that abundantly clear in the tone of her question. "Is something wrong?"

Phelan glanced back with a look of irritation. "Nothing for you to worry about, my dear."

This was definitely not the answer that Cordelia wanted. She stood up and walked the length of the gondola so she was standing beside Phelan and the steersman. "Then why are you changing course?"

This time Phelan did not even bother to look round. He stared intently at the steersman's instruments. "I'm afraid the trip to Manhattan has been aborted."

Cordelia really did not like the sound of this. "What? Why?"

"We have new orders. We are to fly directly to Baltimore."

"Isn't that a little close to the front?"

"Nothing to worry about. We'll still be a long way from enemy-held territory."

"Why do we have to go to Baltimore of all places?"

"I'm afraid it's a need-to-know situation, my dear."

"And I don't need to know?"

"That's unfortunately how it's going to have to be."

ARGO

"You should have both continued to be afraid. Now the two of you are quite dead. You know that, don't you?"

Argo moved so he was between Bonnie and the stranger. "You'll have to deal with me first."

"And how are you going to deal with anything, boy, now that I'm standing on your clothes and weapons?"

Then Bonnie spoke, and to Argo's surprise, she did not sound in the least afraid. "Damn you, Yancey, how the hell do you do that? How do you just appear out of nowhere?"

"That's the real secret, isn't it? Maybe you would have learned it if you'd been paying attention instead of fucking in the water."

"Actually, we weren't fucking in the water, we were just fooling around, and, for your information, we'd already made good and sure that there wasn't a Mosul for miles."

Argo looked at Bonnie in amazement. "You know this character?"

Bonnie nodded. "Argo Weaver, meet Yancey Slide."

She waded quickly out of the stream and bent down to retrieve her shirt. Argo did the same, grabbing quickly for his clothes and struggling into them with all the speed he could muster, feeling profoundly embarrassed to be naked in front of such an impressive and legendary figure, and feeling even more awkward and inept as he tried to pull his pants up his wet legs. "I've heard a lot about you from Bonnie."

He glanced at Bonnie for some kind of help, but none was forthcoming. He saw she was taking her time, appearing totally unconcerned at being naked in front of Slide. A pang of jealousy added itself to all of Argo's other confusion. Had Slide and Bonnie been lovers? Perhaps they were still, and, if that was the case, how was Slide going to react to having found the two of them romping naked in the stream? He had hardly erupted into any kind of possessive rage, but, then again, Slide did not seem the kind to erupt into any kind of extreme emotion; he seemed more likely to take any vengeance he needed quite at his leisure.

"Do you dream, Argo Weaver?"

Argo managed to get his pants up and buckled his belt. Before he put on his shirt and boots, or answered Slide's question, he stuck his pistol in his belt to assert at least a minimal equality with the dangerous-looking stranger. "Yes, I dream. Doesn't everyone?"

Slide's voice was a total contrast to his fierce and formidable dress and appearance. It was soft, like a whisper from a tomb, but it compelled the listener to listen hard. "And how do you dream, Argo Weaver? Are your dreams pleasant, or are they nightmares?"

Argo slipped into his shirt, and, for the first time, he looked into the face of Yancey Slide. He immediately wished he hadn't. Beneath the brim of his hat, Slide had the visage of a corpse. His skin was pale like parchment, his cheeks hollow, and his eyes were dark and deep-set in his head, so they peered as if from hiding. Even the laugh lines that surrounded these socket eyes were so deep-etched that they seemed to have a sinister depth. He wore his sideburns long, in the style of gamblers and bunco artists, and his hair hung clear to his shoulders in greasy ringlets. Argo tried to hide his reaction by answering the question as best he could, but he doubted that he concealed anything. "There's plenty for nightmares to feed on these days."

Slide smiled a smile of strange, otherworldly sadness, and nodded. "Now that's the indisputable truth. Does any single dream recur?"

Argo glanced at Bonnie. "Do I have to answer these questions?"

Bonnie was buckling on her gun and knife, otherwise fully dressed apart from her cap and coat. "Oh, yes, kid, you really do. They may not make sense, but you should answer them if you know what's good for you."

"Yeah, there's one dream that I have a lot. It's not so much a dream, but a face that kinda floats in front of me."

"A face?"

"The face of a girl."

Bonnie laughed. "Yeah, it would have to be a girl."

"What does she look like, this girl of your dreams?"

"She has red hair and that pale skin that goes with it, the kind that freckles in the sun."

Slide glanced at Bonnie. "Does that mean anything to you?"

Bonnie shook her head. "Not a damn thing, but I'm certain he's the one that Miramichi was talking about. He's from my home village, and all the rest fits."

"He was a virgin?"

"Oh, yes."

Argo's jaw dropped. He flushed pink with embarrassment that Bonnie and Slide should be talking about his sexual experience or lack of it like he wasn't even there, but then the exchange became even more mortifying when Slide continued. "And did you relieve him of that burden as Miramichi advised?"

Bonnie nodded. "Yes, indeed. It was practically no trouble. He took to it like a duck to water."

Slide emitted something between a laugh and a wheeze. "So I saw."

Argo started to protest. "Listen . . ."

Bonnie cut him off. "Pipe down, Argo. This is much bigger than your feelings, or you wanting to look like a man."

Slide looked at Argo. "What do you know about the other three?"

"The other three? What other three?"

"You don't know what I'm talking about?"

"I don't have a clue."

Bonnie stepped in. "I don't think he's that far evolved yet."

"What are you both saying?"

Bonnie shook her head. "It doesn't matter. Don't worry about it. It may come to nothing."

"But . . ."

Slide looked up at the sky. "We have to get out of here. Enough time's been wasted beside this damned stream. I have to rendezvous with my Rangers, and besides, there's also a storm coming in from the ocean. It should hit the coast soon after nightfall."

He began to walk quickly away, not even bothering to look back, simply assuming that Bonnie and Argo were following in his duster-flapping wake. Argo fell in beside Bonnie, also looking up at the sky. "What did he mean there's a storm coming? There's not a cloud in sight."

"There'll be a storm. You can always trust Yancey on the weather."

"And all that other stuff?"

"You're just going to have to wait on that. It's definitely not my place to explain."

JESAMINE

"Hey, girl. You girl. Concubine girl."

An old African woman with almost blue-black skin was gesturing to her, but Jesamine could not imagine why. The old woman was standing by the goat pen and feeding scraps to the half-dozen animals that were kept there. A few days earlier, when Jesamine had passed by that way before, there had been more goats in the pen, and she could only assume that the flock had been reduced by the Mamalukes' well-known taste for goat's head soup. Unaware of their intended fate, the remaining ones wagged their tiny tails and bleated at the old woman who was feeding them. Jesamine sympathized with the goats, but at the same time she envied them. As she saw it, both she and the goats were living on time borrowed from men who meant them ultimate harm. The only difference was that the goats knew nothing of their fate, while she could all too easily imagine hers.

"Are you talking to me, old woman?"

"That's right. I'm talking to you, girl. And the name is T'saya, not 'old woman.'"

"And mine's Jesamine, not 'concubine girl.'"

"Okay, Jesamine, now we understand each other, come over here and talk with me."

The woman talked and looked as though she was either a slave or a bonded servant who had been brought across the ocean just like Jesamine, but that seemed a lot of effort to expend on someone who only tended goats. Maybe she was also a cook, with a special knowledge and expertise in Mosul and Mamaluke dishes.

"That's right, girl. I cook for the bastards. That's why they keep me around. If you're going to prepare goat, the first thing is that the goat gotta eat right while it's still in the pen. If the goat eats crap, it's going to taste like crap when it's cooked up and comes to the table. Know what I mean?"

Jesamine was startled, but she hid it as best she could. The old woman could have been reading her mind. "I think I know what you mean."

She walked around the pen until she was standing next to T'saya. The woman handed her the stalk of a plant with broad leaves and an odd, sweet smell that Jesamine did not recognize. "Feed that to the coffee-colored little fella. His fur's about the same color as your hair."

Jesamine did not exactly like to be compared to a goat, but T'saya was right. The colors did match. She held the plant while the goat munched happily on it. T'saya nodded. "I raise them, I feed them, I love them, then I kill and cook them."

"That can't be easy."

"Did anyone say it would be easy?"

Jesamine shook her head. "No, no one ever said that. Not to me."

"So, what you doing around the animal pens, Jesamine?"

"Just taking a walk."

"Smelling another kind of animal from the usual ones?"

"Maybe."

"Must be nice to have the time in the day to take a walk. I sure don't."

Jesamine did not take kindly to being judged. "And where are you around midnight, T'saya?"

"I'm sleeping in my cot."

"Well, I'm not, so it all works out."

The goat finished the plant that Jesamine was holding, and started bleating. T'saya handed Jesamine another that was different and smelled akin to mint. "You're the one who sings, right?"

"That's right."

"And you're the one who's been having the dreams, right."

"What?"

Again Jesamine was shocked. Had Kahfla been talking?

"No, girl, no one's been telling tales on you. I just know what I know."

"And how do you know what you know?"

T'saya turned and faced Jesamine full on. "Because I'm a dream-teller, Jesamine, concubine girl. I was once a dream-teller and a dream-weaver, but you can't weave dreams in a place like this."

Jesamine was suddenly very uneasy. "How do I know you're not a Zhaithan snitch, old woman T'saya?"

T'saya laughed long and loud, as though it was the funniest thing she had heard in a week. "Do I look like a snitch?"

"Does a snitch ever look like a snitch?"

T'saya roared again. "You've got a point there, girl. You've got a good point there, but what have I got to snitch on you about? All you've done is feed the poor little goat. You've got more on me than I've got on you." She stopped laughing and suddenly looked serious. "I'm making you uncomfortable, aren't I?"

Jesamine concentrated on the goat. "A little."

"I mean, that's how the bastards control us, isn't it?"

"Am I supposed to answer that?"

"You think the Ministry men will appear and drag you away if you agree with me?"

"I've seen it happen."

"Then I'll just tell you what I know. That way you can take your time deciding if you trust me, and maybe you'll come back and talk some more."

"Why are you doing this?"

T'saya held out a bunch of turnip greens to a black-and-white goat. "Because if I don't read dreams, girl, I ain't nothing but a slave feeding, killing, and cooking goats."

"So tell me what you know."

"You've been dreaming about two young men. One's a Virginia boy, brown hair, snub nose, kinda goofy-looking. The other's a boy from Hispania, a good-looking kid with big, dark eyes. The two of them are walking like parallel with each other, but with a high wall between them."

Jesamine could only nod. T'saya had described exactly the two young men who had appeared in her recurrent dreams.

"Well, those boys are real, Jesamine, girl. And they're coming closer. Very soon they'll be here."

Jesamine was really frightened now. She wanted to see if Kahfla was still back at the pavilion, or if she had been taken and the information tortured out her. She was the only one to whom Jesamine had told her dreams. If the story had not come from Jesamine, T'saya was exactly what she claimed to be, and that was equally scary. Despite herself, Jesamine had to ask. "And when those boys get here? What then?"

T'saya shook her head. "That's yet to be revealed, but I figure it won't be long in coming."

Jesamine looked furtively round and saw to her horror that two Mamaluke cavalrymen were standing some distance away, apparently looking at her and T'saya. Had she been set up after all? T'saya followed her eyes and sensed her fear. "You better go, girl. Come back when you've thought about what I said. I know I spooked you by calling out like that, but there's something going on around you that I sense is important."

"But I don't want to be important."

"That's a choice none of us gets to make."

"I have to go."

"You go, girl. Sashay a little as you walk away. That'll be enough to throw off them Mamalukes. They're more likely to be looking at the goats, anyway."

Jesamine took a deep breath. "I'm sorry I was so suspicious."

T'saya put a hand on her arm. "You be careful, Jesamine."

"I always try to be careful."

"A storm's going to come tonight."

Jesamine looked up. "There's not a cloud in the sky."

"You believe T'saya. A storm's coming, and coming fast, and that storm's going to bring changes."

"Changes for the better, or changes for the worse?"

"That depends on your point of view, doesn't it?"

CORDELIA

Cordelia could hardly believe what had happened. She felt like she'd been hijacked by these bloody airmen. Manhattan was one thing. That she could accept. "But Baltimore?"

Phelan Mallory frowned. "What's wrong with Baltimore?"

"What happens when we get there?"

"We rendezvous with the cruiser *Cromwell*. I think I can tell you that much."

"The *Cromwell* is already sailing into Baltimore? It was only just announced at the meeting."

"The navy doesn't wait for a public announcement to deploy its ships. The *Cromwell* has been on what's euphemistically called a training exercise in the Northern Ocean for almost three weeks now."

"I suppose I'm still a little naive."

"You are, my dear."

The NU98 was running due south, parallel to a red sunset over the American interior. The view from the windows of the gondola was spectacular, but right at that moment Cordelia was hardly interested in views. She was starting to feel completely out of her depth. "What's going to happen to me? If I show up in Baltimore, I'm likely to be court-martialed."

"How can that be? You're attached to our delegation."

"In Albany. Maybe I could have gotten away with a quick jaunt to Manhattan, but I wasn't supposed to be flying all over the country."

Phelan looked regretful but stern. "There are more important issues here, Cordelia."

She was about to become angrily abusive, but then she realized he was right. At the same time, Hamilton code began spluttering from the wireless. The operator looked up at Mallory. "We have contact with the *Cromwell*, Skipper."

"Where is she?"

"Laying off Kent Island and ready to steam on into Baltimore harbor."

Phelan turned to the navigator. "And what's our position?"

"We should see the Susquehanna River below us at any minute, and, after that, it's a bare half hour until we touch down at Dundalk Field."

Phelan smiled round at the crew. "So we're looking good, lads."

Looking good continued for all of five minutes, right to when the wireless operator spoke again. "I'm getting another flash from the *Cromwell*, Skipper."

"There's a change of plan already?"

"No, sir. It's a storm warning."

Cordelia did not like the sound of this. "This thing can't fly through a storm, can it?"

Phelan ignored her. "Where's this storm coming from?"

The operator looked confused. "That's the problem, Skipper. It doesn't make any sense. It's supposed to be blowing down from the northeast, but when we left Grover's Mill, we had a promise of clear air all the way, and we haven't seen a sign of anything."

"Send a request for confirmation to the *Cromwell*."

"Aye, Skipper."

He tapped urgently on his send key and then waited. In little under a minute, a response came back in Hamilton code. The wireless operator didn't look any happier. "Storm confirmation, Skipper. They're getting their information on ship-to-ship from an Albany destroyer, the HMS *Bounty*, that's off Long Island and already riding it out. It's like it suddenly conjured itself out of nowhere. It's big, and, just for good measure, it seems to be exactly following us."

Cordelia peered out of the nearest window but could see nothing except the same sunset that had been there earlier, only now further advanced. Phelan had done the same and seemed equally mystified. Cordelia was even less happy now. She did not think an airship captain had any right to be mystified and still hold his command, particularly of an airship on which she was a passenger, but for the moment she did not say anything.

She might be scared, but that was no reason to panic or behave like a lily-livered dunce. She was the Lady Cordelia Blakeney, and although the Lady Cordelia Blakeney had never taken her role in the Royal Women's Auxiliary very seriously up to that point, it was only because seriousness had so far not been demanded. How serious could one be when only required to run errands that a ten-year-old could do and, beyond that, just look decorative and sexy for the amusement of powerful men? She had not been called on to display courage, fortitude, or intelligence around Albany Castle and the War Office, but that did not mean that she could not summon these resources if she needed them. She was a soldier of Albany and the descendant of a fine family. The one was a position and the other a heritage that insisted she rise to the occasion, and it hardly mattered if the occasion happened to be her own misguided presence on an airship being threatened by a critically dangerous storm. She would straighten her spine, stiffen her upper lip, and neither whimper nor cry.

Phelan moved up to the steersman. "Make a smooth ninety-degree turn, Lars, so we can see what's immediately astern."

The steersman nodded and spun the wheel. Everyone except him moved the windows that would look to the north when the turn was completed, and even before the NU98 had swung the full ninety degrees, everyone except the steersman let out a low-voiced reaction. The bombardier, who had done nothing all flight, was the loudest, and he voiced what everyone else was thinking. "Holy shit! Where did that come from?"

Where indeed had it come from? Cordelia had no idea how to judge distances in the air, but the huge mass of dark and menacing thunderheads looked perilously close.

The bombardier did his best to sound calm and serious. "How soon will all that hit us, Skipper?"

Phelan shook his head. "It's impossible to tell. We have no idea how fast that mass is moving. I suspect fast, from the way that it seems to have appeared out of nowhere."

Cordelia continued to stare at the storm. It looked like some huge vaporous fortress in the sky, and unfortunately the fortress was capable of movement, perhaps swifter movement than the NU98. Cordelia noticed spasmodic flickering at the base of the cloud formation. "What are those flashes?"

The bombardier answered. "That's lightning, miss. It looks like a bad one."

Mallory looked a warning at him. "Put a cover on that, Sam."

"Sorry, Skipper."

He faced the crew. "We're going to have to try and outrun it, lads." He turned to the steersman. "Set a course south and east, Lars."

"South and east, Skipper. Does that mean we're abandoning Baltimore?"

"We can't moor under those conditions."

"South and east it is, Skipper."

Now Phelan turned to the engineer. "Fuel?"

"We're okay at the moment, but we were only fueled for Manhattan. It depends how far we are going to have to run and how fast the storm's chasing us."

"Let's concentrate on outrunning the storm and see what happens after that."

The engineer shrugged, and Cordelia sensed a growing fatalism among the crew. Maybe it was what made this brand-new breed of aviators able to do what they did. The navigator was looking worried. "If we run south, we don't have too much running room before we're over enemy territory or heading out to sea."

Phelan Mallory looked resigned. "If the storm catches us, we won't care what territory we're over. Let's concentrate on dodging those thunderclouds and work our way back as best we can when we're clear of it. Unless anyone has a better idea."

None of the crew seemed to disagree. Phelan nodded. "Okay, so nose down, full power, and hope for the best."

The engineer leaned on his twin throttle levers, and the noise of the engines noticeably increased. Phelan turned to the wireless operator. "Try to raise Baltimore, and send our position and intentions. You better warn them that we might be going into enemy airspace."

ARGO

Slide marched ahead, a half-dozen paces in front of Argo and Bonnie, plotting their course by some means that Argo was completely unable to fathom. He did not make use of a compass, or any kind of map or chart, and, even when they were once again moving through woodland, he never stopped to look around or check his bearings. He simply walked quickly on, like a man on a familiar street, assuming that his two companions would automatically follow. Yancey Slide was proving to be such a mystery, and posed so many questions for Argo, that he could not help quizzing Bonnie about the man, if indeed Slide was a man at all. He knew it was probably a mistake, but he was unable to curb his curiosity. He quickly learned, however, that his original assumption had been correct. To ask was a mistake, and Bonnie was more than capable of curbing his curiosity for him. Each time he asked, in a semiwhisper, so their strange leader and guide supposedly could not hear, she either rebuffed him or treated his query as if it were a joke. With nothing else to do but tramp through the rapidly darkening woods, Argo had become more and more frustrated. Finally, unable to stand not knowing any longer, he blurted out the question that had been on his mind from the start.

"Did you ever sleep with Slide?"

Bonnie's first response was a combination of impatience and exasperation. "Fuck, Argo, don't you ever stop?"

"Well, did you?"

At that point she turned oblique. "I don't think Yancey ever sleeps."

"You know what I mean."

Suddenly Bonnie was angry and spoke loud enough for Slide to clearly overhear. "If you're wanting to know if I ever fucked him, Argo Weaver, the answer is no, I never did. So you can put a cover on your teenage jealousy. The truth is that I probably would have done if he'd ever asked or given me so much as a sign that he was interested, but I've never seen Yancey Slide show any interest in sex. Not what you'd call normal sex."

Slide also showed no interest in the conversation behind, so Argo continued to press the point. "What's that supposed to mean? 'Not what you'd call normal sex'?"

"It means you can go on wondering about him, because that's as much as I'm going to tell you. If you want to know more, ask him yourself."

For the first time in what had to be at least two hours, Slide recognized the presence of the pair behind him. "What are you two chattering about?"

Bonnie, who had clearly had more than enough of Argo's interrogation, replied with the maliciousness of a petulant schoolgirl. "He wants to know all about you. What you do, what you are, what your preferences might be."

"Preferences?"

"That's right, preferences."

"And what did you tell him?"

"Nothing, except that he should ask you."

Slide halted and turned. His eyes seemed to gleam in the fading remains of the woodland light. "So you want to know about me, do you, Argo Weaver?"

For one horrific moment, Argo felt as though Slide was about to do something fierce and inhuman, like angrily revealing all in a single and terrifying visionary assault that would sear Argo's mind and leave him twitching and brain dead. At the same time, though, a deeply buried instinct told Argo to stand his ground. His voice faltered, but he looked directly into the depths of Slide's infinite and frightening eyes. "Do you blame me?"

"This is not the time, boy. Right now we need to avoid the Mosul and reach a refuge from the coming storm. The questions and answers must wait until a later time."

The moment was suddenly past. Argo would never dare boast that he had faced down Yancey Slide, but he did continue to look right at him. "You assume I'll follow you, but I'm allowed to know nothing about you?"

"I'm simply telling you that this is not the time for explanations. We are nearing the agreed rendezvous with my Albany Rangers. If we come in chattering like three monkeys, they are quite likely to take us for a band of Mosul and open fire. They will be expecting me to arrive in silence."

Argo knew he was being told to keep quiet, but he could not resist a rebellious final shot. "The silence of the grave?"

Slide's eyes glowed briefly, but then he smiled. "Perhaps. If that's the way you care to think of it."

Before Argo could say any more, Slide turned on his heel and resumed walking on as before. Argo and Bonnie had no option but to follow, although, as they fell into step, Bonnie treated Argo to a sidelong grin. "You did alright there. Yancey, with all his magic tricks and the eye business, has it far too much his own way. It's not often that someone stands up to him."

"I thought for a few seconds there he was going to blast me."

"One word of warning, though."

"What's that?"

"Wait a good long time before you try anything like that again, okay?"

Ten minutes passed, and the woods became quite dark. Slide moved un-erringly, but Bonnie and Argo had to pick their way carefully to avoid trip-ping on roots and fallen branches or stumbling blindly into undergrowth. Slide entered a small clearing and suddenly halted, raising a silent hand for the others to do the same. He stood for a moment, and, although Argo was too far away to tell for sure, he seemed to be sniffing the air. Then he let out a strange, hardly human sound, somewhere between a whistle and a whisper. A much more mortal voice immediately responded. "Is that you, Yancey?"

"It certainly is."

"And how was your day?"

"It was uneventful."

"Are you alone?"

Slide glanced briefly back at Argo and Bonnie. "No, I'm not alone. I picked up a couple of strays along the way, but they come from the right bloodline."

The exchange might have sounded like oddly pointless conversation, but Argo was certain that it was a prearranged set of questions and re-sponses that would tell whoever lay in wait, presumably one or more of Slide's Rangers standing sentry, that he was coming in of his own free will and not under any kind of duress. Had the answers been any different, the area would most likely have come under withering fire. Slide gestured to what looked like an outcrop of rock at one end of the clearing, indicating that Argo and Bonnie should move in that direction. As they came closer, three figures suddenly rose from the rocks where no figures had been visi-ble before. They seemed to detach themselves from the very landscape, and Argo knew that these must be the legendary Albany Rangers, and it did not take a genius to instantly appreciate that they were very good at what they did, and their reputation was well deserved. Each of the three held a lever-action repeating shotgun of a kind that Argo had never seen before, but he knew that, in a firefight, they had to be more than a match for any Mosul with their muskets or breechloaders. The Rangers carried their weapons pointed to the sky but in a way that left no doubt they were ready for immediate use if anything untoward might occur. The middle man of the three advanced to greet Slide. "Hey, Yance."

"Hey, Jeb Hooker."

"Any problems?"

"Not a one. You guys?"

"Everything's as it should be with us."

Slide and the Ranger clasped hands and quickly embraced, clapping each other on the back. When they separated, the Ranger looked at Bonnie and Argo. "Who have you brought back with you?"

"I found Bonnie in a stream. You remember Bonnie, right?"

"Is that you in the dark there, Bonnie Appleford?"

"It sure is, Jeb."

Now Bonnie and Jeb embraced. "How the hell are you, Bonnie?"

"I'm fucking fine, and even better for seeing you, Captain Jeb."

Now the Ranger Bonnie called Captain Jeb looked in Argo's direction. "And who's your young friend?"

Slide answered this question. "He's Argo Weaver, recently out of Thakenham, and it could be he's one of the Four, only it's too early to be sure."

Argo did not know what Slide was talking about. The "Four?" So far Bonnie had said that he might be "significant," Slide had asked him about the "other three," and now it turned out that he might be one of the "Four." Slide spoke the word as though, when written, it would be capitalized. Argo was confused as hell and more than a little scared, but right there and then hardly seemed the place to ask questions, especially after his earlier confrontation with Slide. The Ranger captain moved towards him, extending a hand. "Glad to meet you, kid."

Bonnie interrupted. "He doesn't like to be called 'kid.' "

The Ranger inclined his head. "I'm sorry." They shook hands, and the Ranger corrected himself. "Glad to meet you, Argo Weaver."

Up close, Argo saw that Captain Jeb Hooker was a tall, lean man in his early thirties, with large, capable hands, close-cropped sandy hair, a week's growth of beard, and the kind of eyes that seemed permanently narrowed below a just-as-permanently furrowed brow. He was dressed in a forest green tunic with a high hussar's collar and two vertical rows of un-shined military buttons. On one shoulder he wore the bars of a captain, and on the other the Rangers' insignia with its half-moon emblem and the motto *We Own The Night*. Around his waist was a broad military belt that supported a sheathed, saw-edged Jones knife and a small cache of Mills' bombs. A heavy revolver hung in a shoulder holster beneath the open tunic, under his left arm, while a bandolier of blue and copper shotgun shells was draped across his chest. The hilt of a second, smaller knife protruded from the top of one of his high hunter's boots. Although Argo had never seen a human being so loaded for destruction, the Ranger greeted Argo so warmly that he briefly stopped feeling like the new kid in the neighborhood who knew nothing. "I don't mind being called 'kid.' It's just that Bonnie does it too much."

Hooker laughed and nodded. "Yeah, that one's got herself an attitude, all right. We learned that the last time she was with us."

Slide curtly broke up the pleasantries. "Let's take the party inside before the whole forest knows we're here."

Hooker gestured to the two Rangers still in the rocks. "Billy, Conrad, you're still on watch. Stay alert, you hear?"

"We got it covered, Captain. Don't worry about us."

"Come in and tell us when the rain starts."

"We'll do that."

Slide followed the Ranger captain to a dark space in the rocky outcrop and ducked into it, vanishing from sight in what had looked, up to the instant of his entry, like nothing more than rather deep shadow. The captain followed him, but, instead of going into the hidden entrance, he stood to one side and ushered Bonnie and Argo to go first. "Watch your step there. It's kind of uneven, and the rock surface is slick in places, but it broadens out farther back, and then you get to the light."

Argo followed Bonnie into the space and found himself feeling his way forward in total darkness. Then, up ahead, Slide moved a heavy canvas sheet to one side, and he saw the orange glow of an oil lamp. Slide beckoned to the two of them to hurry. "We don't want the light leaking out and giving this place away."

Beyond the canvas that served as not only a highly serviceable blackout drape, but also as a protection against the chill of the night air, the narrow passage widened out into a sizeable cave. As Hooker replaced the drape, Argo looked around in wonder. The Rangers had created a functionally cozy hideout and hidden base for themselves and their operations deep in enemy territory, and, as their motto claimed, they really did seem to own the night. Argo let out a low but awed whistle. "This place is amazing."

Bonnie nodded. "I doubt even a Seeker could find it."

"What's a Seeker?"

"Just hope you never find out."

By a mental headcount, Argo saw that six Rangers currently occupied the cave, plus the two who stood guard outside. He, Slide, and Bonnie made the number up to eleven, and, if the sentries returned, the cave would approach being uncomfortably crowded. Some rudimentary furniture had been installed, two mattresses that had been dumped on the rock-and-dirt floor, along with an incongruous easy chair and a kitchen table on which stood cooking utensils and a small kerosene stove. All presumably had been scavenged from some ruined or abandoned building near the cave. By far the majority of the space in the cave was given over to the storage of supplies. Ammunition boxes and cases of canned military rations were stacked in an approximately organized fashion against the cave walls, along with a two-and-a-half-inch mortar and a portable, tripod-mounted version of the famous and fast-firing Bergman gun. Argo looked at the Bergman gun with interest. He had never seen one before, but he had heard tell of them. The Bergman gun had, according to even the legends of the occupied territories, done much to even the odds when the Albany forces had held the numerically superior Mosul at the Potomac, and its rapid-fire capability had gone on to help maintain the ensuing standoff.

The oil lamp that provided all of the shadowy light in the cave stood on top of one of the highest stacks of boxes. Argo wondered how the Rangers had dragged so much stuff there right under the noses of the Mosul. Had they been dropped from some kind of flying machine? The six men in the cave were all variations on Jeb Hooker: different shapes, sizes, and ethnic backgrounds, but they seemed to have the same calm, hard-bitten confidence of their leader, and, like their leader, not one had shaved in a week or ten days. They all either wore the same forest green tunics with the Albany Ranger insignia or had stripped down to boots, pants, and faded, red flannel undershirts. All had shotguns, carbines, or pistols close to hand, and if they were taken by the Mosul, they would go down as soldiers, not bandits or spies, fully armed and wearing the proud symbols of their regiment. Argo had never seen men like them before. His father, as he remembered him, had been brave, but the cause his father had rallied to would prove lost in a matter of weeks. Jackvance Weaver and the tens of thousands like him had been carried along by patriotic fervor and very little else, hardly knowing the ultimate consequences of their actions.

These Rangers knew exactly what they were doing and had plainly evaluated what the outcome might be. They had no illusions that any gods or goddesses were on their side or looking out for them. They had no illusions that right would always eventually conquer might, or good would prevail over evil. They put their faith in weapons, tactics, and the element of surprise, rather than the righteousness of their cause. They were killers, and as killers, they had sacrificed a part of their humanity to defend humanity itself. In return, they had gained a calm and a confidence that enabled them to do their work with a grim and methodic precision. Argo had seen Mosul killers, and they were in no way the same as these Rangers. The Mosul killed because they could, because they relished the sense of power that came with acts of slaughter. The Rangers relished nothing, except perhaps their sense of comradeship and that, in the risks they took and their destruction of the enemy they fought, they served and preserved some semblance of civilization even though they might employ the techniques of savages in the process. Argo could scarcely believe that he was among such people.

The Rangers all knew Bonnie, and Hooker proceeded to introduce Argo. "Lads, this is Argo Weaver. Argo, this is Barnabas."

Barnabas was a short, dark man with a full beard and the look of a perpetual malcontent who had only found himself a sense of purpose by enlisting in the Rangers. He nodded. "How you doing, kid?"

Hooker continued. "Penhaligon and Cartwright."

Penhaligon and Cartwright looked like two farm boys, but case-hardened by a ruthless process of training. They said nothing.

"That's Steuben on the mattress, and the one in the chair is Madden."

"Hey there, Argo Weaver, pull up an ammunition box and sit down." Steuben had broad shoulders, a bullet head, and bright blue eyes. Argo would later learn that he was the humorist of the outfit. Madden was skinny and withdrawn, with blond hair and beard and a black bandanna wrapped around his head. He simply nodded and went on working on the edge of his Ranger-issue Jones knife with a small whetstone. In the civilian world, he would probably have been deemed crazy and dangerous, but, as with Barnabas, enlistment in the Rangers had provided him with a home and a method that made his madness an asset. Argo accepted the invite and sat on an ammunition box that placed him beside Slide and Bonnie. He again looked around the cave and commented to no one in particular. "You guys seem fixed to stay here for a while."

It was Steuben who responded. "You know what we say in the Rangers? Hold the position until you've won, you're dead, or you're ordered out."

After Steuben's remark, no one in the cave spoke for a long time. The Rangers had no need to fill the silence with unnecessary conversation. They seemed totally attuned to the idea that their lives were lived in moments of violent and frenzied action that punctuated long, numb periods of protracted waiting. When they had nothing to occupy them, it was almost as if they could slow down their internal perception of time. Argo, on the other hand, had no such capacity for silence, and too many mysteries nagged for him to remain quiet. After holding his peace for as long as possible, Argo turned to Slide and spoke in a low voice. "Would it be appropriate to talk now?"

"Do I detect a hint of sarcasm, young Weaver?"

"Maybe an understandable impatience."

"And what are you so impatient to talk about?"

"Perhaps about this 'Four' you've mentioned, and why you think I might be one of them."

Slide, in turn, looked at Bonnie. "You want to field that one? It was your information that set all this in motion in the first place."

Although the Rangers made no comment, every eye was now on Bonnie, who slowly nodded. Even she seemed in step with the Rangers' ability to wait. "I was wondering when you were going to get round to that."

Argo shrugged, maybe intimidated, but not silenced. "I'd like to know what I might be a part of. Surely it's only fair to fill me in."

Bonnie took a deep breath. "Yeah, I guess you're right. No one has really figured out the complete picture, but I can tell you the story so far, for what it's worth."

The Rangers seemed, without actually moving, to draw closer. If nothing else, it would be an entertainment for them. Bonnie looked at them a little apprehensively, but started anyway. "It all began with an aboriginal wisewoman called Miramichi, a windwalker who runs communications between the Appalachians and Albany and Ranger groups like you guys. For maybe a couple of months past, Miramichi had been having these dreams about four young people who were somehow connected, but very separate. At first she said nothing. The dreams were too fleeting, too insubstantial and lacking in definition and detail, and she had also learned the hard way how resistant you military sons of bitches are to matters of the Other Side."

She paused to look round at the Rangers. Tough as they were, they looked away or stared down at their boots. Argo felt as though he had come in on a long-standing disagreement and did not quite understand. "Would someone like to tell me what this is all about? The Mosul have no problem reconciling this world and the other. You don't live long under the Zhaithan if you don't grasp that fact as fast as you can."

Steuben spread his hands, defending both himself and his comrades. "What can we tell you, kid? We were trained in the material world, and we fight in the material world. Where we come from, the Other Side is Goddess stuff."

Bonnie was outraged. *"Goddess stuff?"*

Steuben moved quickly to head her off. "Hey, hey, we don't not *believe*. We know the signs are all there. We've seen the Seekers and the Mothmen and the Dark Things, and we know all about the Mosul conjurers. Maybe we should have been trained in the Arts from bootcamp, but we weren't. We're just grunts who got so good at our trade with gun and knife that they made us specialists. We ain't comfortable around the wiggy shit. It ain't our business, and we try to keep a distance from it."

Bonnie's mouth was set in a stubborn line. "Yeah, well, we can't all fight completely in the mortal world, can we? Some of us aren't given the choice." She looked at Slide. "And what do these material Rangers think you are, Yancey? What tidy piece of denial enables them to live with your wiggy shit and makes this alliance between you and them possible?"

Slide had been sitting on the cave floor with his long, spider-skinny legs folded in front of him in a meditative posture and his back to the cave wall, but he had slid down the wall when Bonnie had started arguing with the Rangers, making himself as small as possible, and with his hat tilted so far forward over his eyes, his visible face was reduced to a jutting cigar and part of an unshaven chin. Even his voice sounded muffled. "Go on with the story, Bonnie. You won't reform these heathen materialists this night, or for many nights to come."

Argo saw what was going on in the cave. The Rangers might be fearless and very capable slayers in the real world, but in the places where reality faltered, they became uneasy. He hoped it wasn't a too-human oversight that would cost them dear sometime in the future. Maybe that was why Slide was with them. To even the balance between the real and unreal. But Argo wasn't overly interested in the argument. He wanted to hear the tale of what they thought he was, and he said so. "Yeah, go on with the story, Bonnie. If it affects me, don't I have a right to hear it?"

Steuben made nice. "Yeah, come on, Bonnie, tell the story."

Bonnie stared angrily down at the floor, but finally looked up with a scowl. "Okay, okay, for the kid, I'll tell the story, but you bastards better start figuring this 'wiggy shit' into your fucking calculations pretty fast or you'll be served on toast when you run into Dark Things for real. Word is that, because Hassan can't match our technology and firepower, he wants such overwhelming numbers that he's even putting the Dark Things and the Mothmen into the field, like he did at Richmond."

While the Rangers looked uneasily at each other, like men faced with a fact they were pretending to ignore, Steuben tried to joke Bonnie out of her attitude by getting down on his knees. "Just tell the story, Bonnie, and stop busting our balls. I'm fucking begging you."

Bonnie sighed. "Okay, okay. Like I said, at first Miramichi had nothing more than vague feelings, and faces in dreams. She knew that there were four young people, all around your age, Argo Weaver, or perhaps a little older, who had a very unusual mutual empathy."

Argo frowned. "Mutual empathy."

Bonnie nodded. "Miramichi called it a *takla*. We have no comparable word for it."

"I don't understand."

"Neither really do we."

Penhaligon, the Ranger with the farm-boy face, had one boot and sock off and was inspecting his foot. "There used to be a story that if Albany was ever in mortal danger, four magicians or wisemen would come."

Cartwright, the other farm-boy Ranger, spat in the dirt. "There used to be a story that if Albany was ever in mortal danger, Henry Morgan's drum would start beating all by itself, but I don't hear nothing."

Argo was now so confused that he looked to Yancey Slide for enlightenment, but Slide said nothing, and so Bonnie continued. "Then exactly thirteen days ago, Miramichi had a much more fully formed vision. The four became the Four, and the Four were coming together. Two boys and two girls, and they would very soon find each other in the realm of the Mosul, and, when they found each other, they would play a crucial part in the overthrow of the empire of Hassan IX."

Cartwright looked at Penhaligon. "So you got your four magicians, boy."

Penhaligon was about to come out with a retort, but Hooker's scowl shut him up. Jeb Hooker, after firmly keeping out of the Goddess stuff— wiggy shit argument, was now taking an interest. "And this time the woman Miramichi reported the vision?"

"She told a few of us in Communications, and a report went to Albany. Luckily, someone in Dunbar's office was bright enough to take it seriously, and we were ordered to pursue it. Meanwhile, Miramichi had already conducted a seeking ritual and found that Argo was wandering aimlessly about in the forest, and she could only assume, since she was intensely aware of his presence, that he must be one of the Four from the previous dreams."

Hooker looked thoughtfully at Argo and then back at Bonnie. "And this Miramichi sent you out to reel him in?"

Bonnie looked at Hooker a little curiously. "Yeah, I was sent out to get him. I did a night-ritual in which we chewed the mushrooms and danced the feathers, and she showed me where he would be and how certain conditions would need to be fulfilled. And then Slide was contacted, and his part was to bring us here."

Steuben raised an eyebrow. "These certain conditions? What were they all about?"

Bonnie regarded the company joker through bleakly narrowed eyes. "You don't need to know."

Slide filled in Steuben's blank. "She fucked him. She was young Weaver's first. She took his virginity."

The Rangers guffawed loudly, and Argo wished the ground would swallow him. Steuben leered. "Same old Bonnie."

Bonnie glared at the Rangers. "Fuck you all."

Only Hooker was not joining in the general merriment and actually seemed to be waiting for it to subside so he could ask some questions of his own. "Miramichi was told that the Four were 'to play a crucial part in the overthrow of the empire of Hassan IX'?"

Bonnie nodded. "That's correct."

"Was she told whether this role would be positive or negative?"

Argo couldn't believe what he was hearing. "I'm sorry, Captain Hooker, but I'm on the run from the Mosul, and if you don't . . ."

Bonnie cut him off. "Shut up, Argo. I know where Jeb's going with this. It's right that he should. He has to protect Albany, and he has to protect his men." She faced Hooker. "Miramichi was led strongly to believe that the influence of the Four would be a positive one. Of course, we had to consider the reverse. It would have been criminally stupid not to, and Miramichi is neither criminal nor stupid. It was decided that if Argo should turn out to be a Zhaithan asset, it would still be better to have him under our physical control."

Argo was suddenly very angry. "You know what I am, Bonnie. My daddy died at Richmond. You knew me in Thakenham before the Mosul even came. Tell them. I'm not working for the Zhaithan. I hate them."

Slide pushed up his hat. "Do like Bonnie says and shut up, boy. You could be a Zhaithan asset and never even know it. You could hate them like poison and still be a pawn in their mission."

"I don't even know if I'm good or bad?"

Bonnie sighed. "We assume you're one of the good guys. But it's something else we don't know for sure."

An ice-cold claw gripped Argo's chest, and for a moment breathing was difficult. He wasn't trusted by anyone in the cave and would never be trusted until he could prove himself. As though echoing his shock, a mournful rattling wail that was the sound of trees being stirred by a gusting wind penetrated the blackout. It sounded as though a storm of some power was brewing. This was confirmed a few moments later when Conrad pushed his way into the rear part of the cave. His overalls were wet, and now the sound of drumming rain could be heard. "There's one hell of storm getting up outside, Captain. You want me and Billy to stay out there?"

Hooker shook his head. "No, stay here; dry out and get some food." He looked round the cave. "Steuben, you've been having a good time tonight. Get a slicker and relieve Billy."

Steuben protested. "Why me, Captain?"

"Some poor son of a bitch has to keep watch, and I couldn't see anyone more deserving."

When Steuben left and Billy returned, the raising of the blackout let in the roar of torrential rain and trees in violent motion, punctuated by claps of thunder. Bonnie turned to Slide. "Conrad was right. That is one hell of a storm."

Slide did not answer. He sat with his fingers pressed to his temples and seemingly lost in thought. After a minute or so, he spoke to no one in particular. "One of our airships is in trouble."

CORDELIA

The storm hit the NU98 like a giant fist coming out of the darkness. The gondola lurched, and Cordelia thought for a moment that it had become detached from the main fuselage and the supporting gasbags. She believed that she had screamed, but with the combined howling of the wind and the engines, and the pounding of the rain, it was impossible even for her to tell. At the front of the gondola, both the steersman and Phelan fought with the wheel and the trim levers, trying desperately to keep the wallowing dirigible on a level course. Phelan had already ordered Cordelia and the crew to strap in, and they sat secured in their seats by canvas restraints with leather and brass fastenings. The feeling was one of complete helplessness in the face of the raging elements. Aside from the efforts of Phelan and the steersman, only the engineer had a function, jockeying the throttles of the two racing engines. The wireless was broadcasting nothing but grating static, and the navigator had no function except to hope, although all his calculations seemed to be that they were well into enemy airspace already. The airship yawed and wallowed sideways like a small boat riding a raging sea. Lightning flashed in stroboscopic shudders of blinding white that seemed to be all around them, just beyond the mica windows, and the windows themselves threatened to burst inwards as they were pounded by wind and rain.

Phelan yelled to the steersman. "Try to bring her round into the wind. We'll be blown backwards, but we'll be taking the brunt of it head-on, and there'll be less chance of her breaking in half."

Phelan and the steersman were supported by individual harnesses attached to solid steel rings in the gondola's ceiling. Without them, they would have been thrown all over the cabin, and the NU98 would have floundered out of control. Not that they exactly had the dirigible reined in even though the two of them clung to the fighting wheel. "That's the problem, Skipper. I can't feel the wind coming from the same direction for two straight minutes."

The navigator had turned in his harness and was looking out of the nearest window, twisting his neck and craning down, trying his best to see what was below them. "I got to tell you, Skipper, it looks like we're running out of altitude. I think I see treetops. Try to ride the gusts to get some height. We may only be a hundred or so feet up."

Phelan yelled something back, but it was lost in a deafening roll of thunder. The NU98 seemed to be spinning, and a terrible ripping noise came from above them that sounded as if the fuselage was coming apart. The steersman shouted a warning. "I think we're losing the skin, Skipper."

"I can hear it."

The engineer joined in with more bad news. "I've got a fuel warning light on the port engine, and the starboard can't have much longer to go."

"I hear you."

"You're going to have to put her down, Skipper. That's all we'll have power for."

"Can you think of any other options?"

"Nary a one, Skipper."

"Then we're going in. Relax your bodies as much as you can. Try to stay loose."

Cordelia decided that was the most absurd advice she had ever heard. She braced herself as best she could. The NU98 again spun horizontally, and at the same time rolled from side to side. At the apex of one of these semi-barrel rolls, she also found herself looking at the ground beneath them, and, in a lightning flash, she saw the tops of trees creating the illusion of an uneven meadow that was uncomfortably close. Almost immediately, something scraped along the floor of the gondola. They could only have lost more height and brushed the treetops. Then the whole gondola was tilted violently sideways, and Cordelia was thrown against the safety straps. If she was going to die in the airship, she did not want to watch. Neither did she want her entire life to flash before her.

RAPHAEL

They were riding towards the strangest storm that Raphael had ever seen. They had spotted the sinister tower of clouds about an hour before sunset, way to the north, and, since then, it had borne down on them like a vast threat all through the fading of the light. Underofficer Melchior had watched its approach with an increasing resignation. "It looks like we're going to be treated to a wet night, lads."

Prior to seeing the storm, Melchior had been congratulating the company on their good luck at having been assigned a truck to carry them up the Continental Highway from Savannah. "You lads are having it easy. In the old days, the Provincial Levies ran all the way to the fight, whipped along with horsehide flails. It was supposed to toughen them up. Now you get to ride in the lap of luxury."

Raphael did not exactly consider the thirty-six hours he and his comrades had spent in the open back of the lurching, vibrating truck to be the lap of luxury. The soldiers in the back were at the mercy of the elements and shaken and bounced until they feared that their kidneys were ruptured. The engine had overheated in the middle of the second day, and the squad had been ordered out to squat or lounge at the side of the road while the driver and his relief frowned into the smoking petrol engine and scratched their heads, and Melchior debated with another underofficer, who was also riding up front, whether they should stay with the truck or continue in the direction of the front on foot, in a forced march. All along the long road from Savannah, they had passed other vehicles similarly broken down, and they had laughed at their stranded passengers as they chugged by, leaving a choking cloud of dust and exhaust. Now it was their turn to wait and to be mocked and eat the dust of the constant traffic rolling to the Potomac. Most of the others in Melchior's squad, working on the comfort principle that it was better to ride than to walk, were hoping that the truck would be fixed so they would spared a long, footsore march. Raphael was the exception in that he figured that he would prefer to walk. They were en route to the front, where only combat and a quite probable early death awaited them. Raphael was in no hurry to arrive at such a grimly terminal destination. Indeed, for the duration of the breakdown, Raphael had simply relaxed and put his mind in the neutral moment, so he could enjoy lying on a dusty grass bank and not being expected to do anything at all. He might have stayed that way until either the truck was restarted or the decision to march was taken had not Pascal, who was lying beside him, rolled over and whispered urgently to Raphael after making sure that no one was paying any attention to them.

"I'm going to desert."

Raphael sat up and looked around. "What? Now? You'd be spotted. It's broad daylight, and there are too many people milling about. Don't forget there's a reward for singing out when you see someone trying to sneak away."

"I don't mean now."

"So when?"

Pascal shrugged. "I don't know. After dark. When a chance presents itself. You want to come with me?"

"You're crazy. You won't get more than a couple of miles. You think the MPs and the Ministry of Virtue don't have patrols all the way up and down the highway? And even if you did get away, you'd be totally on your own. To the natives, we're all Mosul, and they hate us."

"I don't want to die at the front."

"You'll die worse if the Zhaithan take you as a deserter. Better a clean bullet than torture and then the flames."

"Who's to say it'll be a clean bullet? You've heard Melchior's stories about guys laying wounded in shell holes for days, all alone and dying by inches."

Raphael did not have time for this. He had been through all the same horrors in his own mind, and would, without a doubt, go through them again, but he did not need to take on Pascal's panic. "Get a grip, man. You're going to spook yourself."

"So you wouldn't come with me if I went?"

Raphael shook his head. "Not a chance." Pascal looked so worried that Raphael quickly put his mind to rest. "But I won't rat you out if you try it. You have my word on that."

Right then the truck's engine had coughed a number of times and ground back into life. The driver seemed to have found a formula for reanimating the machinery, but it came to Raphael as a very mixed signal. It signified the end of this short respite from traveling, but it got him off the hook of having to listen to Pascal's plans to go on the run. Then Melchior was shouting for them all to get back on the truck, and both Raphael and Pascal rose wearily to their feet.

With the rain about to start at any minute, the traffic grew more dense, with more vehicles joining the flow. More delays were encountered, and more cursing and arguing ensued. The acetylene lamps used by the Mosul vehicles after dark were not noted for either their brightness or efficiency, and although the military police struggled to keep the highway moving, they struggled in a chaotic gloom. Conditions were not made any easier for those caught in the snarling jams of traffic by the fact that different squads of MPs, distinguished by their orange helmets, had very different sets of priorities on different sections of highway. They had passed one checkpoint where the officers were screaming at drivers to keep the traffic flowing at all costs, but, just three or four miles up the road, they encountered another checkpoint at which the MPs were ordering all cars and trucks to pull to the side of the road. Something was coming that took overriding precedence, and all other travelers had to wait at the side for it to pass. Melchior had immediately recognized that a holdup of this kind would only happen if someone or something of great importance was traveling on their road. "Keep your eyes peeled, boys. You might be about to see something right here that will rock you in your boots."

All through basic training, Raphael had tried to figure out how rumors in armies were started, and how they traveled so far and so amazingly fast. The first scuttlebutt explanations of why they were stalled at the side of this stretch of the Continental Highway came after only a couple of minutes as they sat in the dark amid the throb of idling motors and billows of exhaust fumes created because most drivers were reluctant to cut their engines out of fear they would never get them started again.

"Hassan IX. It's him. Hassan IX himself will pass right by us."

The first rumor, however, did not take and had a very short vogue. The majority refused to believe that the emperor was coming, and that story was quickly replaced by one more lurid and frightening. An overheard conclusion that better suited the mood of the majority was swiftly passed along by each company's regular sayer of doom. "I swear, I heard two officers talking. It's Dark Things; they're saying Dark Things are coming. Dark Things with their Mothmen are going to be passing right by us."

The tale ran down the line like a shudder, and even Melchior seemed to buy it. "If it's Dark Things we got, then you callow youth are in for a very irregular experience."

Some in the squad seemed a little too eager for the irregular, like the four from the Lowlands who would have been offering odds on the arrival of actual Dark Things had not Melchior held up a warning hand. "Don't wish for what you later won't want."

Speculation and quasi-facts ran riot as raw replacements asked hardened veterans to tell all they knew about the Dark Things and of what they might be capable.

"Don't ever look directly at them."

"They can permanently blind you if they catch you staring."

"They can fry your brain if they catch you staring."

"They have this flash that burns clear through your eyes."

"They can swallow a man whole in one gulp."

"When they get worked up, they give off this poison gas."

"Don't look directly at them."

Starting with the trucks back down the road some way to the south, a hush fell on the line of vehicles, an eerie dwindling of conversation followed by silence that moved quickly up the highway like an advance warning. The hush was trailed by the glow, an unhealthy orange aura in the night, that appeared way down in the distance but moved up faster than any human formation of marching men. Despite all the warnings, and without exception, everyone in the waiting vehicles looked. At the same time, the first drops of rain fell, splashing on the surface of the road, the warm hoods of trucks, and the helmets of young soldiers. No one in Raphael's outfit had been issued with special rainwear, no slickers, ponchos, or ground sheets, even though autumn was coming on. Right at that moment, though, no one in the truck would have bothered reaching for a slicker if they had one. All were transfixed, unable to look away. Even Melchior sounded awed. "I don't know what they do to the enemy, but they scare the shit out of me."

Where the rain hit the radiance, it instantly boiled, shrouding the

Dark Thing formation in its own unearthly cloud of steam, but it wasn't enough totally to conceal the bouncing geometric lines of the Dark Things themselves. It just made them, and the Mothmen that fluttered above them, even more indistinct than they were already. As they came closer, Raphael could see that they were outwardly nothing more than pitch-black gelatinous blobs with a smooth and shapeless, sacklike exterior that sweated beads of dark red liquid like very old blood. They moved with a bizarre bouncing motion that was ungraceful, uncanny, and unpleasantly comedic. An overcharged young soldier must have seen the same funny side of the Dark Things, because, a few trucks down from that of Melchior's company, someone started laughing, normally at first, but then rapidly rising in pitch as hysteria clawed its way loose, and only stopping when someone slugged the laugher. Or so it sounded to Raphael, and it must have sounded the same to Melchior, because he spoke quickly and softly to calm the men under him, knowing full well that hysteria was dangerously contagious. "Easy now, lads. Let's not be getting away from ourselves."

Once he felt he had them under control, he screwed home his advantage. "Just think yourself lucky you won't see one burst tonight."

"Burst?"

"In battle, sometimes, when they take a hit, they burst. Things come out of them, and it's very nasty."

The Mothmen were harder to describe. If any human equivalent could be used, the Dark Things were supervised by and apparently under the command of hovering Mothmen. As their name indicated, they were winged beings, with spindly humanoid bodies supported by two pairs of huge, mothlike wings, but their form seemed to shimmer and shift as though they were a great deal less in this dimension than the shapeless blobs. As Raphael watched, one of then detached itself from the main mass and rose into the air on fast-beating wings, carrying its own orange aura with it. Even with one of the flying things out on its own, he could not make out many additional details. It glittered and sparkled, and it didn't help that the glow around the single Mothman looked brighter than the more generalized illumination around the Dark Things. The Mothman rose to around thirty feet in the air, hovered for a few moments, and then sank back to the main formation. To Raphael, that action resembled nothing more than the Mothman acting as a lookout, rising in the air to see what was ahead.

Raphael's attention was suddenly wrenched away from speculation on the nature of the Mothmen when one of the gelatinous Dark Things, with no prior warning, sickeningly confirmed an earlier rumor. A shapeless black blob suddenly broke formation and bounced to one side, at a full right angle to its original direction, and landed on a unfortunate soldier, completely enveloping the man before he even had the chance to cry out or scream. The Dark thing appeared to eat and wholly digest him in little more than the blink of an eye. It bounced again and was right back in the line as though nothing had happened. Now everyone watching knew how the Dark Things supposedly fed, and how they really could swallow an entire man whole, and in one gulp, but Raphael had more to think about than just the Dark Things' eating habits. In a split second, during the moment of the attack, he had been subjected to a brief vision in which even more unnameably impossible entities, with angular, disgusting limbs, slime-coated and seemingly without bones, and huge, vulture heads that pulsed with dimly obscene energy, marched in ranks against an unintelligible landscape of rods and cones. Raphael knew by some weird instinct that what he was seeing was a fourth-dimensional being translated for a three-dimensional world, and, with his vision, he had taken a step closer to the untranslatable. What he failed to fathom was why he should have had the vision, what it meant, and why it had been his at all. The experience left Raphael feeling shaken and strange, and the same seemed to apply to all those in the truck with him. After the Dark Things had passed them, Melchior moved down the lines of men seated on either side of the truck, looking each in the face. "Anyone here having an adverse reaction to our allies from the Other Side? No? Anyone not feeling himself?" He stopped in front of Raphael. "What about you, boy? You look like you were just butt-fucked by a drunken Mamaluke."

"I saw something . . ."

"You fainted."

"Honest, Melchior, I swear. I saw something."

"You saw the Dark Things, and you fainted."

Melchior was so insistent that Raphael realized it was time to stop his own insisting. "I did?"

Melchior pushed his face into Raphael's. "You did. Because if you had done anything other than just faint, I would be compelled to turn you in under a new encyclical from the Ministry of Virtue that demands all underofficers be on the alert for what is now known as 'heretic sensitivity.' I am expected to report any man who shows an adverse reaction in the presence of any manner of Otherness. But since you only fainted, no report needs to be filed. Too many faint to make it worth their while mounting an inquiry. Seeing things, on the other hand, might be worthy of investigation, and even you must know something about the Ministry men's investigative techniques."

"Yes, Underofficer. I know what they do to get the answers they want."

"So what happened to you, young Vega?"

"I saw the Dark Things, and I fainted."

"You owe me one, Vega. So don't go doing a runner on me, see? And tell your buddy Pascal to keep his big mouth shut."

"Yes, Underofficer. Thank you, Underofficer."

Melchior treated Raphael to a final penetrating look and went back to his seat in the corner just behind the partition that divided them from the driver's cab. It was gradually dawning on Raphael that Melchior was very different from Y'assir, and, in the person of the squat, burly, and heavily scarred Mosul, they might have a squad leader actually willing to keep them alive for as long as he could.

Another hour passed before the traffic jam created by the passing of the Dark Things and the Mothmen was sorted out and the truck was once again on the move. Where the anticipation of the coming of the Dark Things had produced nothing but wild chatter, in their wake no one seemed to want to utter a word. They rode in silence through a wet, dreary, and uncomfortable night in which Raphael could do nothing but hunch forward as dirty water ran down his neck, soaked his greatcoat, and collected on the bed of the truck around his feet. The memory of the strange, approximate vision of how the Dark Things might look in their own world had left him with a hundred questions and as many new fears running round in his head. Try as he might, he could neither come up with any answers nor quell his own panic at new concepts like "heretic sensitivity." He recoiled from the thought that there was something special or unusual about him that might mark him in the eyes of the Zhaithan. He already had his determination to draw and his art as a potential means to betray himself in a moment of carelessness or showing off. The idea of having heretic sensitivity sounded ten times worse.

Although absolutely nothing could erase the vision of the Dark Things, the sight that presented itself about an hour and a half after they had again started rolling up the Continental Highway was able to push it to the sidelines of his fear. It was a recruit named Raoul, an Hispanian like Raphael, who had first alerted everyone to the apparition in the sky. Raoul was at the end of the line that faced Raphael, suffering the discomfort of sitting next to the tailgate of the open truck, and, only supported by another body on one side, being forced to constantly cling onto something to stop himself from toppling out. He had looked up, his jaw had dropped, and he had pointed in amazement. "Holy shit, will you all look at that!"

For a moment, Raphael thought the Mothmen had come back, but then he saw that Raoul was pointing at something much more substantial. The airship looked enormous, close to a hundred feet long and clearly in trouble. The silent, silver craft was much too close to the ground, and, as it drifted over them, it spun on its long, cigar-shaped axis as though out of control. Melchior was instantly on his feet, clinging to a vertical support in back of the driver's cab. "The bastard's coming down!"

Raphael could make out lettering on the side, NU98, and the star of the Norse Union. "It's Norse."

Melchior stared up as though he had a personal loathing for aircraft. "The bastards must have sneaked over here to drop a few bombs on us, maybe cut the highway. And it looks like they got screwed up, either by the storm or some of our own ground fire."

"I thought the Norse Union was neutral."

"They were, but who the hell knows? Maybe they finally came out on the side of Albany. We're the last ones to hear stuff like that."

The airship vanished from sight behind a stand of trees on a low rise. A few seconds later, a terrible, protracted crashing could be heard even through the wind and rain, and a orange gasoline fireball blazed briefly in the air and then continued to burn as a glow beyond the high ground. "That's it! They're down!"

Melchior immediately turned and banged on the top of the driver's cab. "Pull over! Pull over, right now."

In front and behind, other trucks were doing the same. Melchior turned to his men. "Quite a night for adventure we're having. Best we wait here and see if they need us to hunt down any survivors."

CORDELIA

Cordelia had no real memory of the impact. She recalled pieces of the side and the floor vanishing from the gondola before her horrified eyes. She also remembered being upside down and hanging in the safety straps, and, round about the same time, huge pieces of what looked like flapping fabric flying past her. The next thing she recalled was lying on her back, feeling wet and peering into an indistinct darkness with something burning in the distance. Then Phelan's face was in front of her with blood running from a cut on his forehead just below the hairline.

"Cordelia?"

"Yes."

"Are you okay?"

Cordelia failed to understand the concept of okay. "Have we crashed?"

"Yes, we've crashed, and we've got to get out of here. Can you move?"

"No."

Cordelia's strongest memory was how, in the face of death, she had still been her. Her personality had remained as it was, and, in what could still be her last minutes, she could view even total disaster with a certain aloof detachment. She was rather proud of this and just wanted to lay as she was and relish this pride for a while. She definitely did not want to go anywhere.

"Is anything broken?"

"Me. I'm broken."

He was feeling her arms and legs, and she was tempted to giggle. "Taking liberties, Captain?"

"Nothing's broken that I can find. I think you're in shock."

"I think I have a right to be."

He waved a blurred hand in front of her face. "How many fingers am I holding up?"

"Damned if I know and damned if I care."

"Can you stand?"

"What's burning?"

"One of the engines."

"Why is it such a long way away?"

"It became detached when we first started to plough through the trees. We were lucky. That's the only fire. Try and stand, Cordelia."

"I don't want to."

"Cordelia, try and stand, okay?"

"You're a bore, Phelan."

To humor him, she tried to sit up. Pain crashed in on her, and reality right along with it. Nothing might be broken, but she was profoundly battered. Also, she was lying beside a crashed airship, and, if what the navigator had said right before the crash was correct, she was deep in enemy territory. "Oh, good Goddess. This is really fucked up, isn't it?"

Phelan tried to help her up, but she impatiently waved him away. "Okay, okay, I can manage. I think I enjoyed it more being in shock."

Cordelia stood for a while, swaying a little, and then she looked around and marveled that not only she, but what appeared to be the entire crew, had made it through apparently unscathed. The airship itself had fared much worse than its crew and passenger. The gondola had remained halfway intact, but pieces of framework and fuselage were scattered for a good hundred yards, through a mess of uprooted and broken trees, along a path that led in the exact direction of the flames still roaring from the one burning engine. Cordelia could see how the punishment sustained by the NU98 itself might have saved those flying in it by taking the impact of the crash in easy stages. "Does anyone have a drink?"

The rain was still falling, and Phelan brushed water from his wet hair and beckoned to the wireless operator. "Keats, do you still have that flask?"

"Sure do, Skipper."

"Bring it over here. The lady needs a drink."

"I don't blame her."

Keats the wireless man handed Cordelia a stainless steel flask with the insignia of the Norse Air Corps engraved on the face. She took a pull on it and let out a sigh as the warmth of Scotch whiskey coursed through her. "I needed that." She eased a bruised shoulder, aware for the first time of the rain and the fact that she was soaked to the skin. Somehow neither was high on her list of pressing problems. "Do we have some kind of plan?"

Phelan looked unhappy. "I'm afraid our only option is to walk out of here. That's why we have to get out of this area as fast as we can. The Mosul can hardly have missed seeing us go down, and they could well be on their way here right now."

The navigator joined Cordelia, Phelan, and Keats. He was carrying a first-aid kit, and also looked unhappy. "We may have less time than we think, Skipper."

Phelan turned sharply, wanting no more bad news. "What do you mean?"

"I don't know for sure. It was all happening a bit fast. But I think I saw something right before we hit. I think we crossed the Continental Highway just a little bit back."

"Damn!"

At that moment, the bombardier and one of the gunners emerged from the wreck of the gondola. The bombardier had three holstered pistols slung over each shoulder and was carrying a light carbine. The gunner held another carbine and hefted two heavy rucksacks. "We've cleared out everything in the small arms' locker, Skipper, and we've got all of the emergency food and medical supplies."

Phelan nodded. "Okay, pass out those weapons, and let's start moving out. Where the hell is Coburn?"

"He's seeing if there's any way he can stop the Mosul getting the other engine intact. He's trying to set fire to it."

"Tell him to get back here. He's not going to be able to get it burning if he hasn't managed it by now, and there's no way he can blow it up."

Keats pocketed his flask and hurried off to get the engineer. As the weapons were passed out, Cordelia found herself being ignored. The guns were being given to the men, but nobody had offered her one. "Don't I get so much as a pistol?"

Phelan hesitated, and that was too much for Cordelia. Her tone sharpened. "Aren't I, as a lady, supposed to shoot myself rather than be taken alive? How am I supposed to do that if I don't have at least a pistol?"

Phelan gestured to the bombardier. "Give her a pistol."

The bombardier held out a belt and holster. "Do you know how to use it, Lieutenant?"

Cordelia's impatience with men as a breed exploded. "Yes, I know how to use it. I've been shooting guns since I was five, damn it."

She might have elaborated, but at that moment Coburn and Keats came out of the darkness. Phelan nodded. "Okay, let's get going. We'll take turns humping the supplies. Seck and Hodding, since you've got them already, you can take the first shift. Two hours, and then you pass them on."

The bombardier and the gunner shouldered the packs. Cordelia buckled the belt with its holstered pistol around her hips. For the first time, she was able to take a head count of the crew, and this caused her to frown. "I thought there were nine of us. How is it I only see seven?"

Phelan avoided her eyes. "Lars and Olaf didn't make it."

"They what?"

"They weren't as lucky as we were. They died on the first impact."

"Oh, no."

"It happens."

Cordelia was genuinely ashamed of herself. "And I've been pouting and complaining when two men were dead?"

"You were in shock. You've just been through an air crash."

"That's no excuse. I'm sorry. Where are they?"

"The bodies are still in the wreck."

"You're just going to leave them?"

"We neither have the time nor the implements to bury them." Phelan turned quickly to the men. "Right, we're moving out. Single file. Keats, take the point, Coburn, bring up the rear. Cordelia, stay close to me, and everyone look sharp. The Mosul may be uncomfortably close."

With the orders given, and nothing else to say, the survivors of the wreck of the NU98 walked away from the wreckage and into the dark and the rain of the forest. As the crash site was swallowed up by the darkness, except for the unhappy beacon of the burning engine, Cordelia glanced at Phelan. "And so we move into a new phase of our adventure."

Phelan smiled despite himself. "I hope you can go on thinking of it like that."

JESAMINE

Jesamine eased herself out from under the dead weight of Phaall's arm. He had returned to his quarters so drunk that he had actually passed out during her attempt to give him the sex he'd demanded just minutes earlier.

She was faced with a choice. She could either slip away and hope that Phaall did not revive any time soon and start demanding to know where she was, or she could remain and listen to him snore like a pig for maybe the rest of the night. She walked, naked but for the jewelry at her wrists, neck, and ankles, to the other side of the colonel's quarters, to the chest where he kept his schnapps. The night had been long and hard, and she badly needed a drink, but before opening it, she glanced back to see that Phaall was still sleeping like a large, sweating corpse and not showing any signs of coming to. Her jewelry tinkled as she moved, but that would not be noise enough to wake the colonel. Fully reassured, she opened the chest and removed an already opened bottle. Fortunately, Phaall was not the kind who measured or otherwise recorded the consumption of his alcohol. If some was missing, he would simply assume that he had drunk it himself. Usually, when she stole her master's booze, she drank it straight from the bottle, but with the colonel out cold, she indulged in the luxury of a glass. An hour before, the man had been pouring liquor over her breasts and licking it off. The use of a glass represented a kind of payback. Using a glass made her at least feel like a whore who was bought and paid for rather than a slave who was merely owned.

"Don't let him catch you doing that."

The voice took Jesamine completely by surprise. She knew enough not to cry out, but she did almost drop the bottle. "Reinhardt. Where the fuck did you come from?"

"He's got orders. I have to wake him."

Relieved, she sipped her drink. "You won't wake him now. He's out cold. Doomsday couldn't wake him. That's why I'm stealing his schnapps."

"I have to wake him. It's important."

"What's important?"

"I can't tell you that."

Jesamine used her decorated nakedness to full advantage. She only had to undulate a little and she had the manservant's full attention. "Of course you can. You tell me everything."

"Not this."

" 'Not this,' Reinhardt, 'not this'? What do you mean, 'not this'? What's so important about 'this'?" She leaned closer so Reinhardt could smell what perfume Phaall had left on her. "Do you like me like this,

Reinhardt? You want me to do it to you right here, while our drunken pig of a master snores on?"

Reinhardt backed away. "Don't talk like that. You could get us both hanged."

Jesamine followed him, again closing the gap between them. "Suppose I sucked you off while he was right there in the room, Reinhardt? Doesn't that excite you just one little bit?"

"You're drunk."

"Not too drunk." She giggled and stuck her tongue out at Phaall. "Not as drunk as him."

"Cut it out, Jesamine."

She instantly stopped acting drunk and self-destructive. "Then tell me what these damned orders are."

"Okay, okay. An enemy airship crashed, right in occupied territory."

"Where?"

"Real close. Twenty-five miles down the Continental Highway."

"No shit?"

"No shit."

"He's always wanted one of those engines."

"That's what makes it so important."

"So wake him."

Reinhardt looked pathetically at Jesamine. "Will you wake him for me?"

"Fuck off. Wake him yourself."

"He's liable to get violent. He'll be beating me before I so much as say a word."

Jesamine shrugged. "We all have our burdens to bear."

"Yeah, but you could wake him in a way that wouldn't set him off."

"Are you crazy?"

"You couldn't have survived this long without knowing all the tricks."

"While I preform the tricks, you watch, no doubt?"

"If you did this for me, I'd owe you big time."

Jesamine realized that Reinhardt was genuinely afraid of rousing the drunken colonel. "Big time?"

"Big time."

"You'd better not burn me on this."

"Just do it, and I'll get you anything I can."

With a definite reluctance, Jesamine stretched out beside the still-snoring Phaall. She lay for a minute, aware that Reinhardt was watching, before she rolled over and pressed her body against his back. She started by blowing in his ear and whispering softly. "Wake up, Colonel, baby. There's a wonderful surprise waiting for you."

Phaall's breathing changed, and he grunted. Jesamine repeated the process, this time also stroking his thigh with one soft hand. "There's a wonderful surprise waiting for you."

Phaall grunted again and opened his eyes. "Waaa?"

"Now, I know you're probably still drunk and don't feel so good, but listen carefully, because you're going to like what I say."

Phaall tried to clear his head. "What?"

"An airship crashed."

"An airship."

"That's right, an airship."

"What kind of airship?"

"An enemy airship."

Phaall sat bolt upright. "Where?"

"About twenty-five miles down the Continental Highway."

For one so recently drunk, Phaall was fast to his feet. "Twin fucking gods! Reinhardt? Where is the damned man hiding now that I want him?"

"I'm here, Colonel."

Phaall was taken by surprise by the closeness of the response. "Where did you spring from?"

Reinhardt seemed about to blurt out that he'd been there all along, but Jesamine urgently shook her head. The colonel did not, however, have the patience for a reply. "Field uniform, boots, belt, sidearm. Then get out of here, tell Hartz and Waldheim to put the entire regiment on alert and ready to move out on my order."

"Yes, Colonel."

"Don't stand there like a limp prick, man. Move! Move!"

In a state of near panic, Reinhardt fetched Phaall's field kit and then hurried from the room. Jesamine pretended to luxuriate on the bed as Phaall quickly dressed, swaying a little from the booze still inside him. After he had pulled his pants up, he hurried to the schnapps locker and took out the same bottle from which Jesamine had helped herself. He looked at it, and for a moment she thought he was going to accuse her, but, true to prediction, he shook his head and then took a long pull. After which he wiped his mouth, belched, and glanced at Jesamine. "I'll be gone for three or four days."

Jesamine played devastated. "That long, my master?"

"Maybe longer. I'm going to have one of their bloody engines, and my career will be made. I will be out of this cursed swamp and back in the Ruhr inside of just three months if I can pull this off."

Now Jesamine really had something to luxuriate about. Three days without Phaall was a divine blessing, and more would be a miracle. "I'm very happy for you."

"Yes, well, happy or not, you can stop laying around like a whore in heat and get the hell out of here. My officers will be here in a minute, and I don't need you distracting them."

Without a word, Jesamine gathered up her scanty outfit from the night before and made her exit. Going back to the pavilion half-naked was a little humiliating, but that was more than compensated for by the knowledge that she would be left alone while Phaall lead the Mosul search for any serviceable parts of the aircraft that may have survived the crash. She had learned from Phaall just by eavesdropping how lamentably lacking the Mosul were in aviation technology and how much her colonel wanted to be the one to capture an aircraft engine complete and intact. He could be away for a week or more. Who knew what Jesamine might accomplish in a week? A week in war could sometimes be a lifetime.

ARGO

A large boulder was rolled into place, concealing the entrance to the Rangers' cave hideout from all but the most intense scrutiny. The rain continued to fall, and although it was not coming down with the same drumming force as at the wild height of the thunderstorm, the downpour would also help conceal all signs of their secret occupancy and the tracks they might leave as they moved out into the forest. As they tramped through the waterlogged woodland, with Hooker right behind the point man, forcing the pace, Argo felt a little strange to be part of this single file of hard men and highly efficient killers. Not as strange, however, as he had felt when, back in the cave, Yancey Slide had started receiving the silent messages. Bonnie had been the first to notice that, beneath the black hat, Slide appeared to have vacated his body. She had quickly gestured to Jeb Hooker. "Slide seems to be out on the wind."

Hooker had scowled. "I'll lay odds that it's something to do with that bloody airship."

Bonnie nodded. "The Norse are probably shitting themselves. The last thing they want is the Mosul getting hold of the debris from the wreck and shipping it back to the Ruhr for back-engineering."

Hooker stared at the limp and apparently lifeless Slide. "I dread it when he goes out like this."

Bonnie smiled wearily. "At least he's quiet."

"It's the return I dread. It usually means we go rushing out to find ourselves in a new circle of hell."

Slide's eyes suddenly opened. "A new circle of hell, Jeb? I think we can arrange one of those for you."

As Argo watched, Slide's body seemed to reinflate with life. While the Rangers looked on with expressions that were far from happy, he flexed his muscles as though reacquainting himself with his body's fit. Finally he looked down at Bonnie. "Yes, young lady, you're absolutely right. The talk in the wind was all about the bloody airship."

Bonnie squirmed uncomfortably. "When you're out there, you can hear us back here?"

Slide was dismissive. "Only at a distance. Like voices in another room."

"I'll have to remember that."

Hooker interrupted. "What's the story on the airship?"

Slide seated himself again. "Well, it's down."

"Where?"

"Near the Continental Highway, twenty or thirty miles south of what used to be Alexandria."

"Relatively close to us?"

Slide did not answer. Instead, he looked round with an expression of fatigue at the assembled Rangers. "Does anyone have a drink? Walking the wind takes it out of a body. What about you, Steuben? You always have a bottle stashed." Steuben sighed, rummaged in his kit, and handed Slide a flat flask. Slide took a pull on it and grimaced. "You're down to drinking fucking 'shine, Steuben? I though you had better taste than that."

Steuben shrugged, avoiding Hooker's curious gaze. "I drink what I can find."

Bonnie was sitting cross-legged, and she shifted her weight impatiently. "Are we going to discuss Steuben's taste in booze all night, or are you going to fill us in about the damned airship, Yancey?"

Slide had recapped the flask and returned it to its owner. "The excursion seems to have been something of a mess from the very start. The NU98 took off from Grover's Mill, bound for Manhattan down the Taconic Valley, which should have been simple enough. It was sunny, with little wind, and very little to worry about, except, along the way, they received new orders. They were to forget Manhattan and head for Baltimore, where they would rendezvous with a Norse cruiser called the *Cromwell*."

Hooker frowned. "What was that all about?"

Slide spread his hands in a "search me" gesture. "No one knows. It seems to be the well-kept secret of the Norse delegation in Albany, and they aren't telling."

"And did they make the rendezvous?"

Slide shook his head. "No way. They set a new course and swung out across the Jersey Barrens and headed south to where, unknown to them, the storm was waiting for them like a set and loaded trap. The *Cromwell* tried to warn them by wireless, but by the time they did, it was too late."

Steuben looked up. "What do you mean the storm was waiting for them?"

"It was not only waiting for them, but it performed some highly unorthodox and wholly inexplicable maneuvers, as if it was chasing the NU98."

Now Hooker's face had taken on a worried expression. "Are you telling us the Mosul have someone or something that can control the weather?"

Slide beckoned to Steuben for a second look at his flask. "Not the Mosul. More the high-echelon Zhaithan. Advanced telekinesis of a high order is really all it would require."

He fumbled in his pocket for a cigar, found one, held it up, and then let it go, allowing it to float unsuspended in midair. When he was sure everyone present had seen what he was doing, he retrieved the cigar, put it in his mouth, and lit it with a flame that he kindled on the very tip of his right index finger. Being used as an organic radio seemed to somehow energize Slide and even invest him with a certain reckless need to show off. Bonnie, on the other hand, was not impressed. "Do we have to sit through the magic act?"

Slide ignored her. "The principles behind kinetic weather control are the same as the ones that govern my little party trick. The only difference is that the energy needed to move a storm would be incalculable. I would not like to try it myself, and any entity that did would probably only do it once. The effort would be enough to kill both man and demon. As I told Bearclaw and the Lady Gretchen, I sense the hand of Quadaron-Ahrach in this business. Either Ahrach or a very close and highly trained disciple."

Bonnie looked up in surprise. "You really talk to the Lady Gretchen and Bearclaw Manson?"

Slide seemed puzzled that she should even comment. "Of course. Why not? I always do if the importance warrants it. Go to the top has long been my motto. The king has made the two of them jointly responsible for paranormal operations, after all. And if I'm not paranormal, who the fuck is?" He puffed on his cigar and continued. "If Ahrach and his inner circle have come to the Americas, we need to prepare ourselves for a protracted show of highly unnatural warfare."

Hooker exhaled unhappily. "I was afraid of that."

Argo was confused and felt that he should admit it. "Who's this Quadaron-Ahrach?"

Slide's eyes narrowed. "I don't recall inviting questions."

Argo was too tired to be intimidated. "It's the only way I get any answers."

Slide bear-growled deep in his throat before he replied. "Well, Argo Weaver, this particular answer is that Quadaron-Ahrach is a disgustingly ancient, black-hearted hunchback, who also happens to be the High Zhaithan. I would have thought his reputation was such that he would even have been known in Thakenham."

Argo swallowed hard. "The High Zhaithan?"

"The High Zhaithan, the one divine servant of Ignir and Aksura."

"We weren't even allowed to know his name."

Had it not been suggested to Argo that Slide was a demon of some kind, he would have accepted him as an exceptional magician, frighteningly skilled but still essentially human, but once the idea had been planted that Slide was something other that a man, the possibility of his otherness became more and more plausible.

"There's something else that might be of interest to you, Argo Weaver. The airship supposedly had a crew of eight, but also a unofficial passenger. An Albany RWA lieutenant called Lady Cordelia Blakeney. Seemingly she was enjoying a brief liaison with the NU98's captain, a young aviator called Phelan Mallory, and went along for the ride."

Argo was uneasy. "Why should that interest me?"

Slide smiled. "Because she has red hair and that pale skin that goes with it, the kind that freckles in the sun."

"You're suggesting that this Lady Blakeney is another one of the Four?"

"It's a possibility we can't rule out. Despite her title, she is only a few years older than you and a long way from being a virgin. If she somehow turns out to be the face in your dreams, we have to take the idea very seriously."

Bonnie had been thinking. "Might that mean the Mosul were after her and not the airship?"

"That is something else to be considered. To expend all the effort it would have taken to conjure and direct such a massive storm just to obtain some airship parts is hardly the way of Quadaron-Ahrach. If, on the other hand, he had information on the existence of the Four, it would be exactly the thing to attract his attention and motivate him to bring his magickal big guns to bear."

Silence reigned after Slide had finished speaking. The Rangers were avoiding looking at each other, aware they were not only in the presence of seriously wiggy shit, but also that it was becoming an increasing integral part of the mission. Bonnie pondered silently, and Argo tried to make sense of how what he was being told clashed so radically with the way he felt. In no way did he feel like one of a quartet so paranormally powerful and elevated that it was simply known as the Four. He was just a country boy, Mother Nature's son and straight off the farm. About the only thing he felt right at that moment was totally out of his depth.

Finally Jeb Hooker treated Slide to a long and appraising look. "Why do I feel that we have yet to hear the punch line?"

Slide blew a perfect ring of cigar smoke. "That's because I haven't told it to you yet."

"So let's have it."

Slide replaced the cigar in his mouth. "The long and the short of it is, we now have to saddle up and move out."

Hooker's face was bleak. "I was afraid of that. And where are we moving out to?"

"The first idea was that we should head for the wreck of the NU98, destroy it before the Mosul arrive. After that we would track the survivors, if there were any, and bring them across the river to safety."

Hooker was already shaking his head. "That's absurd. We'd never make it. The Mosul are right on top of the wreck. There's no way we could get there first."

Slide smiled. "I totally agree with you, Jeb. That's why I vetoed the idea."

"And instead of that?"

"We can assume the Mosul will throw a tight dragnet around the crash site. If there are walking survivors, the odds are that they will be picked up very quickly. There's nothing we can do to help them in the early stages, but if they do manage to elude the first Mosul search, we might be able to intercept them and bring them in. Presuming that they are going to head north for the river and Albany, we should head for the estimated point at which our two paths would be most likely to cross."

Hooker thought about this. "Suppose the Mosul get them straightaway and wind up with all the marbles: the survivors, this Lady Blakeney of yours, and the parts of the airship?"

Slide's smile twisted. "You're going to like this part."

"Oh, yeah?"

"In that eventuality, our orders are to assess the viability of a raid to free the survivors and destroy the airship parts."

"Did you think that one up?"

Slide smiled and shook his head. "That came from your own War Office."

Hooker rolled his eyes. "Shit."

"Who promised you it'd be easy?"

"All this is going down a stone's throw from the big camp by Alexandria.

In fact, that's where both the parts and the prisoners would be taken."

"Right."

"So does anyone in the War Office know that's not just a camp, that it's the central supply and replacement depot for the whole of the Mosul front, and it's a fucking *city*?"

Slide was unconcerned. "The bigger the place, the greater the confusion. If push came to shove, we could slip in and slip out of there without them even knowing about it."

"Damn you, Slide."

It was the first time that Argo had seen Slide grin. "And fuck you, Jeb, for acting like a timorous old woman. I know you love a challenge."

Hooker exhaled noisily. "Okay, okay. You win. Let's look at a map." He turned to the Rangers. "The rest of you get packed up for a brisk walk in the country."

Steuben was unable to leave it at that. "A walk of what duration, Captain?"

"Who the fuck knows, Steuben? Who the fuck knows? All I can say is you'd better bring all of your booze stash."

Bonnie also had a question. "What about me and Weaver?"

Hooker was happy to pass that enquiry along to Slide. "That's a good question, Yancey. What about Bonnie and Weaver?"

Slide was already unfolding a map. "They come with us."

"All the way?"

"All the way."

"Even if we have to go into the Mosul camp?"

Slide smoothed out the map. "All the way. I can't be leaving them on their own."

Thus Argo found himself hiking through the wet night, part of the same watchful single file as a crew of grimly determined Royal Albany Rangers armed to the teeth and even carrying a selection of their heavier equipment, including the mortar and the Bergman gun. The rain had eased off in comparison to the earlier downpour, but it still pattered on the overhead foliage, and the leaf mold underfoot squelched like a soaked sponge. Half-seen things inhabited the shadows of his peripheral vision, and Argo fancied that he sensed what he could only describe as a swirling of unfocused dark forces in the air around him. He could still dismiss it as his imagination, the combined product of fear and excitement, but the more he learned, the harder that became. He walked directly behind Yancey Slide. This was how Slide had ordered it. As they had emerged from the cave, a hard-claw hand in a leather glove had fallen on his shoulder. "You belong to me, Argo Weaver."

"What?"

"Stick close to me whatever happens. You're in the care of Yancey Slide now, boy, and woe to him who fucks with you. All I ask is that you don't get in my way."

Argo knew Slide was deadly serious, and he nodded accordingly. "I'll do my best." He turned and watched the Rangers loading up to move out. "You think we'll run into the Mosul?"

Slide nodded as he checked his guns. "It's highly in the cards."

Argo pointed to the strange pistols. "What are those things."

Slide smiled. "You noticed them, did you?"

"I've never seen anything like them."

Slide replaced the first pistol in his shoulder holster and then spun the second before dropping it into the one on his hip. "That's because they're a pair of Colt 1911A1s and not really from this world. Over time, I've grown so used to them that I tend to bring them with me each new place I go."

Slide seemed to enjoy tantalizing Argo with the idea that he was something other than human, but Argo tried not to rise to the psychological bait. Instead, he gestured toward his stepfather's pistol stuck in his belt. "If we're going to go up against the Mosul, I could use a better weapon than this old thing."

Slide took the perpetual cheroot out of his mouth. "What are you saying, boy? You're eager to get in to your first fight? You think you're ready to mix it up?"

The mockery was back in Slide's voice, and Argo didn't like it. "I know I can't keep up with the Rangers, but I'd sure like to be able to defend myself."

Slide conceded that Argo had a point. "You're right, Argo Weaver. That G and J Bolton cuckold's special in your belt is going to be worse than useless in a firefight." He turned, but the Rangers were already forming up to move out. "Nothing can be done about arming you right now, but as soon as we get a pause, we'll have you checked out on a shotgun or a carbine, so you at least have a fighting chance. In the meantime, let's move. For a while, at least, you will have to keep up with Rangers."

The Rangers set a tough pace, and after the first hour of tramping through the rain, Argo began to suspect that what set the Rangers apart from other men, even other soldiers, was not their valor or their training but their infinite tolerance for discomfort and tedium, hunger and lack of sleep. Ever since he had run away from Thakenham, Argo had been going without food for long periods and also not finding all that much time to sleep. Although the Rangers had fed him, the news of the airship crash had come just as he was hoping to close his eyes. The merry-go-round had started up again, and now he found himself soaked to the skin and part of a forced march into an immediate future that was shaping up to be both desperate and dangerous. On the other hand, he in no way mourned the passing of his previous life. Indeed, Thakenham and its people, with their fear and poverty and their passive acceptance of Mosul brutality, seemed like a million miles and a thousand years away. Argo could no longer see himself in that context. A part of him might want to fall out of the line and curl up at the base of the nearest comforting tree, but he entertained no desire to go back to his old life. In fact, despite being wet, cold, and weary, he was also quite pleased with himself. In less than a week, he had made good his escape, and, admittedly more by luck than judgment, he had penetrated to the very heart of the fight against the Mosul in occupied territory. Bonnie had taken his highly unwanted virginity, and he now appeared to be under the protection of no less a being than Yancey Slide, who, if all was to be believed, held high-powered telepathic conferences with the elevated of Albany. Could he in any way have done better? The idea of being one of the mysterious Four was extremely daunting, but even that extended the promise of more curious and exotic adventures to come.

As Argo fought off tiredness and forced his aching legs to keep moving, he covertly observed how the Rangers were holding up. They marched with an easy rhythm that looked set to carry them to the end of the earth if need be, but their faces were strangely blank, as though locked in their own thoughts. Argo's best guess was that they had the knack of retreating into their own minds and distancing themselves from the external discomforts of the grueling march. Argo tried to do the same. Certainly he had plenty to occupy his mind when he felt himself flagging. For instance, right at that moment, he could ponder how Yancey Slide was able to move through the heavy autumn downpour without getting wet. Argo had first noticed this anomaly about twenty minutes into the march, but the darkness had made it hard to be absolutely certain. As the rain eased down to a drizzle, though, and as the first grey of dawn began to show in the eastern sky, he could see quite clearly that Slide had been walking in the rain for hours, and not so much as his cigar was damp. He seemed to have placed an invisible barrier between himself and the weather at a discreet, half-inch distance from the fabric of his clothes, the tips of his gloved fingers, and the low crown of his wide-brimmed hat. All that gave him away was a faint halo shimmer where the droplets of precipitation evaporated to nothing when they touched the magickal shield. That Slide could manage to keep the rain off him with such seeming lack of effort was more than enough to push Argo over the edge into fully believing that Yancey Slide was a demon or some kindred entity not of his world.

RAPHAEL

After standing in the rain for some forty-five minutes waiting for an officer to show up, the arrival of three infantry majors in a captured Army of Virginia steam car had transformed the idle ranks of wet and gloomy replacements into a hive of shouting activity. Underofficers had removed the screws from the boxes of rifles on which the recruits had sat for the duration of their journey up from Savannah, and each man was being armed for the first time since he had set foot in the Americas. Normally this issuing of weapons would not have taken place until they had arrived at the front and been assigned billets on the line. The Mosul did not trust their Provincial Levies with weapons while they were still on the way to the front, but the crash of the airship constituted a recognized emergency, and the replacements needed to be armed so they could be drafted into the search for wreckage and survivors. The fear of an uprising or mass armed desertion was outweighed by the need of the moment. When the lids of the boxes had been removed, they saw that they were being given breechloaders and not the hated muskets. Maybe not the brand new Krupps for which they had hoped, but at least reconditioned Teuton cartridge-and-ball guns. Time was when the squad had worried that they were not going to be given guns at all, and to see them was a relief in itself since it constituted at least a tentative promise that they were not going to be directly assigned to human-wave charges and unarmed suicide squads whose only function was to use up enemy ammunition. The breechloaders were not, however, going to be given to them without a ration of Melchior's gallows humor. "Each man kiss the Twins before he gets his weapon."

Melchior expected each man to kiss the tin dog-tag on the chain around his neck, on which was stamped his name and serial number, and that also carried the image of the Twin Deities Ignir and Aksura. These had been issued at the very start of basic training along with the first cotton uniform and the Yasma. The recruits were supposed to wear the tokens until death.

"Kiss the Twins before you touch the bamsticks, lads, for these are dead men's guns you're taking, my boys, scavenged bamsticks gathered from the battlefields where the fallen no longer needed them and reconditioned for your replacement use of. So each man kiss the Twins before he gets his weapon."

Melchior grinned as each man took his rifle with extreme caution and a few hesitated superstitiously before grasping the stock or barrel. Raphael could see more method in the underofficer's madness. The squad was treating the weapons very carefully. The idea had been planted in the conscripts' minds that their rifle was a sacred object and not to be misused or mislaid. The ammunition was handed out with less ghoulish ceremony but more urgent instruction. "Live rounds, ten per man. I don't say make every shot count, but, if called on to open fire, at least attempt to frighten the enemy, and, above all, don't load before ordered. You all hear me? If I catch one of you silly bastards with one up the spout before you're told, it's a formal flogging. You all got that?"

With what Raphael was learning to recognize as the stop-start irrationality of large armies, all the fuss and panic with which the rifles were issued and ammunition dispensed suddenly dwindled to nothing. The underofficers had done what was required of them. They had armed the men and revved them up to go hunting these on-the-run Norse fliers, but now they were forced to idle and wait while orders were debated. He could see why, according to Melchior's cumulative utterances, underofficers considered themselves the superiors of all commissioned officers up to at least the rank of colonel. The three infantry majors, as far as Raphael could read their body language from a distance, could not agree on the best way to implement the search and had apparently been given no detailed orders. A waft of their conversation had been enough to let slip the information that some Teuton colonel of engineers was on his way with men of his own, but he might not show for an hour or more. In the meantime, the three majors seemed more afraid of committing to a course of action with which the colonel might find fault than allowing any survivors of the crash to escape. The underofficers from the various transports waited together in a separate group, showing their contempt for the majors' indecision as openly as they dared.

Eventually the pressure to do something outweighed the fear of doing the wrong thing and orders were given. The men from the trucks would advance into the woods in separate squads, but once they were in the trees they would fan out into a long, single skirmish line and sweep through the forest in the direction of the crash site, deployed to search and capture. Once the majors had given the word, the underofficers hurried back to their respective trucks to put the plan in motion. Melchior was already shouting to his squad when he was still ten paces away from them. "Form up, lads, single file, rifles slung and unloaded. This is it. Your first taste of action, and since you outnumber the enemy at least twenty to one, it's a nice, easy walk in the woods, if you can manage not to be shooting each other."

CORDELIA

They were caught completely without warning. The rain had fallen away to little more than a drizzle, and the first streaks of dawn were showing somewhere to the east over the unseen ocean. The trees around them were tall pines, and to be in among them was like being inside a pungent, resin-scented cathedral where the thick trunks rose like supporting pillars as far as the eye could see and the overhead canopy was sufficiently dense and high to prevent extensive undergrowth. Visibility was better, and they hadn't seen hair nor hide of the Mosul for maybe an hour. Cordelia was starting to believe that the worst was over for them, and that they were on their own in this stretch of woodland, but then the flash had come, the puff of smoke, the first report, and a musket ball had slammed into a nearby tree trunk, smashing bark with a blood-chilling crack. The second and third shots flashed, and then the firing grew into a ragged volley. Somehow the Mosul had anticipated the route they would take and had managed to position themselves so they were already lying in wait for the survivors from the NU98.

A high hissing sound filled the air, so close to Cordelia that she knew it was the passing of angry, fatal slugs of lead and copper. The men were reaching for their pistols. Coburn had his carbine up and was firing into the billow of smoke that marked the Mosul position, pumping the ejector of his gun after each shot and screaming abuse as he fired. "Fuck you, you bastards! Fuck you! Fuck you!"

Meanwhile, Phelan was attempting to shout over him. "Everyone down! Take cover! Get down!"

Cordelia needed no such order. When the first shot was fired, she dropped instantly to the ground and then wormed her way to the shelter of a nearby tree trunk. Only then did she draw her borrowed revolver and wonder what to do with it. Cordelia had not realized that combat would be quite so fast and so highly chaotic. She had fondly imagined there might be a form of foreplay during which the participants might brace themselves and decide a course of action. Maybe that was how it was during formal battles, but in the woods and on the run, the firefight had blazed out of nowhere, without preamble or warning. Everyone, including Phelan, had dived or slid into some kind of cover, but Coburn, clearly furious at what was being done to them then, and all that had gone before, including the destruction of his beautiful airship, was still on his feet and firing. Phelan shouted to the engineer. "Get down, man! Hold your fire! You're just wasting ammunition."

Like most warnings in the field, it came moments too late. Coburn spun round, his gun flying from his hands and flecks of blood spraying from the right side of his chest. He dropped to his knees, crying disbelievingly in a voice of surprise and shock. "Oh shit, oh shit! They've killed me!"

The second bullet hit him in the back and pitched him forward. Seck made a dive to try and pull Coburn into cover but had to duck back when bullets kicked up pine needles all around him. Phelan was shouting again. "Leave him, man! He's dead, goddamn it."

Around the moment that Coburn was shot, Cordelia realized to her horror that these Norse aviators had never been in an actual firefight before. They were as much novices in the realm of flying bullets as she was. They had maybe trained for such a contingency but had never confronted the real thing. They might even have been through a crash landing before, but they were complete neophytes when it came to ground combat. They were all blazing away at where they believed the Mosul positions might be, except for Hodding, who was already reloading, Cordelia herself, who was not prepared to so much as raise her head, and Phelan, who was still trying to get his men under control. "Hold your fire. Hold your damned fire. There's nothing to shoot at. Wait until the bastards show themselves."

When the fliers stopped shooting, so did the Mosul, as though one of their officers had given the same angry order as Phelan. In the quiet after the gunshots, Cordelia heard the whinny of an unhappy horse. The idea of a horse took her quite by surprise. She had imagined they were facing a detachment of foot soldiers. Cavalry had not occurred to her, although it made perfect sense. A troop of cavalry could have moved fast through the woods to cut off the survivors' retreat if the Mosul were truly determined to take them. At that point, a chill gripped Cordelia's stomach. In the context of the Mosul, if you said "cavalry," the next word was automatically "Mamaluke," and, all through her childhood and school days, the Mamalukes had been the subject of an entire canon of gruesome horror tales. At first it had been nursery screams at fables of how the Mamalukes drank blood and ate babies, and later it was the dormitory tales, told after lights out, breathless schoolgirl whispers of multiple rape, foreign objects, and brutal perversions, with the bound, stripped, and helpless victim murdered afterwards unless she was extremely attractive, and then she might find herself carried off to be used and debased in endless sexual slavery. The standard advice to the woman confronted by Mamalukes was always to save the last round in her pistol for herself. Cordelia suddenly found herself having trouble with her grip on reality. She had managed to accept the storm and the crash of the airship. The escape through the woods had been unpleasant, but that, too, was simply another part of the adventure, and everything would be alright in the end. The deaths of the two crewmen had given her pause, but she had still been alive and could continue to hope. At the prospect of Mamalukes, something inside her went into violent denial. This could not be happening to her. It was not written in the

Lady Cordelia Blakeney's destiny that she should save the bullet for herself. She was special, she was exceptional, and she was definitely not the kind to be raped, sodomized, and murdered by Mamalukes. Surely even a Mamaluke would recognize that she was too much of a prize to be killed and cast aside. Yet how would they know? She was soaked and muddy, and her clothes were torn. Right then she was a prize in filthy disguise who could easily be overlooked.

Cordelia was so shocked to catch herself considering playing the whore to save her own skin that she spoke out loud to herself. "Are there no limits to how much of a slut you'll become if it means your miserable survival? Does honor mean nothing?" She thought about this and decided, when considering the alternatives, it did not mean that much. "Honor is for the living, so what's so damned dishonorable about staying alive?"

"What did you say?" Phelan was close enough to have heard her speak.

Cordelia didn't even have to think of something plausible to tell Phelan. "Did you hear that horse?"

Phelan nodded. "Yeah. What do you think about it?"

"That could be dismounted cavalry in front of us."

"Or just a mounted officer and a squad of infantry."

Cordelia liked the sound of the last statement. It greatly diminished the chances of Mamalukes. "You think so?"

Phelan tried to be reassuring. "I only heard one horse."

Further discussion was cut short by a voice from the Mosul positions, amplified by a megaphone of some kind. "Airmen of the Norse Union, your resistance is pointless. You are outnumbered, and the imperial forces of Hassan IX are positioned both in front and behind you. You cannot escape."

Cordelia quickly glanced back the way that they had come. She could see no sign of Mosul behind them, where they had just walked through unscathed. Earlier, in the dark and rain, shortly after they had left the immediate area of the crash, Mosul had been everywhere. At Phelan's command, they had all lain prone in the wet leaves while lines of searching Mosul swept the forest. Some passed only a few yards from them, so close that Cordelia had managed to make out one or two faces. The soldiers hunting them looked like raw recruits, holding weapons that were still awkward in their hands and moving so nervously that they could clearly spook at their own shadows. The fugitives had crawled and couched and held their breath, protected by the noise of the downpour and the poor visibility, until the enemy all seemed to be behind them. From that point on they had not seen hide nor hair of their foes and were starting to believe they would have no more trouble until they reached the river and had to negotiate the Mosul lines in order cross into friendly territory. It was only then, with their vigilance somewhat relaxed, that they had walked into the ambush.

Cordelia hissed to get Phelan's attention. "I think he's lying."

"What?"

"I think the Mosul with the megaphone is lying. I don't believe there are more of them behind us."

"What are you saying?"

Cordelia decided it was time to take charge. "I think if we pumped all the fire we could into them, and then ran back the way we came, we might be able to give them the slip in the confusion."

The Mosul with the megaphone tried a fresh approach. "Airmen of the Norse Union, you have no reason to fear us. Once we are assured that your incursion into our sovereign territory was accidental, we will return you unharmed to your own people. The Norse Union and the empire of Hassan IX are not at war."

Phelan looked towards Cordelia. "Do you believe him?"

"I don't have to believe him. I'm from Albany, and I am definitely at war with the empire of Hassan IX."

"You want to try running?"

Cordelia was becoming less and less impressed with Phelan's leadership skills. He might be a master of the skies, but on solid ground he was starting to seem seriously out of his element. She rolled her eyes, but he was not close enough to see her exasperation. "Why else would I have made the suggestion?"

"Hold on."

Phelan crawled from one tree to the next so he was closer to Keats. No Mosul took a shot at him, and he seemed to be explaining Cordelia's plan to Keats. Keats rolled closer to Seck to pass the orders down the line. Seck told Hodding and so on. Now Phelan moved back to near Cordelia. "When I give the order, fire a couple of shots into the Mosul position and run like hell. We'll obviously be scattered, so we'll have to find each other again after we've given them the slip."

"You really want to do this?"

"I can't think of anything better."

Cordelia was not encouraged that the men were so willing to go along with any scheme of hers just because they had no better idea. Why the hell were they open to her suggestion? What did Cordelia know? She was no combat veteran. She had spent her entire war on a modification of the same social whirl she had frequented in peacetime. "On your order, then?"

Phelan sounded anguished. "One more thing, Cordelia . . ."

Cordelia sighed. "I know, I know, save the last round for myself."

The megaphone began to set time limits. "Airmen of the Norse Union, we have been patient, but we are not about to wait all day for your answer. You have invaded our airspace and must surrender to our custody to give an account of yourselves. If you continue to refuse, we will have no alternative but to take you by force."

Phelan sprang to his feet, and, pointing his revolver with both hands, started blazing away at where he imagined the Mosul to be. Cordelia, still believing it was madness to be listening to her, followed suit. She fired two shots and then turned and fled. At first she did not look back. She simply ran, one pace in front of panic. Shots rang out, and the hissing was in the air again. One of their number cried out, but still Cordelia did not look back. She expected a rifle bullet or musket ball to smash into her own spine with the same force with which they slammed into the trees around her. The muscles of her back cringed in anticipation of the pain. How much would it hurt? She only turned when she heard a sound that was even more threatening than gunfire. The drumming of hoofbeats on the forest floor meant that her plan would come to nothing. They could not outrun cavalry.

The first thing she saw was that cavalry was perhaps a slight exaggeration. Just eight riders were galloping full tilt between the trees, whooping and yelling and either waving sabers or brandishing long-barreled revolvers. Infantry men raced behind them, rifles held high, and sprinting to be in at the kill. They seemed to be treating the capture of the fugitives as nothing more than a fine day's sport. They could just as easily have been hunting deer or wild boar. Keats was running slightly behind and to the left of Cordelia, and one of the leading horsemen had picked him as a target. Keats tripped and fell, but recovered and started running again. Unfortunately, the delay was enough for the horseman to catch up with him. A saber flashed, and Keats was knocked from his feet, but he scrambled up again, with blood pouring down his face, and staggered as though stunned. He appeared to be alive, however, and the cavalryman must have been using the flat of his sword. Two foot soldiers ran up to him and seized the wireless operator by the arms. The obvious intent of the Mosul seemed to be to take them alive, but Cordelia didn't have time to speculate. A rider was coming hard, and directly at her.

She resigned herself to the fact that she was as good as dead already and aimed her revolver. As she looked down the barrel of the pistol, she saw more clearly than she had ever done before. The horse was a heavyset bay with a dark mane and tail. It's nostrils flared with the shared excitement of the gallop. The whites of its otherwise black eyes were just visible, and foam flecked the corners of its mouth where the bit cut in. The rider's uniform was dark blue with silver buttons and red tabs at the collar and cuffs. His pale, elated face beneath the peak of his busby told her immediately that he was Teuton and not Mamaluke. A long-barreled cavalry pistol was in his right hand, but he was making no effort to aim at her. Maybe they really were to be taken alive.

Cordelia squeezed the trigger of her revolver just as she had always been taught. The gun bucked in her hand, but she had missed, and horse and rider were almost on her. She pulled back the hammer and fired again, but still could not hit the moving target. Did she have two shots left, or only the one? She was damned if she could remember, but, whatever else might happen, she was not about to blow her own brains out here in this dreary, wet forest in front of so many onlookers. She did not feel that unlucky. At the last minute, she tried to sidestep the horse, but the rider skillfully swerved his mount so its flank struck Cordelia and sent her flying. The gun was jarred out of her hand, and with it went the last chance to preserve her maiden's honor. Now she would have to take the chances of the living and not settle for the certainties of the dead. She lay winded for a few moments and then attempted to scramble to her feet but immediately found that this was not possible. A circle of Mosul infantry surrounded her, with cheap uniforms, flat, stupid faces under ugly cooking-pot helmets, and sharp bayonets pointed at her chest, the points too close for her to do anything but give up.

Cordelia moved to a sitting position and spread her hands to show she was unarmed. "Well, boys, it looks like you've got me. I give up. I surrender."

One of the Mosul nudged his comrade and smirked. They had only just realized that they had captured a woman.

F O U R

ȴ

ARGO

"Follow the sound of gunfire, Captain?"

"Follow the sound of gunfire, lads. It's some ways off, though, and I doubt we'll be in time to do any good."

"But head for the thick of it anyway?"

Hooker nodded. "Head for the thick of it anyway."

The first flurry of shooting ceased and was replaced by some indistinct shouting. The Rangers called it as they saw it, knowing that this was a situation where every man's expertise was respected. As was so often the case, Steuben offered his opinion first. "Sounds like it's our Norse boys, and they've got themselves pinned down."

Barnabas listened as best he could while they were still on the move. "I can't make out the words, but that sure sounds like negotiating to me."

Hooker cut the conversation short with an order. "Step it up, lads. If there's a standoff, we might just make the difference."

Despite having walked all night, the column of Rangers quickened pace. Day had dawned and the rain had stopped, and all that remained was a dawn pall of mist that would almost certainly disperse as the sun climbed in the sky. Argo felt dead on his feet but was determined to keep up, come what may. The column had been climbing for some time, winding round the contours of an undulating landscape of woods and fields in cautious, well-spaced single file until they entered a stand of pines that seemed to go on for many acres and found themselves crossing a forest floor almost devoid of undergrowth save for a scattering of ferns.

Another flurry of ragged small arms' fire bounced among the muffling trees, making it hard to pinpoint the exact direction. This firing was more protracted and then fell away into short and scattered volleys and then stretches of silence punctuated by ominous, isolated pistol shots. The Rangers exchanged grim looks. Even Argo could understand that such a pattern of firing had to indicate that one side in the fight had been overrun and was being finished off. Hooker clearly concurred with the majority. "Hold up, men. I think we just missed being in the nick of time. Take one minute."

The entire column dropped to a crouch, breathing hard and saying nothing. The silence was complete. No more shots reverberated through the pines, and Hooker shook his head. "I think we can assume that our Norse boys are either killed or captured."

Penhaligon, the Ranger with the aw-shucks face of a farm boy, drank from his canteen and spat among the fallen pine needles. "We still have to take a look, Captain."

"I know still we have to take a look, but we're not going rushing in there willy-nilly after all indications of resistance have ceased. We're going to go in with all care. We have no idea of what we're walking into, so we're going to take another minute. Then we're going to lock and load and move in, but dispersed and ready. Like I said, take another minute, and then, gentlemen, the Rangers will become really invisible."

They all rested for thirty seconds, but then Ranger hands went, almost unconsciously, to their weapons, compulsively checking. At the full minute, Hooker rose to his feet. "Madden, are you okay to take the point?"

Madden still looked like a psychopath to Argo, maybe more so in the field, where he carried his razor-sharp Jones knife in an inverted sheath strapped to the right side of his chest so he could pull it in an instant. He grinned, nodded, and moved forward. "I got it covered, Captain."

"Okay, the rest of you fan out and use the terrain to the full. Like I said, invisible." Hooker turned his attention to Slide. "Yancey, hang back with Bonnie and the kid. Cover our rear with your pistols."

"It won't be the first time."

Hooker took a last look round. "I figure if the fight's over, the Mosul will be pulling out. They could come at us from anywhere. There's nothing I hate worse than stumbling into the opposition by accident."

Slide's grin was not unlike Madden's. "I'll be watching. I've done this before, Jeb."

The Rangers moved forward, adopting the formation of a ragged, line-abreast curve, with Madden out in front of them. When Hooker had said that they were about to become invisible, Argo had thought that he was exaggerating. He had been, but it had not by very much. The way the Rangers slipped from tree to tree and used every gully, hummock, depression, or patch of ferns to their advantage made it impossible to see any one man for a protracted length of time. A sniper would be hard-pressed to acquire a target, and any enemy force not expecting them would be overrun without warning. Now that confrontation was possible, and perhaps even near, the Rangers had the poise of men who knew their business.

After two or three minutes, Madden dropped to a crouch with one arm raised. The other Rangers froze. "I smell smoke."

Beside Argo, Slide also sniffed the air and then quietly exhaled. "Smoke, indeed, plus gunpowder, horse shit, and death."

Hooker moved quickly up to Madden, and the two conducted a fast, low-voiced conversation, after which the captain gestured to Barnabas, who was kneeling in the cover of a spread of ferns, indicating that he and Madden should scout what lay immediately ahead while the rest waited. The short, dark man nodded, and he and Madden moved forward, leaving Hooker in the point position. Madden came back after maybe five minutes and waved the whole squad forward.

Even though Argo was one of the last to arrive, he saw no less than anyone else of what remained of the encounter between the Mosul and the Norse Union airmen. The Mosul had left the scene maybe as recently as ten or fifteen minutes before, leaving just nine bodies and an expanse of churned-up muddy ground in a clearing. Argo headed for where Slide and Hooker were looking down at the dead. He wanted to see if the red-haired Lady Blakeney, supposedly one of the alleged Four, was among the fallen. He half expected someone to stop him, but no one did, even when he was right there staring into the blank, open-mouthed faces and staring eyes of death. Seven of the bodies were laid out in a neat row, as though ready for transportation. Two Mosul sentries, with their throats recently cut, were less tidily sprawled where they had fallen in their own blood. This unlucky pair had been caught unawares by Madden and Barnabas as they had presumably guarded the bodies, waiting for some kind of transport to be sent to cart the corpses away while the rest of the Mosul force moved out about its business. Madden was still carefully, almost religiously, cleaning blood from his Jones knife. Argo was relieved to find that all of the dead were exclusively male. Of the original seven, three were dressed in Norse Air Corps blue and four in Mosul brown. Lady Blakeney was either a Mosul prisoner or still loose in the forest.

From their overheard conversation, Argo learned that Slide and Hooker shared a similar theory. Slide pointed to the tracks that led away down a forested hillside. "I figure about ten horsemen and maybe twenty infantry, and, since they appear to have gone due west, I'd say that they have a rendezvous on the Continental Highway. Whoever was in charge of this search probably came south from the camp by Alexandria and dropped off search parties at regular intervals. If, as he had rightly assumed, the survivors would head north to friendly territory, all his men would have had to do was to set up lines of intercept that ran east to west, across the possible routes the Norse might take, and the odds were, sooner or later, in the course of their travels, the survivors would stumble into one of them. Whoever's running this show is no fool. It's probably a Teuton engineer who wants the airship to study and the crew to interrogate."

"Poor bastards."

Slide looked bleak. "I guess being a prisoner of the Teutons is marginally better than being a prisoner of the Zhaithan, but not by very much. As you say, Jeb, poor bastards. They might well have been better off dying in the crash."

Hooker noticed Argo looking at the bodies and spoke without thinking. "First time you've seen a corpse, Weaver?"

For once, Argo was able to look at Hooker with a degree of contempt. "I've seen plenty of corpses, Captain Hooker. There were more than enough to look upon once the Mosul came to Thakenham, although most of those were hanged or burned alive."

Hooker sighed at his oversight. "I'm sorry. I wasn't thinking."

Argo considered enquiring if a commander of Rangers was not surely required to be thinking all the time, but Slide seemed to sense this and headed him off. "This boy should be outfitted with a weapon, Jeb. He can't be running around behind enemy lines with a squad of Rangers and only a toting a two-shot G and J Bolton to cover his ass." Before Hooker could respond, Slide pointed to a small pile of captured weapons at a short distance from the line of bodies. "I see a smart Norse light carbine down there that would suit the kid. Why don't you have Steuben clean it up and then show the boy how to use it?"

Hooker, who could hardly deny him anything so soon after his blunder, turned to Argo. "You want the carbine?"

"I certainly do, Captain. It would also seem to make sense."

"You have no problem with a dead man's gun?"

Argo shook his head. He had no problems with a dead man's gun.

CORDELIA

Manacled, helpless, and half-naked, Cordelia found herself lifted bodily and dumped in the back of a Mosul army truck. Her shirt was torn, her stockings gone, her skirt ripped at the outer seams, and she had lost her shoes. She should probably have been grateful that she was still alive and had not been raped, but Cordelia was in no mood for gratitude. She was terrified but keeping her fear in check by also being outraged. In another part of the Mosul turmoil beside the Continental Highway, she could hear Phelan loudly protesting as he was pushed into a steam car, yelling that he was a citizen of a neutral nation, damn it, and should be treated as such. Then three Teuton officers climbed into the conveyance after him, and the doors slammed. Of Keats and Hodding she had seen no sign since they'd been marched away from the scene of their capture. She had expected, perhaps a little foolishly, that a short respite might ensue after the long and dreary hike from the woods where they had been caught. Unfortunately, this was not the case. They had reached the highway to find their arrival a source of great excitement in the chaotic temporary camp of more than three hundred foot soldiers, and maybe fifty horsemen, that could only be the temporary field headquarters from which the search for the fugitives from the crash of the NU98 was being conducted. It was commanded by a welcoming committee of impatient officers—mostly Teuton, and, if she read their insignia correctly, mostly from a regiment of engineers—who seemed to have been there all day and most of the previous night, screaming at underlings and waiting anxiously for news. The captives were brought in to such a level of undisguised jubilation that they could not mistake how their capture had become a very big deal to the Mosul and Teutons. They acted as though they had been waiting forever to capture a downed Norse airship and its crew. Which, although Cordelia did not know it, was the absolute truth.

The two Mosul grunts who had dumped Cordelia in the truck climbed in behind. For a moment she thought the anticipated rape had come. The Goddess knew it would not be difficult. Her hands were pinned at her sides by manacles attached to a thick leather belt that had been strapped round her waist and cinched impossibly tight almost immediately she'd been led into the camp. A collar was buckled round her neck and locked to a light steel chain that was being used like a leash. After all she had been through, she had no reserves of strength with which to fight and could only defend herself with passivity and compliance. *Come on you sons of bitches. Cordelia Blakeney will be an easy lay tonight. She's half-dead but intends to survive.* She had turned down her chance to kill herself when the pistol was in her hand. She had, by definition, opted to live at all costs, and the myths of a lady's honor were reduced to nothing more than that: just pretty myths.

To her surprise and relief, however, the two soldiers only lifted her by the shoulders and pulled her into a sitting position with her back to the driver's cab of the truck. One of them clipped the end of her chain to a steel ring set in the floor of the truck and looked at her warningly. "You jump out, you hang. You understand?"

Cordelia had simply nodded. She understood not only what they said, but that it was quite the wrong time to be talkative or clever. The brace of Mosul hunkered down on either side of her, indicating that they would be her escort for this leg of a journey that seemed to have unspecified but reputed horror at the end of it. From the wear on their uniforms, belts, and rifles, and their generally businesslike attitude, the pair were veterans, who had maybe been in the Americas since the start of the invasion, and their flat, high-cheekboned faces and narrow, unknowable eyes marked them as heartland Mosul from beyond the Black Sea, although Cordelia had noticed that many of the rank and file in the search parties

that had been hunting for them had looked Frankish or Hispanian, raw recruits to the Provincial Levies who had only just been shipped in as replacements and looked fresh off the troopships from Cadiz and Lisbon.
She found she was unable to stop herself from assessing the men and machines around her. It seemed, even though she had not been aware of it,
and had even resisted at the time, that some of what they tried to teach her
in RWA officer school, and all that paperwork she had handled in the War
Office, had rubbed off. She could only hope that, when she arrived wherever she was being taken, such knowledge might, in some desperate moment, give her an edge.

When she and the Mosul were seated, one of them gave the signal to
move by slapping the top of the driver's cab with the flat of his hand. The
truck lurched forward, and suddenly Cordelia was no longer observing
and cataloguing manpower. She was attempting to cling on for dear life as
the truck bucked and bounced over the still-waterlogged ground that had
been repeatedly marched and driven over in the last twelve hours, and she
found that clinging on for dear life was far from easy when one's hands
were in bondage at one's sides. For a moment, she thought she was going
to roll out and be hanged, but the Mosul on her left quickly put a hand on
her shoulder to steady her. Before that, the two had been keeping some
approximate distance. Her escort had clearly been given firm orders to
keep their hands off her, but that obviously did not preclude practical
physical contact between prisoner and guard. Maybe some of that contact, as she had been manhandled through the camp and loaded onto the
truck, had been familiar, if not intimate, but, as they drove away, she was
growing increasingly confident that their grubby intrusion would not be
taken any further. Matters improved considerably once they reached the
highway. On the flat-rolled metaling the ride was smooth, and she found
they had been accorded priority over other vehicles. The truck in which
Cordelia was riding brought up the rear of a small motorcade. Preceding
them was another truck that presumably carried Keats and Hodding, the
car containing Phelan and the three Teuton officers, and a military police
dispatch rider, in leathers, helmet, and goggles, riding a smoke-belching
gasoline cycle.

The use of three vehicles to transport four prisoners was an indication
of the emphasis the Mosul seemed to be making of keeping the survivors

of the NU98 isolated, as though they were afraid they might attempt to whisper some coded order or instruction or formulate an escape plan with secret hand signals. They had been separated in the very aftermath of the ambush and kept a distance apart ever since. Not so much as eye contact had been permitted during the long and dreary journey from the scene of their capture to the Continental Highway. Cordelia's hands had been bound in front of her and the long end of the same rope attached to the saddle of the cavalryman who had brought her down. Cordelia had wondered at the time if the Mosul were sufficiently primitive so that, by some barbarous right of capture, she now belonged to him. In the matter of prisoners, the enemy sure must surely be, if not more civilized, at least more centralized. Phelan was also roped behind a cavalry horse, but so far back in the line that he and Cordelia could not speak to each other. Keats and Hodding must have marched with the infantry. As their captors moved out of the ambush point, the four of them were forced to pass a line of bodies, Mosul and their own, as if it were being made clear to Cordelia how her assumption that orders had been given for them to be taken alive had only been partially correct, and, of the five crew who survived the crash, only Keats and Hobbing remained up and functioning in addition to herself and Phelan. The others had been shot in the last frantic dash to get away, except, of course, for Coburn, who had been killed in the first phase of the ambush. Cordelia knew she was at least partially responsible, but too far into shock to feel guilt.

When they reached the Continental Highway, Cordelia had been led into the center of the camp by her personal captor like the first walking trophy from the hunt. He had turned his horse and jerked her rope, showing her off to the soldiers who stared at her like some exotic specimen and the officers who roughly pushed their way to the front and then did exactly the same. Her attraction was greatly diminished, however, when Phelan was brought in, and the Mosul and Teutons all flocked to him. Phelan's uniform marked him as the captain of the NU98, and the senior officer, and volumes were said about Mosul worship of authority by the way in which he was instantly surrounded and the questions that were shouted at him. As the captain, the Mosul assumed he would have all the answers. As they had walked through the forest, before their capture, Cordelia had attempted to persuade Phelan to lose his insignia, fully knowing that he would never consider doing such a thing. She was learning how her lover was a classic case of one who did what he imagined was expected of him rather than what was sensible.

For once, Cordelia absolutely did not mind not being the center of attention. In the current circumstance, the least attention was the best attention. The men were being driven off for interrogation, and she was merely being driven off. So far, the extreme misogyny of the Zhaithan had worked to her advantage. Their contempt for women was strong enough among even the Teutons that it resulted in what Cordelia saw as a blind spot to the potential hazard of a woman considered unimportant. But let them go on thinking she was a girl and therefore of no use to them for as long as they liked. It might prove the window to her ultimate revenge. The idea of revenge obviously begged the question of where and to what they might be taking her. She had asked her two escorts, but, as she might have expected, their response was an uninformative, "You'll see soon enough."

What they might actually do with her if she was of so little importance was something Cordelia probably should have avoided pondering. Madness lay in that direction. She could not, however, help suspecting that she might be destined for one of the grosser Mosul forms of officers' and gentlemen's entertainment. She imagined the story of what might become of her as an item in an Albany society gossip column. *Will Lady Cordelia Blakeney become a Mosul concert party?* A society of men would hardly want her to go to waste. She might be muddy and disheveled right there and then, but she cleaned up exceedingly nicely, and, if some form of erotic servitude was to be her role in the immediate future, she would grit her teeth, think of Albany, and look for a soft spot that could be manipulated to open doors to more elevated forms of survival or even escape.

The dispatch rider's cycle came equipped with a siren, and he used it to warn other traffic to pull over and let them through. For Cordelia, from her handcuffed, backward-facing vantage point, the ride up the Continental Highway was like a review of the Mosul army on the move. Trucks stacked with supplies and trucks loaded with men were all moving north, and very little was going south. Most of the men in the trucks were the same raw Provincial Levies who had made up the numbers in the search parties. In a possible precursor of what might be the shape of things to come, a recruit yelled something obscene at her from one of the transports they passed, but, straightaway, an underofficer jumped up and smacked him for his impertinence. So good manners still counted for something in the ranks of Hassan IX? She doubted it. More likely the boy had been told to sit still and keep quiet, and it was more about discipline than the way a soldier should treat a lady. As they pulled ahead of the truck in question, she suddenly noticed another recruit was staring at her with huge, dark eyes, eyes that seemed to draw her in with their infinite sadness, and, for a moment, something that she did not understand, but she was certain came from outside her, clutched at her breath, and she had to fight down a sob which she would, in just seconds, be at a loss to explain. Not at as much of a loss, however, as she would be to explain the voice that, just a moment later, would say just two words, clear but as though from a great distance.

"Lady Blakeney!"

RAPHAEL

A military policeman on a gasoline cycle with its siren howling and a car and a truck in its wake was rapidly overhauling the line of slow-moving troop transports. Someone or something of importance was coming through. Maybe the survivors from the airship had finally been caught. Raphael and the rest of the squad had been pulled off the search some hours earlier. For a while they had stood around and waited while their officers wondered if they could be put to any further practical use, but then it had been decided that enough idiot replacements were wandering around the Virginia woods on a collective fool's errand, and Melchior had ordered them back on the truck to resume their interrupted journey to the front. When Melchior had used the phrase "a walk in the woods," he had intended it as a metaphor. In reality, that was all that it had been. A long, squelching march through the wet forest, burdened with their newly issued rifles, during which time they had been given no chance to use the new weapons, even as a threat, and had seen nothing except other searchers moving as purposelessly as they were, unless you counted the couple of brief but impressive glimpses of the crashed airship. They had not been permitted to savor the sight, however. The wreck, like the skeleton of some huge metal mammoth with shreds of silver fabric attached to its bones, was surrounded by crack Teuton troops, well armed and full of self-importance, who had quickly moved them on before they could see too much.

Their transport slowed and moved to one side so the cycle, followed by the car and truck, could roar past with imperial speed. The squad, glad of any diversion on the long road from Savannah to the Potomac, had turned their heads to watch the vehicles pass, idly looking for an explanation as to what all the fuss was about. But then, suddenly seeing the figure in the back of the truck, they craned with much more urgency. Sitting between two guards was a young woman with pale skin and red hair. Her hands were locked down at her sides in a restraining belt, and a collar and chain were fastened around her neck. Her hair was matted, and her clothes so torn that one of her breasts was fully exposed. One of the Lowlanders turned in his seat, leaned out of the truck, and yelled an obscenity. Melchior was instantly on his feet, in front of the Lowlander, legs braced against the swaying. He smacked him hard on the side his head, below the protection of his helmet. "Did we ask to from hear from you? Was your opinion sought? Or were you just demonstrating your ignorance?"

The Lowlander rubbed his ear and blinked. "It was just a bit of fun, Underofficer."

"*Fun?* Did you hear me give any order for *fun?*"

The Lowlander did not have the sense to just shut up. He insisted on defending himself, which, to Raphael, set new outer limits in his already clearly demonstrated stupidity. "But she was a prisoner, Underofficer."

Melchior smacked the Lowlander again. "She was what?"

"I . . ."

Smack!

"I can't hear you!"

"I didn't know . . ."

Smack!

"What?"

Smack!

"I didn't know, Underofficer."

Melchior straightened up. "You didn't know. That's your trouble, lad. You never know. You don't know anything. You don't know that woman's name, or who she might be, or what she might be. You don't even know enough to know that when you don't know, you keep fucking quiet."

At first Raphael had been totally confused. Why should Melchior get so irritated about a few words shouted at a woman who was so obviously a prisoner and quite helpless? Then it slowly dawned on him that a lesson was being taught to the whole squad. In the dangerous world of Mosul combat, anything could be an enemy ruse or a Zhaithan loyalty trap. The lesson being taught was that you never reacted or spoke without thinking, and you did nothing to reveal or draw attention to yourself. Melchior had said it all in his last eight words. *When you don't know, you keep fucking quiet.* That might be the very key to survival. The realization had come slowly to Raphael, not because he was loud, coarse, and ignorant like the Lowlander, but because his last long look at the girl in the truck had left his head spinning. She was one of the two women from his recurrent dreams. He had never expected to see her, but there she was, alive and in the flesh and being driven up the highway under what was clearly close arrest. Without committing the crime of assuming too much, he was certain that she was one of the survivors of the air crash for whom they had been hunting. The multiple coincidences alone would have been enough to keep him preoccupied all day and long into the night if the terrible, wrenching sense of irrational loss he experienced, as the truck carrying her had pulled away and been lost in the distant traffic, had not overshadowed everything else.

ARGO

Argo dreamed of a world of fire, a cavernous place of glowing red and leaping shadows where salamanders slithered and danced in the hot coals, a sinister hunchback presided, and black, shapeless things moved among the leaping, breathless flames. The overcast of smoke was filled with dull metallic flying machines of all shapes and sizes but that he knew instinctively were both dangerous and evil, fell transport for even more terrible weapons. Huge land juggernauts ground forward, crushing charred and brittle skeletons beneath iron wheels and steel treads, taking their implacable firepower to a yet-unseen conflict that was almost as old as time. Argo had no question that his dream had brought him to a battlefield so old, a darogad so constantly fought over, that a simple excavation of the smoking ash with the toe of his boot would easily unearth a corroded weapon or a venerable skull. A single name was whispered on the superheated air. Quadaron-Ahrach. It infiltrated the roar of the conflagration and the rumble and reverberation of distant explosions with the insistence of a holy mantra. Quadaron-Ahrach, Quadaron-Ahrach. And even without conscious intervention, Argo had no doubt that two long years under the Mosul occupation had left any number of hooks planted in his mind on which the enemy might exert its strain. Quadaron-Ahrach, Quadaron-Ahrach. The heavy-handed Zhaithan reprogramming of Hassan IX's conquered peoples had plainly sown the seeds of the images he was now seeing, but, where once he might have been at their mercy, he now stood tall and faced the fire. A tunic of the Albany Rangers was draped over his shoulders, and the garment was torn and charred as though it had already been through a lifetime of conflict. A sword was in his right hand, a pistol was in his left, and he defied his enemies. He was less than clear about whether his defiance was the recklessness of the potential victor or the desperation of the last stand, but either way he was not yoked by his previous fear.

Without any logical transition, he found himself on a bridge, a narrow span carved from living rock that arched across a seemingly bottomless volcanic abyss. Smoke rose on either side of him, and he knew it was vital to his survival that he cross to the other side. The chanting was now even louder. Quadaron-Ahrach, Quadaron-Ahrach. It rose from the chasm beneath like a tectonic grinding. Quadaron-Ahrach, Quadaron-Ahrach. Three figures appeared at the other end of the span. The smoke made it hard to see, but they seemed to be two girls and a boy, waving, making wide and urgent gestures that he should hurry to them. They were also shouting something, but it was drowned out by the booming from below. Quadaron-Ahrach, Quadaron-Ahrach. Argo started forward, moving as fast as he could on the narrow and slippery surface of stone, but the bridge immediately began to vibrate. Cracks appeared under his feet, and fragments of dust and rock were shaken loose and dropped away into the vast fissure. Argo realized that he was not going to make it across to where the other three waited, and, with that realization, the final break occurred. The bridge shattered and fell from under him. He had one chance to scream before he plunged into the burning depths, struggling to wake. "Lady Blakeney!"

Out of nowhere, reality became Yancey Slide standing over him. "You surface from the nightmare calling her name?"

Argo blinked. "What?"

The sun was high, and his formerly damp clothes were quite dry. Re-call came back with a mighty solidity. He was with the Rangers. They had emerged from the forest, and finally, indicating an outlying copse at the top of a long slope of open meadow, Hooker had ordered the team to halt and rest until after sunset. While half the squad kept watch, the others relaxed, removed their boots, inspected their feet, changed their socks, and ate cold food straight from the open can because Hooker was not prepared to risk the smoke from a fire. Argo, feeling dead on his feet, had taken off his jacket and, using it as a pillow, immediately fallen fast asleep.

He had woken dehydrated. Maybe that was what the world of flame had really been about. A part of him still believed that dreams should be read most of the time with a stark simplicity. He struggled to sit up. "I need something to drink."

As though in anticipation of his need, Slide was holding a canteen. "Here."

Argo took the canteen, swallowed, and shook his head. "The dream was so damned vivid."

"It could mean you're getting close to something. What did you see?"

Argo wondered how long Slide had been standing over him, if he had been waiting for him to wake so he could question him about his dreams. "I saw fire all around me. I think, though, that could have been the sun, and the fact that I was thirsty."

Slide dismissed the too-rational interpretation with a gesture of impatience. "What did you *see*?"

"I saw flames, and I saw a bridge, and, on the other side of the bridge, three people beckoned, a boy and two girls. I can only suppose they were the others of this Four you keep talking about."

Again, Slide did not want to hear Argo's commentary. "You crossed this bridge?"

Argo shook his head. "No. I tried to, but the bridge collapsed under me, and I fell. That's when I forced myself to wake."

"You fell calling out the name of the Lady Blakeney?"

The question compelled Argo to face the idea that he been studiously avoiding. He had called the name, and she had been in his dream, of that he was certain, but it was a certainty he would have preferred not to accept. Accepting it meant accepting that he was enfolded, maybe for the rest of his days, in levels of strangeness and abnormality that he could not even imagine. His old world and his old ways of thinking were breaking down, and he was entering the fearsome country of Yancey Slide, whether he liked it or not.

"And what did you hear in this place of flames?"

By some new instinct, Argo instantly knew what Slide needed to hear. "Quadaron-Ahrach was named by name."

Beneath the brim of his hat, Slide's eyes narrowed. "Was he indeed? That may not be at all good."

"It was all through the dream like a chant. *Quadaron-Ahrach, Quadaron-Ahrach.*"

Slide scowled. "Don't speak his name quite so freely, boy. He may be old and frail and only human, but his power is never to be underestimated."

Argo would have liked to have sat and thought about all that had just transpired, but Slide indicated that he should get to his feet. Constant motion appeared to be part of the training process for whatever Slide seemed to expect was to come for him. Slide gestured to where Barnabas, Steuben, Madden, and Penhaligon sat in a circle. Steuben was wiping down a light carbine with an oily rag. "The Rangers have something for you."

Steuben beckoned. "Here you go, kid. The captain said fix up the piece for you, so fixed it up I did."

As Argo approached, with Slide behind him, the Rangers all got to their feet. "You've been lucky here, boy. It ain't every irregular in this war gets an almost new Norse carbine, straight out of Birmingham. I could almost have kept it for myself instead of the ton-weighing piece-of-shit Albany issue I'm toting, but that wouldn't have been the way of it, now would it? Wouldn't have been right to get it for myself, like."

Steuben held the rifle in both hands, and a sense of rough ceremony descended on the gathering. He offered it to Argo. "Here you go, Argo Weaver, your first firearm as an irregular in the ranks of Albany."

Argo took the weapon and turned it over in his hands. "Is that what I am? An irregular?"

"You look pretty irregular to me, boy."

Madden spoke, and Madden did not speak often or to no purpose. "Kiss the butt of the dead man's gun, Weaver. Pay the respect to the last poor bastard who carried it."

Argo did as Madden instructed. He lifted the gun, inclined his head, and touched his lips to the oiled wood of the carbine. As he did so, he swore he could hear the gates to the world of Yancey Slide slam closed behind him. But when he'd run from Thakenham, had not he always known that from there on no turning back would be possible?

JESAMINE

The sun was setting, and Jesamine hurried to be inside before the darkness closed on a camp that was becoming increasingly strange and violent through the watches of the night. As the buildup of troops grew in intensity, the camp grew right along with it, until the place now spread and sprawled over such an area that it was becoming close to unmanageable. When people referred to the central base at Alexandria as a city under wood and canvas, they in no way now exaggerated, and the infrastructure of that city was being taxed to the point of collapse. Water and sanitation were already a problem, and on warm autumn days the stench was such that, on land that bordered on a swamp in the first place, old-timers feared that a cholera epidemic might be close at hand. By far the most serious disease so far, at least as Jesamine saw it, was the boredom that progressively gripped the minds of the men. Men whose only purpose was to fight had been idle for far too long. The scarcely bearable tension of waiting for the big push across the river was bursting into wild and negative outbreaks of indiscipline and insanity. Mamalukes fought with Teutons on a nightly basis. A concubine in another regiment had been gang-raped by a run-amok Mosul rifle company. Drunkenness was on a dizzying upswing, with a foul homebrew as the intoxicant of choice. Stills and blind pigs popped up all over the place, but for every manufacturer or illicit retail outlet the MPs and the Zhaithan shut down, three more opened up in its place. Rumors that mysterious Chinamen were delivering opium to the Mamaluke officers abounded, but Jesamine had seen none of that supposed traffic for herself. Drunken foot soldiers, on the other hand, seemed to stumble all over the duckboard walkways, the wooden sidewalks, or lie sprawled in the clinging mud that choked the thoroughfares between the endless lines of tents, and she had overheard more than one underofficer predicting that they would see a mass execution before the week was out.

Jesamine had made use of the free time she had now that her colonel was away in search of his precious airship to take a walk to the goat pens to let T'saya know that she trusted her, as far she trusted anyone, and that she wanted to talk some more. Even on that fairly brief excursion, she could see how the camp was growing out of all proportion. She noticed that the stand of willows where she and Kahfla had secretly pleasured Reinhardt, currying favor with the master's manservant, had gone, cut down to make room for even more lines of horse pens and drab green tents. She hardly missed the secret meeting place. She had spent too much time on her knees, at Reinhardt's feet in its dirt, to wax nostalgic, but on the positive side, although the location of the trysts was no more, she continued to reap the benefits of the favors curried. None more than the ones earned when she had woken Phaall on Reinhardt's behalf with the news that the airship had crashed. The most beneficial part of Reinhardt being in her debt was a pass that he had obtained by the simple subterfuge of slipping it in with a pile of routine regimental orders that Phaall did not have the patience to read before initialing his approval. While Phaall was away in the woods, and although he did not know it, she was legally permitted to reside in his quarters, eat his food, drink his booze, and also come and go as she pleased. She was merely awaiting her master's return from the field and organizing a joyous reception when he rode home victorious. It was, after all, the traditional duty of the concubine in time of combat, and no one should ask any questions once the pass was produced.

That, at least, was the optimistic theory, and it held good until, in the comparative safety of the Teutonic officers' section, she turned a corner and saw the two Zhaithan priests in the sinister garb of the military wing waiting in front of the wood and canvas exterior of her colonel's quarters. In their black cloaks, red and black tunics, spiked and turban-swathed helmets, and with holstered pistols and sheathed ceremonial daggers on their belts, they radiated such an aura of menace that no simple written pass could stop Jesamine's stomach from turning to ice. She had trusted T'saya and her hallucinogens, and now the Zhaithan were waiting for her. She had been the classic gullible fool, seduced by illusions of possible power, and the old woman's talk of "the big game," into believing there might be any life except this one, and now she would pay for seeking such hope in the fire or on the gallows.

"Are you the concubine?"

Jesamine did not have to act the required part of brainless fear. Her mind was limp after all it had been put through that afternoon, and the panic of the stupid came quite naturally under the circumstances. "Yes . . . my lords."

"Where is Colonel Phaall?"

The question was slightly reassuring. They wanted Phaall and not her, and their information was painfully out of date. T'saya had not betrayed her, and their secret was safe. "He and most of his regiment have gone south to bring back the crashed airship, my lords."

The Zhaithan's faces were hidden behind veils of fine mesh chainmail that hung loosely from the insides of their helmets. It created the illusion of talking to men without faces.

"He didn't return with the prisoners?"

Maybe their information was not as dated as she had assumed. Now she did not have a clue what the Zhaithan were talking about. Phaall had returned? Panic now came at Jesamine from both sides. "I know nothing of any prisoners. If Colonel Phaall has returned, I haven't seen him, although I am hardly the first he'd tell."

One Zhaithan looked at the other with a degree of small, unpleasant triumph that indicated an earlier argument. "I told you she would know nothing."

The other treated Jesamine to a hard look. "You know nothing of any prisoners?"

"No, my lord. I already told you . . ."

He cut her off. "You've heard nothing of three men and a woman who were supposed to have arrived here earlier today?"

"No, my lord. I've neither seen them nor heard talk about them."

"And where have you been all day to hear talk, woman?"

"While my colonel is away, I have been taking lessons in food preparation."

The questioning momentarily lapsed as a crew of lamplighters moved down the row of officers' bivouacs, putting a match to the gas lamps and oil torches, but it resumed the moment they were out of earshot. "And there's no talk of special prisoners among the women of the Teuton officers? No gossip?"

"No, my lord. I swear. Nothing."

The two Zhaithan exchanged glances. The one who had spoken to

Jesamine shrugged and then turned back to her. "There is no need for your colonel to hear of this conversation. As far as he is concerned, it never took place. You understand me, girl?"

Jesamine did her best to look frightened and humble and keep all trace of sarcasm out of her voice. She dropped a deliberately demeaning curtsy, but was secretly very relieved. Once again the Zhaithan and the Teuton Engineers were in a pissing contest. That at least was nothing new. "Yes, my lord. I completely understand you."

The Zhaithan walked away like the lords of damnation they clearly believed they were, and even passing officers avoided their veiled and hidden eyes. They might have cautioned Jesamine to silence, but their very presence outside Phaall's quarters was information that would quickly be disseminated on the rumor mill to all ranks of the regiment. She hurried inside, her heart still pounding. She quickly poured herself a schnapps, before even lighting the interior lamps, and dropped onto the bed. She did not care if Phaall walked in right at that minute. Even he would understand when she told him the Zhaithan had been looking for his prisoners. He would know where her loyalties lay and not begrudge her the schnapps. As she now read it, the mysterious prisoners were presumably survivors from the crash of the Norse airship. Phaall and the Teutons had them, and the Zhaithan wanted them. Phaall presumably wanted technical data from them. Why the Zhaithan wanted them was anybody's guess, except maybe to put them to the torture and see what happened.

Jesamine's day had started out well enough. She was temporarily free of Phaall and had a pass that permitted her to go anywhere and do anything she liked, within the limits of her situation. She had lain in Phaall's own bed until late morning, relishing the luxury of quiet and privacy, and then, after a couple of drinks, resolved to go and see T'saya. Her dreams were becoming more vivid and more complex with each passing day, and although she did still fear a possible Zhaithan trap, she knew she had to talk to the old African woman at least once more in the hope of making some sense out of what was going on. The day was sunny and bright, and everything was at least partially drying out after the torrential rain. The camp did not smell so bad, and the walk to the goat pens had been almost pleasant, except that, when she reached them, she saw plenty of goats but no sign of T'saya. Rather than just wait around in the hope the old woman might appear, she had asked a younger slave pushing a wheelbarrow of manure if she knew where T'saya might be. The slave had mutely pointed to a lopsided shack made of scrap wood, tar paper, and corrugated tin a short distance away, where smoke rose from a stovepipe chimney. The smoke made perfect sense. What had T'saya said about the goats? *I raise them, I feed them, I love them, then I kill and cook them.* The smoke from the chimney had to be the visible evidence that T'saya was inside taking care of the cooking phase of her dealings with the goats. It seemed from that moment the whole tone of the day took a turn for the unexpected and became a series of multiple and highly unwanted shocks.

Jesamine pushed open the door to an interior so dim it was almost impossible to see on first entering from sunlit day. She heard T'saya before she saw her clearly. "Is that you, concubine girl?"

Jesamine laughed. "It's me, Jesamine, if that's what you mean."

As her eyes grew more accustomed to the dark, she saw that T'saya was giving all her attention to a large cooking pot that was simmering on a wood-fired range. She was stirring the contents carefully with a long wooden spoon, and every so often she would stop and taste the result, adding a little more salt or various herbs from a rack of containers beside her. "So you decided to come and talk to me?"

"You don't seem surprised."

"I figured you'd get around to it despite all of your fears."

"My colonel went away."

"To look for his long-desired airship?"

"How could you know that?"

"Girl, I hear pretty much everything that goes on around here." She stepped back from the range and indicated the vapor rising from the pot. "And what I don't hear, I can read in the steam."

"I thought while my colonel was away I could maybe take some time to work out what was going on with me."

"When the Goddess spares you, she usually spares you for some reason."

"You think I'm being spared here?"

"You think you got it hard then, girl? You think you got it hard eating the best of food, stealing your colonel's booze, sleeping in a soft bed, and all you're called on to do is lay under the fool and look interested in his huffing and grunting?"

Jesamine resented being quite so freely dismissed as a pampered slut. "We on our backs also serve."

"Well, all that's about to change real soon."

"You seem very sure of that."

"I am very sure of it, child. Make no mistake about that. The signs are all around you."

"What do you mean, all around me? I can't see anything."

T'saya gestured for Jesamine to move closer. "Step up to the range, girl. Look into the steam and tell me you don't see anything."

Jesamine did as she was told, but although she stared hard, she could see nothing but perfectly ordinary steam and smell the meat and spices. "I don't see anything."

T'saya frowned. "Nothing?"

"Nothing at all beyond what anyone might expect."

T'saya shook her head. "Maybe the seeing isn't your gift. Or maybe you're just not far enough along yet."

Jesamine turned away from the heat of the range. She was becoming hopelessly confused. "How can my entire life be about to change if I'm not far enough along yet?"

"Events don't wait until you're ready for them. They come at you, ready or not. You know what I'm talking about?"

Jesamine unhappily shook her head. "I don't think I understand any of this. You read my dreams and tell me something's about to happen, but you can't say what?"

T'saya moved to where two chairs faced each other across a small preparation table. She pulled out one and sat down, indicating that Jesamine should take the other. "Take the weight off your feet, girl. These things don't all happen at once."

Jesamine sat as she was told. On the table between her and T'saya were a chopping board, an assortment of knives, more jars of herbs and oils, and a tin biscuit barrel with a scratched picture on the lid of idyllic rural Virginia, before the conquest, with a mill and millwheel. Beside the biscuit tin was an unlabeled bottle of something that looked uncommonly like alcohol. As if in confirmation of its contents, T'saya reached for the bottle. "I think maybe you need a drink."

Jesamine nodded. "I think maybe I do."

T'saya produced two glasses but also delivered a warning. "This ain't your fancy Teuton lah-dee-dah schnapps now. This is homebrew, with a few little additions of my own that help to clear the mind, you know?"

"I think my mind could do with a good clearing."

T'saya poured two shots, but, before pushing one across to Jesamine, she picked up a small shaker bottle filled with an oily green liquid. She shook a couple of drops into each glass which immediately turned the contents cloudy. Jesamine looked at T'saya questioningly. "Wormwood?"

"Something similar, plus some extras of my own."

Jesamine picked up the glass and looked at it carefully before drinking. "Is this going to give me visions, old woman?"

T'saya laughed. "Are you afraid of visions, concubine girl?"

Jesamine shook her head. "No, I guess not. Not if I learn something." And, having committed herself, she swallowed half the glass in a single gulp. All of T'saya's additions did little to mitigate the harsh burn of the moonshine, and perhaps made it taste more bitter than the rotgut normally did in its raw and unadorned form. "Damn."

"I told you it wasn't smooth like the good stuff."

"T'saya, my friend, I don't want to offend you, but there's smooth, and there's rough, and there's this stuff."

"We all don't have colonels buying our liquor for us."

Jesamine turned the glass in her fingers, studying the paint on her nails and summoning the courage to finish the shot. "You're sure this is going to give me visions?"

"You just sit awhile, and you'll see everything."

T'saya rose to her feet to check on whatever was in the pot. Jesamine closed her eyes and drank down the rest of the glass. She also tried to stand, but found herself swaying, half out of the chair and wondering why she had bothered to get up in the first place. "What have you done to me, old woman?"

"You wanted to see visions."

"I didn't want to get drunk as a skunk."

"Sometimes that's the price you have to pay."

In previous encounters with what were claimed to be hallucinogenic concoctions, the visual illusions had been slow in coming, only sneaking up on her once she had decided that nothing was going to happen and it had all been a burn. With T'saya's brew, the abstract shapes and saturated colors rushed in fast and mean, closing on Jesamine like an assault of impossible form and brilliance. "Wow!"

T'saya came back from the range and looked into her face. "You getting it, girl?"

"Oh . . . *am* I getting it."

T'saya resumed her seat. She seemed completely unaffected, and Jesamine tried to remember if the African woman had drunk her shot or not, but failed to summon the short-term memory. Instead, she looked round at the undulating patterns that flowed across the walls and floors of the magickal hovel. "This is all so pretty."

T'saya's voice sounded a long way away, but also stern and serious. "If you want more than just pretty hallucinations, you will have to focus."

Jesamine wanted to giggle. "But I'm in fairyland. Why would I want to focus?"

T'saya leaned forward and took Jesamine's right wrist in her hand. Jesamine felt the roughness of the older woman's hard-worked palm against her skin and smelled the garlic on her breath. T'saya was pulling her in, and, for the first time, Jesamine realized that this was no easy interlude of intoxication. She was suddenly frightened and attempted to pull away. "What do you want from me?"

T'saya's grip tightened. "I want focus, concubine girl. Focus, Jesamine, focus and tell me what you see."

"The black hunchback is watching." Jesamine could now hear her own voice. It was also far away, and what it was saying seemed to have little to do with what she was seeing or thinking. *She had not seen a hunchback; except, the moment that thought passed through her mind, he appeared in a place of fire and dense smoke, a bent and contorted figure twisted in a huge, carved chair like a throne for some ruler of the damned. The hunchback looked from left to right with glowing eyes, but somehow he was unable to see Jesamine or T'saya, and T'saya's voice was instantly reassuring.* "That old hunchback has his spies and his watchers, but he can't see us."

"He's looking for us. Why can't he see us?"

"Because he's a fool."

"A fool?"

"We operate in his blind spot. He only sees the men. He believes women cannot be a threat to him. He thinks we are beneath him, so he overlooks us."

The vision of the hunchback receded and was replaced by a formation of four gold stars interconnected by glowing lines of force. T'saya and Jesamine still sat in the shack where T'saya did her cooking, but, at the same time, they were in another place where meanings were multiple and stories could be told long before they happened. As the stars and force lines appeared, Jesamine heard herself utter two words in a language she was certain she had never known.

"Mnabe Ctseowa."

T'saya nodded. "They call it a *takla* here in the Americas."

"Or just the *Four?*"

"Can you see the *Four?*"

The formation of stars abruptly changed position so Jesamine was looking at it from a radically different perspective. "I can only see the *three* because I am *one.*"

T'saya pressed hard. "Can you see the three? Can you see them, girl?"

Jesamine was suddenly very tired. "I only see the stars."

"Don't give up now, Jesamine. One last try, okay?"

Figures began to form behind the stars, but they were without faces or distinguishing features. The reality of the shack began to reassert itself. "I can't see."

"Try harder."

"It's no good. I don't have the strength."

T'saya's voice revealed a trace of impatience. "Of course you have the strength. You always have the strength when the need is strong enough."

"Wait!"

The kaleidoscope in Jesamine's mind stopped spinning, and she saw clearly. T'saya tightened her grip on Jesamine's arm. "What is it?"

A red-haired girl with white skin, frightened but proud, was shackled and struggling between two soldiers. "I can see her, but she can't hear me, and she can't turn and look at me. She is a prisoner. We can't help her."

"Look for another. If we can't help her, look for another."

"He is a soldier. He is near, and he knows me, but we can't find him. There will be so many soldiers. How the hell do we find him in time?"

"What of the other boy?"

"How do you know of the other boy?"

"I know."

"He comes, but he does not know me."

"But he's the one from your dreams."

Jesamine nodded. The effort of the vision had caused her face to fall slack. "He is surrounded by soldiers, but he is not one of them, although they have given him a weapon. But they are soldiers of the enemy, soldiers from across the river."

"That need not be a bad thing."

"A girl is with them, a girl who knows much. She is not one of the Four, but she has powers. And . . ."

"And?"

Jesamine's previously dull and drifting expression was suddenly animated by fear. *"A demon!"*

"Can you describe the demon?"

Jesamine started shaking her head and refused to stop. "No, I can't. I can't look at it. I won't. If I look at him, he'll see me."

T'saya spoke gently. "Then describe his shadow."

Jesamine continued to shake her head. "He casts no shadow."

"Look closer."

"I can't. I'm afraid."

"Just relax and let the shadow come to you."

Jesamine finally stopped shaking her head. She placed her hands flat on the table and let out a long sigh. "I can't do this any more."

"One final effort."

Jesamine took three deep breaths and closed her eyes. "The demon wears a hat, a black hat, and he carries a strange sword and weapons not of this world."

"Do you see his eyes?"

"They are deep-hidden in his head."

T'saya let go of Jesamine's wrist and laughed out loud. "Deep-hidden in his head?"

Jesamine opened her eyes. "This is funny, old woman?"

"Your boy who has a weapon but is not a soldier is with Yancey Slide."

"Who's Yancey Slide?"

T'saya rose from the table. "Yancey Slide is Yancey Slide, girl."

"I'm hooked up to folks who walk with demons?"

T'saya moved to the range and poured hot water into a cup. "Yancey

Slide is no Mosul demon. He's a law unto himself, and, if your boy is with him, it means we're all playing in the big game."

"But I don't want to be playing in the big game."

"Jesamine, you don't have a choice. If you find yourself in the big game, all you can do is sit down and play the hand you're dealt. You know what I'm saying?"

"I don't even want to be dealt a hand."

T'saya placed the cup in front of Jesamine. At first the younger woman did not move. She simply stared at the colors in the steam that rose from it. "Drink that down. It'll help clear your head."

"What is it?"

"Just herb tea, with a little something extra."

"More magick additives?"

"Just do as you're told and drink it."

Jesamine picked up the cup by its cracked handle and put it to her lips. "Concubine girl always does as she's told."

T'saya looked at her coldly. "Don't be taking on an attitude. Not with me."

Jesamine sipped the tea, and, as T'saya predicted, she immediately felt, if not better, certainly a good deal more normal. The hallucinations faded, and she found herself once again in the reality of T'saya's kitchen. "Damn."

"We just learned a lot."

"You can fucking say that again."

"We went in deep."

"You can say that again, too."

"Woman, you did good. You even surprised me." T'saya pulled the biscuit barrel towards her, removed the lid, and offered it to Jesamine. "Eat something."

Inside were a half-dozen small honey cakes. Jesamine took one and put it her mouth. She felt drained. "So I'm one of this Four, this *Mnabe Ctseowa*?"

T'saya sighed. "Don't look on it as a burden, child."

Jesamine chewed wearily. "How am I supposed to look on it?"

"Maybe like you've got three on your side who don't have no choice but to be on your side."

"Are you telling me that I have a power?"

"Awesome, seen?"

"But you had to force me to do everything."

"You just needed the encouragement to start."

"But now I have to find these other three?"

T'saya shook her head. "I think you should just stay put, girl. It's my belief that they'll be coming to you sooner than you even imagine."

"So I do nothing?"

"You listen for the voices and follow any strange new impulse. Those are the only highway signs, but, at the same time, be very careful. You will be going through some powerful changes, and the world doesn't need to see that. In fact, if you're feeling okay, you ought to be getting out of here right now. You can stay if you want, but now that we have our bet down, we don't need to be undone by a detail, like some nasty-minded snitch who may have started wondering what we've been doing in here all this time."

Jesamine did her best to gather her wits in preparation for the outside world. She stood up, expecting to experience difficulties, but the herb tea seemed to have preformed its designated task, and aside from a little dizziness, which was probably just from the alcohol, she felt physically fine. She turned, kissed T'saya, and moved to the door. As she opened it, T'saya stood up.

"You be careful, now, you hear?"

"Oh, I hear you."

As Jesamine walked back past the goat pens, she looked covertly for signs of potential loitering informers. A couple of possible candidates presented themselves, but neither appeared worth taking seriously. Somewhere in the distance she heard drunken singing of a raucous song in some ugly provincial dialect, with a chorus that sounded like "When I was shagging poor Betty." Wasn't enough malfeasance going on in and around the camp to make a big deal over two chicks drinking a little redundant? The answer to that question had been so close to coming back in the negative when she had discovered the cloaked and helmeted Zhaithan waiting for her in the twilight that fifteen minutes and two glasses of schnapps were required for Jesamine to truly grasp how close she had been to coming mentally unglued when she had first seen the men from the Ministry of Virtue. Most slaves only spoke to the Zhaithan one time, and that was when they were taken away to be killed. As an officer's concubine, she had learned a measure more of sophistication but still could only act anxious and abject in the presence of the Ministry men on the rare occasions they were invited to the Teuton officers' mess. She had been sufficiently afraid of the Zhaithan when she had nothing on her conscience but illicit drinking, petty larceny, and masturbating the manservant. After her afternoon in T'saya's hovel, she was now guilty, beyond any shadow of a doubt, of, at the very least, wanton psychedelia, necromancy, and plotting the actual downfall of Hassan IX. From the whipping post or a fast hanging, Jesamine had graduated to an infinitely prolonged and intricately agonizing death, should they take her alive, and she had grave reservations as to whether she measured up to any of the million unknowns that seemed to be bearing down on her. After being property for as long as she could remember, could she really start thinking and deciding and making choices not only for herself but for others? She sincerely hoped that another of the Four could handle spiritual authority better than her, and that at least one of them was not already broken down by Zhaithan conditioning.

T'saya had counseled her to do nothing. She had told Jesamine to wait, to let it all come to her, but T'saya had failed to warn her, and maybe even failed to understand herself, how short that wait would be. The urgent whisper beyond the canvas-covered veranda provided evidence the wait was over. "Jesamine?"

"Kahfla?"

"Are you on your own?"

"Yes, and drinking the colonel's booze. So get in here fast before anyone sees you."

Kahlfa slipped silently through the door, still looking wary at the prospect of being in the quarters of a strange officer, even though that officer was miles away. "Hasn't anyone wanted to know what you're doing here?"

Jesamine poured Kahfla a schnapps. "Relax. I got a pass that covers me for everything."

"Reinhardt?"

"The ever-horny Reinhardt. He loves me. I even have an excuse for having you in here."

"You do?"

"We're planning for our masters' return, if anyone wants to know."

Urman, the cavalry major who owned Kahfla, was also down at the crash site with some of his light horsemen. Although the mission was ostensibly that of the 4th Teuton Engineers, it did not prevent Phaall from bringing along some of his drinking cronies, and the men under them, in some manufactured support role, or, once there, stop them all from having a damned good time under canvas in the country.

"Well, I came as quickly as I could."

"What?"

"I came from the pavilion as fast as I could without being too obvious."

Jesamine had no idea what Kahfla was talking about, but she did not like the sound of it. "The pavilion?"

"You haven't heard? I thought you would have known all about it."

"Known all about what?"

"The new bitch in the cage."

"There's often a new bitch in the cage."

"They brought her naked and in chains with a transport requisition."

"Well, that's to be expected. There'll be more of the natives being brought up here, now the brothels in Savannah are slowing down as the men are all moved to the front."

"The requisition said she was the private property of one Colonel Helmut Phaall."

"What?"

"Do you think he's replacing you?"

That was any normal concubine's very first thought, and always-lurking fear, but Jesamine had ceased to be any normal concubine, and the memory of her vision was stronger than her ordinary self-interest. "Does she have pale skin and red hair?"

Kahfla frowned. "How did you know that?"

Jesamine had already made a dangerous slip. No matter how close they had been previously, Kahfla could know nothing of the business at hand, if only for her own protection. Jesamine recovered as best she could. "I heard some men talking. What's she supposed to be? One of the survivors from the crashed airship?"

Kahfla nodded. "That's right. There were four of them, three men and a woman. They took the men to the Lady knows where for interrogation, but dropped the woman off at the pavilion. I guess they assumed that

she was just along for the men's amusement and didn't know anything."
Again she looked puzzled. "But I thought you hadn't heard about her."

Jesamine now was making it up as she went along. Lying to Kahfla
made her extremely uncomfortable, but there was no way to avoid the deception. "I didn't think anything of it because I didn't know she was addressed to fucking Phaall."

"So what are you going to do about it?"

"There's not much I can do, is there?"

Now the idea that Phaall might actually be replacing her was finally
cutting through the revelations of the afternoon. If she was headed for the
concubine scrapheap, sold off to a junior officer or worse, it would seriously undermine any grandiose plans for the future. "I suppose I should go
and take a look at this bitch in the cage. I might as well know what I'm up
against."

At least that statement was the unvarnished truth.

CORDELIA

Lady Cordelia Blakeney was naked in a cage. To add insult to injury, the
cage was so low she was unable to do very much but crouch on all fours
or lie in a fetal position on the less than clean blankets in the bottom of
her cramped prison, and, since so many people seemed intent on coming
and looking at her, she found the fetal position too exposed and vulnerable, and spent a lot of time crouching. Over the past few hours, after her
enforced ride up the Continental Highway, manacled in the back of a
Mosul army truck, she had been stripped, photographed, hosed down,
and finally brought to her current confinement. All through these tribulations, she had demanded vocally to be accorded the status of a prisoner
of war, but none of the Mosul men that she had encountered paid her
any more attention than would have been given to a yapping dog being
moved from one place to another. Cordelia was not sure whether the
near-pornographic photographs or the hosing down with cold water had
been the most degrading part of the experience. Was it worse to be
stripped naked and forced to pose for a lieutenant with a huge brass and
polished wood plate camera while his brother officers stood around like
huntsmen displaying their catch, or to be soaked and buffeted against a

cement wall by the jet of a fire hose while passing infantrymen stopped, stared, and guffawed? She did not, as yet, have the objectivity to decide, but the one thing she could not claim was that her capture was proving uneventful.

The place in which she finally found herself had the general air and appearance of a nomad bordello somewhere in the Mosul's Asia Minor homelands. It was crowded with women who were mostly young, and, for the most part, passingly attractive, although many had a sluttish resignation in their pose and posture. A scantily clad availability seemed the general theme of the dress code, and that, along with the claustrophobic lines of narrow beds, lockers, and bundled-up mosquito netting, told Cordelia that she had been brought to a congregation of bawds, concubines, body slaves, or whatever might be the current terminology among the hordes of Hassan IX, and she was expected to become another of them. The large pavilion was clearly where the women lived rather than plied their trade, and presumably, when their masters in the officer corps required service, the girls were summoned to the men's own billets. The tent itself had originally been designed and constructed as a much larger and mass-produced version of the traditional Mosul *urrt,* but after two years of being rooted by the Potomac, the tribal pavilion of the endless grasslands had taken on some permanence in its construction, with the addition of a wooden frame, floor, and roof. The place certainly smelled the way Cordelia imagined a military bordello would smell: of musk and misery, bodies and bad perfume, dirty underwear, old laundry, stale cooking, nagging fear, and the pervading damp of the bottomlands beside the river. The only part of her current situation that she didn't totally understand was why she was the only one in a cage, but she suspected it was some kind of orientation by ordeal, and sooner or latter she would be released, clothed, and put to the flatback work of the captive strumpet. How Cordelia felt about this prospect was something she had yet to consider. She was, as far as possible, restricting her worry to the trauma of the moment, and, very wisely she thought, crossing her bridges only when she came to them. She considered it the only way to preserve her sanity, and, as a prisoner of the Mosul, she needed all the sanity she could preserve.

After her trial by firehose, her two-man escort had announced, "We take you to the women," and by that, she discovered, they had meant the pavilion and the cage. Cordelia had taken one look at the place and the assembled females, and she had stopped all protest and complaint and re-solved not to say a further word until absolutely compelled to speak. In the meantime, she would be quite happy to let them think she was retarded or did not speak their language. The less these broads knew about her, the better. These camp followers had seen it all and done it all and could spot a phoney a mile off. This marquee of velvet-choker servitude was definitely not the place to reveal that she was not only an enemy, but an enemy aris-tocrat. Although now playing mute, Cordelia still constituted something of a novelty in the big tent. How much did Mosul bedwarmers and cocksuck-ers, with their bangles and garters, have to laugh at or look down on any-way? A tall, dark, full-bodied woman who seemingly went by the name of Ravenna had stared at her for some time, with such open evaluation that Cordelia had decided she could only be a snitch or a lesbian, or maybe both. In the police state of the Zhaithan, all could be turned informant if enough pressure was applied. The irritatingly infantile twin blondes had been more openly amused by her predicament, and, breaking off from painting blue streaks in each other's white-gold hair, had made playground jokes about natural red hair that Cordelia had heard during her third year in Goddess school. A small Hispanic woman had actually wanted to poke Cordelia with a stick, but Ravenna had warned her off. The pecking order in the brothels of a religious police state was something Cordelia was going to have to learn.

Cordelia might not have paid any attention to the honey-colored girl had she not tried so hard to conceal her surprise. That she had then con-sulted the paperwork that had come with Cordelia had made her interest even more plain, as did the subsequent swiftness of her exit, and that all the time she had been keeping a wary eye on Ravenna. Once the girl had left, Cordelia had to assume someone elsewhere was being informed or warned, and she could only wonder if the honey-colored girl's hurry to get away had been official or personal. It took fifteen or twenty minutes for Cordelia to learn that it had been personal. That was the time it took for her return with another woman who looked so much like her that the two of them could have been cousins, if not sisters. As they entered the pavilion and advanced determinedly in the direction of the cage, the dark one called Ravenna moved to intercept them. Cordelia could not hear the conversation, but it went backwards and forwards between Ravenna and the second honey-colored girl, and on two occasions it became quite heated. Gestures were constantly being made in the direction of Cordelia and the cage, so she knew she was the center of attention. At one point, the paperwork that had come with her was again brought out and examined closely. The second honey-colored girl had pulled out some papers of her own, and documents were compared. In the end, some kind of compromise was reached and a short brunette was dispatched from the pavilion in a way that seemed to suggest that a person of greater authority was being summoned.

Cordelia, having spent much of her young life at least pretending to be a person of greater authority, was not altogether happy about this until she saw that the person of higher authority was a junior lieutenant, a worried young Teuton little more than a pink-faced boy who had hardly begun to shave. She almost smiled at how the women of the tent seemed to know exactly what they were doing. He was precisely the kind a shrewd crew of slatterns could manipulate to their will without him even being aware of it. Presumably the junior lieutenant had some kind of responsibility for the running of this tent of women, although he seemed awkward and ill at ease among the inhabitants. He could only be new at the task, and this was more than confirmed when he listened in turn to Ravenna and the second honey-colored girl, inspected the paperwork, and even paid some attention to a few other women who gathered around to put in their dinar's worth. An older, more seasoned officer would have never allowed the women to waste so much of his time. After some thought, and summoning all of his none-too-secure air of command, he gave the two honey-colored girls a key and waved them to the cage while he talked some more to Ravenna, as though explaining his decision to her.

The second honey-colored girl unlocked the cage and spoke to Cordelia with quiet urgency. "Do exactly as I tell you, and please don't make any fuss or we'll all be in the very deepest shit."

The first honey-colored girl was not looking too happy about what appeared to be happening. "Are you sure you know what you're doing?"

"You're going to have to trust me on this, girl."

"If anything goes wrong, it'll be a whipping or worse for all three of us."

The second girl was tense. "Nothing's going to go wrong unless you stand here for another ten minutes arguing instead of fetching her some clothes and getting out of here."

"I've never seen you like this."

"Just get the clothes, okay?"

"Okay, okay."

Once the first girl was out of earshot, the second looked hard at Cordelia. "I understand you've not been saying anything, and that was probably smart, but I know a great deal about you, and I've come to get you out of here, because the Zhaithan may be looking for you, and you need the direct protection of my colonel."

Cordelia was dumbfounded. At first glance the honey-colored girl seemed a premium dollymop, yet she rapped out her instructions like a veteran guard sergeant. Only closer examination revealed the intelligence in her pretty painted face. Cordelia knew she had to trust her, not only because she seemed to have everything under control and actually appeared to be rescuing her for reasons she could only suppose would be revealed later, but also because, from the second Cordelia had first set eyes on the girl, she had been gripped by a strange déjà vu, as though she had known the second honey-colored girl all her life, or maybe in another. Before she could reply or ask any kind of question, the first girl was back with a bundle of clothes that she thrust at Cordelia. She did not say anything, but her expression and body language clearly demonstrated that she still believed she was involved in an outbreak of a bad madness, that she had only gone this far out of friendship and was rapidly approaching her limits. Cordelia ducked out of the cage and dressed hurriedly. The donated clothes were an odd and hastily grabbed mixture: a cotton shift, a man's work shirt, a pair of sandals, and some very lewd knickers that contrasted oddly with the utilitarian drabness of the other garments. Except for the knickers, it was hardly an outfit for vamping, but at least Cordelia was out of the cage with her nakedness clothed, and according to her self-imposed policy of one minute at a time, it had to be an improvement.

The second honey-colored girl gripped her arm and steered Cordelia through the pavilion. "Okay, so let's get out of here. My name's Jesamine, by the way."

"Jesamine? That's a pretty name."

"Let's just concentrate on making our exit, okay?"

Without looking left or right, and ignoring the curious stares of the other women, Ravenna's clear resentment, and the very possible chance that the junior lieutenant might change his mind and reverse his decision, Cordelia allowed herself to be led in the direction of the wood-framed double doors that constituted their way out and passed through them with a considerable sense of relief even though she had no idea what was happening to her or what might present itself next. As she stepped out into the night with Jesamine beside her and the first honey-colored girl, who had yet to introduce herself, bringing up the rear, Cordelia assumed their troubles of the moment were over. Unfortunately, the worried young officer took it into his head to follow them outside.

"Jesamine?"

The girl called Jesamine cursed under her breath and turned, quickly tilting one hip and turning on a professionally seductive smile.

"Something else, Lieutenant Kemper?"

The boy lieutenant was uneasy, fearing that he had done the wrong thing. "I'm trusting you in this matter, Jesamine."

Cordelia was quite familiar with his kind. She had encountered them even before the war. They came from military families and were raised in fearsome cadet schools that left them knowing very little beyond war, sodomy, and career politics, and certainly nothing about women, or any world beyond their own narrow perspectives. The ones she had met in Albany had been hopeless enough, but she could well imagine the Teutons were ten times worse with all their religious complications and having the Mosul as overlords.

Jesamine made her voice deliberately sexy. "I know, Lieutenant. I am very grateful, and I'm sure Colonel Phaall will be even more grateful when he returns."

Kemper moved towards the three women. "If she escapes, you do know how much trouble you'll be in?"

Cordelia decided it was time she let Jesamine and her friend know that she was not completely helpless. She followed Jesamine's lead and regarded Kemper as though he was the most desirable male she had ever encountered. "I'm not going to try to escape, Lieutenant. I mean, where would I go? I'm a spoil of war. I'm happy to be alive."

Kemper took them both completely seriously and smiled a gauche and idiotic smile that he probably imagined made him look like a man of wit and experience. "I may have to come and check on you girls later."

Jesamine acted as though the idea left her breathless. "You'd really do that?"

"Indeed I would. I know my duty."

"Then please, Lieutenant, do your duty. We'd like that, so much. It'd make us feel so very safe, and you know we've got nothing to hide from you."

The boy puffed up before their very eyes. "Of course, other responsibilities may call."

Cordelia played her part almost without thinking. "Oh, no. Don't say that."

"I fear it's the price of conquest, but you never know. Perhaps I will, perhaps I won't. We'll see, won't we?"

As the lieutenant turned and walked away, Cordelia almost had to clap a hand to her mouth to stop herself laughing. That the fool should feel the need to impress a couple of camp followers was bad enough, but that he felt the need to do it with such a display of junior pomposity was even worse. After he strutted back the way he had come for a few paces, Jesamine called after him. "Lieutenant, can I ask you something?"

"What's that?"

"Do you know how long the colonel's going to be away? How long he's going to be leaving us all on our own, sir?"

"I think you should be prepared for him to be gone at least a week. The tone of the telegraphs he sends back to division imply that he's having a fine time down in the woods."

As soon as Kemper had walked past the pavilion and out of sight, Cordelia and Jesamine both succumbed to a sudden fit of giggles, a release of fear and tension that they were oddly able to share even though they knew nothing about each other. Jesamine had to lean on Cordelia's shoulder to catch her breath. "He's going to come and check on us for sure, and we're going to have to fuck him to keep him distracted."

That started them giggling again, until they noticed that the other woman stood tense and stone-faced. Jesamine straightened up and wiped her eyes. "What's up with you, Kahfla, girl?"

The one whose name was Kahfla shook her head, and her voice was hard and tense. "You two are going to have to fuck him on your own. I don't know what's going on here, but I've gone far enough."

Cordelia took a step back. Too much was suddenly in play, and she knew nothing about it. All she could be was an object again. This was not her fight. Jesamine tried to make light of what was going on. "What's your problem, girl? Our officers are gone. We're just having a bit of fun, drinking the colonel's schnapps and sleeping in his bed and getting away with it."

"This is more than a bit of fun. You're up to something. Don't try to con me, Jesamine. I thought we went deeper than that."

Jesamine's face hardened. "I thought I asked you to trust me."

Kahfla pointed to Cordelia. "Why her? She's not about schnapps and getting away with it."

"I asked you to trust me on that."

Kahfla was shaking her head. She was not going to be won round. "I'm sorry, but now *you're* going to have to trust *me*." Jesamine started to protest, but Kahfla stopped her. "Oh, you don't have to worry. I won't say a word. You know I'd never rat you out, but I get off the ride right here. You feel like you're self-destructing, Jesamine. It happens. I've *seen* it happen. Women get crazy, like they don't care any more, and I don't want to be around it."

Kahfla suddenly turned and fled for the pavilion, leaving her friend staring after her. Cordelia decided to remain absolutely silent until Jesamine was ready to share her next move. Finally she sighed and took Cordelia's arm. "We go this way."

They walked in silence for a while past rows of officers' tents and huts that were largely silent with most of the regiment away in the south. Jesamine was silent and hard to read, and, in the end, Cordelia felt she had to venture a question. "Her name's Kahfla?"

"Yes."

"She seemed, how can I put this tactfully? Jealous of me?"

Jesamine was suddenly angry. "You're asking if we took some comfort in each other? Even though it's a flogging if the Teutons catch you at it and maybe a hanging if the Zhaithan get in on it? Unless you happen to be doing it on the floor of the mess like the twins, and then it's free drinks and a round of applause? Is that what you're asking me?"

Cordelia made firm eye contact with Jesamine, telling herself that the woman was only scared. "I'm really in no position to ask anything, now am I?"

"You're from Albany, right?"

"I'd be a fool to answer that, now wouldn't I?" Cordelia maintained eye contact. It seemed to be working. Jesamine was calming down but still had some pressure of anger left. "I meant what I said about having to fuck that baby, Kemper."

Cordelia did not respond, and Jesamine treated her to a look that was both withered and withering. "Please don't tell me you have a problem with that."

Cordelia shrugged in her borrowed rags. "I have to admit a lack of professional experience, but I learn fast. I fully intend to do everything that's needed in order to survive."

She put enough implied threat into the statement to warn Jesamine that, although she was in no way a seasoned whore, she was far from innocent, and, if she was from Albany, she was still a belligerent.

RAPHAEL

"So you lads had a Mamaluke as a gunnery instructor?"

The four from the squad who were following Melchior across the city nodded. "That's right, Underofficer. He was called Gunnery Instructor Y'assir."

"Mad fuckers, them Mamalukes. One time in Sebastopol I saw one walk into an inn carrying a severed head."

Pascal, who had probably been selected for the expedition so Melchior could keep an eye on him after his talk of deserting, made the necessary astonished response. "A severed head?"

"That's right, boy, a severed head. I swear to the Twins. He's holding it by the hair and there's blood dripping all over the place. The thing couldn't have been dead for more than a few minutes, a half hour tops. He bangs it down on the counter and starts yelling at the innkeeper to give his friend a drink."

Melchior had been given some drinks himself. The squad had found a bivouac in the vast, sprawling camp, but no rations had been forthcoming, and, resorting to time-honored initiative, the veteran underofficer had taken a party out to scavenge for supplies that consisted of Raphael, Pascal, a Teuton called Sheg, and Raoul, who had first spotted the airship. Food had proved hard, but alcohol was easy. As they moved along the muddy thoroughfares of the apparently endless canvas city, drunk men in dirty uniforms were stumbling with one- and two-gallon jugs under their arms, charging half a dinar in imperial scrip for a swallow. Melchior had taken five or six swallows before he launched into the story of the Mamaluke with the severed head.

"So the innkeeper very rightly figures his head's going to be on the counter, too, if he doesn't find a way to keep this Mamaluke satisfied, but he makes the mistake of using logic on a Mamaluke who's been drunk for the best part of a week. He tries to explain to him that his friend the head is irrevocably dead, and the very last thing he needs is a drink, in this world, at any rate."

Drunk or sober, Melchior seemed to know his way through the strange and temporary world of the camp by the Potomac. Raphael and the other three from the squad who'd been chosen for the foraging mission followed him as he made his way between Mosul *urrts* and conical Teuton field tents, past bunkers and around dugouts and hooches. Through a swamp night of drifting mist lit by gas lights and the occasional electric globe, plus torches and flaming braziers made from old petrol drums that added a mix of acrid smoke to the fog from the river, they crossed lakes of viscous mud on creaking wooden walkways and slipped through the mighty shadows of silently parked, armor-plated battle tanks that stood silent and waiting for their guns to be uncovered and their cold steam boilers fired up for the eventual push into Albany. The camp was certainly the largest human assembly that Raphael had ever seen, far bigger than any of the towns of his childhood, but with that strange air of military impermanence, the sense that it, and its hundred thousand or more inhabitants, could, at any moment, be uprooted and moved elsewhere, leaving only scarred earth, abandoned refuse, ditches, and old latrines as evidence of their having been there.

"Of course, the Mamaluke isn't having any of this. He's telling the innkeeper that his friend the severed head will be fine. All he needs is a drink. And since the Mamaluke by now has his hand on the hilt of his sword, the innkeeper decides it's a good time to abandon logic and go along with the insanity, so he asks what the severed head is drinking. And the Mamaluke tells him that the head's drinking arak, so the innkeeper pours a double shot of arak into one of those terra-cotta cups they use for liquor in Sebastopol and sticks it in front of the severed head. That sets the drunken Mamaluke off again, and he starts demanding how the fuck is the head going to drink when he doesn't have any hands or arms?"

Plenty of liquor seemed to be available in the camp by the Potomac, but precious little food. All of Melchior's best contacts were either searching for themselves or holding on to what provisions they had, and many were of the opinion that the general lack of supplies was more than just the usual Mosul foul-up, and that rations were being deliberately held back. Every one of them had a theory as to why this should be. Some thought it was deliberate profiteering, that a corrupt clique of officers, probably Teutons, expecting a hard and drawn-out fight with Albany, was secretly stockpiling food to make huge profits when winter came and the army could well be starving. Others saw it as a disciplinary measure, and that supplies would not be forthcoming until the wave of drunkenness had run its course. Melchior appeared to agree with the ones who saw the shortages as a sign that the push across the river was only weeks, maybe just days, away. A venerable, one-eyed musketeer claimed he had served under any number of bastard generals who cut off their men's rations before an assault on the principle that starving men will do a lot if they think there's a meal at the end of it. Theories, however, did not solve the immediate problem. The quartermasters were giving out next to nothing, while the black market was devoid of anything but homebrew and rotgut. Melchior freely admitted that theft might become a consideration. "We fight for the emperor, but we steal for ourselves." While he kept up his stream of long-service tall tales, Raphael could see that he was not at all happy.

"At this point, our innkeeper has to be given an award for having some balls on him. He looks the Mamaluke straight in the eye, and he tells him, 'I just pour the stuff. I don't help nobody drink it.' "

"So what happened to him?"

"What happened to him, boy? Well, I'll tell you. For a moment, all of us watching thought the Mamaluke was going to whip out his scimitar and cleave the poor bastard in two, but, instead, the Mamaluke starts laughing. And he goes on laughing and repeating what the innkeeper had said, 'I just pour the stuff. I don't help nobody drink it,' while all the time he's got the severed head and he's pouring arak into its mouth. He throws down a bunch of money, and, still laughing, he takes the bottle from the bartender and goes right on pouring, still slopping arak into the mouth of the head as he stumbles out of the door and ceases to be our problem anymore, except for the trail he's left of blood and arak."

Raphael was at a loss to know how to respond to this, and his companions seemed the same. Seeing this, Melchior smiled. "If nothing else, it's a lesson in how the direct approach can be the best way to deal with the mad, drunk, and homicidal."

As they continued to walk, Raphael noticed that they had moved into a markedly different sector of the camp. The bivouacs were larger, more substantial, and better maintained. The streets were cleaner, better lit, and more sections of wooden sidewalk had been installed as protection against the ever-present mud. Seeing his charges were uneasy, Melchior explained. "We're in officers' country now, lads. Just walk like you've got a purpose, a reason for being here, and know what you're doing. Pull that off, and you can get away with murder. If you look like you're in the right place, you become invisible to officers. They assume you're supposed to be where you are, and after that they don't see you. If anyone stops us, let me do the talking."

Raphael and the others had no intention of doing otherwise. Melchior had handled all the previous halts, checkpoints, and encounters with the military police and the Ministry of Virtue. Each time they had been stopped and quizzed as to what they might be doing, he had told what amounted to the truth, the only deception being that he phrased the story in a way that made their mission sound sanctioned and legitimate instead of at their own increasingly illegal initiative. Melchior was so plausibly confident and devoid of guilt, or even concern, that the MPs and the Ministry men seemed to buy what he said with only minimal questioning, and Raphael began to believe that maybe authority figures listened more to the tone of what was being said than the content.

They had been walking in "officers' country" for maybe ten or fifteen minutes without finding anything too promising, and the recruits were becoming sufficiently accustomed to the sights and sounds of the camp to remember just how hungry they were. Raphael thought that very little was going to distract him from the rumbling of his disgruntled stomach, but then, as they were crossing an intersection, the sight of three very attractive women talking with a Teuton lieutenant was enough to remind him that, as long as he might have been without food, he had been out the company and even the sight of women very much longer, and these women were young and, to his eye, so stunningly desirable they set his impulses groaning. Then one of the women moved so her face was to the light. It was the girl from his dreams and his drawings, the one with red hair, whom he had previously seen manacled in the back of the truck on the highway, and then a second of the women half turned, and, to his open-mouthed amazement, she, too, was from his dream. He knew he was not mistaken, even though the presence of the two of them together made no sense at all, unless he was finally losing his mind and starting to hallucinate. He wanted to do something, to run to them, to blurt out to them that they had been in his dreams even before he had crossed the Northern Ocean, but enough of his vital grasp on the real world still remained for him to imagine how such an outburst would be received and what would happen to him when he was assumed to be nothing more than a lust-crazed madman. Yet Raphael had to do something; he could not just walk on regardless.

Unfortunately, that was exactly what Melchior and the other three were doing, until the underofficer turned and barked at Raphael. "Stop staring at the officers' whores, Vega, if for no other reason than you're making yourself obvious."

"Is that what they are?"

"That's what they are, lad, and, as such, absolutely no concern of yours."

As Raphael caught up with the others, he looked around desperately. He saw a sign on a post. It simply read "RQ-38." He supposed it was some kind of designation of this particular area of the camp. He would remember it, and, at the first chance he could find, he would slip away. He would ignore the possible consequences, do everything to find both this place and the women from his dreams.

ARGO

"We're moving into a high-traffic area."

"It's the highway. The Continental Highway is the lifeline between Savannah and the front. They have it covered by constant patrols, minefields, killing zones, even Dark Things. The Mosul have all kinds of stuff for maybe a mile or more out from the road itself. Mainly it's to catch their own deserters and any guerrillas from the mountains looking to mount an attack on the transports."

"So what do we do from here on in?"

Hooker looked round with slow circumspection. "We proceed very, very carefully. We're heading into the dark heart of the Mosul invasion."

The Rangers rested in the shadow of a low rise beyond which the sky was lit by a dull orange glow and the stars were obscured by a dirty haze. They had been on the move since sunset, and it was now past midnight. Previously the night air had been clear, washed down by the recent rain, and Argo had looked up twice to see autumn shooting stars streak across a section of sky. The closer they came to the huge Mosul encampment by Alexandria, however, the more polluted the night became, and first hints drifted on the breeze of the stench created by a combination of swampland, massed humanity, untreated sewage, belching vehicles, and thousands upon thousands of open fires. During a noticeably pungent waft, Argo had turned to Slide. "That's got to be some damned camp."

Slide had nodded. "You'll more than likely see it all for yourself once we cross that ridge. I can't remember much to rival it for sheer, disorganized size."

Argo could find nothing to say to that. He still could not quite believe that he was not only marching with a band of Albany Rangers, but, in a matter of minutes, he'd be looking directly at the largest concentration of the invaders' armored might in the Americas, bigger now than even the port of Savannah. And if that was not enough to boggle his mind, the fact that the huge hostile camp was going to be his eventual destination performed the stunning function. Slide had received the orders through the psychic link to Albany that most of the Rangers preferred not to think about. They were going in; a black-bag job in the heart of enemy darkness. With all of their considerable stealth, they were going to infiltrate the Mosul camp, rescue any survivors from the NU98, and either bring them home or destroy any and all salvaged parts of the airship. On the way out, they also had the option of causing all the collateral damage they could. Even the Rangers were a little daunted by the prospect of worming their way into such a density of the enemy. Steuben summed up the collective hesitation. "Ain't that kinda like being ordered into hell to fuck the Devil's wife while he ain't looking?"

Madden did not see the problem. "Shit, Steub, it's child's play to get lost in a big place like that."

Barnabas picked up the same theme. "Sure, Steub, it's a piece of cake. Nobody knows anyone else, and they're all milling around like wet hens, each new replacement trying to find his own ass."

Hooker had not seemed so convinced that the task was either child's play or a piece of cake, but he had his own solution. He smiled wickedly at Barnabas and Madden. "Since you two are so damned confident, go scout that ridge for me, will you?"

The pair shrugged, dropped their packs, hefted their weapons, and slipped into the night. As they moved out, Madden drew his knife. All the Rangers were good, but Madden and Barnabas were the squad's masters of invisibility.

Argo wanted to demand how they thought he felt if a Ranger like Steuben had reservations about stealing into the Mosul camp, but he said nothing, partly to save face and partly because he didn't think he had heard the whole story. In addition to the rescue of the NU98 survivors, he was sure that Slide, and maybe Albany, too, had more goals for this mission than just those that Slide had told to Hooker. He guessed that some of those plans might involve himself and the Lady Blakeney. This had all but been confirmed when his and Bonnie's role in the operation had been discussed. Hooker had been all for leaving Bonnie and Argo behind and arranging a rendezvous location close to the river, where they could all reunite and then be transported across when the Rangers headed for home and safety, but Slide had overridden him. Bonnie and Argo would come along, but Slide was less than precise about what their function might be. He seemed to be expecting a lot to be taken on trust, and when Bonnie made no protest, Argo could hardly express any doubts about walking into the biggest Mosul camp on the continent. Bonnie's attitude was that she was with the Rangers come what may, but Argo was certain that both Bonnie and Slide expected a new phase of their search for the rest of the mysterious Four to play out beside the Potomac.

That was, of course, if they made it to the river in the first place.

Barnabas was back in a matter of minutes with news that cast a shadow of doubt over even that first objective. "We got Mosul, Captain."

"Where?"

"Up on the ridgeline, a guard and two engineers manning a heliograph. They seem to have a regular little relay station set up. They've got a tent, cooking facilities, everything."

"Are they still standing and blissfully ignorant?"

Barnabas nodded. "They act like they don't know there's a Ranger this side of the water. Madden was for cutting straight to the wetwork, but I told him it was your call."

"Can they be laid down quietly and with no fuss?"

"They won't know what hit them."

"Then the two of you hit them, and let's put the heliograph out of commission and move on."

Slide drew the oriental sword from the sheath on his shoulder. "Wait, I'll come with you. I want to see this heliograph for myself."

Neither Hooker nor Barnabas made any objection, so, as Barnabas again vanished into the night, Slide followed. Once he had gone, Hooker glanced at Bonnie. "Yancey feeling the need to do some of his own killing?"

Bonnie was noncommittal. "Who knows with Slide?"

Hooker signaled to the rest of the squad to follow at a distance. The moon was up, brightening the hillside and complicating the approach, and he gestured in the Rangers' own sign language for no sound and maximum caution. They rose like ghosts from the grass and advanced, weapons at the ready. Argo and Bonnie brought up the rear. Then, as the Rangers moved silently forward, the sound of a gasp and a brief scuffle told them that the element of surprise, and the blades of Madden, Barnabas, and Slide, had done their work. The main party reached the top of the rise to find the heliograph that Barnabas had described and Madden standing over two bodies. Closer inspection would reveal that the corpses' throats had been cut from ear to ear. Slide, meanwhile, was pulling his sword from a collapsed, four-man ridge tent and wiping it clean on a loose fold of canvas. He had first sliced the guy ropes to drop the fabric of the tent on top of its occupant and then skewered him through it as he thrashed around helplessly in what was going to be his voluminous shroud. Even in his methods of death delivery, Slide made perverse choices. He was also so certain of his work that he simply sheathed his sword and walked away to inspect the heliograph without inspecting the body, commenting pedantically to no one in particular, "Hassan's big problem is communication, and it will doom him in the end."

He looked the twelve-feet-tall heliograph up and down. It was essentially a steel tower supporting a moveable mirror, capable of using reflected sunlight to send a dot-dash code to the next relay post down the long road to Savannah or the shorter distance up to the Potomac. He examined the polished steel, umbrellalike reflector that was at that moment folded back against a chance night wind, and then he leaned down to peer into the base of the device, where, cloaked in canvas against the weather, a heavy bank of nickle-iron batteries and an electric arc had been installed to make night transmission possible. "If they've got this thing set up on a permanent basis, it means that the telegraph stations along the highway are jammed with more messages than the lines can handle, and they're using this junk as an even slower alternative."

He straightened up and smiled sardonically. "The Zhaithan have such a holy fear of wireless technology, they're going fuck everything up for Hassan. Which is good for us, except it pushes the vile and hunchbacked Quadaron-Ahrach further and further into the field of windwalking and talking on the dimensions."

At which Bonnie chimed in, "And that's where the next battle's going to be fought, boys. In the nether places, with what you men-in-denial like to call the wiggy shit."

She seemed about to deliver a post-incident lecture when she was interrupted by Barnabas. He had been pulling the canvas off whatever was inside the tent with the man that Slide had killed. Now he turned and spoke sharply to the others. "I don't want to worry anyone, but there's packs and bedrolls for four in here, and we've only got three stiffs."

The Rangers froze. The ground was not secured after all. A possible lone enemy was on the loose. But where the fuck was he? Taking a shit, back at camp sick, or deserted two days ago? Or was he already running to raise the alarm? Weapons were leveled, and each Ranger turned slowly, but no one had an answer. The order to first establish a perimeter didn't have to be given before the Rangers were doing exactly that, deploying spontaneously, in silent agreement, but already too late. The shot came out of nowhere. The surprised Mosul had probably fired in response to the Ranger's sudden and deliberate moves. The canteens he was carrying, dropped at first sight of the enemy unit, would testify how he had been sent to get water from a stream at the bottom the rise and had been toiling back up when he spotted the Rangers before they spotted him. He had crouched down, probably hoping to creep away unseen., but then the Rangers had discovered him by his absence, and he must have decided to pick off at least one before he ran.

At the sound of the shot, everyone dropped into a crouch, except Bonnie who collapsed suddenly, like an unstrung doll. She was hit. The cry went up. "Bonnie down!"

Slide was instantly beside her. He ripped the glove from a skeletal right hand and felt her pulse. Then he let out a strange, soft howl that had to be one of rage and loss, and shook his head. "Bonnie is *dead*."

While Argo reeled from shock, Slide was instantly on his feet. He looked directly at the fourth Mosul, seeing him immediately as he stood in the moonlight, desperately reloading his weapon, snapping cartridge and shot into the cumbersome breechloader. Slide's sword was out in a single sweep, and he advanced on the man at an inhumanly fast gait. The Mosul could only be given a certain brutal credit that he did not simply come apart or turn and flee as a vengeful, angry, and grieving demon bore down on him with a naked blade. Instead, he went right on loading his rifle. He snapped the lock closed with what must have been critical relief. Slide was so close that the man did not even have to aim. He simply fired from the hip. Slide broke stride, staggered slightly as the bullet hit his body, but then swung his sword in a fearsome horizontal backhand stroke, like a Frank executioner, so the man's head came cleanly off. Argo had never seen a man killed with a sword before, and shock collided with extra shock, plus an odd and hollow rejection of a vengeance that came so quickly behind Bonnie's still-unaccepted death. But Slide was also shot, and he immediately proved that it was no superficial wound by sitting down abruptly on the grass in front of the spread-eagled body of the headless Mosul.

Argo ran as fast as he could to where Slide sat bolt upright staring fixedly ahead. He dropped to his knees beside him and stared anxiously into his face. Slide's hat had been lost during the decapitation, and Argo could see at once that the demon's eyes were closed. Argo could not read pulses, but all instincts told him that Slide was either dead or very close to that abyss.

The front of Slide's work shirt was a soaked mass of what looked in the moonlight like blue-black blood. His sword lay on the turf beside him. His shoulders were slumped, and his hands hung loosely at his sides. Somewhere there was a missing glove that Slide had not bothered to replace after using his bare hand to discover Bonnie's lack of a pulse. Argo turned and shouted to the Rangers. "Quick! Over here! I think Yancey Slide is dead, too!"

Bonnie was dead. Slide appeared to be dead, and Argo suddenly realized that, in addition to all the other implications, he was now alone with the Rangers, who still did not absolutely trust him. He could suddenly see that his only options were now to go right on into the enemy camp with the Rangers or to be left on his own. That was if they did not decide simply to dispose of him as too much of a suspect nuisance.

FIVE

〉

JESAMINE

Jesamine sprawled on the bed with yet another schnapps in her hand as Cordelia dug further into the costume trunk. They had already amused themselves by painting each other's faces, and now they were selecting their finery for a harlot's masquerade. Cordelia pulled out an item that Jesamine had not seen or worn in a long time. Cordelia wrapped it experimentally around her waist but then had trouble with the three buckles that fastened it in the back. "This is excruciatingly tight."

Jesamine's speech was a little slurred. "It's supposed to be excruciatingly tight. It's designed to nip your waist in and leave you unable to breathe."

"Will you help me with it?"

"Come here."

Cordelia sat down on the bed and turned so her back was to Jesamine, who rolled over and then leaned forward to fasten the first of the three buckles. "The times I wore that for the loathsome Phaall, it brought out all of his least-pleasant impulses."

"Is Phaall really that loathsome?"

"He isn't the worst, and he isn't a Mamaluke, but otherwise he's a pig."

Cordelia giggled. She had drunk almost as much schnapps as Jesamine. "That's the best that can be said about him? He isn't a Mamaluke?"

"That can sometimes say a lot in this place." Jesamine started on the second buckle. "Breathe all the way out, girl, and suck your stomach in hard. I told you it was supposed to be tight."

The garment in question could be viewed as either a narrow waist synch or a wide belt. It was made from soft purple leather, decorated with spirals of tiny gilt rivets, and stiffened with panels of a less flexible hide. As Jesamine had so far read her, Cordelia appeared to have decidedly imperious tastes when dressing for the boudoir. She had already selected a pair of pale gold silk stockings and was now counterpointing it with the purple leather. Jesamine knew she wasn't only of Albany—something that, as yet, she had very wisely not admitted—but she was also highborn of Albany. Of this, Jesamine was in no doubt. Cordelia's efforts at anonymity had been good, and would have passed any casual inspection, but, over the few hours they had spent together, and as the schnapps took hold, she had revealed her origins in any number of minor but significant trifles of accent, mannerism, and attitude, all the small signs that it was impossible to conceal over a protracted period. Even in her current and extremely precarious situation, she managed to maintain a certain inherent authority, and from the way she sat, right there and then, she betrayed that she was very accustomed to having someone help her to dress. This Cordelia was an Albany lady, no mistake about that, but also an adventurous spirit, or how else would she have been riding around in an airship that by all accounts was on a secret and dangerous mission? By any logical criteria, Jesamine should have taken an immediate dislike to the woman, but instead she felt a strong affinity for her, which really made no sense, but was there anyway. Attraction was not the right word, although a degree of that might figure in the mix. Maybe the term was empathy, but that was not a word that Jesamine used with any great frequency. Teuton officers were not partial to concubines who showed off too extensive a vocabulary, and an immoderately smart mouth could bring rapid retribution.

"Colonel Phaall can be overly handy with his belt and his riding crop. I know there are those who claim to enjoy their stripes, but I'm not one of them."

Cordelia's voice sounded constricted as Jesamine pulled the final strap tight. "He makes excuses to punish you?"

Jesamine leaned back to inspect her handiwork. "He doesn't need excuses. He thrashes me because it thrills and pleases him. At least he's quite open about that."

Cordelia stood up and flexed her hips, testing her newly cinched waist. "Your colonel isn't so unique. There are plenty on the other side of the river who share his taste."

"Even in Albany the women are beaten by the men as part of the sex game?"

"Sometimes. And sometimes the reverse."

Jesamine had heard of such things but never encountered a man with those kind of desires. "I think I might rather enjoy such a reversal."

The corselet seemed to have deepened Cordelia's voice and made it more husky. Or maybe the schnapps was having that effect. "My dear, there are men who'll beg to be collared and chastised by a beautiful woman."

Cordelia had now selected a gilt choker and was fastening it round her throat. This lady of Albany was proving to be less and less what Jesamine would have expected. On the Mosul side, they were told so little about the enemy across the river, and much of what they did hear were the patently impossible lies of the Zhaithan propaganda machine. According to the Zhaithan, the women of Albany were loud and promiscuous harridans who made midnight blood sacrifices to a corrupt and hideous earth goddess. Cordelia hardly seemed a blood-sacrificing harridan, although she did portray herself as unashamedly experienced. She finished fastening the choker and posed for Jesamine. "How do I look?"

"Maybe just a tad too exposed."

"You think so?"

"Girl, all you are wearing is a corselet and stockings."

Cordelia giggled. She was almost drunk. "I've never had any complaints about that, darling."

"A few secrets should be kept in reserve."

"Are you saying put on more so he has something to tear off?"

"That's one way of looking at it."

"What would you suggest?"

"I think you need maybe one more item. You don't want to be offering yourself as completely vulnerable, girl, even if you are."

"But that Kemper isn't going to be like your colonel, is he? I mean, he's little more than a damned baby."

"He'll probably have some little baby pig fantasies just waiting to be fulfilled."

Cordelia again rummaged in the trunk. "I'll have him eating out of my hand."

"Your hand?"

"Believe me. I'll have him on his lieutenant's knees."

"Are you sure you won't be the one on your knees?"

"As I've said, I'll do what it takes, but he's young and unsure of himself and probably totally lacking in imagination. He may find it a relief just to do what he's told."

"You've met Teutons before?"

"No, but I've met soldiers before. What they call the junior officer class." Cordelia took a deep breath. "He really is coming here, right?"

Jesamine was in no doubt about that. "What do you think? Like you say, he's a baby. He's a callow lieutenant who's barely started shaving. His colonel's away in the field, and his colonel's personal sluts have invited him to come up and see them. You think he won't show? Damn, girl. He'd be afraid not to show."

Cordelia pulled out a length of gold damask and draped it around her shoulders like a wrap or stole. "Better?"

Jesamine nodded. "Better."

She hugged the fabric to her body, flashed it open and then concealed herself again. "Modesty and availability all at a gesture." She frowned. "Where did you get all this stuff?"

Cordelia wasn't the only one who was dressed to command. Jesamine had picked out a simple, low-cut slip, slit up each side to above the hip, and matching, wedge-heeled sandals with ribbons that tied around her ankles. The extra height from the shoes meant she would be taller than Kemper. "Like everything else, it came from the officers' black market. I guess it was captured and looted from all over. But I really don't think about things like that anymore. I just wear the stuff because it pleases Phaall and his cronies. It's the concubine's path of least resistance."

Cordelia picked up a mask of peacock feathers and held it up in front of her face. "We don't have this kind of selection in the shops in Albany anymore. Before the . . ." Cordelia faltered.

Jesamine filled in the missing word. "Conquest? Is that what you were trying to say?"

"I was going to say 'invasion.' Before the invasion, lavish was quite in

vogue, but in wartime, one is expected to be a little more frugal and practical. I hear the Norse use all their silk for parachutes."

Jesamine frowned. "What are parachutes?"

"These umbrella things that airmen use when they have to jump out of
a falling airship."

"And they're made of silk?"

"You can't get silk stockings for love or money." She grinned. "At
least, you can't get them for money. Sometimes love will do the trick."

A chill fell between them. "You only talk like that, girl, because you
still believe you can choose what you wear or who you fuck."

Cordelia at least had the grace to realize she had been insensitive. "I'm
sorry."

Jesamine knew it was pointless to be upset at Cordelia. She was adapt-
ing as fast as she could. "It's okay. I'm just feeling sorry for myself. Come
and sit down here and have a drink."

Cordelia seated herself on the bed, close to Jesamine but not touching
her. Jesamine poured more schnapps. "We'll be drunk as nubians on shore
leave by the time Kemper gets here."

"And do we care?"

"I don't think we do."

Jesamine sipped her schnapps. "Did you have to use one of those parachutes?"

Cordelia laughed and shook her head. "You know I can't answer that."

"What I don't know I can't tell, right?"

Cordelia nodded. "Isn't that the best way? Let them torture it out of
me rather than you."

Jesamine lowered her eyelids. "You realize you just revealed that you
are from Albany."

Cordelia sighed and sadly shook her head. "I'm no good at this, am I?"

"Don't be too upset. I've known all along."

"That makes it even worse."

Jesamine sipped her schnapps and openly studied Cordelia's face. The
features were finely chiseled; her lips full but intricate, her nose small and
delicately precise, her forehead high and deceptively fragile. Her eyes
were large and dark, but only a fool would fail to see the intelligence and
calculation and think them innocent. Jesamine had never seen such pale

skin, and she stared at the faint blue veins that pulsed beneath its surface. Cordelia was looking at her in the same way, and without any conscious design or considered intent, the two of them moved towards each other until their faces and their lips were so close that to kiss each other became so inevitable that it had to be. Suddenly they were in each other's arms, holding one another as though for dear life and desperate solace. Cordelia's words came out like an unbidden sob. "Please hold me, Jesamine. I'm trying so hard not to be afraid."

Jesamine stroked her red hair. "You're doing very well for a beginner, child."

Cordelia looked up at her, pushed back her hair, and laughed the kind of laugh that is used to hold back tears. "I am, actually, aren't I?"

They kissed again, still holding onto each other as though, if they pressed close enough, their two bodies together could form a perimeter to exclude the outside world, and they went right on holding and kissing until the unexpected and intruding voice jerked them out of the embrace. "Isn't that illegal?"

Cordelia sat up and, hitting the metaphoric ground running, smiled wickedly. "It isn't if you quickly join us, Lieutenant Kemper. We can claim we were doing it just for you. Like those twins who perform in the officers' mess."

Jesamine had to admit that Cordelia was fast. She might have let slip the admission of being from Albany, but she had remembered the twins. Kemper's eyes were already about to bug out of his head, and the invitation made further mincemeat of any discipline or reason he might have retained in the face of the two outrageously clad and painted women disporting before him with criminal abandon. Jesamine and Cordelia rose from the bed as one, like sirens moving in for the kill on an already lured victim. "Can we offer you some schnapps, Lieutenant Kemper?"

Kemper suddenly seemed to have problems with his breathing and the formation of sentences. "Yes, please. Thank you. That would be nice. I mean . . . yes."

In her high-heeled sandals, Jesamine was indeed taller than Kemper. She leaned on his shoulder and breathed in his ear. "Relax, Lieutenant Kemper."

While Jesamine fed the boy schnapps, Cordelia worked on the buttons of his tunic and then eased it off him. Together, they pulled him out of his boots and stripped him of his britches and his long johns. Their efforts revealed a boyish body that was not, in the abstract, totally unpleasing and at least went halfway to making the task they had set themselves less distasteful and arduous. Jesamine had no precise idea what exactly might be gained from the two-woman seduction of the young lieutenant. She had made the suggestion that he came to Phaall's quarters on the spur of the moment, initially to distract him from questioning them further, and also as a chance of an eventual but undefined advantage. She had played him the same way she regularly played Reinhardt, only for higher stakes. Kemper could be a possible friend, or a mark for blackmail, a contact in the lowest of high places, and maybe a fool who might be looking the other way when they attempted escape to Albany. The two girls had not talked about escape, but Jesamine knew it had to be uppermost in Cordelia's mind, and, to her Albany lady's arrogance, it might even seem possible. Whatever happened, if Cordelia made a break for the river, and across to freedom, Jesamine would be with her.

They fed Kemper as much schnapps as he would take and then laid him back on the bed. Jesamine was surprised to find that, just as Cordelia had predicted, in the intimacy and sweaty, perfumed privacy of the threesome, he took quite quickly to the idea of doing what he was told. As they moved their bodies against his, stroked and caressed him, and kissed him in places Jesamine was certain he had never been kissed before, the suggestion only had to be made, between their exaggerated whore-moans of faux delight, and he would willingly comply.

"Yes, oh, yes, Lieutenant Kemper. Right there, ah, right there, and oh, please, so slowly."

"That's right, baby, just like that. You don't have to say a word. We know what you want."

"We know what you want before you even want it."

"Just like I'm showing you, Lieutenant Kemper. Put your mouth right there."

"Harder, boy, harder. Show the slave that you're her master."

"Turn over, Lieutenant Kemper. You're going to like this."

Kemper moaned helplessly.

"That's right, boy! Like it! Like it good!"

He moaned again, longer and louder.

"Now tell me you like it, Lieutenant. Tell me you like it, boy."

"I . . . like . . . it."

Then a moment came in which Jesamine found herself face to face with Cordelia, damp hair hanging over both their faces, lips wide, hands and tongues almost touching across Kemper's panting, writhing body. They were both manipulating him with their mouths, and the two of them felt their breathing fall into a single rhythm, and their hot breath mingle. Their eyes seemed to lock and widen, each pair drawing in the other. Jesamine felt herself floating in a way that was unprecedented and had nothing to do with drugs, alcohol, or even sex. She was rising above the mundane reality of the bed and young man and going to some other place. It was not unlike the place to which T'saya had sent her, except no potions were needed and no effort was required on her part. Strangest of all, Cordelia was rising with her, and there seemed to be a lessening of the sense of individuality and separation between them. Was this *Mnabe Ctse-owa*? Was this the *takla*? Were two of the *Four* now conjoining? And if so, to what place were they going, and when, if ever, would they return?

ARGO

"Quick! Hurry! Over here! I think Yancey Slide is dead, too!"

Steuben was the first to arrive beside Argo, followed almost immediately by Penhaligon. "What happened?"

Argo stared at Slide's inert body, sitting upright but otherwise inanimate. "The Mosul, the one that killed Bonnie, he got off a shot before Slide decapitated him."

Penhaligon examined Slide, and Steuben walked a few paces on and looked at the headless Mosul. Penhaligon gently moved aside the flap of Slide's duster to expose his bloody chest. "He took a bullet, sure enough."

Argo nodded, trying not to panic, but his head whirled. Previously the world had been dangerous but exciting. Now it was going clear to Hell. "He killed the Mosul, but then his legs just gave way and he sat down, just like he is now. He isn't moving at all, and there's a lot of blood. Is he dead?"

Penhaligon looked at Argo in amazement. "Hell, boy, Slide's shot, but he ain't dead. Don't you know about Yancey Slide?"

"Know what?"

Before Penhaligon could answer, Slide's eyes opened, and he suddenly spoke. *"Vyfaik fhscak cwkvi cwhga ca arjahqh ni ja vsisdujd. Myk ca cwkvi ooon. Vyfaik a vyfaika. Ni ja. Ni haj ja."*

Argo stared at Slide open-mouthed at this sudden and unintelligible stream of words. Then Slide's head turned and looked straight at him. *"Myk ca ni ja?"*

"What?"

Slide was making an effort to focus his eyes. Then he spoke as though the previous utterances had never happened. "Death is for humans, Argo Weaver. I am merely shot, although it's still an occurrence that I don't take fucking lightly." He glanced at Penhaligon. "Tell Hooker to break out that lump of opium and the pipe that I know he always carries. This hurts like a motherfucker, as they say in other parts."

Steuben shook his head. "The captain ain't going to give his opium up to me. He isn't even going to admit he's got it. If you want it, you're going to have to ask him yourself, Mr. Yancey Slide."

Penhaligon tried to be helpful. "There's some morphia in the medical kit."

Slide weakly shook his head, but a little of the old fire had crept back into his eyes. "I don't want morphia, lad. I need the smoke that calms after being shot through the heart. Hooker is going to have to break loose the little cache he keeps for emergencies."

Argo was still gazing wide-eyed at Slide, reeling from the horrible pileup of disaster on disaster. Bonnie was dead. Slide had seemed to be dead but then had come alive again, and then talked in some strange and demonic language. Finally, after he had demanded opium, Slide now turned his attention to Argo. "And what the hell is the matter with you?"

Before Argo could answer, Hooker arrived and knelt beside Slide. "What's all this about opium?"

Slide coughed dark blood, as if to make his point. "I either have to let this body heal or get another one, and I prefer not to be walking looking around like a squat and warty Mosul or a big-nosed Mamaluke. The only problem is that the healing hurts like hell, so break out the dope, Captain Hooker, sir."

"What makes you think I carry opium?"

"Damn you, Jeb, I know you do. So don't mess with me. I'm hurting."

"Can you move?"

Slide managed to shake his head. "No, I can't. It takes a little time to restore an exploded chest cavity. I feel like I gave birth to an alien."

"What?"

"Nothing. Wrong world. Just give me some time and some dope, man."

"How much time?"

Slide sighed. "Half an hour, twenty minutes minimum."

"Two shots have been fired, Yancey. Every Mosul unit in earshot is going to be coming this way."

"I'm well aware of that, friend, but it doesn't alter my situation, so give me the damned opium and get your boys ready to pull out, possibly under fire. Unless you want to leave me out here to suffer, old buddy, old pal . . ."

Hooker held up his hands. "Okay, okay." As Steuben and Penhaligon exchanged glances, he pulled a small oilcloth-wrapped package from inside his tunic and handed it to Slide. Slide unwrapped it, revealing a small brass pipe in the shape of a dragon and a small box of the same alloy. Steuben and Penhaligon seemed set to watch, but Hooker glared at them. "Don't you two have anything to do right now?"

"Orders, Captain?"

"Okay, get back up the ridge and get the others good to go. I need to talk to Slide. Have the mortar assembled and ready to fire on the run. And Penhaligon?"

"Yes, boss."

"I want you on the Bergman. A fire point by the heliograph. That's where any Mosul will most likely be headed."

Penhaligon nodded. "Covering fire as the others move out?"

"You got it."

"And then?"

"And then we bring you out under cover of small arms and mortar."

The Ranger nodded. "By the book, a one-over-one play."

"You can handle that?"

"That's what they pay me for."

"Okay."

Penhaligon and Steuben climbed swiftly back up the rise, and once they were out of earshot, Hooker scowled at Slide. His tone was less than encouraging. "This is a mess."

Slide extracted a dark brown ball of opium about the size of a pea from the copper box, rolled it between his fingers, and inserted it in the pipe. "Everyone was careless. We should have checked for the fourth man, but what's done is done."

Hooker nodded. "I have to get my boys away from here in one piece, and then try to go on with the mission."

Slide kindled a flame at the end of his finger. It guttered as though there was no power left in him. "So we're going to have to split up here. You and your boys do what you can, and Weaver and I will slip away in the confusion. I just need time to mend a bit."

This was the last thing that Argo had expected. He thought they were set to stand or fall with the Rangers. "What?"

Slide sucked on the pipe and then exhaled. "This would be a good time to keep quiet, boy."

Hooker rose to his feet. "You'll get all the time and all the confusion I can give you, Yance."

"I appreciate that."

"Where do we rendezvous?"

Slide did not seem concerned. "In the Mosul camp, if we both make it. If you're there, I'll find you."

Hooker nodded. "Oh, yeah, Yance, you'll find me. Probably in the middle of some unholy shit-storm, if history means anything." He shook his head resignedly and turned to join his men.

Although Slide had told him to keep quiet, Argo felt he had a right to know what this separation would mean. "We're going into the Mosul camp? Just you and me?"

"That's right. Just you and me." Slide winced, and his voice grew nasty. "Just you and fucking me, and we're going to find Lady Cordelia Blakeney, and the Four will be united, and we'll win the fucking war and both be heroes. Now shut up and let me smoke this pipe."

"And what about Bonnie?"

Slide was growing irritable. "What about Bonnie?"

"Are we just going to leave her here?"

"The Rangers will bury her if they can. If they can't, her body will be left for the Mosul."

Argo was dumbfounded. "No!"

"What would you do, boy? This is war. In the early days, the Rangers made a whole big deal about never leaving anyone behind, until whole companies were being wiped out trying to bring home the dead. They had to face reality, just as you are going to have to face it. The dead are dead, and beyond our help, and the living can all too easily join them if they embrace romantic but fucking silly ideas."

The statement stopped Argo in his tracks, and a long interval passed before he spoke again. When he did, his voice was smaller, and he was not thinking about what his rights were anymore. "So it's just you and me?"

Slide dragged on the pipe again and nodded with total finality. "And all of the gods help the both of us."

That the Rangers did not immediately depart was not just an extreme favor to Slide. Slide would later explain it to Argo. "Hooker also needed some time and confusion for himself. He needed to know where the first Mosul detachment was going to come from, so, while Penhaligon held them off with the Bergman gun, the rest of the Rangers could move around behind them, grease the whole bunch, then melt into the landscape before any more could arrive. With dead all over the place, and the hillside chewed up by mortar shells, it was going to take the next bunch of Mosul a while to figure out what exactly had happened. And they'd be moving up very slowly."

Thus Argo sat silently with Slide while the Rangers peered into the darkness and readied themselves for a seemingly inevitable firefight and Slide made his unbelievable and inhuman recovery. Twenty minutes passed in this way before Slide gestured to Argo. "Give me my sword, will you, boy?"

Argo retrieved the oriental sword from the grass, and before he handed it to Slide, he felt an odd tingle as he held it. He noted the oddly shaped blade and fanciful, batwing guard. Slide took the sword and used it as a support as he attempted to climb to his feet.

"Do you need me to help you?"

"No, I have to do this myself."

Slide groaned a little but managed to stand, and, after taking a number of deep breaths, he started up the rise to where the Rangers waited, wheezing as he climbed. Once at the top, Slide returned Hooker's brass pipe and box, rewrapped in their oilskin. The two men embraced, and Hooker seemed about to say something when Madden hissed a warning and Penhaligon tightened his grip on the stock of the Bergman. "Sounds like we got company, Captain."

Immobile as statues, the Rangers listened. Sounds of movement were coming from somewhere in the distance, the slight rattles and footfalls of soldiers on the move, but Argo could not tell exactly where they might be. Hooker whispered a warning to Penhaligon. "Don't fire until you've acquired."

Penhaligon all but chided his commander. "I've done this before, boss."

A moment after he had spoken, a flare burst above them. The Rangers all did their best to be invisible, hugging the ground to appear as nothing more than hummocks in the grass. The flare burned briefly and then dropped into the darkness at some midpoint between them and the advancing sounds. Hooker gestured to his men, indicating they should move out fast along the ridgeline, just below the crest, to outflank the enemy unit. Only Penhaligon stayed to hold what had previously been their position. Slide indicated to Argo that they should follow. "But when they turn, we keep on going straight."

The Bergman gun opened up with the characteristic single-second, chugging reports of its revolving multiple barrels.

"They must be coming up the far side of the hill."

Penhaligon fired in three- and four-shot bursts, husbanding his ammunition, confident that the Mosul had nothing to match his firepower.

Hooker gestured silently to move.

The other Rangers were running, crouched low, already swinging round, using the terrain to outflank the Mosul.

"Ready the mortar."

Argo could have remained and watched, but a seemingly reinvigorated Slide took him by the arm. "Let's go, boy."

Keeping the firing at their backs, Slide and Argo moved quickly into the darkness. The Bergman gun chopped on relentlessly, and shouts and two different sets of screams came from the Mosul attackers. Then, after a couple more minutes, they heard the muffled sound of a mortar being fired. Both Argo and Slide paused at the sound and waited the five seconds or so until the explosion of the detonating shell followed. The sound of the lone Bergman was replaced by the chatter of carbine fire and the bark of repeating shotguns. The cracks of the Mosul breechloaders sounded as though they were being overwhelmed by the superior firepower of the Rangers.

"Let's move, Argo Weaver. It sounds like our boys have the upper hand. We have ourselves to worry about."

The pair hurried on, making for the cover of a small copse at the foot of the hill. A second and third mortar shell exploded somewhere behind them. Once among the trees, Slide paused, leaning on a trunk for support. Argo stared at him anxiously. "Are you alright?"

Slide nodded. "Yes. Give me a moment. I was on the move a little too quickly, that's all."

Finally Slide straightened up. A final flash and one more mortar detonation brought about a cessation of the unseen firefight. After a short interval, three sharp reports that sounded like pistol shots provide the last punctuation. Slide raised his head. "Hooker and his boys seem to have done what they set out to do. By now they'll be doing the melt-away."

Argo was having trouble keeping up with what was endlessly unfolding all around him. "Those last shots?"

Slide looked hard at him. "This is not a time to be taking prisoners." He turned and sniffed the air. "And it seems that our Rangers may well be away in the nick of time."

"Is something coming?"

"You don't sense it?"

Argo listened and peered into the dark. "No, I don't. What do you hear?"

Slide stared at him again. "I don't have time to train you, boy."

Argo did not like the sound of this at all. "Train me for what?"

"You're going to have to start using your abilities if you're going to survive what's in front of us. Focus, damn it."

Argo noted that Slide had said "if you're going to survive." Slide seemed instantly to know the direction of his thoughts. "Don't worry about me, Weaver. I'm the demon Slide. I will survive, but I can't carry you on my back through the next round. Can't you feel it through the very earth?"

But Argo still felt nothing, and shook his head.

"Cavalry, Argo Weaver. A squadron of heavy cavalry, if I'm not mistaken."

Now Argo could feel the faint drumming of hooves through the ground under his feet. "I think I feel it, if the feeling's not just suggestion."

"You feel it. It's no suggestion. If I wanted to suggest something, it would be more than just a vibration under your toes. Focus on the sensation and how much it's able to tell you."

The very first faint hint of dawn was imperceptibly lightening the eastern sky. Somewhere out over the great Northern Ocean, it was already day.

"They're coming from the west, from the Continental Highway, riding into the start of the dawn."

For the first time that he could recall, Argo heard Yancey Slide sound encouraging. "That's good. You're getting it. Can you see them?"

"See them? No. It's too dark."

"Not with your eyes. See them with your mind. Follow the hoofbeats, make a picture to go with the vibrations."

Argo closed his eyes and concentrated. Nothing happened, much as he had expected, but Slide was not finished. "Just relax. Don't try so damned hard."

Argo blanked his mind as best he was able, and, to his amazement, he saw. Shadowy forms of horsemen, seen in his mind, a full minute before they appeared on the crest of the next rise in the open, undulating country. They turned out to be impractically flamboyant Mamaluke Lancers, with white capes streaming, and they were coming at the gallop. Guidons and pennants flapped below the tips of the traditional lances, although, as a concession to modern times, half of them were carrying carbines. They had not, however, abandoned the high and fearsome, winged and plumed helmets for the contemporary protection of camouflage, and steel cuirasses gleamed beneath the long riding cloaks that made them look like ghost riders in the Virginia dawn.

Argo turned urgently to Slide. "So what do we do? Stay put here and try to blend in to the shadows?"

"We can do better that. We can become invisible."

"Like the Rangers?"

Slide shook his head. "No, really invisible."

If the situation had not been so serious, Argo would have laughed. "Maybe you can, but . . ."

"Just now you thought you couldn't see the Mamalukes."

"But invisible? That's not real."

"And what exactly, Argo Weaver, is fucking real?"

"Invisible isn't real. Whatever way you look at it."

"Shut up and stop getting in your own way. If one of them comes too close, just will yourself out and up. Just out and up. That's all you need think to take yourself out of the picture that their eyes are receiving."

"I . . ."

Slide was suddenly stern and towering. "I ordered you not to speak, boy. Will you still demand reasons even now that the bloody Mamalukes are all but on us?"

The lancers had plainly been steeplechasing to the firefight, following the sound of combat, but, now the guns had stopped, they were directionless. They wheeled to a halt, uncomfortably close to the copse that concealed Argo and Slide, and seemed set to remain there until they knew more. Four troopers were dispatched at speed to scout the high ground in front of them, the rise that Argo and Slide had just descended. Almost as an afterthought, the troop commander ordered two more of his horsemen to take a look under the trees. The two moved out from the body of the troop, and Slide whispered four words before lowering himself into the cover of the undergrowth. "Up and out, boy."

Up and out. How could anything so impossible be stated so simply? The two Mamalukes were still negotiating the outer low branches of the copse, and Argo had to fight down a panic that screamed that he should run. The brace of enemy smelled of horse and sweat and leather. They were close enough for him to hear the harnesses creaking and see the steel of the buckles, spurs, and stirrups gleam. The riders' lances were held in gauntlets that extended to their elbows, and they had to duck low to peer

into the darkness of the copse. Seeing that they would not be able to negotiate the trees and the undergrowth while still mounted, one of the Mamalukes handed his lance and reins to his companion. Drawing a saber
from the scabbard behind his sheepskin-covered saddle, he swung down
from the horse. First removing his high, winged and plumed helmet, revealing himself as hawk-nosed, shaved-headed, and with a full drooping
mustache, he pulled a revolver from a holster on his belt, and, with sword
in one hand and pistol in the other, he advanced towards where Slide and
Argo crouched motionless.

Argo took a deep breath and did as Slide had ordered. *Up and out.*
Again the miraculous seemed to occur. Argo was suddenly seeing the scene
in the copse from two separate points of view. One was his normal perspective and the other was a more colorful and hallucinatory vision with
bright rainbow shimmers along and around the edges of anything on which
he tried to focus. The point of view of this strange new way of seeing also
appeared to be rising, floating up to a place where the intruder did not
threaten. *Up and out.* Argo floated half in the world that he had always
known and half in somewhere new. *Up and out.* With what he now found
himself thinking of as his earthly vision, he saw the lancer coming closer
and closer. He could hear his breathing and feel the tightness of the Mamaluke's grip on his weapons. He could smell the tobacco on the man's
breath and found himself staring at the high, over-the-knee tops of his
heavy and highly polished riding boots. He all but felt the slight tug as the
rider's cape snagged a bush.

*In the other weird new world of up and out, he saw all of that, but so much more.
A brand new sky was above him, arched with lingering trajectories of multiple moons.
In this extraordinary realm, none of the angles and spacial relationships made sense
according to the way he previously had seen the world. The Virginia woods and open
hillsides were all around him, except they now danced with a unique fragmented light,
and other alien landscapes of rods and cones and things that he was unable to describe,
even to himself, rose at fourth and fifth right angles from them. Thinking entities both
hideous and beautiful, some simultaneously, moved over the impossible surfaces. Time
itself was not as Argo had known it. It was either a fraction of a second ahead or an
equal fraction behind his old world, and, with other impossible factors added, and even
vaguer and more insubstantial impressions of what might be the future or the present
being somehow overlaid with afterimages and echoes of the past.*

He could see himself, and Slide, and the enemy horseman. He could see his thoughts and those of the lancer like a colored aura, except the colors were ones that he had never seen before and were nothing like the blues, yellows, and greens, and all the tones in between, to which he had forever been accustomed. Only Slide had no such glow around him, only a dark demon essence. Beyond the copse, he could sense the thoughts of the other riders and even the horses. Farther afield, he sensed the bodies of the recently dead, Bonnie's among their number, and the fugitive Rangers, purposeful but scattered, making their way to a prearranged map reference where they would regroup. Argo was also not alone; two more like himself, golden-glowing and together, moved sinuously one on the other, while another was seeking like himself, but wrapped in a blanket of frustration, loss, and fear, and all three were too distant for Argo to reach. Much as he was loath to admit it, he knew beyond a shadow of a doubt that these were the rest of the Four.

Above all, Slide had been right.

His instruction to "take yourself out of the picture that their eyes are receiving" now made absolute sense. Argo could do it. He simply reached into a possible future and removed himself and Slide from the exact moment in time when the Mamaluke looked at them. For the enemy lancer, they simply did not exist.

"All secure in here."

The man's mounted companion nodded, and the one on foot pushed his way out of the copse. Argo had done it. He had gone *up and out* and saved them both. He wanted to talk, to babble, to ask questions, and to look more at the unearthly dimension that had opened up for him, but the Mamalukes were far from gone. The one who searched the copse rejoined his partner, replaced his helmet, mounted his horse, took back his lance, and then the two of them trotted back to the main body of horsemen. The lancers then did nothing except wait, until Argo thought he would go crazy. Then, not a moment too soon, a horn blared from someplace up on the ridge. The call was clearly a prearranged signal from the quartet of scouts, because, the moment they heard it, the entire troop of lancers spurred their mounts and took off at the gallop. Slide stood up and watched them go. Then he turned to Argo. "So you did it, didn't you?"

Argo was still breathless. "I went into a place, but I didn't understand any of it, the why, the how, the where. I don't have a clue what I did."

"And you may have to resign yourself to the possibility that you never really will."

RAPHAEL

Raphael lay in his blanket on hard and cold ground that was covered with just a thin, damp groundsheet. He stared up at the canvas just above him and ached. He yearned for the two women. He could see their faces; he could see their bodies; he was excited by the scanty clothing they had been wearing when he had seen them. If he had dared admit how he was feeling, Melchior would have had a word for it: *cuntstruck*. Melchior used the word a lot, but it wasn't that. The longing he felt was not one of crude lust or raw teenage frustration. It went far deeper, so deep, in fact, that it seemed to emanate from a place that he totally did not understand and could not locate inside himself. It was not that he wanted to fuck them, and he was not the victim of any kind of what others might call puppy love. He did not know the names of the two young women, although he suspected the one with the red hair was the Lady Blakeney, she of the strange name and title that he had inexplicably uttered back there on the highway. Raphael's only consolation was that his preoccupation with the women was so strong that it pushed the awareness of his hunger, discomfort, and fear to the back of his mind. His stomach rumbled, the ground was bone-chilling and unyielding, and his muscles ached from marching and being bounced in a truck all the way from Savannah. He was exhausted, and yet, tired as he was, sleep refused to come. The women seemed to be willing him to find them. But he only had the enigmatic sign near where he'd seen them, that had read RQ-38, as his single clue.

Elsewhere in the tent, Sheg, the Teuton conscript, was snoring loudly in what amounted to a drunken stupor. Sheg had, along with Raphael, Raoul, and Pascal, been one of Melchior's foraging party, the one that had found precious little in the way of food but plenty in the way of alcohol, and had been regaled by the underofficer with tales of drunken Mamalukes. They had been able to steal nothing in the Teuton officers' section of the camp, beyond some table scraps, and a four-hour excursion had yielded only a sack of turnips, four loaves of bread, some yams, and two scrawny chickens that had come courtesy of a rather unorthodox transaction on the part of the now sleeping Sheg. Sheg had revealed himself as not being adverse to offering himself sexually. Oddly, at least to Raphael's somewhat sheltered mind, Melchior had accepted this as a legitimate means to an end. In addition to the chickens, Sheg had also scored two bottles of just-about-drinkable railroad gin, but he had insisted he should keep them for himself since he was the one who had gone to all the trouble, and hence his current booze-coma. "I mean, you guys didn't have to suck off those three bastards, did you?"

Raphael found himself drifting. He hoped it was, at long last, the onset of sleep, but it was not the same merciful dimming of the light and waning of wakefulness. As he stared unseeing at the angled canvas of the tent's interior, it seemed to shimmer and melt. Could it be that, after all the Mosul training and conditioning, all the marching and abuse, his mind had finally given up? He felt himself rising, detaching from his body and entering a new world.

To his horror, he found that he recognized the place into which he had entered. He had seen the strange angles, the grotesque and nameless colors, and experienced the sense of distortion and overlapping time before. The lividly streaked alien sky, the up-curving horizon, the rods and cones, and the impossible crystalline structures had all been in the frightening vision that had come unbidden to him as the formation of Dark Things had bounced past him on the highway and the Mothmen had fluttered above. Again his unexplained instinct told him that he was seeing a small section of the fourth dimension, and, somewhere nearby, the same impossible entities marched in ghostly ranks. He had been alone in the vision brought on by the Dark Things, but he could feel that others were hovering somewhere that was at one and the same time close to him but beyond his vision. And he knew, as unbelievable as it might sound, that they were the two women of his preoccupation, the Lady Blakeney and the other with the honey skin and dark eyes that he had seen so often in his dreams, on the pages of his drawings, and then, for real, in the Teuton officers' section of the camp.

The women were not the only ones, however. He also sensed a young man like himself, also tired and also afraid, and who had briefly moved into the same dimension to save himself from some present and mortal danger. The knowledge of these others also did not stop at them merely being there, although that was enough of a shock on its own. A connection existed between the four them. Raphael did know what it meant or why it should be, but he had absolutely no doubt that it was.

No connection existed with the fourth human that he was sensing in this place of dimensional distortion. Quite the reverse. It was a hunter, and it was after Raphael and the others. It could not quite place their location, but it desired them, *and it was seeking them and, again without doubt, intended them no good. This fourth being was a hunchbacked figure that radiated a refined and long-honed evil. It also had the power to command the denizens of this world, and Raphael could tell that it wielded a terrible power, and, new and inexperienced as he was to all this, he would have no chance if it ever located him. He might well have lingered too long in this unasked-for netherworld already.*

As if in confirmation, he saw a Mothman coming in his direction. It was acting under the instructions of the hunchback, of that he was certain. The form and features of the thing were clearer than they had been back on the highway in what Raphael thought of as the real world, but his view of it was still more a matter of impression than of acute observation or clear-cut detail. He could see what appeared to be four beating wings attached to an insectoid, segmented body; he could see a pair of what looked to be black multifaceted eyes on either side of a vertical slit of a mouth, surmounted by a pair of long prehensile feelers or antennae that ended in fluttering digits that might have served as hands or fingers. What looked like powerful mandibles extended from the lower part of the head and, if relative size and proportion meant anything, could snap a man of his build in two. That the Mothman was coming in his direction, and possibly coming for him, was also a matter of relative size and proportion, but Raphael did not have such objectivity. He was sufficiently sure that he was in this place by mistake, that he was in peril and must get out as swiftly as possible. Far beneath him, he could see his corporal body in the wretched Mosul tent, and he willed himself downwards in a plunging, controlled dive to what he still, for better or worse, thought of as reality.

Raphael groaned and rolled over on the cold, damp groundsheet, dragging his blanket with him. None of the other conscripts even bothered to look at him as a spasm forced him to curl into a tight fetal ball. Stomach pains had become endemic among the Provincial Levies, and it was assumed that Raphael was either suffering hunger pangs or stomach cramps from what was literally rotgut booze, but the truth was that, as he had plunged by effort of will out of the strange other world in which he had found himself drifting, the Mothman had slashed at him with its mandibles, and although the attack had caused him no physical damage in the world of the Mosul camp, the residual pain was excruciating. The only mercy was that it seemed to ease as quickly as the dimension of Mothmen, hunchbacks, and what he was already beginning to think of as his three mysterious companions, faded to a dreamlike unreality. As the pain subsided, he tentatively uncurled his spine and, at the same time, recognized that nothing was as it should be. A bizarre and terrible door had now opened twice for him, and the stuff of dreams was making disturbing incursions into his waking life. He had seen the vision on the Continental Highway, and now, here in the wretched tent that he shared with the other cannon fodder, he had returned to the same place. He had no means to fight what was happening to him, and he was not at all sure that he should. The only consolation in all this, and what might perversely be his only source of strength, was that he had absolutely nothing to lose. He had the supreme advantage of being able to work on the assumption that he was dead already. Melchior was a good squad leader and would do his best to bring his men through the coming assault across the river and into Albany with as few casualties as possible, but Argo knew the odds were against them. Their chances of living through the campaign were slim to none in the armies of Hassan IX, where the taking of massive casualties was a time-honored battle tactic.

The only other factor that he had in his favor was that it seemed, in the grotesque dimension from which he had just fled, he had three potential friends and companions who, if he could only make himself known to them, might prove stronger than Pascal, Raoul, the shameless Sheg, or any of the other men in the tent with whom he might shortly be risking his life. He suspected that the same doors were opening for these other three, and that they might well be experiencing the same fear and confusion. A link seemed to be trying to establish itself between them, almost as though the four of them, if united, would be greater than the sum of their parts. Maybe they, too, were seeing the hunchback and running from the Moth-men, and, if they were together, they might have the capacity to stand and fight and perhaps, dare he say it, prevail. If he could find them in this hungry and brutal world of mud and threat and drunken soldiers, the hopeless odds might be redefined in their favor.

Raphael threw off his blanket and reached for his boots. He pulled them on, laced them, and then quietly stood up. No one paid him any attention as he slipped into his greatcoat, placed his helmet on his head, and picked up his rifle. He moved as routinely as he could, like a sentry going on guard. In his pocket were two contraband rounds of ammunition that he had, by a quick sleight of hand, failed to turn in after the foray into the woods to see the airship and look for the airmen. Picking his way between the forms of the sleeping men, he ducked out of the tent. Once outside, he took a deep breath of the night, despite that it smelled little better than the stench within. Soon it would be dawn and reveille, and shouting officers and braying trumpets would be rousing the camp to its daytime mode of chaos. If he was going to find the two girls, he would have to hurry and look exactly like just one more anonymous soldier going about his duties. He hitched his rifle a little more comfortably on his shoulder, trying not to think about how, with his first step, he had become a deserter.

"Vega!"

The sound of his name caused him to jerk and turn. His first thought was that Melchior had caught him, and now, at the very minimum, he would have a flogging to add to his burden of woe, but then he saw that it was only Pascal.

"Keep you voice down, you idiot."

"Where are you going?"

Raphael looked about tensely. He could not waste time talking to Pascal. He had to get away. "I don't know. I may be attempting to desert. I may be looking for food, or I may just be looking."

"Can I come with you?"

Company in his folly was certainly a temptation, and two men going about their business might be more plausible than one. "We may only be walking into a hanging."

Pascal did not care. "We're going to fucking die anyway."

"That's pretty much the conclusion I came to."

"So?"

"You may not like the places I intend to go."

Pascal's hopeless look made his words almost unnecessary. "Listen, I'm past caring."

And Raphael relented. "Then get your stuff quick. Deserters must move fast."

CORDELIA—JESAMINE

The two of them were one, and shuddering waves of pleasure rolled through what felt like a new and mutual nervous system. Cordelia and Jesamine, indivisibly intertwined, had become an exaltant and triumphant celebration of how, after all the mysteries, miseries, frustrations, and tantalizing dreams, they had finally and completely found each other. The joy of connection even allowed them to forget that this joyous and ecstatic conjoining was happening in a place so fundamentally foreign and unknown that, by most normal criteria, they should have been scared out of their minds. Their wildly rising spirits had merged under a blazing sky crisscrossed by what looked like racing and multiple-ringed moons and double and triple stars that left trails of light in their wake to mark their passage. Towering assemblies of cones, spheres, and cylinders reached for the moon-filled sky from an undergrowth of uppointing crystal fingers, and it was impossible to say whether they were the constructions of those who dwelled in this place or the natural products of a very unnatural environment, but the linked minds of Jesamine and Cordelia were too blissfully euphoric, rapt and enraptured in the throes of something close to extended orgasm but, at the same time, very different from the merely sensual, for them to question how or why or where they found themselves. The illusion was that the transport of delight would continue to infinity, and time, as they once had known it, was subject to a complex distortion and seemed either a fraction of a second ahead or an equal fraction behind the world as they knew it, and with an impossible complication of vaguer and more insubstantial impressions of what might be the future or the present being somehow overlaid with afterimages and echoes of the past.

Even in a place where time did not appear to be either regular or linear, though, the shock wave of exultation must sooner or later succumb to entropy and, first, level to a plateau, then break down entirely, its fuel of passion spent, to a fond and beloved ember. The details of their circumstances began increasingly to claim the attention of Cordelia and Jesamine.

"Have you been here before?"

"Have you been here before?"

To speak was redundant but habitual, and when they did, they spoke together, with one as an echo of the other.

"I believe I have."

"I know I haven't."

"What is it?"

"What is it?"

"I think this place is one turn of the screw beyond our own."

Cordelia and Jesamine quickly discovered that, in combination, one with the other, they could bring at least some of this place of the paranormal into manageable perspective. A measure of what they saw could only be imposed by their own minds. They certainly did not believe it was in any kind of objective reality that they walked on amber sand along the margin of a wine purple ocean, splashing in the shallows with strange jewels adorning their wrists and ankles and chaplets of golden blooms upon their brows, or that they floated like twin fleecy clouds above an idyllic landscape of orchards and rolling hills. These could only be a product of their own fantasies and desires for comfort and safety, hallucinatory representations of the solace and elation that they found in each other. They could enjoy these phantasms in the first wonder of finding each other and discovering the strange and wholly unexplored powers that their joining had unleashed, but they knew they must not forget or fool themselves that all would continue as perfection and remain so, then, now, and forever. Powerful good was present in this place, but, at the same time, a deep and threatening evil lurked somewhere at the periphery of all their wonderment. They had also not left the real world behind. This dimension that had opened was no hiding place. Far beneath them, the hideous encampment by the Potomac still stank and breathed in fetid anticipation of slaughter. The evil empire of Hassan IX was still poised to hurl itself on the defenders of Albany. Their bodies were still pressed against that of the unpleasant young Teuton officer like the memory of a pornographic charade that was simultaneously being acted out along a different but parallel track of time as they bargained sexual favors for a slim advantage in their struggle to survive.

As if to reinforce the presence of all the intruding negatives, and to prove that bliss could, at best, be momentary in such a time of conflict, blue-black clouds formed out on the oddly curved horizon of the purple sea. At the same time, a vortex of dust swirled up way down along the imaginary beach. Cordelia and Jesamine could perceive a djinnlike figure moving within the sandstorm, coming in their direction and obviously meaning them no good. The rider in the vortex was the same hunchback that Jesamine had seen on her own in the vision that T'saya had induced, but Cordelia actually knew the name.

"Quadaron-Ahrach."

"Quadaron-Ahrach."

"We have to leave this place now."

"We have to leave this place now."

"I don't want to."

"I don't want to."

The hunchback in the sandstorm was moving closer.

"We must."

"We must."

"Now."

"Now."

The smell of swamp and bodies and cheap whore's perfume enveloped them. Cordelia had Kemper's penis in her mouth, and Jesamine was close by with her tongue lapping his scrotum. His cock was thick and engorged, and, unaware that the women had ever left him, he writhed with unattractive porcine pleasure. Kemper had the fingers of his left hand twisted in Cordelia's hair and was forcing her to swallow more and more of him. The shock of return to this reality of total debasement was enough to cause her nearly to gag, but much more jarring and unpalatable was the sudden wrenching separation. Cordelia and Jesamine were once more isolated in their individual minds and bodies. A priceless gift had been taken away from them, and all that was left was a memory and the awareness that they somehow must get away from Kemper, and the environment of those like him, so they might conjoin again and explore what was so obviously a vast potential. Jesamine was one step ahead of Cordelia in this. She knew that she had to take Cordelia to T'saya. The old African woman would know what to do. Maybe T'saya could again use the herbs and potions to send them back to the dimension they had so recently fled, and maybe she would have something with which they could defend themselves against the waiting dangers. Quadaron-Ahrach might be the High Zhaithan, and his powers might be legendary, but they, too, had powers, and if they could only learn to use them in what time they might have left, they could carry the fight to him. Back in the Mosul camp, back in Phaall's bed with the naked and contemptible young lieutenant, it all seemed totally impossible, but they had been to a place where the impossible was the norm. Cordelia raised her head and looked directly at Jesamine, quite as though she was able to read her thoughts. Cordelia would be willing to chance anything. What, after all, did the two of them have to lose?

ARGO

"She went down so fast."

Slide went on walking, staring straight ahead, and, when he eventually replied, his voice was cold. "That's often how it is. Death in war proceeds according to its own timetable. Soldiers do not die with hands clutched to their breasts, exclaiming 'Goddess, they have killed me.' That only happens in plays."

"I've never seen a play."

"Never?"

"Of course not. Before the Mosul came, I was too young, and afterwards there were no plays."

"Then you have something to look forward to, don't you?"

"You think so?"

"You should hope so."

Again they walked in silence. The sunrise had come, and morning was upon them. It was a dangerous time to be traveling in heavily occupied territory, but Slide had explained that they really had no choice. They needed to put as much distance between themselves and the scene of the firefight as they could. The Mosul would be using the bodies and the scarred ground left by the encounter as the obvious central starting point in their search for the Rangers, and, although the enemy was probably unaware that Slide and Argo had been with them, they had no plausible excuse for being who they were, or where they were, and armed into the bargain. If they could not shoot their way out, their capture would be as big a prize as an entire company of Rangers if Slide was recognized. They had, however, found a sunken road leading in the right general direction that afforded them a degree of cover. Overhanging trees guaranteed that they would not be spotted from a distance, and Slide, with his apparently supersensitive hearing, and Argo, with his new but rapidly developing perceptions, had been able to spot other travelers coming in the opposite direction well before they spotted them. Twice already they had crouched in the overgrown ditch that ran along one side of the road, once while a platoon of Mosul infantry had slogged past, moving from one unspecified point to another, dusty and tired but singing an obscene marching song in a dialect so thick that it made the words scarcely recognizable. The second dive for cover had been at the approach of a chain gang of slave laborers, formerly free Virginians, yoked at the neck, linked by leg irons, and guarded by four soldiers and a whip-wielding overseer, unfortunates with shaved heads and emaciated bodies who had absolutely nothing to sing about.

Slide, after the chain gang had passed and was out of sight, seemed to soften somewhat. It was possible that, in his own way, he was also affected by the death of Bonnie Appleford but had looked beyond his own form of demon grief and finally become aware how heavily the death weighed on Argo's mind. It seemed as if he were attempting, in his own inhuman way, to offer what comfort he could. "You have to accept that those close to you are going to be killed in action, my boy. It's an inescapable fact of combat."

"How do you simply accept that someone can be there one minute and no longer exist the next?"

"Did I use the word 'simply'?"

"No."

"On the battlefield, loss goes with the territory."

"She was a soldier, right?"

Slide nodded. "She was a soldier."

"And brave."

"I considered her exceedingly courageous."

"And she slept with me for the cause?"

Slide sighed. "Get off it, boy. She slept with you because she so desired. That was her way for as long as I knew her."

Argo could not help, however, blurting out a small measure of his grief and confusion. "But did she desire me? Did I mean anything to her? Or did she do it just to fulfill some aborigine's prophecy?"

Slide's face hardened. "This is about her, Argo Weaver, not you. Mourn her, but leave her memory in peace. Don't dwell upon all the things you wanted to hear from her."

Argo shook his head. How could he not dwell on all of the unsaid words? "We hardly even talked."

"To be in love in wartime requires a very selective memory and a moratorium on what might have been. Bonnie, if anyone, knew that."

Slide stopped and abruptly raised his hand, than signed to Argo to edge to the side of the road. Once in the shadows of the leafy overhang, he sank into a crouch. Argo could sense nothing coming towards them, and frowned. "What?"

"There's a river up ahead, and a bridge. I think it may be guarded."

"Should we double back?"

Slide shook his head. "Let's ease on up a piece and take a look."

For some time, the sunken road had been descending a shallow but noticeable incline and, at the same time, becoming gradually less sunken. As they crept quietly forward, it reached a level with the surrounding pasture and then actually ran along a raised embankment to a brick-and-ironwork bridge that crossed a small and meandering river.

"You sense anyone?"

Argo concentrated the way he had back at the copse, but this time the answer came to him immediately. The simple but unquestionable fact, but with no accompanying vision. "Two men, under the bridge. In the water, out of sight."

"Anything else?"

"They're doing something, but I can't clearly see what."

"And?"

Argo focused again. "And horses, but they're not with the men. I don't get it . . . Wait a minute. The horses are tethered on the other side."

Slide grinned dangerously. "Sounds to me like a couple of calvary men taking a dip after a morning's ride."

Argo nodded. "That could be it."

"With any luck, they'll have dropped their drawers on the bank and we'll catch them taking the waters naked."

Argo shook his head. "I can't tell. They seem close to each other, embracing or something."

"So what are we waiting for, Argo Weaver? Let's take a look. May happen we can steal their horses and ride the rest of the way."

Argo blinked. He had become so accustomed to ducking and hiding, he needed a few seconds to make the switch to the idea of taking the initiative, but he still followed Slide as he advanced cautiously up the road. As they approached the bridge, Slide drew his oriental sword and one of his odd, flat pistols, and, when they were just a few yards from the first brick supports, he pointed to two neat bundles of clothes on the grass of the riverbank, topped by carefully folded silk turbans and a pair of highly polished spiked helmets. The word came out of Argo like a gasp. "Zhaithan."

"So it would seem. The military elite, if I'm not mistaken. All the more satisfying for us to bring them down."

With those words, Slide strolled almost casually to the riverbank. Argo knew it was hardly the time to protest or debate the course of their action, but he had lived so long under the occupation that the idea of even facing two elite Zhaithan terrified him. On the other hand, the current circumstances dictated that he had to follow with his still-unfired carbine at the ready. At the last minute, Slide turned and signaled silently that he wanted no gunfire. The carbine and pistol were for threat only.

Argo might have been conditioned to fear the Zhaithan, but absolutely nothing could have prepared him for the sight that met his eyes. In the shadow of the bridge, and up to their thighs in water, two men in their mid-twenties, one a good deal taller than the other, were holding onto each other in blatant and flagrant sexual delight. Slide all but laughed out loud. "Maybe you didn't know enough to recognize what they were doing, young Argo." He raised his voice and spoke to the men in the water. "I believe, gentlemen, the charge is 'for unlawful carnal knowledge,' the origin, in fact, of the handy verb 'to fuck'."

Argo did not believe him. Surely the charge would be rendered in Old Mosul, and that would call for a totally different mnemonic. It was hardly the time, though, for such details. Slide again spoke over the sound of the water, pointing his pistol at the same time. "I'm sorry to interrupt the passion, gentlemen, but it would be a good idea if you both separated and raised your hands."

The two Zhaithan sprang apart but then quickly recovered from their guilty shock. When they saw that Slide was neither from the Ministry of Virtue nor a superior officer, they stared at him in amazement. "Do you know who we are? You can't threaten us. Are you quite insane?"

Slide's grin broadened. "Insane? Possibly, but I have a loaded pistol, so I can definitely threaten you. In fact, that's exactly what I'm currently doing. I'm threatening your lives, and also suggesting you take me extremely seriously, sane or not."

"What do you want?"

Slide ignored the question. "Oddly enough, I met my young friend here under the same circumstances, naked and disporting in a stream. Of course, he was with a young woman, but it still seems a bit like history repeating itself."

Even naked and under two guns, a Zhaithan could still lack patience, as was proved by the one who made the angry demand. "What do you want of us?"

Slide gestured with his pistol. "I want you to come out of the water very carefully." Then he laughed. "But I suppose it would be hard to be anything other than careful, seeing as how you're both jaybird naked."

Under the muzzles of Slide's pistol and Argo's carbine, the two Zhaithan waded to the bank with looks of outrage on their faces, something that caused Slide even more amusement. "Considering you young men were just apprehended in a situation that I believe is a hanging offence in your army, you should maybe be thankful to bloody Ignir and equally bloody Aksura that it was just a couple of freebooting guerrillas that caught you. Is it true that a terrible steel device, a kind of expanding phallus, is used for executions in cases like yours?"

The two Zhaithan reached the bank and climbed it dripping. "What now? Is it money you want?"

Slide's smile faded. "Money? What would we do with money? No, my friends, our motives are a little more personal than that. One of you Mosul bastards just killed my friend and this boy's lover, so you might say what we want is payback."

The sweep of the sword took Argo completely by surprise, and the first of the Zhaithan probably never knew what hit him. The blow was not as clean as the one that had felled Bonnie's killer, and the head did not come completely off. Instead, it dropped to one side, still attached to the crumpling body by a narrow strip of flesh. The second Zhaithan stood as though paralyzed, only making a move to save himself when it was far too late. Slide was already performing a balletic spin, which ended when he ran him clean through. The naked Zhaithan fell to his knees and then toppled and fell as Slide ripped out the steel. He then pulled a rag from his pocket and wiped the blood from the blade, at the same time looking enquiringly at Argo. "You feel better? A life for a life? In fact, two lives?"

Argo thought about this and shook his head. "No, I don't feel better. Maybe I should, but I don't."

Slide nodded. "That's the problem with revenge. It doesn't really have the desired effect. It doesn't bring back the fallen." Suddenly he was brisk and businesslike. "Quickly now. Get into the smaller of those Zhaithan uniforms. And hook up that chainmail thing on the helmet. When it's in place, it completely hides your face."

Argo could think of few things more repugnant than putting on the hated Zhaithan uniform. "I . . ."

Slide gestured impatiently. "Yes, yes, it scares the shit out of you, but it's only a suit of clothes like any other. And what better way to infiltrate the Mosul camp than in a costume that everyone fears and no one questions? Hurry it up, boy. Get into the uniform, and let's make off with those horses."

CORDELIA

The night had been long, and they had slept into the day, and, indeed, Cordelia only woke when she did because Jesamine was shaking her. "Come on, sleeping beauty, get up. Quit your sweet dreams and drag your ass out of that bed. It's well past noon, and you and me have things to do."

"Do?"

"That's right, do."

Cordelia sat up and rubbed her eyes. She felt hungover, intimately abused, and the bad taste in her mouth was not all schnapps. "Has Kemper gone?"

"He scuttled out of here hours ago. He was to afraid to linger. He kept compulsively checking the door, and, each time he heard a sound, he thought it was Phaall returning."

Cordelia looked around. If Kemper was gone, she did not want to think about him or the night before. She just wanted to take a little time to recover from all that had happened to her. She had been in an air crash, held prisoner, then spent the night giving herself to the disgusting little lieutenant. She knew that she was probably lucky to be alive, but now that Jesamine seemed to want to rush her into a whole new and unknown day, she momentarily baulked. "So what do we have to do? You have some kind of duties or something? I'm not certain I can move."

"You're going to have to move, girl, and move now."

"Why? I thought Phaall was going to be away for days."

Jesamine was already dressing for the outside world. "We can't count on that, and besides, there's someone we need to see."

"Need to see? What do you mean, need to see? Is there some other officer I'm going to have to fuck to stay alive?"

Jesamine's previous sympathy wilted at Cordelia's outburst. "You don't remember what happened to us last night?"

Cordelia avoided Jesamine's eyes. "I was trying not to think about it. I was pretending it was a dream."

In this, Cordelia was telling the absolute truth. She had been doing everything she could to keep from thinking about the purple beach and the shared hallucination and the passion that she and Jesamine had exchanged. She most especially did not want to think about the name that she had uttered as the hunchback had come at them down the beach. The name of Quadaron-Ahrach, the High Zhaithan, could evoke fear even in Albany. His knowledge of the black arts and the dark places was generally accepted to be superior to those of even the Shaman Grey Wolf and the Lady Gretchen, if for no other reason than that he was fully prepared to embrace and make allies with the forces of unearthly evil, where Grey Wolf or the High Priestess of the Goddess clearly would not. Any business that involved not only strange and prolonged hallucinations of such power, but also the name of Quadaron-Ahrach, was more than enough to scare Cordelia so deeply that she would hide from the idea any way she could. Cordelia might have been willing to ride in an airship, and even raise a pistol to the Mosul cavalry, but the machinations of the Other Side filled her with a profound unease. She had, of course, worshiped the Goddess since she was a small child, but that had been more an affair of ceremony and tradition, candles and pretty blue dresses trimmed with white lace. She had never embraced such Sunday trappings as any profound and functioning belief system. She had always gone her merry way and saw no cause to bother a deity with her problems. To believe devoutly in anything but themselves was not the way of Cordelia and her kind. The lower and middle classes were devout, while she and those like her adopted a pose of aristocratic cynicism, but she knew she could not remain cynical after what she had experienced, and the adjustment would take a little time. Time, though, was something that Jesamine was not about to allow her.

"It was no dream, baby."

"I was afraid I was losing my wits."

Jesamine shook her head. "You are not losing your wits."

"I'm glad of that, at least."

"You may not be when you hear what I've got to say."

Cordelia did not like the sound of this at all. "I don't understand."

"You'd better sit up and pay attention, girl, because I am going to pour you just one drink, and, then, as quickly and succinctly as possible, I will tell you everything I know."

Cordelia said nothing as Jesamine moved to Phaall's liquor chest and frowningly held up a bottle. "We need to get away from here before Phaall returns, if for no other reason than he will certainly whip us both bloody when he sees how much of his booze we've gone through."

"Is there coffee here in the realm of the Mosul?"

Jesamine searched for glasses. "There is, but we don't have time for coffee. We'll have to make do with schnapps." She found what she was looking for and handed Cordelia a shot of raw spirit, and then Jesamine sat down and told her everything that she knew about T'saya and the Four, the previous experience with T'saya's rotgut psychedelic, and how she could only think that, in the first odd and illogical affinity they had felt for each other, and then the subsequent conjoining in the night, a first bond was being forged. She went on to repeat all that T'saya had said about the Four, including the crucial fact that it would require the two young men to complete the quartet of power.

"We are two of the four?

"Of the Four. That's what T'saya said, and after all that has happened, I'm not inclined to doubt her."

"And that's where we're going? To T'saya?"

"Do you have a better idea?"

Cordelia shook her head. "Right now I don't have any ideas at all."

"So shall we get dressed and go?"

"To T'saya?"

"To T'saya."

"Last night you said your colonel would protect us."

"That was last night."

"And now?"

"If the vision said anything, it's that we can only rely on ourselves."

"And this T'saya?"

"And T'saya."

One other facet of the hallucinations that had yet to be mentioned still disquieted Cordelia. It was the physical bliss that she had apparently derived from the conjoining with Jesamine. Except for a half-grown, schoolgirl crush, a dormitory embrace and some shuddering and heavy breathing, Cordelia had taken her pleasure exclusively from men since she had been of age, but her experience with the honey-skinned girl, who was right then squirming into a shapeless cotton kaftan suitable for the outer world, had turned all that on its head. "Jesamine?"

"What?"

"Are we lesbians?"

Jesamine smoothed out her kaftan and then leaned over and kissed Cordelia on the forehead. "No, girl, I don't think we're lesbians. We may, in fact, be something far more dangerous to these bastards than lesbians."

RAPHAEL

Reveille had come and gone and daylight was on them. Raphael and Pascal walked through the camp, rifles over their shoulders, doing their best to look like two grunts going about their routine and fully authorized business and not the frightened AWOL recruits they really were. Just after reveille had sounded they had come upon a formation of Mosul footsloggers, in the worn greatcoats of veterans, paraded in dressed lines for a company punishment. The unfortunate victim was stripped to his long johns and strapped by his wrists and ankles, and a leather belt around his waist, to a tall iron tripod that both boys knew was specifically designed to hold a prisoner immobile while he suffered a military flogging, branding, or mutilation. In this case, the sentence of the drumhead court-martial being meted out was a simple flogging, fifty lashes, as they would learn later, delivered with a cat-o'-nine-tails, with small steel studs inserted in each of the thongs of the implement, and, although this was one of the milder disciplines inflicted on Mosul troops in the field, the chance remained that the recipient might not live through it. Raphael and Pascal had arrived on the scene after the punishment had already commenced. A lieutenant delivered a slow count while a burly underofficer, tunic off and shirt sleeves rolled to reveal hairy, muscular arms, swung the fearsome whip.

"Twenty-one!"

Blood was running down the prisoner's bare back from the whip's deep and horizontal lacerations, and it had already soaked into the off white undergarment. A leather gag was thrust into the man's mouth so he could utter no sound except a muffled grunting gasp as each blow fell. His body twisted but was held fast by the tightly buckled restraints.

"Twenty-two!"

A second man, also half-dressed, and confined in a wooden yoke, knelt white-faced and watching, waiting to be the next up on the cruel device. The tradition in the Mosul ranks was that, in such a case, the most guilty of the pair was the one who waited, so he could watch and imagine his own coming pain as his accomplice suffered. Pascal grasped Raphael by the arm. Both boys had felt the cut of the cane at the training camp across the ocean and seen it applied to others, but that had been nothing like what they were now witnessing. "Let's get the hell out of here."

"Twenty-three!"

Raphael nodded, but he could not resist turning to another gawker who had stopped to watch from behind the formally assembled ranks of the victims' own company. "What did the two of them do?"

The man just shrugged. He did not know and seemed not to care, but another bystander volunteered the information. "AWOL and thievery, from what I heard when the charges were read."

"Twenty-four!"

Now Pascal looked even more unhappy. As yet they had not stolen anything, unless their rifles counted as purloined official property, but they were definitely AWOL and had been since Melchior had presumably called the roll once the squad fell in after being roused by reveille. Raphael knew that Pascal was imagining himself bound to the triangular frame with the strip of leather clenched between his teeth, and he was all but doing the same himself.

"Twenty-five!"

"Okay, let's go."

They moved on as slowly as they could, not wishing to attract attention to themselves, but, as soon as they were away on their own, out of earshot of any eavesdropper, Pascal turned and faced Raphael, wide-eyed and close to panic. "We could go back. Melchior would understand. The worst we'll get is just a beating if we get back now."

Raphael looked bleakly at Pascal. First the damned fool had demanded to come with him, and now he was losing his nerve. Sure it was traumatic to walk without warning into a public flogging, but surely that was all the more reason to run from the Mosul and all they stood for. "Just a beating? You think so? You saw that poor bastard."

"They wouldn't do that to us."

"This is the front, boy."

Pascal's eyes grew wider still. "I should never have come with you."

Raphael snapped back angrily. "Did I ask you to come with me?"

"Why did you decide to run at all? Back on the road you told me that there was nowhere to go."

Raphael was not about to tell Pascal that he had deserted to look for two women he had seen in a dream, and then once briefly in the flesh, but, mercifully, he found that he did not have to. The conversation had taken them as far as a particularly muddy intersection where a new commotion was attracting attention. Where the flogging had been an ordered and largely silent affair, with the only sounds being the officer calling off the strokes, the hiss and crack of the whip, the gasps of the victim, and low-voiced conversations among those observers in the rear of the ranks, this was a shouting, chaotic, almost slapstick spectacle. A slipping, straining team of eight mules slithered and brayed as a gun crew beat on their backs, trying to make the protesting animals drag a six-inch howitzer with huge iron wheels through the sucking, man-made mire. A fuming, red-faced artillery officer was busily enlisting every able-bodied onlooker either to get his back under the gun carriage and push or to help turn the spokes of the great wheels, and it was only a matter of moments before he spotted Raphael and Pascal as likely candidates.

"You two, get over here."

The last thing Raphael wanted was any contact with an officer, and he quickly reacted with imbecilic surprise. "Us?"

"Yes, you, damn your eyes!"

"But we have orders, sir."

"Fuck your orders. Get on that wheel and lend a hand."

Faced with no choice, the two of them stepped down from the wooden sidewalk and into the mud to join the men laboring to move the massive fieldpiece. An angry underofficer shoved Pascal bodily to join the men pushing from behind, while Raphael was ordered to the nearest wheel. To be down in the mud, hungry and breaking his back, was hardly what Raphael wanted, but, on the positive side, he was separated from Pascal and his frightened complaining, and also, for the moment, completely anonymous. As he hauled on one of the thick iron spokes, he glanced at the man next to him. "What's going on here?"

"They're moving the guns up to the forward positions."

Raphael looked back the way the gun must have come. Two more of the big cannons and two more teams of mules were waiting until the first gun had cleared the deep mud of the intersection before they ventured into the quagmire. "Does this mean the attack is going to happen for sure?"

The man looked at Raphael as though he must be a complete idiot. "Haven't you heard? Hassan himself, may his name be blessed, has landed in Savannah. He will be here sometime tonight."

ARGO

Slide shook his head. "Hassan isn't coming here."

Argo frowned. "Then why are they all saying it? That's all we're hearing."

"By any realistic calculation, Hassan IX is over a hundred years old."

"What?"

Slide seemed to enjoy delivering these tidbits of shock. "That's right, kid. It's just another of those things that's never mentioned in the world of the Mosul."

Argo could only fall back on a well-used admission. "I don't understand."

"It'll be a double, boy. One of maybe a dozen."

"But how is that possible?"

"How is what possible?"

"That no one puts two and two together and figures out that doubles are being used whenever the emperor makes a public appearance?"

"Did anyone you know put two and two together?"

"But that was Thakenham. We knew absolutely nothing."

"You think there are other, more enlightened and informed parts of the Mosul Empire where truth and sophistication are the order of the day and the minds of its subjects are not ordered and controlled by the Zhaithan and the Ministry of Virtue?"

Argo considered this. "I suppose not."

"Our best information is that Hassan himself goes nowhere and sees no one, except an inner circle of his closest advisors, his most trusted generals, and his seventeen sons."

"He has seventeen sons?"

"The real number is closer to fifty, but a lot have been executed over the years, usually after they've taken it into their heads to hurry along their inheritance by plotting to overthrow the old man. The story goes, and I tend to believe it, that now only magick, medication, and blood transfusions keep the blessed emperor alive."

Argo and Slide were now deep in the Mosul camp, but, on their tall thoroughbred horses, and dressed in their stolen Zhaithan uniforms, no one so much as looked at them, let alone questioned what they might be doing. Fear of the Zhaithan was so complete that no one in the camp had even questioned the small anomalous details that might have given the two of them away. They had no need to worry that their faces did not fit. The chain mail that hung from their stolen helmets hid them from all observers. That the uniforms were less than a perfect fit was also no problem. All lack of tailoring was covered by the voluminous black riding cloaks, as were Slide's two highly unorthodox pistols. Keeping their old clothes also proved no problem. The Zhaithan saddles came complete with saddlebags with plenty of capacity to hold their bundled garments. Rather more risky was that Slide would not give up his oriental sword, and Argo was equally reluctant to jettison the Norse carbine given him by the Rangers. It was, after all, a prize weapon and a dead man's gun. Thus, the sword hung from Slide's saddle in place of the dead Zhaithan's saber and the carbine was laid across the pommel of Argo's saddle.

While turning out the saddlebags to make room for their things, Slide and Argo had made what was, for Argo at least, a very pleasing discovery. The two Zhaithan had been well supplied with food and drink for whatever journey they had been making. Bread, sausage, and smoked meats were packaged in greaseproof paper, and these were accompanied by two quart bottles of robust Teuton beer, a corked jug of a dark wine that was good if overly resinous, and a box of American cigars. Apparently the Zhaithan's religious piety did not preclude an indulgence in creature comforts, and, once they were far enough away from the bridge that had been the scene of the double slaying, Argo, who seemed to have been hungry for most of the days since he had left Thakenham, had made himself what was an extremely satisfying picnic, while Slide, who appeared to only eat as a social requirement, but had a need to drink and smoke that was both definite and infinite, went straight for the wine and cigars, judging the latter acceptable and the former good if too Hellenic, a word that Argo had never heard before.

As they continued to ride deeper into the camp, Argo thought that Slide had concluded the lecture, but apparently he had not. "Back in another place and another time, I was involved in an assassination attempt on that old bastard."

Argo could hardly believe what he was hearing. Some of his Thakenham conditioning that Hassan was near-divine and unassailable still lingered. "You personally took a shot at the Emperor? How was that possible?"

"It was a long time ago."

"But you did it?"

"Well, to tell the exact truth, I didn't fire the gun. The actual shooters were two guys called Harrelson and Lee Oswald. The plan was to kill him during a state visit to a city called Sarajevo."

"And they missed him?"

"Oh, no, they didn't miss him. In fact, it was a hell of a piece of shooting, considering the Immortals were all round him, covering him from every angle. Oswald hit him in the small of the back, and Harrelson nailed him clean with a headshot that lifted a section of his skull and blew away half of his brain in a bloody pink cloud. All in front of maybe ten thousand people. The man was dead before he hit the floor of the carriage, but then we found out that the man wasn't really Hassan."

"How was that kept quiet?

"It wasn't. Another Hassan was on television within forty-eight hours, proving that the wound had only been superficial.

Argo was mystified. First "Hellenic" and now television. "Television? What's television?"

"Something from another place that you'd best not worry about, Argo Weaver."

Slide winced and shifted in his saddle. Although he hadn't admitted it since he had smoked Hooker's opium, Argo suspected that the Mosul wound still caused him some demonic version of pain, but, pain or no pain, it did not stop Slide dropping these tantalizing hints of other worlds beyond the one they currently inhabited.

"So what should I worry about?"

"If I was you, Weaver, I'd be worrying whether Quadaron-Ahrach will be part of this display of encouragement for the troops."

Argo frowned. "Is that likely? I mean, would they really risk sending the High Zhaithan across the ocean and into a war zone? Even in Thakenham we knew that he was extremely ancient and had lived far in excess of any normal human lifespan."

"You're learning to think more like a tactician."

"And less like a bumpkin?"

Slide smiled. "I didn't say that."

"But really, he wouldn't be sent here, would he?"

"Quadaron-Ahrach isn't sent anywhere. If he comes here, it will be of his own accord and by his own decision and not because of any order from the emperor. And if he comes here, it won't be for such a mundane purpose as merely encouraging the troops for an assault on Albany, but because he senses there's a threat to his power here in the Americas, a threat of which you and I may very well be a part."

And there ended the lesson, leaving Argo with considerably more to worry about than when he'd asked his first simple question about how the Mosul camp seemed to be buzzing with rumors of Hassan's impending arrival. Worry, hunger, and sleeplessness had become Argo's constant companions since he escaped into his new life, but, bit by bit, he felt as though he was learning to deal with the three attendant miseries. He now took food and sleep when and where they presented themselves, and he attempted to counteract the nagging of worry by reminding himself, not always successfully, that the unexpected constantly lay in wait, and that for him to predict or anticipate the worst would only serve to drive himself crazy. He had managed to doze for a while on the ride to the camp, but then they had begun to encounter patrols and checkpoints, and he had been forced to remain fully awake and with his wits about him. Once more he learned the lesson of how pointless it was to dwell on possible and potential dangers. He had, for example, considered the infiltration of the Mosul camp a near impossibility, but then, out of the blue, he and Slide had stumbled across the pair of Zhaithan committing aquatic sodomy under the bridge, and their problem had been solved. His next fear had been that his impersonation of one of the Zhaithan elite would be so implausible that he and Slide would be stopped and arrested at the first roadblock, but that had been proved equally groundless as they were hastily waved through, not only by Mosul guards and military police, but even rank-and-file Zhaithan, without so much as a demand for them to show papers, passes, or authorization of any kind.

As the two of them had neared the vast area of the camp, the Virginia woods and fields that had so far been the backdrop to Argo's adventure had given way to a landscape that was more akin to a derelict tract of hell. The road they traveled had crossed the still-scorched earth of a battlefield from the combat of two years earlier, acres of ground where the subsequent growth of nettles, brambles, and incongruously bright poppies had yet to disguise the half-collapsed trenches, the shell craters, the corroded hulks of burned-out steam tanks, juggernauts, and battle wagons, and the rusted barbed-wire entanglements where the fragments of the skeletons of both men and horses, and ragged pennants of faded flags and uniforms, remained like time-defying relics. Along the same road, they encountered more modern horrors, and their horses snorted at the bloated and fly-blown bodies of men, presumably deserters, rotting on crosses and gibbets, either hung or crucified, and left on exhibition as a warning to those who still lived. Many of the decayed cadavers wore crudely painted signs around their necks. *Deserter, Defeatist, Heretic, Thief, Coward, Sodomite,* and *Spy*. He had seen and heard all of these words in Thakenham, but the last one chilled him. At the very least, he was a spy himself. The camp itself was much as Argo had expected it, with lines of drab tents and sour-faced uniformed men in constant motion, although nothing had quite prepared him for the stench and the all-pervasive mud that was being increasingly churned to the consistency of a thick and disgusting porridge by the mass of infantry and ordnance on the move. Slide and Argo were repeatedly forced to halt their horses and wait while large cannon were dragged past by a combination of men and mules, all headed in the direction of the river. The second time this had happened, Argo had glanced at Slide. "These are the final preparations, aren't they?"

And Slide had confirmed the thought with a nod. "You got that right. The guys across the Potomac better be bracing themselves."

For one who claimed he had never been in the Mosul camp before, Slide navigated unerringly, although, of course, Argo had no idea to where exactly he was navigating. They did, however, seem to be making for the higher ground, which at least meant they were leaving behind the worst of the mud. They reached a section of the camp where the bivouacs were larger and looked more comfortable and the traffic on the street was considerably less than on the thoroughfares where the guns were being moved. Slid halted and sniffed the air. "Do you smell something?"

Argo looked at him as though he was crazy. "Over all this stink?"

"Concentrate, lad."

Argo tried again. "Goats, maybe?"

Slide smiled. "That's exactly what we're looking for."

JESAMINE

Jesamine and Cordelia, swathed in long kaftans and with veils in place, followed the same route that Jesamine had taken on the two previous occasions when she had visited with T'saya, but this time they found it blocked by a Zhaithan checkpoint. "Oh, shit."

Cordelia looked at her sharply. "What?"

"I usually go up that street, but the fucking Zhaithan have it blocked off, and they're checking everyone's papers."

"But you've got the go-everywhere pass."

"But you haven't, and I don't know how well it's going to hold up for the both of us. In fact, I don't know how well it's going to hold up for me, now the Zhaithan seem to have a beef with Phaall."

"So what do we do?"

Jesamine pursed her lips in annoyance. "I guess we have to take the long way round."

"How long's the long way?"

"Long enough. You're going to get a guided tour of the Mosul military."

Cordelia sighed. "I've more than seen the Mosul military, thank you."

"Well, girl, you're going to see some more. I'm not chancing the checkpoint."

As she spoke, two mounted Zhaithan in the black and red uniforms of the elite rode up the roadblock and were waved through without having to produce identification of any kind. Cordelia felt an odd tremor pass through her, but then she was distracted by Jesamine, who spat angrily. "Bastards. With one of those uniforms you can get away with anything."

Cordelia regarded her curiously. "You hate them that much?"

Jesamine nodded. "And you'll come to hate them, too. They are extremely easy to hate when you know that your life can be snuffed out like a candle at their very whim."

Cordelia shook her head. "No, I won't learn to hate them. I won't be here that long. I'll either get out, or I'll die."

Jesamine gave her new friend a long look but said nothing. She knew Cordelia meant what she said but wondered how long her determination would last. "We'd better go. We're going to attract attention standing here like this."

The detour took them out of the officer's quarter and deep into the section of the enlisted men, where the mud was thicker and the smell was worse and they found themselves subjected to catcalls and shouted obscenities each time they passed a group of men with no underofficer to shut them up. After years in which to become accustomed to such behavior, Jesamine was able to ignore the suggestion, lewdness, and insult, but, even with her face veiled, she could see that Cordelia was stiffening with suppressed anger.

The detour also took them past the camp's main parade ground, a large open area in the approximate center of the camp that was used for mass assemblies and religious gatherings but, for the most part, was usually empty except for one or two drill formations or perhaps a group of cavalry officers playing a pickup game of polo on its flat expanse. Thus Jesamine was surprised to find—on this day that, to her, had so far seemed no different from any other—the large open square a hive of activity. Engineers, carpenters, and other specialist craftsmen were hard at work, with their efforts concentrated on two half-finished structures at either end of the field, while prisoners from the stockade, in their distinctive convict stripes, were busy with brooms and rakes cleaning the entire space.

"What the hell is going on here?"

Cordelia stopped and looked around. "This isn't usual?"

Jesamine shook her head. "The hell it is."

"Then what's going on? What are those things that they're building?"

Cordelia had pointed to the nearest construction, and that was the easy answer. "It's the Ziggurat."

"What's the Ziggurat?"

"It's . . ." Maybe not so easy. How the hell did you explain something that you had grown up with to a stranger? "It's like a pyramid, only a bit more complicated. It's a religious thing, a copy of the Great Ziggurat in the Holy City. When it's finished, the Flame will be lit at the very top. It's supposed to find favor in the eyes of Ignir and Aksura. By the look of the base, that one is going to be maybe fifty or sixty feet high and hold a lot of people in its cages, so whatever's happening here is going to be important."

Cordelia pointed to the structure at the other end of the field. "And what's that thing? It looks like some sort of stage or platform."

Jesamine hesitated. "You really want to know?"

"Of course I want to know. Why shouldn't I want to know?"

"That stage, as you call it, will be a gallows, a multiple gallows capable of hanging twenty men at once. Or twenty women."

Cordelia's face was hidden, but Jesamine could see her body grow even more rigid than it had been when the grunts had been yelling at them, and when she spoke, her voice was strained and formal. "And who are the ones to be killed?"

Jesamine could only shrug. "It hardly matters. In addition to encouraging the living to behave, mass executions are also supposed to find favor in the eyes of Ignir and Aksura, so pretty much anyone will do."

A squad of men was unloading wood from a horse-drawn wagon, but, at the sight of the two women, they stopped what they were doing and stared. An underofficer yelled at Jesamine and Cordelia. "Come on, girls, move along. Stop distracting my boys. We've got enough to do before tonight."

"What's happening tonight? Is the shooting about to start?"

"You didn't hear? Where have you girls been?"

"We've been a little busy."

The underofficer permitted himself a knowing leer. "I can imagine you have."

"So what didn't we hear?"

"That *he*'s coming."

"He?"

"Hassan is coming. May his name be blessed. So get lost, okay? We've got work to do in a hurry, or we may find ourselves on the gallows instead of just building it."

Jesamine did not have to be told to get lost. She wanted to be away from the parade ground with all haste, and Cordelia seemed to be in shock and needed to be led away equally fast. She took Cordelia by the arm and began walking away at a brisk pace. Three Mamalukes in white capes galloped across the parade ground and reined to a stop by the men building the Ziggurat. At the sound of the hoofbeats, Cordelia looked round, and Jesamine felt a sudden desperation radiating from her, and, for the first time ever, she heard fear in Cordelia's voice. "Why are they doing all this? It's horrible."

Jesamine tried to find a tone that was somewhere between stern and comforting. "It's how the Mosul ask their gods for a victory. Men will die, the Flame will burn, and . . ."

"And?"

"The whole Army of the Americas, Mosul, Mamaluke, and Teuton alike, will go completely out of its mind."

"What?"

"Listen, I don't want to talk about it. Not here. Not now. Let's get on. This makes our seeing T'saya even more crucial."

ARGO

Argo did not exactly know what he had expected, but he knew it wasn't the tilted-over wood and tarpaper shack, with the smoke rising from a tin chimney, that Slide had just pointed out as their destination. "Are you joking?"

Slide laughed from behind the chain mail mask as he urged his horse forward. "Don't judge everything by the outer appearance, boy. If I did that, would I be riding here with you?"

Even the horses seemed disconcerted as they were reined to a halt in front of the hovel with its reek of cooking and air of long-term dilapidation. They snorted and jerked their heads as though such a slum was beneath their equine dignity. Slide dismounted and looped the charger's reins over a low picket fence that surrounded an orderly, if small and sooty, vegetable patch and herb garden. Argo did the same and then followed Slide to the door of the shanty. Slide pushed the door open, revealing the space inside to be cramped and chaotic, and, in their flowing capes and tall, spiked helmets, Slide and Argo seemed to fill the place as they stepped inside and the old African woman who was its only inhabitant turned from her stove and stared at them as though they were a vision of death itself. For a moment she stood as though paralyzed, and then, in an unbelievably fast lunge, she came up with a long and wickedly sharp kitchen knife. Argo's first thought was that the woman was about to stab Slide, but then he saw that her intention was to take her own life. Slide, however, moved like lightning and grabbed her wrist. "Hold up there, old woman. All is not as you imagine."

With his free hand, he removed his helmet, and the action brought a gasp of furious recognition from the woman, followed by a furious outburst. "You bastard! You dirty demon bastard! You all but gave me a double-damned heart attack. Since when did you join the Zhaithan elite, Mr. Yancey Slide?"

"Just borrowing the clothes, Mother T'saya. My friend and I took the former owners unaware while they were making the beast."

Despite her anger, the woman called T'saya grinned. "I always told you the boys in black weren't as chaste as they liked to pretend."

"And, to our good fortune, you were proved right."

"So what did you do with the buggering bastards once you'd deprived them of their finery?"

Slide shrugged and smiled, almost coyly. "We killed them."

Argo noted that Slide had included him in the credit for the deed. T'saya nodded approvingly. "Then you're still of some use."

Slide then looked to Argo. "Take off that damned helmet and say hello to Mother T'saya, Argo Weaver. She is a great deal more than she appears."

"I'm not your mother, Yancey Slide, and I'll thank you not to address me as such."

Argo extended a hand. "I'm pleased to meet you, T'saya."

T'saya looked him up and down before she accepted his hand, but then she held it longer than would have been normal for a mere greeting. "You're Argo Weaver?"

"That's right."

She turned to Slide. "And he's one of them?"

Slide nodded. "He's one of the Four, as far as we can tell. So far he's passed every test and conformed to every prediction."

"Has he now?" T'saya sat down at her small table and reached for a bottle of deep green liquid. "I think I need a drink after your little surprise."

While T'saya recovered from her shock, Slide took the time for a moment of gourmet curiosity. He lifted the lid of a pot on the stove and sniffed the contents. "Goat?"

T'saya poured three fingers of green liquid into a glass. "Best goat this side of the ocean."

"Still hiding among the Mamalukes and doing the cooking?"

T'saya nodded. "It's worked for almost two years."

"It won't work for much longer."

"The hell you say."

Slide replaced the lid and turned to the business at hand. "You'd better make that a fast shot, old woman. We don't have much time."

"Time for what, Yancey Slide? Are we going somewhere I don't know about?"

"Things are speeding up."

T'saya sighed and shook her head. "I could be getting too old for this."

"You knew you'd have to emerge sooner or later."

"You want to tell me something, Yancey Slide? You want to tell me why every time I have dealings with you I find myself on the run?"

"Stop complaining, lady. Just look on me as the harbinger of change. Your goat business is at an end. This camp will be breaking up. They've sent in one of Hassan's doubles, so the Mosul are going across the river any day, and we have to round up the other three of the Four and hightail it to Albany ahead of them."

"What makes you think I have any intention of going to Albany? You know how I feel about Albany."

"Get over it, girl. The old king's been dead for more than two years."

"Jack Kennedy's still fit enough, though, and prime minister into the bargain."

"You loved Jack Kennedy, old woman."

"So did a lot more."

"I won't deny that."

"So maybe that's why I don't want to leave my goats and go back there."

"Albany is your only hope now. Your goats are history."

T'saya tipped back half of the glass. "I'm just a harmless old cook. My Mamalukes will protect me."

"That's bullshit, and you know it. You're back in the game, and if that hasn't been detected by the Ministry of Virtue already, it soon will be. It's Albany or the Zhaithan."

"What makes you think I'm back in the game, Yancey Slide?"

"Cut the crap, T'saya. This is Yancey you're talking to. Poor me a shot of that green, and let's get out of here."

"It'll cost you one of your cigars."

"How do you know I have cigars?"

"Are you ever without them?"

Slide reached inside his stolen tunic and handed T'saya a cigar. "I wouldn't have this if one of our departed Zhaithan hadn't been carrying a box with him in his saddlebags."

"Something always provides. Even if it's the enemy."

Slide kindled a fire at the end of his right index finger. T'saya put the cigar in her mouth and leaned forward to take a light from the flame with one eyebrow raised. "Still with the demon party tricks?"

The sound of passing riders came from outside the hut, and Argo looked round anxiously. "Shouldn't we be having this conversation on the move, instead of sitting in here?"

T'saya slowly dragged on the cigar, bringing the lighted end to glowing life. "Don't rush your elders, boy. The Zhaithan aren't coming for me yet." She poured Slide a double shot from the bottle. "So we have three of the Four accounted for, and we know they're all in this forsaken place?"

Slide lit a cigar for himself. "You've contacted the two girls?"

"I started the girl Jesamine down the path, and then she found the other one, the highborn from Albany."

Argo placed his helmet on the table, wondering if T'saya was going to offer him a drink. "The Lady Cordelia Blakeney?"

T'saya reached for a glass, filled it, and pushed it towards Argo just as though she had read his mind. In his case, though, she shook in two or three drops of an oily liquid as what he assumed was extra flavoring, something she hadn't done for either herself or Slide. "Is that her name? Well, whoever she is and whatever she is, the two girls bonded last night in the old, old manner. They may not have known it at first, and they may be having trouble accepting it right now, but they're in the place."

Slide picked up a jar of herbs, held it up, and examined the contents. "Bonded, did they? In the old manner?"

T'saya took the jar from him and put it back where he had found it. "You cannot expect better than that, now, can you, Yancey Slide?"

Slide threw back his drink in a single gulp. "And what of the fourth one, the other boy?"

T'saya refilled his glass. "He's the hard one. It seems like he's a soldier, and there are a hell of a lot of soldiers in the immediate vicinity." She gestured to Argo. "Doesn't he sense him?"

Slide took his cigar from his mouth. "Boys don't have the same mutual sensitivity. Their prejudices are too entrenched."

Argo sniffed the green liquid. It smelled foul, and, when he tentatively sipped it, the taste was as bad as the smell had promised. "So where are the girls?"

"Jesamine is the concubine of a Teuton colonel, an engineer that goes by the name of Phaall."

"Phaall?"

"Right now she's lodged in his quarters."

"So we have a Teuton colonel to contend with if we want to get to them. I hope he's fooled by these borrowed uniforms."

"You don't have to worry about Phaall. He's away in the south looking at some crashed Norse airship."

"And will the girls stay put so we can go and get them?"

T'saya puffed on her cigar. "Where would they go? If they went anywhere, they would only come here. More important than that, though, how the hell do you intend for us to cross the river? There's more than a few who've died trying."

Slide smiled the smile of a man who is one step ahead. "It's covered. I came with a squad of Albany Rangers."

"So you're working for Albany full-time?"

"Albany's the only viable ally in these times."

"And where are these top-dog cutthroats?"

"Off about some dirty dog-work of their own. We have a rendezvous point with them and boats to cross the river. That's one reason we can't afford to linger. If we miss the rendezvous, they won't wait for us."

T'saya laughed. "I recall Jack Kennedy telling me something like that. What's the other reason for all this haste?"

"You need another reason? Aside from that the Mosul assault could happen in as little as twenty-four hours?"

"I know you, Slide. I've never seen you so anxious to get away from a war."

Slide took a deep breath. "I also suspect that Quadaron-Ahrach is on his way here with this double of Hassan they're bringing in to whip up the troops."

T'saya leaned back in her chair as though she was one step ahead of Slide. "Quadaron-Ahrach will be here sooner than you think."

"You've located him?"

T'saya shook her head. "You know as well as I do that to locate Quadaron-Ahrach is to let him locate you right back. No, Yancey Slide. I know Quadaron-Ahrach is coming because Jeakqual-Ahrach is here already."

"Who's Jeakqual-Ahrach?" Argo had difficulty forming the words. He was feeling a little strange, and he could only suppose it was the drink going to his head after so little sleep. Not only did the hut seem to be filled with a haze of cigar smoke and the steam of cooking, but the haze was taking on some very peculiar and very vibrant colors. Both Slide and T'saya ignored him, however. Slide was frowning as though, for a change, there was something that he did not understand. "Why didn't I sense her?"

"Because you're a man."

"But I'm not a man."

"You are in that respect, demon."

"Who is Jeakqual-Ahrach?"

Again Slide and T'saya ignored Argo. "If the sister's here, the brother can't be far behind."

Argo repeated the question. "Who is Jeakqual-Ahrach?"

This time T'saya looked up and answered. "She is a poisoner and a torturer, a blackwitch and a bitch from hell."

Slide picked up where T'saya had left off. "She is the sister of Quadaron-Ahrach."

"She's Zhaithan? A woman is Zhaithan?"

"This woman is a very important Zhaithan."

Argo was shocked. "But a woman in the Zhaithan?"

"She's not well publicized. In fact, she's a rather well-kept secret, but that doesn't diminish either her significance or her power."

"But it goes against all that we were ever taught during the occupation. All those verses in the Yasma that they used to repeat over and over. *'You may not suffer a witch to live,'* or *'A woman will choose service or the fire, and she will hide her face from the displeasure of men.'*"

T'saya filled in a third. " *'The disobedient woman is an abomination and shall be cursed and reviled.'* "

Argo shook his head. Not only because the idea of a woman in the Zhaithan hierarchy was so alien, but because he was also having some difficulty seeing clearly. Colors were now drifting across his vision like bright clouds driven by a curling breeze. "And she is the sister of the High Zhaithan?"

Slide answered. "The rumors, such as they are, claim that Quadaron-Ahrach and Jeakqual-Ahrach have a particularly unique relationship, even in the perverse annals of human depravity."

T'saya nodded. "And you have to go to some very rarified places even to hear those rumors."

"It's said they believe they are the incarnation of the twin gods Ignir and Aksura," Slide said.

"Are they twins?"

"That has never been clear."

Some unfocused but also highly unclean pictures were attempting to form in Argo's mind. "And is she a hunchback, too?"

T'saya shook her head. "No, she isn't a hunchback, but that's about all that can be said for the elevated bitch."

Slide held up a hand, calling a halt to the discussion of Jeakqual-Ahrach. "This is not the time for a history lesson. We are wasting time. We have to get out of here."

T'saya stubbed out her half-smoked cigar and placed it carefully behind her ear. "If we have to find the fourth one, the other boy, the one that is a soldier, why can't young Weaver here start by trying to reach him?"

Slide made a motion as though it was out of the question. "His powers aren't that well developed."

Argo could feel himself drifting. "I could maybe . . ."

Although obscene hints of weird, sexually twined twins crowded the periphery of his inner eye, a figure in Mosul drab, muddy and with a rifle on his shoulder, was now in the center of Argo's vision, but before he could focus, Slide made a second dismissive gesture. "We're just wasting time."

T'saya came to Argo's rescue. "I gave him a little something."

"You did what?"

"I gave him something to ease his lack of sensitivity."

Slide's eyes bored into Argo. "You see anything, boy?"

"I . . . don't know. It's blurred. He's frightened. And he's hungry."

Slide scowled impatiently. "That narrows it down to around ninety percent of the grunts in the camp."

T'saya glared at Slide. "Give the kid a chance, damn you." She reached out and grasped Argo by the wrist, and her voice took on a singsong cadence. "Concentrate, boy. Concentrate very hard. Concentrate on the boy who is a soldier."

"I can't see him."

"Try, Argo."

"I can't see him, but . . ."

"Try."

"But he needs direction. He's lost and at a loss. I can maybe tell him a place to go, a place where we can find him. Except . . ."

"Except what?"

"Except I don't know this place. I don't know where to tell him to go."

Slide was urgent. "Tell him, woman. Quickly. Tell Weaver some easy landmark."

"The parade ground, Argo. Make him go to the parade ground."

RAPHAEL

The tin spoon halted just an inch from Raphael's mouth. He had been eating some compressed mess of meat and beans from an airtight can, hunched beside the gun that he had just helped haul to its emplacement by the river, spooning the food down as fast as he could, as though he was fearful that someone would take it away from him. For almost two hours he had slithered, strained, and sweated, moving the heavy howitzer through the mud of the camp, but at least the gunners had fed him at the end of it. Simply to fill his belly was a pure animal pleasure. He knew that the stuff from the can would weigh heavily on his guts later, and probably give him cramp and the runs, but he did not care. It seemed like a year or more since he had smelled, let alone tasted, food, and no guarantee was being offered that he would eat again any time soon. Then suddenly all thought of food and hunger ceased. The voice that sounded in his head was like a personal command from a deity.

The parade ground. I have to go the parade ground. I will find them if I go the parade ground. If I go the parade ground, I will find the Four.

Raphael slowly lowered the forgotten spoon. "What the fuck?"

He knew that he had no way to explain what had happened, and he did not waste time trying. He could not reach for so much as an implausible explanation, and the most flimsy excuses totally eluded him. He was hearing voices. That was the plain fact, and the order was so emphatic that he could not even dismiss it as a bout of madness. Madness did not come out of nowhere with such singular assurance. He glanced at the young Teuton who sat next to him eating with the same famished concentration that had been Raphael's up to a moment before. The Teuton showed no signs of having heard anything. The commanding voice was in Raphael's head alone.

The parade ground. I have to go the parade ground. I will find them if I go the parade ground. If I go the parade ground, I will find the Four.

Perhaps the strangest part was that the directive was phrased as though it came from himself. *I will go to the parade ground.* He gave the command to himself, as though two halves of his brain had divided, and one of those new telegraph lines was strung between the two halves. And what the hell was the Four? Why was the word so obviously capitalized, and why did the sound of it fill him with thrills of both excitement and fear? And why were the girls suddenly so clear in his inner eye? The one thing he did not for a moment dispute was that he would do as he was instructed. Or as he was instructing himself. He might have a thousand questions about the method of its delivery, but he had none about the order. *He would go to the parade ground.* He had deserted from Melchior's squad for no better reason than that he knew he had to find the two girls from his dreams and drawings, and now voices in his head were telling him what to do. Were the girls part of this Four? Was he? He did not know. All he knew is that he would do it. The voice was telling him to go to the parade ground, and to the parade ground he would go.

"Are you going to eat that?"

Raphael was jerked back into the world of guns, the Mosul, and meat and beans. While they been hauling the gun across the camp, he and Pascal had been separated, but now, with the task complete, they were reunited. Raphael snapped impatiently. He might be receiving messages from the devil and have a split brain, but food was food. "Yes, of course I'm going to eat it. We're starving, aren't we?"

Pascal shrugged. "You looked like you didn't want it."

Raphael shoved in two spoonfuls of meat and beans and chewed hungrily. He suspected that the meat might well be old horse or worse, but that did not bother him. Pascal was getting on his nerves. Raphael had allowed the Frank to come with him on the spur of the moment, and only because he had thought company might mitigate his fear and he believed that two of them might be less conspicuous than just him on his own, but so far the boy had proved to be little more than a vacillating burden. Maybe, of course, it was Raphael's own fault. He had not, after all, leveled with Pascal. He had led him to believe that he was deserting to save his hide and to escape the coming assault across the river, whereas in reality, if he could call it reality, he was following a wholly irrational impulse that he did not even understand himself, and, as an added plus, he was now doing the bidding of voices invisible.

"The underofficer in charge of the gun crew says that he's cutting us loose, and we're supposed to go back to our units."

Raphael scraped around in the can for the last morsels of meat and beans. "He said that?"

"What he actually said was that we could fuck off back to wherever we came from."

"And did he say what we were supposed to tell our own underofficers when they want to know why we've been missing for three or four hours and are probably posted as AWOL?"

"Some guy asked him that, and he said we should just explain what happened and there shouldn't be any trouble."

"And you believed him?"

"You don't?"

Raphael dropped the now empty can on the ground but tucked the spoon in his pocket for future use. "It's kind of easy to say. I mean, he got his bloody gun moved. That's all he cares about. He could say anything just to get rid of us."

Raphael stood up and looked around. The gun emplacement was one of about a dozen positioned along a line of low bluffs overlooking the river. The lines of Albany were less than a half mile away, and he could see the stone and concrete defensive walls, the pillboxes and blockhouses, the trenches, the lines of dragons teeth, the steel spikes sticking up from the water, and the entanglements of barbed wire. The formidable defenses forcibly brought home the reality of his situation. In what was now looking like just a few days, thousands, if not tens of thousands, of men were going to die crossing that river, and the odds were well on the side of he and Pascal being among them.

"So what do you want to do?"

Raphael picked up his rifle. It was crusted with mud from where he'd twice dropped it while moving the howitzer and probably would not fire without a good cleaning. "I don't know, boy. As deserters, we're not doing very well, are we? In fact, we're a bit of a fuckup. We managed to get away for less than an hour before we found ourselves drafted into the artillery. And now that the artillery doesn't want us any more, we have the choice of either going back and hoping that Melchior believes our story, or we start wandering aimlessly again, looking for a way out. As I see it, it doesn't constitute much of a choice."

Now Pascal was staring at the Mosul lines. "If only we could get across that fucking river."

"You think the other side are going to welcome us? They probably have a solid stream of deserters, and they probably either shoot them or throw them in a cage somewhere."

"For mercy's sake, keep it down, will you? Someone might hear."

Raphael knew that he was being unreasonable. The voice in his head had disturbed him more than he had initially realized. "Yeah, okay. I'm sorry."

"Maybe we should go back. You know what I mean?"

"I'm far from sure about throwing ourselves on Melchior's mercy."

"You've got a better idea?"

Raphael shook his head and lied. "No."

"So?"

Raphael slung his rifle over his shoulder. Maybe it had not been a lie. To go to the parade ground was hardly an idea. Just a mystery command. "Let's get out of here, seeing as how they've fed us and now they don't want us here anymore. Let's head back into camp and talk about it on the way."

Pascal still plainly leaned to the idea of going back to Melchior's mercy. "One of the gunners told me, if we were going back into the main part of the camp, we should avoid the parade ground at all costs."

"Why?" Raphael only just managed to conceal his surprise and concern. "What's happening on the parade ground?"

"There are gallows and stuff being built for the arrival of Hassan. There are going to be mass executions."

"Then we avoid the parade ground."

Again Raphael was lying to Pascal. He had no intention of going back to the squad, and he was quite determined to reach the parade ground and see if he found the Four as promised, whoever they might be. If the discovery had to be in the middle of a mass execution, that was just too damned bad. And what did it matter? In a day or so the Potomac would be blood red and the whole area a mass execution.

I will go to the parade ground.

ARGO

"The damned horses are eating my vegetables."

Slide unhitched his mount from the fence. "You won't need them again."

T'saya hefted the bundle of things she had gathered up before leaving the cook shack for the last time. "I suppose not. It's kind of hard to grasp. I suppose I never really expected to leave this place alive."

Argo tried to follow suit, but his movements were awkward and uncoordinated. He was still seeing hallucinations from the concoction of herbs and alcohol that T'saya had fed him, and, in fact, now that he and Slide had replaced their Zhaithan helmets, the distortions caused by the chain mail mask made it very hard for him to see at all. He looked at the horse, wondering how he was going to mount it. "Perhaps T'saya should ride while I walk."

T'saya looked at Argo like he was an idiot. "Now that would be really plausible, wouldn't it? A high Zhaithan walking while a slave rides. To really act out the part, you should be dragging me along manacled and with a rope around my neck. The Zhaithan don't lend their horses to old cookwomen."

Slide sighed and swung easily up into the saddle "Now I'm in the middle of the biggest enemy camp in the Americas, the heart of fucking darkness, and stuck with a heavily intoxicated teenager. Did you have to give him so much of that stuff?"

T'saya looked up at Slide as though she found his complaint completely unreasonable. "I actually gave him less than I gave Jesamine, the concubine girl. Seems the girls go in deeper but come out faster. I guess there's no accounting for the metabolism of gender."

After three tries, Argo managed to haul himself onto his horse but still swayed slightly in the saddle. Slide snorted. "He's drug-addled."

"He'll come out of it. A little danger, and the resulting adrenaline will bring him round."

"Danger is what we're trying to avoid."

T'saya sniffed contemptuously. "Like you were never drug-addled yourself, Yancey Slide?"

"Not in a situation like this."

"Oh, no? What about that time in High Barbary when we were trying to give the slip to the R'zooli, and you were fucked-up on ghat and kif?"

Slide's chain mail mask covered his face, so his expression was impossible to read. "That was different."

"How so different?"

Slide urged his horse forward. "We're wasting time. Let's stop the re-criminating and move out, shall we?"

And so they moved away from T'saya's cook shack, demon and boy riding, and the old African woman walking between them, an apparent prisoner of the two phoney Zhaithan in their stolen cloaks and helmets, making their way, as T'saya put it, "first to the bivouac of this Colonel Phaall, and then on to the parade ground to see if young Weaver's message has made it through to the other boy."

CORDELIA

The detour they had been forced to make gave Cordelia a chance to see a major portion of the Mosul camp in broad daylight, and what she saw, even excluding the horrors being prepared on the parade ground, far exceeded her worst expectations. In contrast to the comparatively civilized disposition of the Albany military, the Mosul army was a vast and chaotic convocation of only minimally ordered barbarism. In some parts of the camp, the stench of raw sewage almost caused her to gag, and she wondered how it was that cholera had not broken out months earlier. The majority of the drab rank and file looked ripe for any disease. They were unwashed, un-shaven, and shabby. Their uniforms were shoddy and threadbare, and their weapons outdated and poorly maintained. Many seemed gaunt and under-fed, and still more were the worse for drink. In complete contrast, the of-ficers and the elite units, especially the cavalry, were swaggeringly well dressed, with some still sporting archaically impractical finery from a hundred years ago: lavish gold braid, flowing fur-trimmed cloaks, silk turbans, gleaming cuirasses, absurd plumed and winged helmets in a riot of dazzling colors that would surely make them immediate targets for any Albany marksman worth the issue of his ammunition. Though Jesamine and Cordelia were veiled and shrouded in their voluminous kaftans, Cordelia could feel the two of them being constantly observed by hundreds of pairs of hungry eyes. Jesamine had told her that the Mosul grunts had their own wretched brothels on the margins of the camp, where ugly and dispirited slatterns plied their slave trade from dusk to dawn, but clearly these were not enough to keep the soldiers satisfied, because the two women still walked like moving targets for a constant dull, but hungry and resentful, lust.

Although she had worn a uniform and spent almost two years in the company of heroes, generals, and politicians, Cordelia would never have described herself as a military analyst or expert, but it was plain even to her relatively inexperienced eye that, stacked up against the backs-to-the-wall determination of Albany, or the technical ingenuity of the Norse Union, the Mosul were a desolate and demoralized horde that should have been doomed to go down in defeat. The single and overwhelming consideration that was omitted from this optimistic equation was that the Mosul had the numbers. She had no idea how many men were now quartered in the fetidly endless camp by the Potomac, but she guessed the count could be as high as a half-million fighting men, plus support and supply, and with that numerical advantage it hardly mattered if they looked like the scurvy dregs of two continents going into the fight. The Mosul could lose a hundred and fifty thousand scurvy dregs in the assault on Albany and still come out grimly triumphant. She was also left in no doubt that they were about to engage in the final preparations for that terrible assault and the vast slaughter that would go with it. She and Jesamine had to stop repeatedly and wait as cannon and steam-wheezing fighting machines were moved up to the battle lines, and the rising sense of fear and tension was palpable. Officers and NCOs seemed to be tightening the screws of a brutal control, and Cordelia knew enough to see how such brutality might be needed. The moment when the men were pushed to the front was a time when an imperial army, armed and with little hope of individual survival, was at its most vulnerable to the spark of bloody mutiny. She recalled the history lessons during her RWA training about how the Teutons, fifty years before, had turned on their own officers at the start of an assault during the winter campaign against the Russe under Joseph the Terrible. The revolt had ultimately been put down with savage force and followed by the harshest reprisals, but—in Albany, at least—the Teuton mutiny had been seen as one of the rare cracks in the iron discipline of the Mosul. She could see that every effort was being made to prevent a repeat of such a thing on the Potomac.

Cordelia, of course, knew nothing of the geography of the sprawling camp, but Jesamine proved herself wholly familiar with its tent-lined quasi-streets and muddy thoroughfares, and Cordelia followed, fully confident that her newfound friend and psychic sister not only knew the way to where this woman T'saya lived and raised her goats, but could also steer a course around the numerous roadblocks and checkpoints. To Cordelia this seemed to be a hugely excessive number, and, at each one, men were being pulled out of line at random and hustled away. She also saw a number of groups of prisoners being marched off by escorts of military police and Zhaithan. It looked to Cordelia as though some kind of mass roundup was being conducted, but, being so unfamliar with the ways of the Mosul, she had no real clue as to whether this was some special circumstance or merely an unpleasant routine. After they had passed their third group of frightened and unhappy prisoners, she decided to ask Jesamine. "Is it always like this?"

Jesamine scowled and shook her head. "There's always plenty of security, just to keep up the fear, but right now they want bodies."

"Bodies?"

"You saw the gallows."

Cordelia swallowed hard. She had been trying to forget the gallows she had seen being built on the parade ground. "But the gallows only held twenty. Surely, in a place like this, there must be that many prisoners and more being held under arrest already?"

Jesamine's smile was tired, crooked, and devoid of humor. "The gallows only takes twenty at a time, but there could be dozens of drops."

"Drops?"

"Multiples of multiple hangings."

"Dozens?"

"They could kill three or four hundred, twenty at a time. It could go on for an hour or more. Hassan is coming, don't forget. The Zhaithan want to put on a show. Thus they're rounding up all the deserters, heretics, drunks, and defeatists. They want all the undesirables they can get their hands on to make up the kill quota. The Mosul like their ritual death in big numbers."

"So what makes a man a heretic or a defeatist? What constitutes an undesirable?"

Jesamine stared at Cordelia as though she was innocent to the point of idiocy. "Being in the wrong place at the wrong time, and maybe with the wrong papers."

Cordelia felt an icy band tighten around her chest. Pride would not allow her to expose the sudden breathless fear she felt in front of Jesamine, but she wanted to whimper like a baby. "You've got papers, though. Right?"

"I've got papers that would see us through normal times, but today I'd rather not put them to the test."

"So what do we do?"

"We do what we're doing. We go the long way round so we don't get questioned, and then we see what T'saya has to say."

Eventually they found themselves in an area that seemed to be primarily occupied by a number of Mamaluke regiments. Given the Mamalukes' widespread and highly unsavory reputation, this seemed like a decidedly foolhardy route to be taking, but then Cordelia saw the collection of multicolored, penned-up and bleating goats and realized that this must be where the woman with all the essential knowledge lived and worked. "So this is it?"

Jesamine pointed to a small, sagging shack with a tin chimney. "That's it. That's where T'saya cooks for the Mamalukes."

Cordelia spoke without thinking. "It's hardly an inspiring residence for one who seems to know so much."

Jesamine treated Cordelia to yet another look that a mentor might give to a thoughtlessly dense pupil. "She's survived a very long time for someone who comprehensively flouts Zhaithan law, especially since, as a woman, and therefore already suspect, she could be denounced as a witch at any time. Cooking goat's head soup for Mamalukes may not be a particularly exotic cover, but it sure as shit seems to work."

They were almost to the shack when a young girl, skinny and perhaps no older than ten or eleven, with unkempt hair and dressed in the kind of shapeless smock issued to the most menial of serving slaves, beckoned urgently to them. "You're the courtesan girls, right?"

Jesamine clearly did not think it was the right time to dispute the terminology. "We're T'saya's friends."

"You'd better get away from here."

"What are you talking about?"

"She was lifted."

"Lifted?"

"T'saya, she was lifted. They took her away."

Cordelia saw Jesamine actually turn white. "She was arrested?"

"That's right. Arrested."

"Who took her?"

"Zhaithan. High Zhaithan. The black riders. They come. They stay for a while and then they take her with them. You have to go. You have to get out of here."

"How long ago did this happen?"

The slave girl shook her head. "I can't be seen talking to you. I've said too much already."

Jesamine's face hardened. "How long ago?"

The girl turned to get away from these obviously dangerous young women, but Jesamine grabbed her by her filthy smock and pulled her back. "Tell me how long ago the Zhaithan were here, or by the Twins, girl, I'll beat it out of you. And I'm a concubine woman, so you better believe I know how to give a beating."

The slave girl's eyes became as wide as saucers. "Please, lady, I can't . . ."

"Oh, yes, you can. Now, how long?"

"Not long. Maybe a half hour. Maybe twenty minutes."

"And the black horsemen took her?"

"Yes, the black horsemen. Please let me go."

Jesamine let go her grip on the girl's shift, and she scuttled away. Cordelia took a deep breath. "This is bad, right?"

Jesamine looked slowly around as though she expected other Zhaithan to be lurking. "It's definitely not good."

"So what do we do?"

Jesamine sighed. It was the sigh of one who was always being asked what to do and always being expected to make the decisions. Cordelia felt a pang of unaccustomed guilt. She would have liked to be decisive, but she was a stranger and knew very little. So she was ignorant of the ways of the Mosul—what did Jesamine expect? Cordelia had only been their prisoner for a matter of days. She did not like the way it made her dependent on

Jesamine, but there was nothing she could do about it. Finally, Jesamine helplessly spread her hands. "We have to get back to Phaall's and lay low, at least until another option presents itself. That's all I can think of right now."

"I thought Phaall's was the place we were running from."

Jesamine was growing irritable. "Didn't they ever teach you in Albany that flexibility is the key? It's a slim hope, but if we go back to Phaall's, we're on Teuton turf and that might afford a bit of protection. Maybe we can use these new powers of ours to figure out a means of escape." Cordelia saw Jesamine have a visible idea. "Wait here and keep watch. I'm going to look for something inside the shack."

"Is that wise?"

"If I can find what I'm looking for, it might improve the odds."

"Suppose someone sees you?"

"That's why you're keeping watch. Lean against the shack and try and look casual. If anyone comes, kick the wall behind you. They're so thin, I'll hear you immediately."

With that, she slipped through the unlocked door and disappeared inside. Cordelia leaned against the wall and tried to appear as inconspicuous as possible. A troop of Mamaluke lancers rode past in white capes and winged helmets. From their posture she could tell that they were tired and had ridden a long way. Their capes were dusty, and the plumes on their helmets drooped, and although one of them whistled at her, the majority showed no interest. By the time they were past, Jesamine was out of the shack with a bottle of green liquid that she quickly hid under her kaftan. "That was weird."

"What was weird?"

"The place hasn't been touched. Usually when the Zhaithan arrest someone in their own home, they search the place and smash everything in the process. The shack was exactly as it was the last time I visited her. A cooking pot was still on the stove, and all that anyone had done was to douse the fire."

"Theory?"

Jesamine shook her head. "It beats me."

"So back to Phaall's?"

"Back to Phaall's."

"The long way round again?"

Jesamine grimaced. "You want to go past the cursed parade ground again?"

That was the last thing that Cordelia wanted. As far as she was concerned, the parade ground was the epicenter of all the horror that was choking the Mosul camp like some psychic miasma. "Not in the least."

"Then let's take a look at the roadblock. I mean, we're on our way home. They might just accept our pass and wave us through."

Cordelia and Jesamine walked in silence until they were within about a hundred feet of the checkpoint, and then Jesamine stopped, half turned, and pretended to be removing some imaginary smut from her kaftan. Cordelia played along and helped her. The checkpoint was manned by just two regular military policeman in drab olive uniforms and their distinctive orange helmets. They were checking passes and inspecting soldiers' dog tags, but without any special show of zeal or enthusiasm, and no one was pulled out of line while the two women watched. Mercifully, no suspiciously supervising Zhaithan were in attendance. "I think we might take a chance on it. It all looks pretty lax."

Cordelia had misgivings, but she followed Jesamine anyway. The traffic though the checkpoint was reasonably heavy, and, as the girls had observed from a distance, the MPs were slack to the point of casual in the way they were carrying out their inspections. They waited in a line of assorted pedestrians for two or three minutes, until it was their turn to be scrutinized. One of the MPs looked them up and down, pleased for the diversion of two good-looking women, although they were so totally swathed that Cordelia wasn't sure how the man could tell. "And where are you girls going?"

"We're the property of Colonel Phaall, and we're on our way back to his quarters."

The MP leered. "So the Colonel gets two of you, does he?"

Jesamine placed a hand on her hip, tightening the fabric of the kaftan so her shape was more overtly visible. "The officers get it all, don't they?"

The MP nodded. "Now that's the truth, girl, and no mistake."

Unfortunately, Jesamine's ploy of showing her form had also revealed the form of the bottle, and the MP's eyes went straight to it. He obviously saw the chance for a piece of alcoholic contraband that might be negotiated down to his own personal loot. "Now, what you got there, dearie?"

Jesamine instantly became coy and girlish. "Just a bottle, sir."

"Out with it, girl."

"It's just a bottle of cheap 'shine."

The MP became more belligerent. "I said out with it."

Jesamine reluctantly pulled out the bottle she had brought from T'saya's cook shack. The MP took it from her, held it up to the light, and then removed the cork and sniffed the contents. "This doesn't look like any 'shine I ever saw."

"There's just some herbs and stuff in it."

The MP sniffed again. "Smells like a psychedelic to me." He passed the bottle to his companion. "Doesn't that smell like a psychedelic to you?"

The second MP sniffed and frowned. "Sure smells like something."

Cordelia knew they were in trouble. What the hell had Jesamine brought the damned bottle for anyway? Was it the psychedelic with which T'saya had induced her visions? Jesamine tried to be even more girlish. "You boys could just take it as a gift and check it out for yourselves."

For a moment, it seemed as though the ploy was going to work. The two MPs exchanged glances. For a moment they were both on the fence, undecided, and then the first flopped on the side of by-the-book duty. "Sorry, girls. I don't know what the hell this stuff is, and I can't take a chance. I could let a bottle of 'shine slide, but this shit's weird."

Jesamine tried not to sound completely desperate. "It's just 'shine with flavoring. It's the new thing among the Mosul. Seemingly they picked up the taste in Italia."

"Italia? Now I know you're shitting me."

"I swear."

The first MP's face hardened, and he shook his head. "This is going to have to be booted up to the Ministry. I've got to look out for my own ass."

A crudely wired telegraph was mounted on a post by the checkpoint. It was one of the kind that did not even send words or code but simply rang an electric bell somewhere else by way of an alert. One of the MPs cranked the handle. "You girls are going to have to wait until the Ministry men get here and see what they think about all this."

While the guards were at the telegraph. Cordelia stood close and whispered quickly to Jesamine. "What does this mean?"

"It means we're fucking fried."

The telegraph-summoned Zhaithan took a full half hour to arrive, and, in that time, Cordelia lost count of the times that she had considered simply running but had then looked again at the MPs' breechloaders and calculated how far she might get before she took a bullet in the back. The two Zhaithan who finally showed were definitely not elite. No black horsemen, these. They wore the red-trimmed black tunics, but they lacked the capes, the spiked and turban-swathed helmets, and had no sheathed ceremonial daggers on their belts. They did carry fairly modern carbines over their shoulders, however, and one had a swagger stick under his arm, while both showed at least the start of the sinister Zhaithan arrogance. A part of this arrogance manifested itself as an unwillingness to talk to Cordelia and Jesamine directly. Instead, while the second MP, with his breechloader now unslung, watched the girls, the Zhaithan and the first MP stood off at a distance, examining the bottle and Jesamine's pass and presumably discussing the contents of the former and the validity of the latter. Finally the conversation appeared to be complete, and the Zhaithan approached the girls.

"Names?"

"Jesamine."

"Cordelia."

"Status?

"Concubine."

"Concubine."

"Owner?"

"Colonel Phaall, 4th Teuton Engineers."

"Colonel Phaall, 4th Teuton Engineers."

"He owns both of you?"

This time Jesamine made no joke, and the Zhaithan who was doing the talking continued. "The bottle found on you is suspected of being a proscribed psychotropic, the use of which constitutes heresy. Thus you are detained on suspicion of wanton psychedelia, necromancy, and wandering abroad. You will come with us." He turned to the MPs. "Shackle them."

As the MPs snapped on the indicated shackles that the Zhaithan had thoughtfully brought with them, Cordelia felt sick, numb, momentarily mindless. Again she whispered urgently to Jesamine. "Has this made us part of the show on the gallows?"

The Zhaithan who had done the talking heard her and struck her sharply across the shoulders with his cane. "Keep your mouth shut, whore. You'll be told when to talk."

SIX

𝔳

ARGO

The sound of drums consumed the whole of the vast Mosul camp, and at regular intervals strange ululations split the air. Formations of men were marched into place. Lines of lurid torches burned, and black flags with the red flame device fluttered on the night wind that blew from off the sluggishly moving river. Massed ranks of Mosul, Mamaluke, and Teutons, buttoned, burnished, and shined in their best dress uniforms, formed the human demarcation of a central avenue by which Hassan IX, or, if Yancey Slide was to be believed, the man who was supposed to be Hassan IX but wasn't, would enter from the south end of the camp, cross the parade ground, and proceed to the special and sumptuous pavilion that had been erected and prepared for him, and to the podium in front from which he would address—or at least show himself to—the mustered assembly of his military might in the Americas. To one side of this processional approach route stood the tall and now fully completed Ziggurat, with its soon-to-be-incinerated human sacrifices already chained in place, while, on the other, stood the gallows, its platform so far empty but with more than enough condemned waiting below, in the shadows of the scaffold, to put on a show.

The entry of their lord and emperor was being deliberately promoted to impress, and no device of grand, open-air theatre was being spared in the effort to convince the massed legions of the Mosul Empire that the presence of Hassan in their midst, even though Yancey Slide might condemn him as a double, was nothing short of a guarantee of victory and their ultimate domination of the Americas. The immoderate display might seem excessive to an outsider, but this was a culture had been co-opted by military regimentation and a military religion and totally distorted to serve only their specific purposes. The precise lines and coordinated curves of the close order drill squads with the flaming, smoking torches, directed by the unmistakable parade ground scream of Mamaluke underofficers, set the mood of a powerful, harnessed atavism, and, when the Ziggurat was finally torched, it would be totally clear that while Hassan IX might head an empire, whether he headed a civilization was highly debatable. The Mamalukes provided the spearhead for the lavish martial spectacle. First came the braying trumpeters, the precision torchbearers, and the supertall infantrymen who carried the burning lion standards and the red, green, and gold ensigns of their crack divisions. They were followed by the cream of the Mosul Old Guard in dress green and conical sheepskin *marfouds,* performing a slow goose step with fixed bayonets and rigid spines. The Old Guard did not have the height of the Mamaluke infantry, but they were, at the very least, equal in their unswerving and unquestioning determination.

It was left to the cavalry to bring both pomp and dash to the already implacable circumstance. First the Teuton *uhlans,* with their heavy chargers nodding and high-stepping, their plumed shakos bobbing, and their drawn sabers gleaming, held at a uniformly perfect vertical, followed the Old Guard at a reined-in walk. The Mamaluke lancers that came next swirled their pristine capes and kept their mounts in careful check as some seemed willing to spook at the pair of lumbering, steam-driven battle tanks that entered the parade ground immediately behind them. The tanks caused something of a lull in the ceremonial entry of the emperor. The unwieldy machines took a few minutes to maneuver on their huge, iron-spiked wheels into their designated places beside the reviewing podium from which Hassan would face his army, display himself to them in his armored glory and reaffirm the time-honored promise of hallowed butchery and sanctioned pillage. These mechanical steamers had to reverse and then grind forward a number of times until they stood positioned, not only for maximum effect but also so their side-mounted gun turrets commanded a wide killing ground should the need and eventuality for defensive slaughter arise.

Hassan's Immortals entered with the full knowledge that they and they alone were the cream of the elite, the life-guards of the sovereign. The horsemen were all well over six feet tall, and their grey mounts were all bred from the same bloodline. Huge, gold-plated scimitars glittered in the firelight, and the pounding of the mounted kettle drummers, with lionskins over their uniforms, forced the rhythm of urgency onto all the other drums throughout the camp. Compared to the precise geometry of the Teuton riders and the more flamboyant prancing of the Mamalukes, the Immortals were close to disorderly. Their skill as both swordsmen and horsemen was unquestionable, but their concept of formation was free-form and fluid. They would move in and out of each other's paths, deftly spinning their sabers as they swerved and maneuvered. They would trot forward and then halt and hold back. Their constant and seemingly random configurations made no sense until Argo took into account that Hassan himself rode in the middle of them. The wide, whirling blades and the complete unpredictability of those who surrounded him made any kind of organized attack very difficult. Argo recalled the story that Slide had told of the two assassins Harrelson and Oswald. The Immortals were a constant distraction around their lord that would confound any lone marksman or team of assassins, and they allowed no visible vulnerability to remain open to a sudden and surprise attack.

At the focus of all this protection, Hassan sat calmly astride his own mount, a tall, thoroughbred Uzbekian that was black as night, but he was hard to see with any clarity considering that he was, right then, the center of attention for close to a quarter of a million armed men, and, in a broader sense, the absolute ruler of most of the known world. By all expectations he should have dominated the vast gathering, but, in reality, he remained hidden. In the brief glimpses Argo had between the effective interference of the flashing swords and the deliberately milling Immortals who wielded them, he could see that Hassan, or his double, was a very tall, very slender figure arrayed in surprisingly unadorned but mirror-polished full-body black armor and an almost all-concealing cape with a flame design running up from the hem. The only concession to Hassan's imperial power was a cold coronet of stylized flames that circled the brow of his gleaming black helmet. He rode like a man no older than forty, and, for Argo, this made Slide's contention that he was a substituted double far easier to believe. Even in Thakenham, they knew that Hassan IX was not a young man.

Every so often, the darkly shining figure would nod or slowly raise a hand. The gesture was not that of one who was happy to be among his warriors, it was simply the acknowledgment that his power was being duly recognized. This seemed enough, however, to drive his followers into a frenzy, and a cry of baying welcome went up from the legions.

"Urah!"
"Urah!"
"Urah!"
"Urah!"

The guttural but coordinated shout did not remain confined to the parade ground, but rapidly spread to all other parts of the camp. Argo could scarcely repress a shudder. The drumming and the shouting were transcending the routine horror and day-to-day tyranny of the Mosul and tapping into what felt like a reserve of primitive dread, a place of ancient darkness where fountains of old and primal evil could still be tapped and used. Argo's newly developed senses could detect a rumbling from somewhere deep in the earth, as though the long dead of previous battles were actually moving. A wordless terror wormed through his nervous system, and he knew that he was being pushed towards the brink of an unreasoning panic with no newly learned skill to resist or counter the fear. Then Slide laid a steadying hand upon his shoulder. "Easy now, Weaver. It's just the Zhaithan rattling their oldest magick and delving for the primordial warrior frenzy. Don't let it get to you. It's largely an illusion."

"Urah!"
"Urah!"
"Urah!"
"Urah!"

When T'saya had, on the spur of the moment, designated the parade ground as an easy rendezvous point for the as yet unknown and unnamed boy who was the last of the Four, it had been a unknowing but grievous error. The parade ground had just seemed a large and obvious landmark that even a raw recruit could find. None of them had known that Hassan would be reviewing his troops in martial ceremony the same night in the selfsame location, and Argo could easily have started believing that the arrival of Hassan IX, real or fake, had caused some invisible miasma of foul fortune to settle on the camp, because from that point on, nothing had gone as they had hoped. They had made their way to Phaall's quarters, with T'saya walking between the horses while Slide and Argo rode, still unchallenged in their High Zhaithan disguises, but they had found no sign of the concubine Jesamine or the Lady Blakeney. They had attempted to question soldiers and servants in the vicinity, but these underlings' mortal fear of the two supposed priests-militant prevented any but the most vague and nebulous information from being forthcoming. The most the three of them had been able to learn was that the two women had left Phaall's quarters a few hours earlier, dressed and veiled for the outside world. At that point Slide, T'saya, and Argo were faced with a choice. T'saya had suggested that perhaps the two women had gone to see her, and their paths had unknowingly crossed. Slide conceded that had a certain logic but was unwilling to backtrack. "When they find you gone, they might wait for a while, but they'll be nervous and wanting to keep on the move."

T'saya nodded. "Then we should continue to the parade ground and see if you, Weaver, can find the other boy in the midst of all the ugly hoopla that's going to be building there with the setting of the sun."

Right then, Argo had offered to see if he could sense the two girls, but again he could find no trace of them. T'saya had made disparaging noises at the inadequacy of male inner vision, but Slide had surprisingly sprung to his defense. "When the time comes, he'll do what's needed of him. Don't blame him that your two floozies couldn't stay put in one place."

T'saya had not taken this well. "Expecting him to find one needle in a haystack instead of two? And what about us? Two High Zhaithans and an old African cook? Maybe moving through the streets we can get away with this implausible charade, but anywhere near the parade ground? I don't think so. We look about as fucking believable as two wolves and a fat rabbit taking a stroll."

"Then we're going to have to do something to change your appearance somehow, aren't we?"

Disguising T'saya had been less of a problem than Argo might have imagined, and Slide had demonstrated a clear-thinking skill for improvisation. He had obtained a long, hooded Mosul infantry rain slicker by the simple act demanding that a soldier who had one tied over his rucksack should give it up. He had obtained one of the round cooking-pot helmets by the same method. "You see? No matter how bizarre the order, no one questions a Zhaithan."

Covered in the voluminous and shapeless slicker, hood up, helmet down over her eyes, and a carbine slung from her shoulder that had previously belonged to the Zhaithan whose horse Slide now rode, T'saya would pass all but the most close of scrutinies. She now looked like some tagalong servant of the equally disguised Slide and Argo rather than a prisoner, and although she had been less than pleased with the basic premise of the charade, she could offer no alternative solution, so that was how they made their way to the edge of the parade ground in time for the grand entry of Hassan IX.

"Urah!"
"Urah!"
"Urah!"
"Urah!"

At a slow and stately pace, Hassan and his Immortals proceeded across the parade ground to the podium upon which the emperor would exhibit himself. Even before they reached the raised structure, the Immortals were already dropping from their saddles, ready to ensure that their lord could mount the steps that led up to the platform in complete safety. The horses all moved to one side of the dais, and for a moment, Hassan remained the only mounted figure. He seemed to hesitate before finally swinging down from his charger with a lofty flourish of his dark cape. For some moments, he had sat, hands down, loosely holding the reins, and then slowly turned his head, taking in the men and the horses, the flames, the weapons and armor, both real and ceremonial. The movement was birdlike, albeit a pow-

erful and confident bird of prey, and Argo tried to picture what such a man
could be thinking, because somewhere, beyond all the power and ceremony, a man, if only to a minimal degree, had still to exist. Argo, however, was at a loss to imagine what could be possibly be going on in the
mind of such a figure, be he emperor or arranged impostor. How did it
feel to command such an array, to have men barking their fealty and willing to kill and die for you? Could any shred of common humanity be retained under such circumstances, or was the temptation to believe in one's
own divinity simply too seductive? Had Argo been older, wiser, or more
well versed in the ways of his newfound perceptive crafts, he might have
recognized the thought as the germ of dangerous temptation, the infiltration of a similar destructive seduction, but Argo Weaver was, at that point,
none of those things, so he merely contemplated what it might be like to
rule so absolutely.

"*Urah!*"
"*Urah!*"
"*Urah!*"
"*Urah!*"

Still flamboyantly protected by the Immortals, Hassan IX mounted the reviewing stand, and, as he crossed to the central and focal position, batteries of electric arc lights came on, bathing the dais in dazzling, blue-white
light. This was the first time that Argo could remember seeing electric
light in such massed intensity, and he shared the common gasp of awe that
it brought from the assembled troops. The light was reflected from the
mirror-polished surface of the emperor's armor to further enhance the illusion that he was near to a god incarnate, and Argo marveled that electricity, this most modern of inventions, should be used for a show that
appealed to all that was base, barbaric, and superstitious among the watchers. As Hassan IX raised his arms in salute, a second drama commenced on
the parade ground's second platform, the stage of the death, the multiple
gallows that would for so many that night be the stepping-off point from
this world into the undecided possibility of the next. In the dimmer, more
hellish light of high iron braziers and banks of burning torches, prisoners
in the loose paper shifts of condemned heretics, with ropes already around

their necks, were run onto the scaffold by impatient guards who acted as though they had a quota to meet, and indeed they might. Argo had no idea of the exact mechanics of a Mosul mass execution, but he could well appreciate that it was probably conducted according to some formula of frantic and grisly efficiency. The ropes around the victims' necks were attached to iron hooks bolted to the underside of the gallows' long, rectangular crosspiece. With blows and curses, they were forced into the approximation of a line, catches were sprung, traps opened, and bodies dropped into physical space and mortal infinity and were then cut down like so many sides of beef by crews in among the supports beneath the platform to make room for the next collective drop. As Hassan or his double posed and postured and men and women died twenty at a time, the roar of the troops picked up time to faster, double cadence.

"Urah-urah!"
"Urah-urah!"
"Urah-urah!"
"Urah-urah!"

Again Slide put a hand on Argo's shoulder. "Go past all this. This is just the facade of evil. Go past it and see if you can detect the other boy."

A second line of bodies fell through the traps of the gallows, and the woodwork audibly groaned under the strain of so much deadweight. Argo shook his head. "I don't think I can."

"See through it, Argo Weaver. They have steamships and the telegraph, but what they are resorting to here is nothing short of human sacrifice. Most of the time, I bother very little with what human beings choose to do to each other, but this is a little too primitively bestial even for me."

Argo stretched his concentration and new perception to what felt like its limits, but he could only look anguished and shake his head. "Nothing. I sense nothing. There's nothing here but fire and electricity and death."

"Urah-urah!"
"Urah-urah!"
"Urah-urah!"
"Urah-urah!"

RAPHAEL

The underofficer was yelling at the top of his lungs. "No need to push, there's plenty for everyone!"

The crowd of men, however, paid him absolutely no heed. They pushed and shoved and even threw punches to gain a place closer to the carts from which the loaves of dark bread, the hard sausage, and the jugs of cheap wine and Teuton beer were being handed out on a first-come, first-served basis. Men who, in some cases, had hardly eaten for days, and other men who had been drunk equally as long, were suddenly facing a crude feast but discovering that they were going to have to fight for it. A mule that had hauled in one of the carts spooked at all the shouting, kicking, and gouging men and lashed out with its hind hooves. A cart had turned over in the violent ebb and flow of confusion, and now Mosul, Teuton, and Provincial Levies were rolling on the ground and slithering in the camp mud for tainted beer and a dirty loaf while all around a whole army howled in orchestrated dementia.

"Urah-urah!"
"Urah-urah!"
"Urah-urah!"
"Urah-urah!"

Raphael was hungry, but he stood back from the bloody and rapidly regressing scrimmage as though a part of him would go no further. Some final portion of his humanity was in revolt. Oh, yes, he had been through their basic training. He had been beaten, brutalized, humiliated, and taught to respond like a machine. He had ridden on their troopships and their trucks, and he had seen their Dark Things from Other Places move past in horrific formation while the Mothmen fluttered above. He was even willing to go to his death in one of their human waves, but he was not going to be turned into an animal by Hassan IX and his braying legions. A short Mosul, built like a brick, shouldered past Raphael with a loaf of bread clutched to his chest like a Frankish football. The man's eyes were glazed, revealing a mind that had vacated all else in favor of feral rage. In that instant, Raphael realized that the final sacrifice required by Hassan's empire and its flame banners was the surrender to a blind combat madness. They could break his bloody body, but Raphael Vega was not going to give up his mind. Enough was enough, and he had reached the point of enough.

"Urah-urah!"
"Urah-urah!"
"Urah-urah!"
"Urah-urah!"

Pascal was long gone, stumbling and struggling somewhere in the mud, as mad as any Mosul, and had Raphael not been standing alone, apparently the only man who remained in the camp who was prepared to wrestle back his sanity, he would not have seen the two girls. The previous night, they had been free and seductive; now they were captives and nothing short of wretched and terrified. They rode in a motorized tumbrel of the Zhaithan with a dozen other prisoners and four guards armed with fixed bayonets. Their hands were locked into steel cuffs, and their veils torn away to reveal their faces. No mistake was possible, and, for an instant, he believed that he locked eyes with the red-headed girl, causing a frown of puzzled and unreal recognition to cross her unhappy and frightened face. Raphael's first thought was that the two were being taken to the gallows on the parade ground, but they had no ropes around their necks, and the tumbrel was headed in entirely the wrong direction. In a flash he realized that the tumbrel's destination was the Bunker. Raphael might have been new to the camp, but he had already heard about the Bunker. The Bunker was the name given by the rank and file to the Ministry of Virtue headquarters by the Potomac. It had earned the title partly by the fact that it was one of the few permanent brick and cement structures in the camp and also because its grim vaults and corridors were reputed to extend far under the ground. The Bunker was a place of fear, with tales of torture and human experimentation that had even seasoned veterans swivelling their eyes to find another place to look as they passed by the squat, square edifice, but Raphael knew he had no option but to follow. Somehow he had to achieve the impossible and free the women of his dreams from the clutches of the Zhaithan, and, with no clear idea of exactly how he was going to accomplish such an impossibility, he settled his breechloader more comfortably on his shoulder and quickly followed as the camp roared on.

"Urah-urah!"
"Urah-urah!"
"Urah-urah!"
"Urah-urah!"

CORDELIA

If any consolation at all could be gleaned from entering the headquarters of the Ministry of Virtue, it was that they were way from the howling soldiers and the madness in the camp outside. Not that the Bunker was not consumed by its own insanity. The upper levels came with the complete stamping, shouting chaos of institutional panic. What could only be described as the stage manager of the mass executions taking place on the parade ground, a slight and very verbal Zhaithan superintendent in a scarlet cape, and with a leaning to hysteria, was short of victims and screaming like an impresario under stress. Outside was a traffic of motorized tumbrels and carts pulled by mules filled with the recently arrested coming in and the condemned going out, and the lethal stage manager was hysterically attempting to cut the turnaround time in half. No sooner were Cordelia and Jesamine pushed into the echoing expanse of the very first, ground-level, raw-concrete booking area than he pointed at the entire group of which they were two parts and screamed at the regular army Mosul guards, who, with their muskets and fixed bayonets, were providing most of the threat and muscle for the increasingly chaotic process.

"Three minutes to get that new bunch stripped down, roped up, dressed up, and out to the parade ground. Three minutes and no longer, you hear me?"

A Zhaithan records officer in black trimmed with blue looked up. "You can't send them straight out with no paperwork. How the hell do you think we're going to turn in an accurate death roll?"

This only forced the scarlet superintendent's blood pressure higher. "Sodomize the paperwork, you retard. Just get them out of here. Hang and burn the quota, fake the paperwork, and let the Twins sort out the sinners."

Even in Albany they knew about the Bunker. The Bunker was where spies from Royal Military Intelligence ended their days, a pistol shot in the back of the head if they were lucky. It was where the resistance fighters from the Blue Ridge and the Appalachian partisans were brought and interrogated until they gave up the location of their camps, or they gave up their lives. Cordelia moved in a daze and the unsupported belief that this simply could not be happening to her. The combination of the two kept her just a fraction away from the brink of wordless, screaming terror. She was a lady of Albany, and they would not see her crack, even at the end. She kept telling herself that Lady Cordelia Blakeney surely had a more elevated destiny than ending her days as part of a heathen death spectacle. That kind of horror happened to other people. As she had been coming in, she had caught a fleeting glimpse of a prisoner who looked like a battered and bloody Phelan Mallory on his way out with a rope around his neck. She could not be fully sure it was him and far preferred to imagine that she had been mistaken. That kind of horror might happen to other people, but when one of the other people in question was revealed as a recent lover, it made the idea much harder to believe.

At the same time as the superintendent and the records officer were arguing the fate, or at least the imminence of the fate, of the new intake of prisoners, two Zhaithan in plain black, but with an air of command that could counter anything in the place, even the scarlet superintendent, were carefully and methodically inspecting all the female prisoners who were being brought in. All were swiftly dismissed and consigned to their fate until the two halted in front of Cordelia and Jesamine.

"Names?"

"Jesamine."

"Cordelia."

"Status?"

"Concubine."

"Concubine."

"Owner?"

"Colonel Phaall, 4th Teuton Engineers."

"Colonel Phaall, 4th Teuton Engineers."

The recitation would soon become a mantra. The black Zhaithan nodded and turned to their armed escort of six regulars. "Pull these two out of line and take them to Basement One."

The Mosul moved to haul the two women out of the line, but the scarlet superintendent immediately protested. "What the hell are you doing with those two? I need every flammable body I can get."

One of the black Zhaithan directed a chill gaze in the man's direction, as though he was noticing him for the first time. "These two are Category A detainees."

The scarlet superintendent's eyes widened, and he deflated considerably. "I didn't know."

"Well, you do now."

The Zhaithan motioned impatiently to the regulars, who had paused to see the outcome of the priestly dispute. "Basement One, and the Twins help you if they don't remain anything but perfectly intact."

Apparently the Lady Cordelia was neither for hanging nor burning just yet, and what might be in store instead was excluded from her thoughts as far as that was possible, as was the speculation on how exactly one qualified as a Category A detainee. She shunned speculation, knowing it was not the coward who died a thousand times but the poor bastard with an overactive imagination. They pushed her and Jesamine across the booking area and down a flight of concrete steps with muskets pressed against their backs. Cordelia's kaftan was torn and dragging. It kept threatening to trip her, and she had trouble keeping her feet. In her dogged concentration on the small, moment-by-moment challenges, she began to believe that she might be okay if she could remain standing, and, indeed, maybe more by luck than agility, she made it to the bottom of the steps without falling and found herself in a long, grey, electrically lit corridor with blank cement walls the color of chronic depression. A dozen or more women, all give-or-take young, and equally give-or-take pretty, in various states of torn and abused disarray, stood along the walls, strictly positioned some eight or nine feet apart to make conversation difficult. Seemingly, no chances were being taken with Category A detainees. Each one was assigned a Mosul guard of her own who stood facing her, standing straight against the opposite wall of the corridor, weapon at the ready. For a long time, their only function seemed to be to wait and be afraid. The black Zhaithan had positioned themselves at the end of the corridor, and they, too, waited. Waiting looked to be a major occupation in the religion of Ignir and Aksura.

"*Cordelia?*"

The word came out of nowhere, simultaneously as a whisper in her ear and a shimmer of soft light in her inner vision.

"Cordelia, can you hear me?"

Cordelia concentrated hard. Could the linkage that had been achieved during the act of passion be duplicated in the this long and narrow, tomb-grey anteroom to the Lady-only-knew-what, under the eyes of armed and hostile men? *"Jesamine, I can hear you."*

"Can you respond without speaking?"

Cordelia cursed inwardly. Jesamine's question revealed that she was not hearing her. How could they hope to mesh in this Goddessforsaken underground vault? *"I'm trying as hard as I can. Why can I hear you, and you can't hear me?"*

"Cordelia?"

Was this their first voluntarily induced contact? Cordelia was never to know. At that moment, the black Zhaithan stiffened and formally turned, facing inwards to the stairs. At the same time, one of them barked an order to the occupants of the corridor. "Guards to attention! Prisoners stand straight. Prepare to look upon Her Grand Eminence Jeakqual-Ahrach."

ARGO

Torches were being set to the Ziggurat. The chant of the crowd once again doubled its tempo.

"Urah-urah! Urah-urahha!"
"Urah-urah! Urah-urahha!"
"Urah-urah! Urah-urahha!"
"Urah-urah! Urah-urahha!"

The complex structure of the wooden pyramid that was going to be incinerated to laud, honor, and glorify the Twin Deities Ignir and Aksura was honeycombed with cramped cages, openwork wooden cells the largest of which contained five unfortunate victims and the smallest just a single crouched and lonely sacrifice. All would shortly be burned alive, just as Gaila Ford had been burned alive in Thakenham, an event that, to Argo, now seemed like a thousand years ago. Prior to the formal ignition of the fire, the electric lights that illuminated the reviewing platform had been dimmed. Argo had expected Hassan or his double to make some kind of stirring speech that would inspire his troops to do and die, but that was not the way of the Mosul. It was enough that Hassan should appear before them. He uttered no more than a few dozen words, in a firm but somewhat singsong baritone, but they seemed to be enough.

"Warriors of the Mosul, my brothers, behold us and let all men tremble because we are once more gathered for the Invocation for Victory. We stand on the edge of this wide river, in the shadow of those victories that belonged to our fathers when they marched from the Indus to Hispania with the Holy Twins going on before them, when they marched over the dead of their enemies and the fallen unbelievers to build an empire like the world had never before seen and that would make all who beheld shiver at its terrible majesty. We have now brought that same majesty and the same will to conquest to a new world, and, like the old world, it will fall to the might of our arms. Warriors of the Mosul, my brothers, we have gathered for the Invocation for Victory. In the sure and certain knowledge of the greatness of the victory soon to be ours, let the hallowed flames of the all-powerful Ignir and Aksura at this time be kindled, and let all our enemies fall back in fear from its dread illumination. Warriors of the Mosul, my brothers, behold us and let all men tremble."

An honor guard of Zhaithan elite bearing flaming torches marched to the Ziggurat, and as the lights dimmed on the reviewing platform, a halt and hunchbacked figure in a plain hooded cape, aided in his walking by two Zhaithan attendants, had moved to stand beside the emperor. When Hassan had taken the stage, Slide and Argo had dismounted from their horses and stood with T'saya way back on the edge of the crowd, the two phoney priests holding the reins of their mounts. At the appearance of the hunchback, T'saya and Slide had exchanged ominous glances, and Argo had to ask. "Is that . . .?"

Slide quickly cut him off. "Don't say his name. Now that you can actually see the monster, and he can see you, don't, for any reason, say his name."

The quietly ominous arrival of Quadaron-Ahrach from out of the darkness had caused a hush to fall over the crowd that was little short of uncanny.

The figure of the man might be close to invisible in the gloom, but the awe and fear that greeted his coming said a million times more than any physical impression. Then the honor guard applied the first torches to the wood at the base of the Ziggurat, and a new and even more hideous roar broke out. What had once been mere baying became a violent shrieking and stamping.

"Urah-urah! Urah-urahha!"
"Urah-urah! Urah-urahha!"
"Urah-urah! Urah-urahha!"
"Urah-urah! Urah-urahha!"

The first flames were insignificant, almost harmless, but with the wood of the structure soaked in tar and kerosene, it spread like an angry, all-living, all-consuming totality, horizontally around the base but with tongues of exploratory fire leaping vertically to the higher levels, first following the geometry of the supports and the cross beams but then blossoming into the free-form patterns of rapidly soaring conflagration. Black smoke rose and swooped in the night wind off the river, causing the human sacrifices in their cages to start coughing before they began to scream. A burning figure in a cage close to the ground managed to kick his way free, breaking through the glowing, flaring, half-charred wood and running from the blazing Ziggurat only to be bayoneted by one of a circle of soldiers who formed a perimeter, at a tolerable distance from the heat, for the purpose of containing such possible escapees. Given the same grim choice, Argo supposed the swift stab of the bayonet was preferable to the slower roasting and choking. When the first fire reached the apex of the Ziggurat, it set off a preset pyrotechnic device that blasted the sky with multicolored flares of red and purple radiance. The crowd, which had been watching the burning and death up to that point with a certain awed reticence, erupted once again.

"Urah-urah! Urah-urahha!"
"Urah-urah! Urah-urahha!"
"Urah-urah! Urah-urahha!"
"Urah-urah! Urah-urahha!"

Argo, to his own total horror, caught himself mouthing the cheer along with the Mosul pack. "Urah-urah! Urah-urahha!"

Argo glanced quickly around to see if either Slide or T'saya had noticed. Apparently not, but both their faces were hidden, T'saya's by her borrowed helmet and the hood of her slicker, and Slide's by the chain mail veil of the Zhaithan helmet, so Argo was unable to gauge their reaction to the Invocation for Victory or the way in which he had momentarily succumbed to it. To find himself going along with the barbarian horde was a considerable shock. Slide had already warned him that his newfound perceptions could make him vulnerable, but vulnerable to what? He had assumed that the ghastly circus was nothing more than deliberately barbaric spectacle and induced mass hysteria, but was a more real and multidimensional power at work in this macabre and brutal ceremony than just illusion and madness? Slide was present, and so was Quadaron-Ahrach. The two opposing forces were perhaps more than enough reality for the circumstances. He turned away from the Ziggurat that, with all of its incarcerated humans mercifully dead, was starting to resemble a man-made volcano, and looked towards the review dais. Hassan had left the stage, protected by his Immortals, but Quadaron-Ahrach still remained, attended by only a small squad of Zhaithan elite. Argo found himself staring at the mysterious draped figure as though drawn to the High Zhaithan, and, as he stared, he thought he saw the gleam of red luminous eyes in the darkness under the cowl of the high priest's robe. Such a vision could surely only be an illusion. The distance was too far to see such a detail even if it existed. But even as illusion, it chilled Argo to the core of his bones.

JESAMINE

The order had been curt. "Strip them, and bring the black ropes."

The ropes had turned out to be lengths of the finest braided silk. Even in her cruelty, and in the bleak surroundings of the Bunker, Her Grand Eminence Jeakqual-Ahrach liked to handle beautiful and voluptuous things. The room to which Jesamine and Cordelia had been taken was down a further flight of steep steps and along another cement corridor. The subbasement cell was large, severely rectangular, and plainly designed for a variety of intense restraint. Pulleys and chains depended from the ceiling, and steel rings were anchored in the wall. A thick stainless steel pole ran from one side of the room to the other at a height of about to six and a half feet from the flagstone floor, and it was to this that Jesamine and Cordelia were directed. A young Provincial Levy with a rifle stood guard in the outer corridor as Jeakqual-Ahrach's two black Zhaithan assistants looped the lengths of silk over the pole, knotted the ends around Jesamine and Cordelia's wrists, and then pulled them taut so the two women were hauled up to half-hang and half-strain on tiptoe with their arms stretched above their heads. Jesamine found that the most comfortable position, in a circumstance in which comfortable was a highly relative term, was to drop her head forward, except that, when she did that, she could see the floor had a drain set in its center, presumably so blood and any other bespattering fluids could be easily sluiced away.

Jesamine was scared but resigned. Pain loomed unpleasantly in her future, but pain was hardly an unknown, and neither was the dread and vulnerable feeling of exposure and the humiliating nakedness that preceded it. Such was the allotment of the slave. She had frequently, if privately, been whipped by Phaall, and long ago she had undergone ten lashes in the public stocks. This major humiliation had been back in the days when, taken by the Mamalukes in a routine raid, she had been shipped over the sea and put to labor as a common young house-available in a Cadiz knocking shop and then had been unwise enough to be caught red-handed clipping the purse of a Mamaluke underofficer. The ten lashes, and the other, more intimate chastisements that were administered, bent over a chair in the whorehouse parlor, had been the painful punctuation of her life after she had become the property of the Mosul empire and had also been her primary persuasions that the life of a concubine might be preferable to that of a come-one, come-all thief and harlot. At least she would be consolidating her pain and placing it in the hands of a single oppressor whose wrath might at least be predictable. This thinking had started her on the long road that had brought her to the carnal clutches of Colonel Helmut Phaall, the new world of the Americas, and the banks of the Potomac. With supreme irony, just a matter of hours after she had attempted her escape from both Phaall and the Mosul, she found herself facing what promised to be the worst pain of her life, plus some good odds that she would end that life in this grim cement box, with its pulleys, chains, and overhead steel pole.

"You are fully aware that you gave yourself away, aren't you?"

Jeakqual-Ahrach had returned after the assistants had secured Jesamine and Cordelia. She had walked round them twice and then approached Jesamine from behind. She wore a musky perfume that Jesamine failed to recognize, and her touch had been gentle as she twisted her fingers in Jesamine's straight, dark hair and raised her gaze to the vertical, whispering softly in her ear in a voice like some slight arctic wind that presaged a far worse gale to come. "You should not have done that, girl. To attempt to communicate with your companion in that way when I was so close was very stupid. In so doing, you not only revealed yourself but her also. Your inexperience is pitifully evident."

Jeakqual-Ahrach's age was hard to assess. Superficially she seemed to be no older than her early forties, but if she was, as T'saya had insisted, the full sister of Quadaron-Ahrach, that was hardly possible. She had to be far older. The electrical lights in the subbasement of the Bunker were not kind, and immediately upon this second entrance, she had ordered them disconnected and replaced by the more flattering, and more traditionally sinister, flame-glow of torches. The lace veil that dropped from a gold chaplet of blood red enameled roses that banded her brow had to be the start of Jeakqual-Ahrach's youthful illusion, but in the moments before the change in lighting, Jesamine had noticed a severe tightness in the skin of the woman's face, more than just the physical manifestation of her malign power, that suggested how maybe the knives of skilled surgeons had played a part in the staving off of the ravages of mortality, perhaps along with the ministrations of apothecaries, necromancers, and other specialists at whose function Jesamine was not even prepared to guess. Jeakqual-Ahrach's body was a little full, but nonetheless shapely, and moved with an energy and grace that could only indicate that more was being done to keep her young than mere adjustments of the cosmetic surface. As befitted this strange, secret sibling who was the only female in the high orders of the Zhaithan faith, she was dressed in a black robe, but, as if to assert her femininity, it was lavishly trimmed with red and gold. An embroidered representation of the sacred flame of Ignir and Aksura curled around the entire vertical length of the garment, and the robe was cinched at the waist by a gold, ruby-encrusted belt that displayed the curves of her breasts and hips beneath the soft fabric, curves of which Jeakqual-Ahrach seemed inordinately proud, to their maximum advantage. The belt alone, without even counting the rest of her jewelry, could have fed a large family in any occupied territory for a full span of their collective lives. And if the gold and ruby collar around her throat, the pendant earrings, plus the mass of bracelets and rings, the chaplet that held back her raven black hair, and all the other adornments, were added to the reckoning, their combined worth could probably have ransomed a small city under siege.

Jeakqual-Ahrach released Jesamine's hair and again walked around the two helpless women, this time stopping in front of Cordelia, but still talking to Jesamine. "Is our friend a little smarter? Did she know enough to keep her mind shut, or is she simply even more lacking in the skills of silent communication?"

She moved closer to Cordelia and ran a thoughtful hand over the suspended flatness of Cordelia's belly, as Cordelia bit her own lip. "I wonder which of you will break first, the concubine or the lady? This chamber is soundproofed, so you are free to scream all you want."

Only Jeakqual-Ahrach's hands betrayed the rest of her otherwise youthful exterior. They were veined and wrinkled like those of a woman decades on the far side of forty. In fact, only one of them was exposed. The left hand was covered in a velvet glove, with rings on the outside. Her right hand also did not remain uncovered for very long after she had touched Cordelia. She snapped her fingers, and one of her assistants advanced with a gold tray on which another single and highly idiosyncratic glove was draped. As she slowly drew it on, Jesamine saw that the palm was like a short-bristled brush, except the bristles were short silver needles. Jeakqual-Ahrach seemed aware that Jesamine was watching her, because she turned and moved towards her, the gloved hand raised palm outward so Jesamine could see it more clearly. She lightly stroked the steel brush across Jesamine's breast. "Can you image the damage this could do if used with a combination of force and creative malice?"

"I know the pointlessness of begging."

"At least you understand something."

She moved the steel bristles slowly down the length of Jesamine's body. "I would hazard a guess that you come from one of the tribes that sing, but whose homelands are too close to those of the Mamalukes."

"I sing for my master."

"And will you sing for me?"

"If you want me to talk, I'm helpless. I can hardly tell you anything, because I hardly know anything."

Jeakqual-Ahrach slightly used the glove with more intimate aggression. "I'm not sure I even want you to talk. Confessions are remarkably unreliable. It is my brother's belief that there are four of you."

"We are nothing."

Cordelia spoke with considerably more pluck that judgment. "She's telling the truth. We are nothing more than spoils of war."

Jeakqual-Ahrach responded to Cordelia by gripping Jesamine's inner thigh with the glove and slowly increasing the pressure, so some of the tiny spikes pierced the skin and caused pinpoints of bleeding. "I would not advise you to be speaking out of turn, child. You have no idea if it will be you or your friend who suffers as a result."

Jeakqual-Ahrach released her grip on Jesamine, stepped back, and, at the same time, moved so she was behind Cordelia. Jesamine let out her breath in a quick gasp. Jeakqual-Ahrach was clearly playing the two of them against each other, and Jesamine was guiltily relieved that, for the moment, Cordelia was the one being played, and she was merely left hanging in her silk bonds with an odd-looking graze on her thigh. The fingers of Jeakqual-Ahrach's velvet glove ran through Cordelia's red hair, while the leather and steel one cupped her left buttock. "You are the one from Albany. That's correct, isn't it? The intrepid young officer who dared the ride in the Norse airship?"

Cordelia clenched her teeth and said nothing. Jeakqual-Ahrach pulled her head up and laughed. "Aren't you afraid of me, Lady Blakeney?"

Jeakqual-Ahrach seemed to know a great deal about them, and Jesamine began to feel decidedly queasy. If T'saya had been arrested after all, and that was why she had been missing from her shack and her goats, everything would have been revealed already. Jesamine was under no illusion that anyone, even T'saya, would hold their silent secrets to the grave once the Zhaithan had gone to work on them.

Cordelia took a deep breath and turned her head as far as she could to try and look Jeakqual-Ahrach in the eye. "Of course I'm afraid. I'm very afraid. I'd be a fool if I wasn't afraid in my present situation."

"But still you retain that Albany aristocrat pride?"

Jeakqual-Ahrach tightened her grip on Cordelia's cheek, and Cordelia gasped. "Why don't you tell me what you want of us?"

Again Jeakqual-Ahrach laughed. "Perhaps what I require is simply your submission. You see how I suddenly hold out a last-second possibility of hope?"

"I would have said you had our complete submission right now. We are captive, bound and naked, and you can do whatever you like with us. How could we be any more submissive than we are?"

Jeakqual-Ahrach slapped Cordelia hard. "You seek to bandy words with me, girl?"

Cordelia gasped and twisted against the ropes. Very deliberately, Jeakqual-Ahrach slapped her again, and again Cordelia's body twisted.

"Well?"

Cordelia took a moment to compose herself. When she spoke, her voice sounded strained but still collected. "I was simply hoping that if we gave you what you wanted, it might save the two of us considerable pain. I was seeking to be practical."

"Seeking to be practical?"

"And perhaps seeking to save our lives."

Jeakqual-Ahrach touched the marks on Cordelia's flesh with her velvet hand. "My brother believes that you two, plus two more, collectively command a certain power."

Jesamine watched as a bead of sweat ran down Cordelia's side from her armpit. Cordelia nodded as best she could with within her current confines of movement. "As far as we can tell, he may well be correct."

Jesamine could not believe what she was hearing. Was Cordelia giving in already? Or was she attempting to match wits with Jeakqual-Ahrach despite her seemingly complete disadvantage? Either way, her newfound companion was playing a very risky game. On the other hand, as Cordelia herself had pointed out, they were captive, bound and naked, and Jeakqual-Ahrach could do whatever she liked with them. How much more dangerous could it get?

Jeakqual-Ahrach used Cordelia's hair to twist her head around. "What do you mean, as far as you can tell?"

"You're hurting me."

"Explain yourself."

"What is the point of me telling you what I know if you continue to hurt me?"

"You told me that you were nothing but spoils of war."

"We lied."

"And now?"

"To avoid torture, I'm telling you what I know."

"Which is?"

"That we have sensed a power within us. Jesamine and I have shared certain hallucinatory experiences, but we have a long way to go before we can either control or understand what is happening to us."

Jeakqual-Ahrach rested the spiked glove lightly on Cordelia's breast. "And the other two?"

Cordelia was trembling slightly. "We have never met the other two."

"Don't lie to me, Lady Blakeney."

"I'm not. We have never seen them except in dreams and visions."

Jeakqual-Ahrach moved very close to Cordelia. "Only in dreams and visions?"

"That's all."

She turned and stared at Jesamine. "And you would confirm this?"

"It's the truth."

Jeakqual-Ahrach advanced on Jesamine, but then abruptly stopped. Something indefinable changed behind her eyes, and she made a small bird-like movement of her head that seemed completely at odds with her previously revealed personality. "My brother . . ."

Quickly she righted herself and resumed being the former Jeakqual-Ahrach. "I have to briefly consult with the my brother. I shall be gone for a short while, and then I shall return. In the meantime, you will both learn a first lesson. What we are engaged in here is not the exchange of information in return for the mitigation of pain." She faced Cordelia. "You, my dear, have made an error that is common to many prisoners who pass through my hands. You believed that you could buy your way out of the inevitable with small increments of confession. You failed to realize that this is neither a negotiation nor a transaction, and information and pain are not items of currency. You have no purchasing power in this room with which to escape what was inevitable from the moment you came before me. The pain that you are about to suffer is the pain of transformation. It is the pain that will break you and then recreate you anew as you are rebuilt under my authority and this alleged power of yours is brought under my command and control."

She gestured imperiously to her black Zhaithan assistants. "While I'm gone, I want you to subject the dark one, the one called Jesamine, to a First Stage Physical Infliction. Use the martinet and the new electrical device on her, and let the other one watch in the full foreknowledge that the same or worse will happen to her on my return." Jeakqual-Ahrach smiled at Cordelia. "The army employs a similar psychology in its field punishments. When two men commit an offence, the sentence of the secondary accomplice is executed first, while the primary instigator waits and watches. I have always considered it a technique with considerable merit in that it adds a major measure of guilt on one part, and hatred on the other, to the routinely physical hurt. It severs the ties of loyalty and is the perfect breaker of friendships."

And with that, Jeakqual-Ahrach swept swiftly out of the torture chamber with her robe and perfume wafting behind her. On her way through the door, she snapped an order to the young Provincial Levy on guard in the outer corridor. "Let no one in or out of this room, you understand, boy?"

The Provincial Levy nodded and bowed. "Yes, ma'am."

"Good." Jeakqual-Ahrach was gone, but her voice floated back down the corridor. "One day, my damned brother will learn to wait at my convenience instead of issuing his cursed summonses."

Jesamine was seized by an irrational anger. Cordelia was a stupid, arrogant bitch who had attempted to play games with a creature as overpowering as Jeakqual-Ahrach, and now it was she, Jesamine, who was to be punished for Cordelia's overweening audacity. Cordelia must have sensed her fury, because her apology was plaintive. "I'm sorry."

"Yes, I'm sure you are."

Then Jesamine braced herself as the assistants advanced on her, one swishing a cruelly traditional martinet while the other carried a somewhat phallic glass tube from which wires ran to a scientific-looking Bakelite box with a steel crank handle.

"Just relax. This is going to hurt."

"Why should I relax before you hurt me?"

"It may well be your last chance."

Then, to Jesamine's complete surprise, the two Zhaithan halted with looks of amazement on their faces, and a voice, nervous but insistent, with a distinct Hispanian accent, spoke high and clear. "Touch either of them with any of those things, and I'll shoot you dead."

RAPHAEL

As Raphael followed the two women in the motorized tumbrel, he found that, the closer they came to the Zhaithan's Bunker, the more the disarray was compounded and the confusion increased. The streets around the bunker were choked with trucks, gun carriages, and mule carts, and the tumbrel carrying the girls from his dreams was forced to halt a number of times as the traffic locked up solid. As he fully expected, the worst confusion was centered at the main entrance to the windowless cement block that housed the headquarters of the Ministry of Virtue. Prisoners were being dragged out of the building, clearly destined for the mass executions, while others were being dragged inside to some yet-to-be-specified hell. Some wept, some screamed, and others stumbled stone-faced to their fate, and, all the time, in the background, the madness on the parade ground howled on. Raphael quickly realized that matters had reached the point when much was being handled by simple visual impressions, as in the assumption that a figure that wore a helmet and carried a weapon was a guard, while one that did not was a prisoner. When the girl's tumbrel was finally unloaded, Raphael's best and, in fact, only idea was to tag along with their escort as they were taken inside, and he was amazed to discover that this was all it really took. Once inside the echoing concrete booking area, he found that the place was thronged with more regular army Mosul guards than with Zhaithan. Soldiers just like Raphael stood around with muskets and fixed bayonets, looking bored, tired, or worried and waiting for someone to tell them what to do, while a scarlet Zhaithan superintendent tried to organize the milling crowds, the recently arrested, the already condemned, and the men needed to guard them into some manageable order by screaming incoherently and only breaking off to argue repeatedly with a Zhaithan records officer.

Guards and their allocation, it appeared, were almost as much of a problem as the prisoners. At any given time there was either too many or them or too few. Units had long since been broken up as men shuttled between the bunker and the parade ground, and now escort squads were being formed on the spot by the simple process of Zhaithan officers pointing and yelling. This was exactly what happened to Raphael after he'd been inside the Bunker for only a matter of minutes. A blue Zhaithan had motioned impatiently to him and some Mosul regulars. "You men! Basement One. There's some Category A detainees being sent down there, and you're to watch them."

Raphael hesitated as though the order did not apply to him, but the Zhaithan obviously intended that it did. "You, boy! That means you!"

Raphael fudged a suitably surly salute, just on the safe side of dumb insolence, and followed the rest of his newly designated squad to a flight of cement stairs. He glanced back. The two girls had been separated from the rest of the prisoners, and they were being moved in the direction of the very same flight of steps. The redhead's kaftan was torn and dragging, threatening to trip her, but they seemed to be otherwise unharmed. The steps led to a long, grey, electrically lit corridor with blank cement walls. A dozen or more young women, some crying, others with their clothes ripped, all give-or-take pretty and all in various states of torn and abused disarray, were lined up along the walls, strictly positioned some eight or nine feet apart to make conversation difficult. The black Zhaithan in charge were taking no chances. Each girl was assigned a guard of her own who stood facing her, his weapon at the ready. One of the Zhaithan waved Raphael to a position against the wall, so he would be guarding the next woman to be brought down the steps, and, to his amazement, she turned out to be the pale-skinned redhead, the one from the truck on the highway, the one who might go by the name of Lady Blakeney. Raphael all but took refuge in superstitious disbelief. What omens and portents were being closed or completed by this happenstance juxtapositioning? The situation went well beyond any possible coincidence or act of fate. He stared into her face, but she avoided his eyes as though he was any other faceless Mosul soldier. She looked like someone who was extremely frightened but holding herself together with a supreme effort of will. He wished that he could say something to encourage or comfort her, but he knew that to speak might well doom the both of them, assuming they were not doomed already.

"Cordelia."

The word came out of nowhere, simultaneously as a whisper in Raphael's ear and a shimmer of soft light in his inner vision. He cautiously looked around to see if anyone was speaking, but no sound echoed, and no lips moved even when one word became five. *"Cordelia, can you hear me?"*

The redhead's eyes swivelled desperately from side to side, and she bit her lip as if to avoid making any inadvertent sound. *"Jesamine, I can hear you."*

The new voice could only come from the redhead, but something seemed to be wrong. The other girl, the honey-colored one with the dark hair, who had to be Jesamine, was not hearing the thoughts. Cordelia, who could only be the redhead, was unable to get through, despite all her efforts. *"I'm trying as hard as I can. Why can I hear you, and you can't hear me?"*

And why could Raphael hear both of them? Some magick that Raphael totally failed to understand was at work here. The only thing he knew for sure was that it was not any Zhaithan magick, but something completely different. He covertly glanced down the corridor to where the two black Zhaithan waited, just in time to see them stiffen and formally face the stairs. At the same time, one of them barked an order to the occupants of the corridor. "Guards to attention! Prisoners stand straight. Prepare to look upon Her Grand Eminence Jeakqual-Ahrach."

A musky and not altogether pleasant perfume filled the drabness of the corridor, and a small woman came down the steps, wearing what, to Raphael, looked like a heretical female version of a Zhaithan uniform and a fortune in gold and jewels. So who or what was Her Grand Eminence Jeakqual-Ahrach? All Raphael could tell was that she was ponderously important, and even that went against everything he had been taught growing up under the Mosul. Despite her diminutive size, she moved with a weighty and impatient authority, as though she was accustomed to being in command of any given situation. According to the Zhaithan law, as it was related to the masses, no woman could achieve such prominence. Such a thing was contrary to the express dictates of Ignir and Aksura and the Way of the Twins, and yet the black Zhaithan who had previously been in lordly command were now obsequious, almost fawning, in their deferential respect. They followed Her Grand Eminence Jeakqual-Ahrach like pet dogs as she moved slowly down the row of young women, scrutinizing each in turn. Taking her time, she reached the end of the unhappy assemblage, thoughtfully turned, and then started back again. She passed Jesamine, and as Jeakqual-Ahrach's back was to her, the honey-colored girl tried another silent call to Cordelia. *"Cordelia?"*

Jeakqual-Ahrach halted, and Raphael knew to his certain horror that she, too, had heard the inner voice, just as clearly as he had. Jeakqual-Ahrach slowly turned and gestured to the Mosul guarding Jesamine. "Room SB101 for this one."

As Jesamine was led away to a door farther down the corridor, Jeakqual-Ahrach stared hard at each female prisoner in turn, as though assessing who might have been the intended recipient of the silent communication. "So, which of you is Cordelia?"

No one moved or said a word, including the redhead, but then three words glowed in Raphael's mind. *"I am Cordelia."*

Jeakqual-Ahrach did not respond. A point had been proved, and maybe a small victory had been won. Raphael could hear Cordelia's mind, but Her Grand Eminence could not.

"I said, which one of you is Cordelia? Whoever it might be is being very foolish in keeping quiet. I can so easily check the records, and the immediate future will prove infinitely worse for whomever it turns out to be."

Cordelia straightened up. "I'm Cordelia."

Jeakqual-Ahrach nodded. "At least you show a modicum of common sense." She glanced at Raphael. "Room SB101 for this one as well."

Raphael was glad that Cordelia did not put up any kind of physical resistance or start crying or screaming. He was not sure what he would have done if he had been expected to move her by force. She followed reluctantly in Jesamine's footsteps, but without protest, and, as they came close to the designated door, Raphael decided to try a dangerous experiment of his own. *"I can hear you."*

Cordelia's step faltered. *"What?"*

Jeakqual-Ahrach, who was walking behind, did not seem to notice anything, and, if she had seen Cordelia's shocked stumble at all, she appeared to dismiss it as simple fear.

"Don't worry. I'm a friend."

"You're the guard, right?"

"Right."

And then they were at the door, and no further communication was possible. Jesamine's guard had taken a position beside the door to SB101 with his back to the wall. Raphael assumed the equivalent position on the other side. He could not see inside, but the first order from Jeakqual-Ahrach did not bode well. "Strip them, and bring the black ropes."

Having set her Zhaithan assistants to work, Jeakqual-Ahrach emerged and went down the corridor to another room. Raphael tried to project a thought through the wall to Cordelia. *"Can you still hear me?"*

The response was clear but trembling. *"Yes."*

"I don't think Jeakqual-Ahrach can hear what we're doing, Cordelia. Unfortunately, I don't think Jesamine can hear us, either."

"Who and what are you? How do you know our names?"

"There's no time to explain, even if I could. You'll have to trust me that I'm on your side and I'll help you when the slightest chance presents itself."

"I should trust someone in this place?"

Jeakqual-Ahrach had emerged from the other room and was returning. Raphael sent a warning thought. *"Quiet now. She's coming back."*

Jeakqual-Ahrach halted before going back into SB101 and looked at Raphael and the Mosul. "I don't need two of you on this door." She motioned to Raphael first and then the legitimate guard. "You stay, and you go back upstairs and make yourself useful."

The Mosul hurried off, as though pleased to be getting out of this unholy subbasement where a woman gave the orders. Raphael remained at attention until Jeakqual-Ahrach was inside room SB101 again. Although the door was left open, he knew that to actually peek inside would be fatal. He did not precisely know what was being done to Cordelia and Jesamine, but he doubted it was good. The place had the unmistakable air of a torture chamber. He heard Jeakqual-Ahrach's voice, he heard slaps, and he heard gasps. He felt a long process of systematic hurt was being slowly initiated. He caught a snatch of dialogue between Cordelia and Jeakqual-Ahrach but could not make out the exact words. Then he heard Her Eminence issuing more instructions to the assistants, and shortly after, she came out and snapped an order at him. "Let no one in or out of this room, you understand, boy?"

"Yes, ma'am."

"Good." Jeakqual-Ahrach hurried off, as though suddenly and urgently called away, but her voice floated back down the corridor. "One day, my damned brother will learn to wait at my convenience instead of issuing his cursed summonses."

A thought immediately came from within. *"You out there. Are you really willing to help us, because it could be now or never."*

Raphael stepped into the doorway and saw Jeakqual-Ahrach's two assistants advancing on the bound and naked Jesamine, one swishing a cruelly traditional martinet while the other carried a phallic glass tube from which wires ran to a scientific-looking iron box with a Bakelite crank handle. Raphael raised his rifle and spoke with all the insistence he could muster. "Touch either of them with those things, and I'll shoot you dead."

The two Zhaithan halted with looks of amazement on their faces. A humble ranker had never spoken to them in such a way before. "Put down the gun, boy. A dozen men will be in here if you fire a shot." Then Cordelia spoke. "The room is soundproof. Just shut the door boy." Raphael did as she suggested, without lowering the gun or taking his eyes off the Zhaithan. They both had holstered revolvers on their belts, and Raphael was ultracautious. He could only thank whatever strange gods now seemed to be looking after him that he had loaded his rifle hours earlier with one of the rounds he had neglected to return to Melchior way back on the Continental Highway.

"Very slowly raise your arms and clasp your hands at the back of your heads. The first one to speak or do anything I don't like is going to die."

Scarcely able to believe what he was doing, and amazed that it so far was going well, Raphael moved quickly behind the first Zhaithan and pulled his pistol from its holster. He felt better with the two guns. At least he was not confronted with the task of holding up two armed men with the threat of just one shot. He swiftly disarmed the second Zhaithan and gave more curt orders. "You, cut down the two women, and you, the other one, you lay face down on the floor."

The Zhaithan torturers seemed well versed in obedience and possessed of no reckless or unnatural courage, and they both did exactly as they were told. Jesamine was the first to be cut free from her silk bonds, and she looked at Raphael with sideways distrust as she stood and massaged the circulation back into her wrists. "Who the hell are you?"

"That doesn't matter. Take this pistol. If either of these holy-born bastards moves, shoot him dead."

"Could I find something to wear first?

"Take the gun first. Survival before modesty."

Jesamine took a deep breath. "Whatever you say. You're the one to the rescue."

Now Cordelia was free and rubbing her wrists. "Do you have any idea how we're going to get out of here?"

Raphael shook his head. "No, I don't."

"You want to repeat that?"

Raphael avoided the girl's eyes. "I have no idea how to get out of here."

"You really planned this well, didn't you?"

"I didn't plan it at all. It was just when I heard your silent words, I knew I had to do something. The fact that I could hear you think clinched it. All I know is that there's some weird connection between the three of us."

Cordelia swiftly put a finger to her lips. "Not in front of the Zhaithan."

Jesamine stood over her former torturers, naked and formidable, with her revolver leveled. "We need to know how long Jeakqual-Ahrach will be gone." She looked down at her prone charges. "Maybe one of you would like to tell us. How long were you supposed to soften us up for before the bitch came back?"

One of the Zhaithan raised his head slightly. "We won't talk to you."

Cordelia gestured to Raphael. "Put your gun to his head."

"What?"

"Put your pistol to his head. The one who won't talk to us. Just do it, boy. Be ready to blow his brains out if I give the word."

Raphael immediately did as he was told. These two girls were not only distractingly nude and gorgeous, but, as he was rapidly learning, ruthlessly tough and implacably bitter. He could only assume that they had learned their attitudes in an even harder school than the bootcamp of the Provincial Levies. Cordelia moved to where the Zhaithan had left the scientific-looking iron box with a Bakelite crank handle and the wires that ran to the phallic glass tube. She experimentally flicked two switches on the top of the box and then cranked the handle. The tube glowed with a pulsing diffusion of violet radiance, and Cordelia gingerly picked it up by the insulated handle. She tested it on her own hand and cursed. "Damn. That hurts like hell."

Jesamine had watched the entire procedure with calm curiosity. "Do you intend to do what I think you intend?"

Cordelia nodded. "I intend to rip his britches down and use this thing on him at maximum penetration. And I won't stop until he tells us everything we want to know."

The Zhaithan who was Cordelia's intended victim cringed away from Raphael's pistol. The man had turned white. "Wait."

Cordelia looked down at him with eyes that were so cold they frightened Raphael. "Wait? Wait? You ask me to wait? Would you have waited if I'd asked the same of you? Would you have waited if I'd begged you?"

"I . . ."

Cordelia bared her small white teeth. "Beg, you bastard. I want to hear you plead."

The Zhaithan was now turning green. "Yes, yes, I beg you . . ."

"And?"

"A First Stage Physical Infliction is supposed to take one hour."

Cordelia laughed nastily. "Did you ever imagine a high and mighty Zhaithan would crack so quickly?"

Jesamine indicated that Raphael should move out of the way so she could take his place. She pointed her own gun at the Zhaithan. "You were going to torture me for an hour?"

The Zhaithan pressed his face to the floor. His Zhaithan superiority was history. Now he whined. "I've told you what you wanted to know."

Jesamine was curt. "You, look up. Look at me."

The Zhaithan looked up, and she slapped him hard across the face with the barrel of the revolver. Her first blow must have broken his nose, because blood immediately gushed from it, but the profuse bleeding did not deter Jesamine from hitting him again, this time across the mouth, and teeth flew. "Scream all you like. Remember the soundproofing." At the sight of his companion being pistol-whipped, the second Zhaithan found a measure of desperate courage and moved as though he intended to get to his feet. Raphael was immediately on him. "Flat on the ground, asshole, unless you want the same."

The extent of the second Zhaithan's bravery was strictly limited. In the face of Raphael's gun, he dropped to the floor again. Meanwhile, Jesamine hit the first Zhaithan a third time and then stepped back. Cordelia glanced archly in her direction. "I guess you needed that."

Jesamine nodded. "I did."

"A lifetime's worth?"

"A small down payment."

The second Zhaithan voiced a last vestige of resistance. "You know you'll never get out of here. The hour you've gained yourselves is only a respite. At best, you perhaps die quickly by your own hands."

Jesamine regarded the man coldly. "The moment before they come for me, I'll put a bullet in you and another one in your partner."

ARGO

At first Argo tried to dismiss the sensation as nothing more than the effects of too little sleep and the herbs with which T'saya had dosed him. A spiral of flame and hallucination was tugging at him, pulling him into the evil vortex of mass hysteria, wanting him to become one with the madness all around. On the gallows, bodies were plunging into space and destiny, jerked into death at the end of their short hempen ropes, while screaming and tormented spirits rose from the burning Ziggurat, howling with the leaping flames, up into an agonized sky. Sweat gleamed on the faces around him, Mosul, Teuton, Mamaluke alike. Eyes were wide and bloodshot, and mouths hung slack. He could feel how some were beginning to be seized by the conviction that they were already dead; that they were already fighting from the spirit world and need have no fear when, tomorrow or the tomorrow after, come one imminent dawn, they would be charging the Albany lines, roaring their war cries and battle hymns into the bullets and cannister shot from the muzzles of massed Albany artillery, fast-loading Norse rifles, and Bergman guns with nothing but a single-shot musket, a bayonet, and an induced madness to protect them. The minds of many in the chanting mob rolled with the roiling smoke and the smell of charred human flesh closer to the foul dimension where the Dark Things dwelled. An increasing number of bottles circulated amid the fire and murder on the parade ground, bottles of not only the routine 'shine and cheap schnapps, but ones with strange herbs marinating in the liquor, angry cousins of T'saya's concoctions. The chanting itself was becoming loose and disjointed, degenerating into a babble and gabble of incoherent rage.

One step to the side in space and time, tendrils of a living, gleaming vapor infiltrated the Mosul throng; a purposefully drifting mist of white death streaked with blood and amber and with holes of black nothingness filling the spaces between the animate wisps. As Argo looked closer, the curls of fog seethed with serpentine forms that slithered and clung to the bony reaching hands and skeletal faces of the fallen who had gone before and died in the first Battle of the Potomac. The dead and disembodied specters drifted over the swaying parade ground, where mortality was the currency and nameless deals were being transacted with the very essence of life itself. A number of undulating vapor skeins appeared bent on engulfing Argo, insinuated phantasms that softly whispered to him in all languages or none, promising him the world and an infinity of powers-that-might-be-his if only he would turn away from all that he had learned so far and . . .

He shook his head to clear it. He had to focus his eyes. This was no time or place to go up and out. Up and out could only take him places even more dread and loathsome. Quadaron-Ahrach had left the stage with his Zhaithan, but his presence lingered over this ululating gala of deadly power and violent iniquity. The vision of the supreme Zhaithan's gleaming eyes had locked itself hard into Argo's mind, and he knew from his newfound instincts that it was this image of the eyes, and the swift, sharp corruption of the mind behind them, that was willing the whispering ghosts to surround him. Argo's problem was that the horror had a strange and seductive buoyancy that was trying to enfold him and then float him, weak and irrational, to where he absolutely did not want to go.

A vibrant energy of discolored orange-yellow was now streaming from the men around him, and in a different part of the camp, as far from the river and the human habitations as it was possible to get, an electric compound of Dark Things bounced and hummed with ugly satisfaction as they sucked in the confluence of the thousands of bonding and expanding streams of stolen lifeforce. Overhead, indistinct winged creatures fluttered like moths as the Dark Things were nourished by this tainted and hemorrhaging power of humanity and they visibly grew stronger and more malevolent as they fed. Some actually perceived him and evilly invited him to join them, promising that they would be his to command if only . . .

Argo needed something easy and human. He needed a shock, a drink, a jolt of physical reality to bring him out of this Other Place and to prevent himself constantly slipping and sliding back into it. He was tired. Without help, he could not resist. He only knew he had to resist, but he was being hard pushed by temptation. He was being enticed with promises of unspecified power to reveal who and what he was even though he was far from certain of that himself.

In the place where he did not want to go, Quadaron-Ahrach waited. The hunchback of previous fearful illusions was again on his throne, and more of the all-consuming sheets of flame danced behind him, a fire of this world combined with the fire of another. But he now leaned forward, gaunt and smiling, with a sinister if shapely female figure in the silhouetted shadows behind him. Quadaron-Ahrach was speaking to him. His thin, ancient lips moved, and although no audible words came, the message was clear. He wanted Argo to come to him. He wanted Argo to join him. If Argo came to Quadaron-Ahrach and pledged his fealty, all would be made good. Argo would not only be safe in the power, but a proud prince among men, with thousands to do his bidding.

A slap of sharp, sudden pain and the wrathful hiss of Yancey Slide brought Argo back to reality. "Stop that! It's getting a grip on you! You have to fight it."

Slide looked to T'saya, who was wide-eyed herself. "He has to get out of here. The boy is being taken over. I believe Quadaron-Ahrach has found him."

T'saya blinked and nodded as though tearing herself away from a vision of her own. "Yes. Yes, indeed. Let's get the fuck out of here."

No sooner had she spoken than the entire picture changed, and any number of spells were broken as a loud explosion was detonated somewhere in the camp, not too far from the parade ground. Men looked angry, puzzled, frightened. Were they being shelled? Was Albany attacking them? Had an ammunition dump accidently blown up? After a moment of puzzled silence, a thousand Mosul soldiers blundered into each other as they looked for weapons or a superior to issue them some kind of orders.

Argo did not know how he knew, but he was certain enough to speak without hesitation. "That explosion came from the Bunker."

T'saya nodded. "It's your crazy damned Rangers, Slide. They've only gone and mounted an attack on the Zhaithan headquarters."

Slide looked from one to the other, but before he could say anything, Argo took control. "We have to go there right now."

"Has something gotten into you, boy, or are you just out of your mind? You want to go to the Zhaithan headquarters in the middle of a crisis?"

"It's where we have to go."

Argo readied his horse and was preparing to mount. Slide put a hand on his arm. "Hold on there, Argo Weaver."

Argo shook his arm free of Slide. "We have to go."

"Have you thought where this imperative might be coming from?"

"It's from me."

"I'm not letting you do this."

For the first time ever, Argo turned and fully faced down Yancey Slide. "I'm going. It's nonnegotiable."

"Big words, boy."

"Big or small, I'm going."

Slide blazed with the force of command. "No!"

Argo was unmoved. Let Slide blaze all he wanted. "Yes."

And the Ziggurat blew up. Later Argo would know that it was an aimed mortal shell, fired by Jeb Hooker's Rangers, but in the moment, as men yelled and burning debris rained down on them, he thought Slide had done it to make his point.

"Nice effect, Yancey Slide, but I think that makes my point rather than yours. I'm going!"

T'saya had ducked when the burning structure spectacularly blew, but then she reached for the reins of Slide's horse. "I don't know about you, Yancey Slide, but I'm going with the boy. This place is under fire. Probably more of your Rangers' games."

CORDELIA

Room SB101 had yielded all that Cordelia, Jesamine, and the new boy, who had told them his name was Raphael, needed to restrain and silence the two Zhaithan. The bloody, bruised, and toothlessly disfigured victim of Jesamine's pistol-whipping posed no threat, and his condition should have been enough warning of what might happen to his companion if he did the slightest thing to raise an alarm, but still no chances were being taken. In addition to being careful, both Jesamine and Raphael seemed to take a shameless, payback delight in gagging Jeakqual-Ahrach's little helpers and manacling them to the wall. Together they had locked the manacles so tight that the circulation in the men's arms would almost certainly be cut off. When the Zhaithan who had not been pistol-whipped protested, Jesamine's lip had curled, and, with a glance at Raphael, she had all but spat in the helpless man's face. "Do I give a rat's ass if your hands turn blue, or even drop off? I don't think so."

Not that Jesamine was willing to totally trust Raphael as yet. The concubine had seen too many Mosul uniforms in her time to completely take the word of anyone who might be wearing one, but that did not stop her sharing some acts of minor revenge on their former oppressors. Cordelia might have felt the same if she only had the young man's word on his defection, but she had seen a small way inside his mind, and that had been enough for her. She had no doubt that he was another of the Four. A short conversation, and a not-too-well-performed exchange of silent images and unspoken ideas, had further convinced her but also made clear that they all had a great deal to learn about their powers and how to use them. Cordelia was now certain that nothing would function properly until the full quartet was together.

This was a fact that Cordelia kept to herself, however. Their strange new powers were their last best hope for finding a way out of room SB101 in less than one hour, and she did not want to plant the idea of failure before they had even started to explore the possibilities. Even where to start was a problem. Raphael knew less than either Jesamine or Cordelia. He had seen the two of them in his dreams, he had made drawings of them in his secret sketchbook, and he had experienced visions in the presence of the supernatural entities called Dark Things, but that seemed the limit of his experience. He had frowned at the two women in mystification when Cordelia suggested that they try for some sort of psychic bond that included Jesamine. "I suppose we could link hands and see if anything happens."

They had tentatively grasped each other's hands and closed their eyes. Concentrating hard, they had found that precisely nothing had happened, and when the attempt had been abandoned, Raphael had looked at the women in all innocence. "You said you were able to form a bond with each other. How did you do that?"

Jesamine hesitated. "It was kind of accidental."

"Accidental?"

Cordelia could not leave him hanging. "It grew out of a sexual thing."

Jesamine nodded, a little overcoyly in Cordelia's opinion. "And we were both very drunk."

The same thought occurred to both Cordelia and Raphael at the same time, and they both knew it. To engage in an erotic threesome right there on the floor hardly seemed plausible, practical, or effective. Not that Cordelia would have hesitated had she thought that it might have revealed a magickal avenue of escape, but the silent stares of the two Zhaithan had been enough of a distraction when they had been just holding hands. To try for some kind of lewd transcendence with those two bastards watching was plainly pointless and would never happen. Not that Cordelia questioned Raphael's willingness to play his part. Without so much as reading his thoughts, she had seen him staring at her and Jesamine's bodies when he thought they weren't looking, and by his covert glances, he clearly indicated that he was interested in more than just their immediate survival. Before he, Jesamine, and Cordelia had immobilized the Zhaithan, they had stripped them of their tunics to give the girls something to wear apart from their ripped and filthy kaftans. The overlarge black jackets still revealed a lot of intimate flesh, and Raphael had continued to look. Cordelia, for her part, also did not view Raphael with distaste. Cleaned up, and with new clothes, the young man, with his large brown eyes, black hair, and olive skin, would have been darkly attractive, and the Goddess only knew how long it had been since he had been anywhere near a woman. Raphael had caught this final thought, smiled with a boyish embarrassment, and Cordelia had giggled. Jesamine was, of course, mystified. "What the hell are you two laughing at?"

"Just a shared thought."

"Why can't I share a thought?"

Raphael diplomatically intervened. "Let's try again and see if we can link the three of us."

They once more joined hands, and, to Cordelia's surprise, something indistinct faltered on the very periphery of each of their minds. Glowing colors like lines of force were bent and tangled as though, without the fourth individual to complete the conjuration, nothing was going to happen as it should, and then, without warning, a fully realized vision fell on Cordelia. She jerked and pulled her hands free of the grip of Jesamine and

Raphael. The illusion not only shocked her with its unheralded suddenness, but it was also someone else's perception. She was looking through the eyes and mind of a stranger.

A vibrant energy of discolored orange-yellow was now streaming from the men around her, and in a different part of the camp, as far from the river and the human habitations as it was possible to get, an electric compound of Dark Things bounced and hummed with ugly satisfaction as they sucked in the confluence of the thousands of bonding and expanding streams of stolen lifeforce. Overhead, indistinct winged creatures fluttered like moths as the Dark Things were nourished by this tainted and hemorrhaging power of humanity and they visibly grew stronger and more malevolent as they fed. Some actually perceived her and evilly invited her to join them, promising that they would be hers to command if only . . .

Then the vision distorted, seeming to slip sideways, and when it returned, the hunchback of previous visions was facing her on his throne.

All-consuming sheets of flame danced behind him, a fire of this world combined with the fire of another. But he now leaned forward, gaunt and smiling, with a sinister if shapely female figure in the silhouetted shadows behind him. Quadaron-Ahrach was speaking to her. His thin ancient lips moved, and although no audible words came, the message was clear. He wanted Cordelia to come to him.

Just as Cordelia felt she was unable to handle what was happening to her, the vision abruptly ceased, and, at the same time, a bomb exploded somewhere very close. Dust cascaded from the ceiling. The electric lights went out in the subbasement, but the light of the burning torches remained. Cordelia stood up as two smaller explosions, closer but deafening, and a burst of gunfire echoed from above. "I think this may well be the cavalry coming to rescue us."

Jesamine looked at her as though she had just lost her mind. "I hope you're right. I've never been too impressed with the cavalry."

ARGO

They forced the horses through the crowd, with Argo leading the way and T'saya riding behind Yancey. As they rode towards the smoke that was rising from the Bunker, they were forced to push through a solid mass of confusion. Behind them, two more explosions ripped upwards from the parade ground, and someone was yelling that the gallows was gone, as if the fact was some kind of loss. Although no one opposed them, the going was difficult as crowds of men in drab green thrashed around in their own disorder and stampeded this way and that according to the dictates of the latest shouted rumor. Some seemed to believe that a preemptive strike was coming from across the river. Others were convinced that it was the Norse Union attacking from the air and scanned the night sky for flying machines. The only mercy in the mess was that the great majority of the Mosul rank and file had not been issued with ammunition. Otherwise, a fearful random slaughter might have broken out as the euphoric high of suggestion, regression, and human sacrifice gave way to panic and irrational terror. Only the fact of having nothing to shoot with prevented men from firing at everything that moved, including each other. The Zhaithan had made scrupulously sure that no man not on duty, on or near the parade ground, had a loaded weapon. Enough dangerous armed mayhem was being caused by the panicking officers who had retained their loaded sidearms. Some, persuaded that a prearranged mutiny was being instigated, had opened fire on troops doing nothing more threatening than desperately searching for their own units and familiar faces, while others had simply blazed their six shots into the night on the principle that doing something was better than doing nothing. For greater authority, Argo had drawn his own revolver and brandished it in the air as he kicked his horse forward to the irrational but certain conclusion the Bunker would provide the answers he had needed for so long.

An eerily familiar sound caused Argo to rein in sharply. The distinctive and repetitive bark of a light-model Bergman gun was echoing harshly from the Bunker. He turned back and stared at Slide and T'saya. "That has to be the Rangers."

T'saya grunted. "You have little faith, Argo Weaver. That's what I already told you."

Argo looked around, suddenly undecided. "If it's Hooker and his boys attacking the Bunker, how the hell do they expect to get out of here? There's a lot of bloody Mosul between us and the other side of the river."

"Something we need to bear in mind ourselves."

Argo was still maintaining a healthy anger at Slide. "It was supposed to be a suicide mission, was it?"

"It's not a suicide mission. The Rangers work on the principle of blow up the whole world if need be and then vanish. You'd be surprised what they can pull off with a little surprise. Here and now they've got more than surprise. They've created total fucking chaos."

In the area around the Bunker, the chaos had actually doubled as the Bergman had opened up. A sudden surge of men came from the direction of the building, seeking cover and, once again, someone to give them an order. No one seemed to care that two mounted Zhaithan and a physically strange soldier were pushing their way in the opposite direction. If the attack really was the work of no more than Hooker and his squad, they had done a destructively miraculous job on the Zhaithan headquarters. A huge section of wall had been blown out, right beside the main entrance. A staff car was burning, and bodies, some whole and others no more than separated limbs, seemed to be scattered for ten yards or more from the point of impact, covered in drifting cement dust, fallen beams, and shattered masonry.

Slide rose in his stirrups and looked over the heads of the fleeing crowd. "Seems like someone did a good job of laying a satchel charge right by the front door." Muzzle flashes were visible in the smoky darkness of the interior, and Slide laughed. "And then they went inside to make it a massacre. You have to hand to Hooker and his boys. They have style."

"The other three of the Four are inside there."

Slide looked sharply at Argo. "What did you say?"

"The other three of the Four are inside there."

"You know that for a fact?"

"The thought came to me, and I said it." Argo had nothing to add. It was exactly as he had told it. He was suddenly in a world without questions, where he could only act on the instinct of the moment.

But seemingly Slide believed him. "Damn."

"We have to go in there."

"That presents a real fucking challenge to not be shot by our own side."

Argo, still without thinking ahead, kicked his horse hard, eager to go and be unable to turn back should his courage run out. He plunged ahead, breaking through the ragged perimeter that some Teuton officers, less drunk and more on the ball than the rest, were attempting to kick and bully into place around the Bunker, while an underofficer and two men were being sent for an issue of ammunition. A brief bayonet charge had been attempted, but it had been cut down by the faceless fire from inside, and Argo's path took his horse's hooves across the still-warm bodies. He glanced back and saw that Slide was following, having been left with little or no alternative. What sounded like a bullet from inside hissed past him. Slide had been right. The challenge really was to not be shot by their own side. When he reached the gaping hole where the entrance had once been, he slid from the saddle and cut his horse loose. At the same time, he ripped off his helmet, and, with revolver in one hand and the dead man's carbine in the other, stumbled shouting into the smoke and gunfire. "Hooker! Don't shoot! It's me, Weaver. I've got Slide with me. Don't fucking shoot!"

RAPHAEL

Raphael and the two girls moved through darkness and smoke, feeling their way along the ways of the subbasement corridor as what sounded like a violent firefight raged above them. Through all of his time in the service of the Mosul, he had heard men mimic the dread sound of the enemy Bergman gun, but he had never heard it for real and fired in anger. He hissed to the girls. "This has to be an Albany attack."

They halted in a crouch, and Cordelia looked up as though trying to peer in the direction of the sound through two floors of cement. Her eyes suddenly opened wide and fixed on a point in front of her. "It's a raid across the river. It has to be the Rangers." She suddenly glanced round at things that Raphael and Jesamine could not see. "The last of the Four is here. He's two floors above us."

Raphael and Jesamine's eyes met. Crazy as Cordelia sounded, they knew they had no choice but to trust what she was saying and not to even question her for details lest they break the link.

"He knows the Rangers."

She started to rise to her feet, but then suddenly dropped back into her previous protective crouch and shook her head. "Fuck."

"What?"

"I lost him."

"Him?"

"I could see through his mind what was going on around him. Just brief flashes. He knew the Rangers personally, as though he had traveled or fought with them, and quite recently, too. He was telling them to hold their fire and not shoot him. We have to go up there. Now. This is it! This is the way out."

"Hold it."

Cordelia shook her head with almost demented determination. "No! We go!"

"But I'm an enemy grunt."

"But you're with me."

"The Rangers may not see it that way."

"I'm the Lady Cordelia fucking Blakeney, and an officer in the RWA. They have to see it that way."

Raphael did not know exactly what Cordelia might be capable of, and plainly Jesamine had not seen her like this before. "Take her word on this, Hispanian boy. Cordelia may be onto something. All that pedigree has to count for something."

"Take off your tunic."

Cordelia had all but barked an order at him, and Raphael was conditioned to do what he was told by officers. But she was also a comrade, so he still felt the right to argue. "I'm only going to look like a Mosul in his undershirt. And you're still wearing those Zhaithan tunics."

Cordelia looked bleakly at him. "I'm not about to go to war naked, my dear. What we have to do is dump our weapons."

"Are you crazy?"

"In a situation like this, it's a matter of first impressions. Under fire, you may not live to give or receive a second one. We have to look like we're surrendering."

A small fire of spilled kerosene provided a light at the bottom of the first flight of stairs. Raphael and Jesamine reluctantly put down their guns and followed Cordelia towards the licking flames on the floor and wall. The stairs were dark, but free of too much debris, and the three made it to the upper basement without incident or encounter. The corridor they entered contained no living person, just a number of sprawled dead. Two of the bodies were those of the other women who had been lined up for Jeakqual-Ahrach's inspection, and they looked as though they had been shot well before the Rangers had attacked. Raphael and Jesamine hesitated, but Cordelia continued doggedly on and even turned back to remonstrate with them. "Come on, we have to hurry. If the Rangers pull out without us, we're dead."

A scuffle at the top of the stairs brought even Cordelia to a halt. A shotgun roared, reverberating damagingly in the enclosed space, and a body flopped and rolled towards them. Raphael had never seen an Albany Ranger before, but he had seen enough artist's renderings of enemy uniforms. He recognized the man for what he was by the broad cut of the shoulders even before he saw the wide, flapped-back lapels and the twin rows of buttons on the forest green coat. The man must have seen Raphael, Cordelia, and Jesamine at the foot of the stairs in the muzzle flash from his gun, because he immediately turned the weapon on them. Cordelia braced herself and spoke in a voice that was clear, controlled, and conversational. "Ranger, I am Lady Cordelia Blakeney, and I urgently need your help."

The shotgun was not lowered, but the Ranger descended two careful paces down the steps. "Lady Blakeney?"

"That's what I said."

"Lady Blakeney from the airship?"

"From the NU98, the very same. You have just rescued me."

Raphael could not believe what he was hearing, and the Ranger seemed to be having trouble believing it, too. "What happened to the others?"

"The others from the NU98?"

The Ranger nodded. "The captain and crew."

"I'm fairly certain Captain Mallory and his crew are all dead. I think the last of the survivors were hanged this very night."

He pointed with his shotgun at Raphael and Jesamine. "So who are these two?"

"They are my companions. It's very important that all three of us get out of here."

The Ranger shook his head. "It's not possible, miss. We can take you with us, but not a couple of additional strangers."

"Between us we have vital information that has to be given to Prime Minister Kennedy. He is a dear friend of my mother."

"They look like enemy prisoners to me, and we're not taking prisoners."

"What's your name, Ranger?"

"Barnabas, miss."

"And your rank?"

"Ranger First Class, miss."

"Well, I'm a bloody lieutenant, Ranger Barnabas, so you will do as I ask."

ARGO

"Hooker! Don't shoot! It's me, Weaver. I've got Slide with me. Don't fucking shoot!"

Hooker's voice came from out of the smoke. "Weaver?"

"Yeah."

"Slide?"

"Don't let the uniform fool you."

"Keep your damned heads down. Some of them still want to make a fight of it."

As Argo dropped to a crouch, a musket ball slapped into the cement behind him as though to illustrate Hooker's point. Two Rangers fired at the flash, and, at the same time, Madden appeared beside Argo, Jones knife in hand. "You're lucky you're you, boy. I was ready to gut you as a Zhaithan."

Now Steuben was on his other side. He clapped Argo on the shoulder. "You picked a hell of a time to show up."

Being back with the Rangers made Argo feel like he had come home. He took his first chance to look around. The interior of the Bunker was part charnel house and part blackened ruin. A short way away, Penhaligon was sheltered behind a fallen section of wall, manning the Bergman. Madden gestured with his knife. "After we'd blown the outer wall, we came back to clean out the place. We tossed in a couple of Mills bombs and then moved inside to finish it."

Slide eased in behind them. "And how do you intend to get out of this killing zone?"

Steuben grinned. "Don't fret, Yancey. We've got it covered."

Barnabas appeared from the flight of ruined stairs. He was moving fast, and three figures followed him. Argo instantly recognized the first one, even though he had never seen her in the flesh before. "Lady Blakeney!"

He started to rise, but Madden jerked him down again. "I don't know who she is, but she isn't worth getting your fucking head shot off for."

Argo was beside himself. "You don't understand. It's them. It's the rest of the Four."

CORDELIA

The Ranger captain was kneeling behind a monolith of toppled masonry. Another Ranger was operating a Bergman gun. The captain scowled when he saw that the Ranger called Barnabas was not alone. "When did you start taking prisoners?"

"These aren't prisoners, Captain."

"Then what the hell are they?"

Cordelia decided to save time by cutting in. She recognized the captain, but he did not recognize her. "You're Jeb Hooker, aren't you?"

"Do I know you?

For sake of impact, Cordelia was blunt and to the point. "You should—you were fucking my friend Coral Metcalfe when you were in Albany on a two-week leave."

"You're Cordelia Blakeney?"

Cordelia made a small, heads-down curtsey. "Believed missing on the NU98."

"And these two?"

"Was the nature of the Four explained to you?"

"Yancey Slide told me what I needed to know."

"We are three of the Four, and the fourth is just over there, with, if I'm not mistaken, Yancey Slide himself."

"And what do you want me to do for you and your companions?"

"Obviously we need to return to Albany with all speed."

The Ranger at the Bergman fired a chugging burst, and Hooker waited for the noise to stop before he responded. "Are you the only survivor of the NU98?"

Cordelia nodded. It was the second time she had been asked that question. She did not want to appear the cold bitch, but so much had happened in the intervening time to make the airship, and even Phelan Mallory, seem a very long way away.

Hooker looked around, doing a mental roll call of his men. "If that's the case, you're probably right. We haven't found the bits of your airship for the Norse, but I think we've done all the damage we can do here. We should hightail it back to Albany as fast as we can." He glanced at Penhaligon, who was scanning the dark interior of the Bunker's ground floor. "How does it look to you? Are we secure here?"

"About as secure as we're going to get, Captain."

"Then let's call ourselves a cab."

ARGO

Madden led and Argo followed, with Slide and T'saya, to where the others of the Four were grouped around Jeb Hooker. He knew it was a significant moment. Indeed, only the future would tell just how significant. Oddly, and as with so many supposedly significant moments, he felt mundane and normal. He still perceived himself as the same scared kid who had fled Thakenham after being beaten by his stepfather, despite all the logic dictating that he had grown and changed in the course of all that had gone down since. The Four approached each other awkwardly, almost with embarrassment. None of them seemed sure of the appropriate way to act. The phrase intimate strangers jumped into his mind, and he suspected it had come from Cordelia. Was she reading his mind even as he thought? He was not sure he liked that. It seemed to be emerging that this Lady Blakeney was the most powerful of the three, although, right at that moment, the redhead of his visions cut a far from powerful figure. She and the other girl had Zhaithan jackets over plain nakedness, and the boy was stripped to his ill-fitting Mosul trousers. They were covered in dust, soot, and sweat, had plainly come through an ordeal that he could only attempt to imagine. He figured that he did not exactly resemble an agent of destiny in his stolen and equally messed-up Zhaithan uniform.

"You could be the gentleman and offer me your cloak, Argo Weaver."

From that day on, Argo was never sure if those first words of Cordelia's were telepathic or spoken. Many would pretend to know, but if Argo did not know, how could anyone else? All he remembered was that he whipped off his cloak with a flourish, at the same time turning to Slide. "Yancey, maybe you should give your cloak to . . ."

"Jesamine."

Slide grinned and handed his cape to the tall, dark-haired, honey-skinned girl. Argo stepped closer to Cordelia and draped his over her shoulders. Pretending she was completely unaware of the stares of the Rangers and the others around her, before Jesamine took the cloak from Slide she slipped out of her Zhaithan tunic and stood nude for a moment as she handed it to the Hispanian boy whose name was Raphael. "Here, you better put this on." Then, with the studied execution of a dancer, she swept Slide's robe out of his hands and around her body. As she made the move, Argo sensed an abrupt flurry of competition with Cordelia for his, and probably everyone else's, attention. His new companions were as flawed and insecure as he was, and that came as a great relief. With Jesamine's jacket over his ill-fitting Mosul trousers, Raphael was the first to speak directly to the other three as a group. He looked at them with grave formality. "We've all come a long way to be here."

The other three nodded, suddenly just as solemn. Without any more being said, hands were extended. In the moment before they all touched, Argo felt a precipitate and breathless reluctance, as if he were giving up a part of himself. Then skin touched skin.

They were locked in a blaze of rectangular gold. The Four had finally located that power that was greater than themselves—or to be more accurate, the power had located them. It gleamed around them, mighty and geometric, but who served whom was probably a matter of individual perception and perspective. The immediate problem was that in this world of golden linear energy and black emptiness, they had no perception or perspective, although mercifully they seemed to retain their individuality. The geometry was beyond inexplicable. Right angles stood at ninety degrees to each other, one upon the next, and on and on in a continuum of compass points that extended to an apparent infinity. The amount they so obviously had to learn about their new potential and this Other Place in which it would be realized threatened to charbroil their newfound collective mind before they had so much as embarked on the journey that was planned for them.

The contact was broken as if by mutual consent. They all knew why, but it took Slide to put it into words. "I'm glad you all remembered how little you know and agreed this was not the place."

Raphael and Jesamine were avoiding looking at Slide, and Argo wondered if some evil, nightcrawling legend had circulated among the Mosul about him. In Thakenham they had never heard of him, but he seemed to be notorious everywhere else. Cordelia seemed to know all about Slide, probably from the talk in Albany, although he wondered if her impression might not be colored by a few flourishes of romance and propaganda. Together or apart, they all had a lot to learn, and nothing should be assumed. Once the contact was broken, Jesamine embraced T'saya and then introduced her to the others. Argo was about to do the same for Slide, when Hooker indicated they had no time for such niceties. "I know you have a lot to talk about, but it's going to have to wait. We have to concentrate on getting out of here." He gestured to Madden. "You want to do the honors?"

Madden opened a knapsack and removed a small satchel charge while looking around the interior of the ruined Bunker until convinced that no more live and armed Mosul were lurking. Then he moved to one of the far walls. As the other Rangers carefully gathered their gear, he laid a charge against a steel door that had to be a ground floor rear exit. "I would suggest you all cover your ears and protect yourselves against falling debris." He then grinned nonchalantly and lit the fuse on the charge. "Fire in the hole, lads."

RAPHAEL

Although the charge that took out the door was far less powerful than the ones that had devastated the main entrance, the noise of the explosion in the confined space was deafening and left Raphael's head ringing. He was allowed no time, however, to recover. Before the smoke had cleared, and while freshly dislodged masonry was still dropping from the ceiling, the Rangers moved out. As they were exiting the freshly blown hole in the wall, a Mosul had suddenly risen out of nowhere and aimed a blow with a short-handled entrenching tool at the head of the Ranger who had set the charges. Weaver, who had his pistol out and already, shot the attacker before he could connect, with a coolness that made it appear as though he had killed almost without thinking. The two men had then nodded to each other. "My gratitude, Mr. Weaver."

"You're welcome, Mr. Madden."

Outside, a staff car and a truck with a closed cab and a tentlike canvas cover on the back roared out of the night, blowing smoke, engines racing, wheels spinning in the mud, and Zhaithan pennants fluttering above the headlights. They had all been instructed as to what to do when the hijacked vehicles arrived, otherwise Raphael would have assumed the automobiles were part of a Zhaithan counterattack. Fortunately, the Mosul outside the building actually did assume that and jumped aside to let them through. A partially formed perimeter had been thrown around the Bunker, and storming parties had been formed, but, as always with the Mosul, supply was the weakness. Ammunition was only just being issued, and, when the Rangers and their charges dashed from the hole blasted in the rear of the Bunker, most of those who could have turned a gun on them were still hurriedly loading rifles and muskets.

The Four were being separated again, almost as soon as they had found each other. The boys were to be riding in the truck with the Rangers, while the girls went into the staff car with Slide, T'saya, and Hooker. As they ran for their designated transports, Hooker was shouting just like every officer Raphael had ever encountered in his less-than-distinguished military career. "Come on, lads, move! Move! Move! Move!"

Helped by Rangers, Raphael scrambled into the darkness of the back of the truck, right behind Argo Weaver, and then, in turn, he helped pull up the gunner with the Bergman whose name, he had learned, was Penhaligon. As the truck lurched away, following the lights of the staff car, a few Mosul loosed off pursuing shots, but, with no time to aim, these went wild. Penhaligon deftly mounted the Bergman on the truck's tailboard and fired a burst that sent the Mosul scattering for cover.

"See how the bastards run." Penhaligon bared his teeth at Raphael. "No disrespect, okay?"

"None taken."

After they were clear of the streets around the Bunker, all problems seemed to cease. No one so much as attempted to get in their way. Penhaligon spat out the back of the track, into the slipstream, and lit the stub of a cigar. "No communications, see? Once we're away from the immediate combat area, every Mosul will think we're Zhaithan on a mission."

JESAMINE

Jesamine sagged back against the expensive leather of the rear seat of the Mosul staff car. She was going to Albany, and only the devils of hell knew what she could expect when she got there. Slide and Hooker were compressed into the front of the vehicle with the driver, while Cordelia and Jesamine sat squashed in the back, one on either side of T'saya. The gasoline burner had been clipped by a musket ball as they raced away from the bunker, but no kind of pursuit was mounted and the two vehicles escaped unscathed. As the staff car plunged and bounced into the night, she learned from the conversation between Cordelia and Hooker that they were driving at speed for the river, where canoes were hidden that the Rangers would use to paddle across to friends and safety. Jesamine had waited years for the chance of escape, but, now that it was here, the sequence of events was moving so fast that she had no time to analyze how she was feeling. Somewhat to her shame, she was reacting to the racing developments, and her lack of control over them, by being irritated by all that was mean and petty. As she sat squeezed in the car, she was gripped by a definite resentment towards Cordelia and the way that she had changed now that she was back among her own people. Now that Jesamine was no longer useful, she appeared to have been discarded.

Her attention was only diverted from this negative introspection when the car, and the truck that followed it, drove right by one of the huge, steam-driven, iron fighting machines. She had often seen the big, lumbering battle tanks from a distance, but she had never before been allowed so close to one of the ungainly products of the forges and factories in Damascus and the Ruhr. Stokers had kindled a flame in the boiler, and the crew watched as they now attempted to raise a head of steam and set the metal monster, with its riveted, battleship body, in motion. As the car rushed by, both the crew and stokers stopped what they were doing and came to attention, obviously believing that the Zhaithan pennants on the staff car meant that someone of significant importance was dashing through the night. Cordelia laughed and looked gleefully at Jesamine. "The bloody fools are probably firing up that thing to go and save the Bunker from its attackers. Little do they know the attackers just drove past them and they saluted."

Cordelia seemed to be treating everything as though it was some marvelous schoolgirl prank and forgetting how, just a short while before, the pair of them had been stripped and ready for torture. Jesamine had never been a schoolgirl. It did not work that way under the Mosul, and she did not have the ability to switch moods quite so capriciously. She wondered if this knack for levity was the prerogative of aristocrats or if it was shared by all in Albany. In truth, Jesamine was daunted by the thought of Albany. She had been a slave of the Mosul in one demeaning capacity or another for as long as she could remember, and she was not sure how well she would adapt to an entirely different world. Of course she did not believe all the horror stories about Albany that were spread by the Zhaithan propaganda machine, but she still had her doubts about how she would survive there. How would people in Albany accept her? Surely they would see her as nothing more than a combination of runaway slave and enemy whore. How would she manage on her own in what promised to be a very foreign environment? Then, finally, Jesamine caught herself. She was not going to be there alone. She would have companions. She was one of the Four, and the one thing that was no longer in doubt was that the Four were real. Cordelia might be irritating, but Jesamine's irritation might only be a shield against the plain fact that she was walking into the unknown with all of her insecurities and lack of self-respect at full jangle. Phaall, and all those who had come before him, had taken great care to beat and bully the self-esteem out of her. Over and over she had to repeat to herself that she was one of the Four, and they were the children of destiny, no matter how hard that might be to believe. They were the Four, and they were a force with which to be reckoned. They were the Four, and the rest was just a reaction to that overwhelming single fact.

Besides, T'saya was also with her, and just the presence of T'saya was a great comfort to Jesamine. T'saya meant she would not be completely shut off from the past, no matter how horrendous that past might have been.

ARGO

Argo could not believe that he had killed a man face to face and, in so doing, entered the exclusive club of men like Madden and Barnabas. He equally could not believe that it had affected him so little. The man had come at Madden out of nowhere, and he had raised his revolver and fired without thought or hesitation. He was taken back to that last night in Thakenham when he had been unable to shoot his stepfather. Things had changed so much since then, and he wondered why he did not really feel any different. In what privacy of mind he still had, he continued to feel like the frightened boy who had run away from the impossible, but he now appeared to be doing the impossible. He was not so desensitized, though, that he would soon forget the flat, sweating face of the Mosul he had shot or the look of pain and resigned chagrin that this was all there would ever be for the poor bastard with more rage than sense. In fact, the memory was still so vivid that he did his best to avoid it by concentrating on the moment at hand and how he was back on the run with the Rangers.

He was not able to see much from the back of the covered truck. The road stretching behind was visible over the tailboard, but even that view was limited by the form of Penhaligon bent over his Bergman gun. Argo, Raphael, and the Rangers did not even see the huge steam tank until they had already passed it, leaving its crew, clearly taken in by the flashy Zhaithan pennants of the staff car, at attention and staring after them. On the other hand, Argo's country-boy nose was not about to let him down. The stench of the Mosul-fouled Potomac was growing stronger and stronger by the moment. The river could not be far away, and their time in the dark flatbed should not be prolonged.

This was confirmed when the truck lurched to a halt, throwing everyone momentarily off balance. Leaving the Bergman where it was, Penhaligon swung over the tailboard and dropped to the ground. Steuben quickly moved forward and handed the weapon down to him and then jumped down himself, glancing back at Argo and the others. "All aboard the skylark, lads. Now we have the boat ride."

The truck had halted under a grove of trees on a small knoll of high ground surrounded on three sides by polluted wetland that was choked with weeds and the skeletons of rusty, shot-to-hell vehicles and beached and beat-up landing craft. Billy and Cartwright were already waiting for them. They had been detached from the rest of the squad to wreak havoc with the mortar, and they had been responsible for the blowing up of the burning Ziggurat, the multiple gallows, and the other shells that had fallen on the parade ground. Having caused the right measure of mayhem, they had made their own way to the rendezvous point and now looked relieved that everyone had emerged from the attack on the Bunker unscathed.

When Hooker walked back from the staff car, he quickly looked around. "What did you do with the mortar?"

"Broke it down and dumped it in pieces, just like you said, Captain."

The next phase of their escape was to make their way, hummock to hummock, across the oily bog to the open water where the Ranger's canoes were concealed and waiting. Hooker took a hand-drawn chart of the route to the canoes from his map case. "I'll walk point on this. Penhaligon, you bring up the rear with the Bergman in case of some bad-luck pursuit."

Penhaligon nodded. "Covered."

"Very well. I want everyone to follow in my footsteps as accurately as possible. The bastards may have dumped mines and booby traps in this mess, so be really careful." He paused for a moment to see if anyone had anything to add. "Okay then. Let's go to Albany."

CORDELIA

The defenses of Albany looked formidable by the light of a smoke yellow half-moon. Massive earthworks, concrete blockhouses, high stone walls, pointed dragons' teeth, and miles upon miles of barbed wire, coiled, strung, and threateningly entangled, all combined to give the impression that the armies of Hassan IX were going to pay dearly for every square foot of ground they so much as touched on the north side of the Potomac. The wire went not only all the way to the water's edge, but continued into the river to become a maze of cruelly submerged, flesh-ripping snares. The night had covered the surface of the water with a layer of hanging mist, and Cordelia pulled her borrowed cloak around herself against the damp and chill. The hem of her less-than-adequate garment was wet and slimy where it had been dragged through the swamp. The party had crossed the odious margins with haste and efficiency, although a number of even the Rangers had missed their footing and sunk at least knee deep in the reeking ooze. The canoes had been swiftly located and launched. They were long, aborigine-style craft of pounded bark and cured leather stretched over willow frames, each with the curved and pointed front and rear design that had made the native people such masters of the American waterways. She had found herself seated in the prow of the lead canoe, and, perhaps due to some still-maintained Ranger idea of gallantry, she was not required to do galley-slave duty. Behind her, Argo Weaver and four Rangers dug in with their paddles, while T'saya and Yancey Slide sat idly in the stern. The demon, it seemed, was with the women when it came to superfluously exerting himself. The second canoe followed with Jesamine in the prow and Penhaligon, seemingly inseparable from his Bergman, in the stern.

The boats were steering a long, downriver diagonal course from one bank to the other, using the current to their advantage and moving east to where the Potomac widened out and the Mosul were not so concentrated along the water's edge. The canoes were painted dull black, and their occupants crouched low, offering as small a target as possible to any enemy picket that might feel like firing on them. Aside from being damp and chilled, Cordelia was also more than a little nervous, and she hoped that someone had somehow warned the defenders of Albany that they were coming. She said nothing, because it probably would have seemed irrational, but her sudden and overwhelming fear was that after having been through so much, she would end up being shot by one of her own, sharing the same ironic and legendary fate that had befallen Colonel Mahogany Jackson, in the oft told tale. When you were killed by friendly fire, that seemed to be all that anyone ever remembered about you.

Cordelia saw the lights when the canoes were at a point a little to the Albany side of midstream. She had glanced back to see that the second boat, with Jesamine in the prow, was keeping up. She was somewhat concerned about Jesamine. While Cordelia had been elated, Jesamine had seemed remote and withdrawn since they had escaped from the Bunker, and Cordelia was wondering if she were suffering from some sort of delayed shock. Cordelia's first and obvious reaction was that the lights belonged to a Mosul patrol boat coming downriver, following their wake, and if that was the case, they were in trouble. The only problem was that the lights of a gunboat, either from the Mosul or from Albany, should have been distinct pinpoints, and these were not. What Cordelia was seeing in the distance was an unhealthy and diffused orange glow. She supposed that this diffusion could have been a result of the low-lying river fog, but somehow she thought not. She leaned close to the Ranger behind her, the one called Steuben. "There's something behind us."

Steuben, whom she had noticed fancied himself a comedian, saw nothing funny about the lights when he glanced back. "I don't think I like the look of that, miss."

"A gunboat?"

Steuben shook his head. "I don't think so."

"What then?"

"I'd hate to say it and then be wrong." He pulled his paddle out of the water and signaled silently to Slide that they were being followed. Yancey Slide looked and then hissed a low warning."Dark Things on the water!"

"Shit! I don't want to be seeing this."

"I'm afraid you are, lad. I'm going to warn the others."

Cordelia questioned Slide in a loud whisper. "Can we outrun them?"

Slide shook his head. "I don't think so."

He waved for Hooker's attention, and, using Ranger sign language, directed the captain's attention to the lights. Hooker gestured to Penhaligon, indicating with a throat-cutting gesture that the Bergman was not a solution. Cordelia wanted to know, "Can the Four do anything?"

Slide was firm. "No, you can't. You don't know enough yet to take on Dark Things in an open boat. They are repositories of pure loathsome rage." Then he suddenly grinned. "Don't worry, though. Even repositories of rage can be punctured."

"Punctured?"

"Let them get a bit closer."

"Who would have sent Dark Things after us?"

Slide drew on his hand-cupped cigar. "Quadaron-Ahrach or his sister at a guess. We pretty much made fools of the Zhaithan tonight, plus we stole two of the Four right out from Jeakqual-Ahrach's clutches. The siblings have got to be spitting mad."

Black spheres were now visible within the glow, and no matter how those with the paddles exerted themselves, digging deep in the water and going desperately for speed instead of quiet concealment, the glow and the spheres came rapidly closer.

"Wouldn't it have been easier to have sent a gunboat? Dark Things seem like an awful lot of effort to catch poor little me." Cordelia knew she was only being flippant to cover up the fear that seemed to be moving up her body to grab for her brain. She could already feel the presence of the Dark Things bearing down on her. The closer they came, the more her flesh crawled and she found it hard to breathe. Unfocused flutterings attacked the edges of her mind with half-formed visions and unintelligible whispers that hinted at fire and darkness, pain and impossible perspectives. Her hands were starting to shake, but she smiled bravely at her own inane question.

Slide at least had the compassion to laugh, and Steuben also grinned despite himself. "Listen, miss, if we can't outrun or run off a Mosul gunboat in the dark, we're in the wrong business. They've brought up the big guns."

Slide agreed. "They want poor little you rather badly, my dear. It's become personal. The evil siblings want to punish us for our audacity. It's not just you Four. They've probably figured out that I'm here, too, and the Ahrachs would really like to get their hands on me."

"You say they can be punctured?"

Slide drew one of his strange and otherworldly pistols. "A bullet from another thread of time, fired by a equally displaced pistol; that should fuck up their nastiness."

"I don't really understand."

Even though the Dark Things had halved the distance between them and the canoes, Slide turned and looked hard at Cordelia. For a moment she could have sworn that his eyes had become almost sympathetic. "Time is like a river, Cordelia. It moves as one, but within in its depths are a million interlocked eddies and moving microcurrents. In the same way, across the breadth of the time stream, an infinity of variations move side by side, similar but with different sequences and different variants of reality. You humans exist in but one of them, and, for the most part, you are unaware that, just a split, sideways-second away, a hundred other Hassan IX's make war with varying degrees of success, and a hundred other Cordelia Blakeney's are caught up in those wars. As you move outwards, at right angles to your familiar three dimensions, the terrain becomes a whole lot more alien and queer, and that's where Quadaron-Ahrach harvests his Dark Things and brings them back here to feed and grow mean on the worst poison of men's minds."

"Didn't you ought to be watching those things and not talking to me?"

Slide grinned. "We have a little time."

Cordelia was sure that Slide was being overconfident, and she was not sure she liked it. The Dark Things were now sufficiently close that she could see they were more than just pitch-black spheres. They were gelatinous blobs, and far from perfectly spherical. The Dark Things had smooth and shapeless exteriors, like thick, living sacs that sweated beads of dark red liquid the color of congealing blood. The three of them rolled across the surface of the river in a tight V-formation, protected by the unhealthy orange glow. Where their undersides touched the water, it hissed and boiled and made it look like they rode on a surface of trailing steam. Slide, however, seemed unworried.

"Let them get a bit closer."

Slide now seemed downright cocky, and Cordelia had to ask, "Are you really a demon?"

"And what's a demon, Lady Blakeney? Just a being who is able to jump the time streams, one to the next, and find a foothold wherever he might land. Now that the Four of you are together, you will learn some of the same."

"I'm not sure how I feel about that."

"Then think about it later. I estimate our foul friends are close enough. Watch and learn."

Slide crouched in the stern of the canoe and aimed his pistol with two-handed care, resting his arms on the upcurve of the gunwale. He fired three times in regular succession, and the pistol responded with a rapidity greater than any weapon Cordelia had ever encountered. He hit the lead Dark Thing three times in a grouping no more spread out than the surface of a small plate, but nothing happened beyond three raised and quivering blisters that appeared on the grotesque and supernatural monster's hide. Otherwise it was not so much as slowed in its rolling. The voices and intruding visions were now more that merely peripheral. They were threatening Cordelia like water about to close over a drowning swimmer. "I thought you said you could puncture them."

Slide scowled and aimed again. "I didn't say it would be easy."

He fired two more fast shots, but again nothing happened, or so it seemed for the space of about ten seconds. Then a small rent appeared in the leading Dark Thing's hide, at first just a tiny split, but rapidly elongating as though under some kind of internal pressure that it could no longer contain. The interior of the Dark Thing became visible and then started to spill out and run down its skin. Cordelia could only think of the inside of a pomegranate as what looked like sticky, dark red, segmented seed pods were vomited from the wound, but she knew the mess she was seeing was not seeds and had nothing to do with reproduction. They hissed when the water touched them as though they contained a powerful acid. The Dark Thing wobbled to one side, seeming to lose all ability to maintain its direction. The other two also spun away from their original course, as though navigation had been some combined process.

It only took two shots to puncture the second Dark Thing, and this one proved to have no pomegranate interior. It deflated like a burst balloon with wrinkled rags of hide flying off to drop into the water and dissolve. Slide whipped out his second pistol and holstered the first. Seven shots had exhausted the clip. The remaining Dark Thing came to a halt and slightly settled a few submerged inches in the water, toadlike, as though considering its next move now that its companions were gone. It slowly changed color from black to a highly offensive purple. Visible pores opened in the thing's hide from which a black gas flowed with a growing pressure and density. Slide cursed as though this was the very last reaction he wanted. He snapped back the slide on his fresh pistol, aimed at the now stationary third Dark Thing, and pumped three bullets into it. Three ragged holes appeared in the body, out from which poured more black gas. The last Dark Thing was fast sinking into the river but spewing as much poisonous vapor as it could before it drowned. Slide shouted a warning as the gas rolled onto them like smoke on the water. "Cover your faces! Don't breathe too much of the black gas. It's been known to drive men permanently crazy."

Everyone pulled coats, capes, and tunics over their mouths and noses, but while they were protecting themselves, the two canoes were dead in the water. Slide yelled again. "Paddle, you idiots. Let's get the fuck out of here!"

Cordelia caught a whiff of the gas. She began coughing helplessly, and black specters invaded her mind. For a moment she thought she was going to lose her reason, but the Rangers, along with Argo and Raphael, had dug in with a vengeance, and suddenly the menace of the black gas was behind them and they were again breathing relatively clear air. The specters in Cordelia's head lost their footing and fell away. At the same time, a signal lamp flashed a repeating pattern from the Albany bank. *One-two-three, one-two, one-two-three, one-two.*

"Is that for us?" Steuben snorted.

"You see any other dumb bastards floating about on the river in the middle of the night?"

One-two-three, one-two, one-two-three, one-two. The canoes turned hard toward the signal, and as they followed the bank, it was soon possible to see a small jetty where uniformed figures stood and waited for them. Cordelia permitted herself a long and heartfelt sigh. Her strange circular voyage of discovery and loss, that had begun as an excitingly romantic day trip to Manhattan, was over. Other even more bizarre excursions might be ahead of her, but, for the moment, she had come home, and, blasé as Lady Cordelia Blakeney might endeavor to appear, the thought of home had a profound effect on her, and she had to get a firm grip on herself to avoid bursting into tears.

SEVEN

RAPHAEL

Vast and elongated drab green rectangles of close-pressed and ordered men, reduced to single cells in a geometric beast, and whose will had been replaced by a single destructive purpose, extended back to some infinity of the morning mist on the other side of the river. The air seemed dead, and Raphael could feel sweat form under the arms of his Albany Ranger's tunic. He could so easily have been one of them, and even though he had now changed sides, no guarantees were being given that any of those present would survive the coming days. After two long years of recuperation, the army of Hassan IX was on the move. Through the night and through all of the previous day, the battle lines had been laboriously formed. Now, as the sun slowly rose in a damp and damned autumn dawn, both sides paused, poised and ready, with the river between them. The Mosul and the defenders on the Albany bank took a long breath before the trumpets brayed, the orders were screamed, and the inevitable artillery opened fire. The Four, now united and recognized as such, stood together, looking out from the crenelated parapet of one of the high stone walls that had been raised along the Potomac to meet the long-awaited enemy assault. Politicians and some of the Albany high command, complete with aides and entourage, stared over the same parapet but discreetly kept their distance from Raphael, Jesamine, Argo, and Cordelia. The more the Four came together, the more Raphael noticed that others tried to keep away from them, or, at least, invent reasons not to come too close. Nowhere in Albany had it so far been doubted that the Four were an asset, a new weapon in the arsenal of abnormal warfare, but even those who sought to use them seemed to look on them as an unholy acquisition, the product of a deal with a demon.

Aside from Cordelia, who was now smartly arrayed in her RWA lieutenant's uniform, the Four were dressed in the forest green tunics of the Albany Rangers. Raphael supposed that the outfits, although they came without insignia, badges of rank, or the famous "We Own The Night" shoulder patches, conferred an honorary status on them as a part of the Albany war effort, although in his case, he was not sure exactly how honorary that status was. To many who were not in the paranormal and mystic loop, Raphael was seen as nothing more than a miserable deserter from the lowest ranks of the Mosul, and, behind his back, he was certain that questions were whispered as to why he was being accorded special treatment instead of being speedily dispatched to an internment camp just like any other unwashed turncoat. Dearly as he would have loved to do such a thing, he even hesitated to sketch the dramatic and mundane vignettes of war lest he be arrested as a spy. The others were hardly treated any better. To the uninformed, Jesamine was a runaway Mosul slave-harlot who appeared to be receiving levels of favor far above her station. Argo was also being viewed as a refugee from occupied Virginia who, despite his youth, had waited far too long before making his escape. Maybe the greatest irony was that Cordelia, who should have been welcomed in Albany with open arms as one of its own, came close to faring the worst of all, and only the intervention of no less than Prime Minister John Kennedy had saved her from being forced into the striped suit of a military prisoner awaiting court-martial.

Immediately after the Four had slept longer and more comfortably than any of them could remember and were sitting down in the kitchen of their new quarters to a breakfast that was nothing short of sumptuous, a stout RWA colonel had arrived with an armed escort and an arrest warrant in her fat fist with Cordelia's name on it. Seemingly, Cordelia's ill-fated ride in the NU98 had been a wilful and romance-driven adventure, a simple but irregular jaunt to the cabarets of Manhattan, embarked on with only the most flimsy official sanction. Colonel Patton had no tolerance for flimsy. As far as she was concerned, Cordelia was merely a deserter who had finally returned to face her judges, and not even a furious Yancey Slide could deflect her from what she all too delightedly considered to be her duty. It was only when Slide went to the very top—and the very top, in this instance, was Prime Minister Kennedy on a visit to the front—that Colonel Patton was sent packing with her guards and her warrant and the most categorical orders never again to bother the Lady Blakeney, who was now crucial to national security. Raphael supposed he was a little disappointed. He had never deceived himself that Albany was a paradise. It was a considerable improvement on the Mosul hell of burning, flogging, hangings, and constant fear and hunger, but it was far from being without its own pettiness, prejudice, and myopic bureaucracy.

On the other side, out across the river, in the spaces between the dull, camouflaged infantry formations, plumes bobbed, banners fluttered, the blades of drawn sabers and the points of lances glittered, and polished breastplates reflected the rising sun as the eager horses of a multitude of cavalry danced and pranced and waited for the charge to be sounded. From what he had learned from Melchior, it would be a long time before the bugles sounded the charge. The cavalry were only there to lend color and spectacle to what would be a grinding slaughter of infantry attrition. These pampered regiments were too pretty and too beloved of their generals to be thrown into the furnace until the wretched bloody infantry had smashed enough of a breach in the enemy defenses for them to gallop in with all the dash and flourish of an assured victory. As always, the foot soldiers were expected to lay the groundwork of annihilation. He wondered where his former squad might be in the sea of green. He wondered if Pascal had made it back and was not dangling at the end of a rope for his absence. He wondered if any of them would live through the day, or if Melchior really could bring the squad miraculously through their part in the assault.

The officers along the wall from Raphael were brought a field telephone. Orders, and probably orders of extreme significance, were about to be given. This was certainly an improvement in efficiency over the Mosul, who, save for a few Teutons, would have used a combination of runners and a heliograph in the same circumstances. What had Ranger

Penhaligon said, spitting out of the back of the truck as they fled the Mosul camp? "No communications, see." The telephone's dynamo was cranked, and the senior general, the slim, thoughtful man who walked with a limp, took the handset. Raphael had yet to learn all the names and the precise ranks, but from the red tabs on his collar, the gold on the peak of his cap, and the way all the others deferred to him, although he seldom seemed to raise his voice, Raphael had to assume that the one who limped was the supreme commander. He was too far away to hear the spoken order, but, from the way the officers covered their ears in its immediate aftermath, he knew what the content must have been.

CORDELIA

Cordelia covered her ears as the Albany guns opened up. When Dunbar had gestured for the field telephone, she knew it could only be to give one order. Field Marshal Virgil Dunbar did not confer or ask the advice of his battery commanders when the enemy was about to launch its attack. All that had been covered long before. Dunbar could only be calling for the opening bombardment, the first move in the long and bloody, slow dance that was contemporary warfare. The roar of the artillery was deafening as ordnance all along the river hurled shot and shell, hot metal and high explosive into the neat geometry of the Mosul array. Star shells burst overhead and blossoming fountains of smoke and flame erupted in a devastating pattern of destruction amid the enemy squares. A shell fell among the gaudy and formal ranks of horsemen, and colors were thrown around like a scattered flower arrangement, while another bisected a long column of infantry. Down on the ground, the carnage must have been hideous, and any reasonable human being might have been forgiven for demanding to know why the armies of Hassan IX did not run away right there and then. Reasonable humans, however, had no idea of the blood lust and blind obedience of which the enemy, Mosul, Teuton, and Mamaluke alike, was capable. She had seen it in the mind of Raphael, who had been one of them; she had also seen it in Argo's mind, who had been caught up in the channeled savagery of Quadaron-Ahrach's ceremony on the Mosul parade ground as, all around him, fighting men were gripped by a howling hysteria and talked in tongues to the twin gods Ignir and Aksura; and she had seen it herself when she had looked into the face of Jeakqual-Ahrach. Far from running away, the Mosul took the Albany barrage as a signal to advance. Trumpets brayed, men roared above the explosions and the screams, drums pounded, and marching songs were bellowed into the face of death as the lines of infantry surged forward.

The artillery bombardment, and the enemy on the move, had at least driven the resentment from Cordelia's mind at how close she had come to being thrown in the stockade after all she had been through, both in the cause of Albany as well as simply preserving her own life. After they had been allowed to sleep, the Four had risen to a communal breakfast shared with T'saya and Yancey Slide, who appeared to have been assigned as their mentors for the duration, although Slide did not eat, just smoked a cigar and watched everyone else. Cordelia found herself sitting down to buckwheat pancakes, bacon, sausage, and three eggs, sunny-side up, and felt it was probably the best thing that had happened to her in a very long time. Unfortunately, as though to prove that all delight comes at a price, Grace bloody Patton, Colonel of Women,́ had marched her corseted, ramrod-stiff bulk through the door with enough MPs at her back to apprehend a fighting-drunk mountain jack.

"On your feet, Blakeney, while I read the charges."

To raise a quizzical eyebrow might not have been the best reaction. Patton had come up through the ranks and harbored a deep loathing for fashionably commissioned aristocrats. Had she known where Cordelia had been and what she had done and witnessed, which, of course, she did not, it probably would not have impressed her, and she would have viewed the entire sequence of events with extreme suspicion.

"On your feet, my girl, and snap to it."

Cordelia had then compounded all previous offences by looking at Patton with irritated contempt. "Can't you see I'm eating my damned breakfast?"

She was one of the Four. She was the vessel of destiny. She might well save Albany before she was through. Who knew of what she might be capable? She felt that she had earned the right not be bothered by the like of Grace Patton, but once again her attitude and handling of the situation may have been less than wise.

"I'm giving you one last chance. One your feet, or I'll have these men subdue and take you by force."

Cordelia was simply not willing to play Patton's game. It was something out of back then, and this was right now. She put down her fork and regarded Patton with a gaze of pure, highborn chill. "I have just come from a place where I was strung up naked with silk ropes for the cause of Albany. I have been in an airship crash and watched the crew massacred. I have fought with the Rangers and faced down Dark Things. And now you want to arrest me? You know something, Colonel? You aren't that different from some of the fucking Zhaithan I encountered. And believe me, Grace, I encountered the very worst."

Patton inflated like a furious bulldog and snapped at her military policemen. "Take her. Drag her if need be. She's under close arrest."

This had been too much for Yancey Slide, and he had removed the cigar from his mouth. "Hold up there a minute, colonel-lady. No one's about to take anyone anywhere, let alone be dragging them."

In the aftermath of Patton's speech, the MPs were already looking a little doubtful. Slide had enough innate demonic authority, whether they knew who he was or not, that the MPs halted, unsure of whom to obey. Patton immediately revealed that she knew nothing of the Yancey Slide legend. Patton glared at him. "And who the hell are you?"

"I'm someone you really don't want to piss off, colonel-lady."

"What's your name, civilian?"

"Slide, Colonel. Yancey Slide."

Day dawned on Colonel Patton, and it was starting to look like a day of reckoning. "You're Slide?"

"One and the same."

Patton stood caught between duty and rumor, but she had been in the thrall of duty too long, and maybe that had put her a little out of touch with practical reality. "I've heard about you, Slide, but it doesn't change anything. That woman's mine. She's a deserter, and she's going to face a court-martial."

The quarters that the Four had been assigned came equipped with a field telephone. Slide put his cigar back in his mouth, picked up the handset, and cranked the handle.

"Let me just make a call on this contraption."

Patton's jaw set. "It won't make any difference. I have a signed warrant here from the Advocate General's office."

Slide ignored her and spoke in the phone. "Hey, central, give me the Top Drawer. Just tell them it's Yancey Slide."

T'saya looked up. "If that's who I think it is, tell him I need to see him."

Slide waited for about a minute. "John, yeah, it's me. I'm sorry to disturb you, but we have a problem down here. I know you planned to come by and meet with us sometime today, but it might be a good idea if you were to make it like right now. We have a problem here that needs to be nipped in the bud." Slide smiled and nodded. "I really appreciate that, John."

Slide hung up the phone and looked round the room. "Okay. Everyone will just stay right where they are, and we'll wait. In fifteen minutes, I guarantee this whole matter will be sorted out. In the meantime, I suggest that you, Colonel, help yourself to a cup of coffee (we have real coffee here for a change), and you, Cordelia, finish your breakfast."

T'saya scowled. "You didn't tell him I was here and wanted to see him."

"He's already well aware of that."

Patton was about to protest, but Slide treated her to a look that might have killed a being of lesser body weight. "All I need is fifteen minutes, Colonel. Is that too much to ask?"

"It won't make any difference."

"Humor me?"

It might have been more dramatic if the door had opened right there and then, but they had to wait not fifteen but an entire twenty minutes before the drama occurred. The wait was clearly worth it, though, because when the door did open, no less than the venerable John F. Kennedy, the prime minister of Albany, entered, guarded only by a single Ranger with a shotgun. The MPs stiffened to attention, Patton looked close to physical explosion, and even Cordelia was surprised, although she did her best to hide the fact. The only ones who did not react at all were Raphael and Jesamine, who did not know any better, since the Mosul had taught them that Albany was a feudal kingdom, and Slide, who seemed to be on the most intimate terms with the prime minister. Kennedy leaned on his cane, assessing the situation in the room. "Am I to understand that you're causing trouble already, Lady Blakeney? You certainly are a great deal like your mother when she was younger."

Cordelia half rose and attempted a perfunctory curtsey. "I'm sorry, Prime Minister. This seems to be trouble left over from before I departed."

Patton had recovered from her shock and was now in the process of deciding that all she was seeing was part of an upper-class conspiracy of privilege and nonaccountability, compounded by Kennedy's famous womanizing. "I'm sorry, Prime Minister, but Lady Blakeney has been posted as a deserter and must answer the charges. If you feel there are extenuating circumstances, you will be free to offer testimony to that effect at her trial."

Kennedy glanced at Patton's MPs. "Would one of you boys be good enough to get me a chair? I am old, and I spend far too much time on my feet."

A chair was found and placed, at Kennedy's indication, between Cordelia and Jesamine. He seated himself and smiled at Jesamine. "Would you be so kind as to pour me a cup of coffee, my dear? I don't think I know your name."

Jesamine smiled alluringly and reached for the coffee pot. "Jesamine, my lord. My name is Jesamine."

"I'm not a lord, my dear. Just a commoner like yourself. Am I right in thinking you're the one who just escaped from the Teutons?"

"That's right."

"You must tell me the whole story some time soon."

Cordelia realized that she was seeing the famous and so seductive Kennedy charm in operation. Even at his advanced age and with his long grey hair, the man had a certain magnetism. When young, he must have been irresistible.

Patton was fuming. "I'm sorry, Prime Minister, but I really have to take Lady Blakeney into custody. I feel enough time has been wasted here."

John Kennedy sipped his coffee. "I also am sorry, Colonel, but I have to tell you that you won't be taking Lady Blakeney anywhere. Greater considerations have to be balanced here than just a minor matter of RWA discipline."

"Desertion is no minor matter."

"We all know that she went for an airship ride, and the train of events ran totally out of control. She has returned to us with vital information and will remain attached to my staff, or the Rangers, for an indefinite period.

Patton huffed. "I can't just ignore these charges."

"Then you will put them on hold, Patton. Perhaps until the war is over. The great leveler of national security has closed over you."

Patton contained her fury, but not to the point that she could speak, especially after Jesamine had stuck out her tongue at her. She turned and made for the exit, followed by her frowning MPs. At the door, she found her voice. "I didn't vote for you, Prime Minister."

After Patton was gone, Slide looked slowly round the table. "I suppose that will serve to keep people guessing and confuse Mosul intelligence."

John Kennedy lit a cigar. "You know, Slide, you have an inhuman nerve. No one asks the prime minister to come to them."

"These are extraordinary circumstances, John."

"That's the only reason I'm here."

T'saya helped herself to one of Slide's cheroots. "You're looking old, John."

"I am old, my dear T'saya."

"You still recognize me?"

Kennedy adopted an expression of ancient innocence. "How could I not?"

"You stood me up a lot of years ago, John."

"And I've regretted it ever since."

"You're a bullshit artist, John."

Kennedy smile sadly. He suddenly looked tired. "That I am. I can't lie to you."

"You could lie to anyone. That's what makes you such a brilliant politician."

"Am I a brilliant politician?"

"One of the most brilliant. Are you still making overtures to Cetshwayo V to start a second front in Africa?"

"Are you still spying for him?"

T'saya's eyes became blank. "I never spied for Cetshwayo."

"No?"

"Cetshwayo is as much of a bloody despot as Hassan IX. If it wasn't for his absurdly traditionalist loathing of firearms and how they spoil the pure nature of warfare as it was conceived by the great Chaka, we'd all be in a mess of trouble."

Raphael and Jesamine glanced at each other. Rumors regularly circulated in the Mosul world of the mysterious and primitive Zulu Hegemony in the southern half of Africa, of how Mamaluke expeditions seeking slaves and ivory had been put to flight by ZH impis, and Teuton prospecting teams had been slaughtered all save one man, who had been sent back to Hassan to tell the tale. Obviously, if the Zulu formations moved north, the emperor would have to pull troops from the Americas to contain their advance, and Albany would be the beneficiary. With the Mosul they were told nothing, and life was severe but simple. In Albany, you heard so much that the world became a large and complicated place.

T'saya smiled. "I may of course have let slip a few crumbs of information to people who were going that way, but I work for no one."

"Twelve years among the Mamalukes, and you work for no one?"

T'saya's smile broadened. "I have my own agendas, John Kennedy."

"And what might they be?"

"Now, wouldn't you like to know?"

Cordelia's eggs were cold, but suddenly she didn't care. Patton had been sent on her way and would not be bothering her again. Slide was able to pull no less than the prime minister out of his hat to protect her. Cordelia was aware that she was important. Not only by birth or connection, but on the strength who she was and these strange new shared powers. She was at the very center of world events. She was sitting at the table with the prime minister of Albany, a reputed demon who could step sideways in time, and a strange old woman who had lived among the Mamalukes to further her own mysterious and probably mystic interests. Later she would find herself standing on the battlements as the Mosul commenced their advance, and only then did she realize that much was going to be demanded of her for all this protection and attention.

As the guns of Albany roared out, and Cordelia began to believe that her hearing was going to be permanently impaired, she looked up and saw a tiny blue object in the sky. A spotter plane was high above the battle. She could picture the excited young man, with helmet and goggles, wrapped in fur and leather against the chill of the heavens, looking down like a visiting angel on the explosions and the carnage, and she was suddenly seized by a sense of loss for her own airman, and the memory of how she, too, had looked down from the clouds at the world below. Then shock gripped her as the plane seemed to falter and fall. *Please, no.* She did not want to witness another crash or be a party to the death of another aviator. The aircraft appeared to be plunging straight down. Had it been hit by a well-aimed or lucky Mosul bullet, or had the machinery somehow malfunctioned? Only when it leveled out and flew straight did Cordelia realize that the pilot had been in control all the time. As the plane skimmed over the Mosul, she recognized its triple-winged triplane configuration from one of the aircraft identification outlines that she had been compelled to memorize during RWA basic training. The machine, known as a Hellhound, had almost certainly been prefabricated in the Norse Union but assembled in Brooklyn, so it now wore the proud shield of the Crowned Bear on its wings and fuselage. The pilot dropped a token pair of small bombs and then climbed again to less dangerous altitudes as his two small explosions were added to the general thunder of fire and flame.

ARGO

The enemy guns were slow to fire in response or even in support of the infantry that was preparing to cross the river in the hardest way possible. The Albany bombardment had been going on for a full five minutes before a line of Mosul howitzers on a ridge to the east tore into the Albany earthworks that were directly opposite them. He could hear men on the Albany side screaming for medical attention, and he knew then that the war, in which no quarter was going to be received, given, or even expected, had started in earnest. The Mosul now swarmed at the water's edge, and, despite the barrage and the hail of small arms' fire that blazed from the Albany banks, engineers were moving pontoons into place and laying prefabricated lengths of wooden roadway to form a dozen or more swaying and makeshift bridges that, when completed, would carry men and machines across the river. The bridgework was a slow, and, in many cases, suicidal task. The bridge builders were instant and obvious targets, as were the squads of riflemen who advanced onto each new section directly it was secure and used it as a firing platform, discharging volleys over the heads of the sappers as the next section was moved into place and they advanced a dozen yards closer to Albany.

The slow chop of heavy Bergman guns cut down the infantry on the bridges like sweeps of an invisible scythe, while the sappers in the water were picked off by sharpshooters or decimated by concentrated rifle fire, but no matter how intense the carnage, more Mosul moved relentlessly forward to take the place of those who had fallen. Gaping holes were blown in the structures by mortar and artillery shells, but the engineers went right back to work like some mutant hybrid of man, ant, and beaver, repairing the damage and, at the same time, extending their agonizingly slow path of conquest. Now Argo could see quite clearly how the Mosul had gained both their fearsome reputation for tenacity and their total control of half the Old World. They never stopped coming and, no matter how many thousands might be cut down, more were always waiting to climb over the dead and continue the attack.

The enemy strategy did not rely entirely on bridging the Potomac to bring its assault troops across. At the same time as the pontoons were being manhandled into place, an armada of rafts, flat-bottomed barges, and low-to-the-water riverboats was being launched all along the Mosul-held bank, and each was loaded to capacity with men and weapons. Some proved overloaded and quickly foundered, sinking humiliatingly in the shallows. More made it to somewhere around midstream but were then sunk by Albany gunners. Some even approached the Albany banks but were either blasted to matchwood by light four-inch field guns firing cannister from the riverside emplacements, or their occupants were hacked to death by the constant coughing of the Bergmans. Within minutes of the start of the assault, the Potomac was a mass of the floating dead and living men struggling desperately to save themselves from drowning between the leaping waterspouts that marked the impact of shells from both sides. A few of the craft actually reached their objectives. Mosul soldiers splashed onto dry ground and dived for any cover they could. The first across lived only a few minutes, with the Albany defenders allowing them no time to even dig in at the water's edge. One squad did have enough time to set up a trench mortar and wreak a degree of havoc before they were blown back into the river.

A steam-driven fighting machine had been laboriously maneuvered onto an especially large raft that was surrounded with huge steel barrels for extra buoyancy and now moved sluggishly out into the current. If the mechanical monster was able to gain a foothold on the Albany side, it would be hard to dislodge and could provide the cover for maybe hundreds of men to reach the north bank and press the attack. A direct hit from an artillery shell smashed the raft, and, as the battle tank majestically submerged, its boiler burst, adding one more explosion of noise to the general cacophony. Argo's life seemed to have gone into high gear since he had arrived in Albany. He had seen Cordelia nearly arrested, and he had met the prime minister, and now he was watching the full might of the Mosul hurling itself at the place that he had so recently accepted as his home.

Argo had never imagined that war would be so loud. The Mosul artillery may have been slow to start, but now every enemy gun seemed to be in action, and, as the earth shook, it was Albany's turn to face the smack of hot metal and the roar of high explosives. The gunners across the river did not seem to be particularly accurate, but, when firing at full strength, there were so many of them that it hardly mattered. With the din of battle all round him, the shells that, aimed too high, whistled overhead and exploded somewhere in the rear failed to connect with Argo as any kind of personal danger. He had no sense of invincibility. He simply did not make the correlation between the sound and the possibility of his own death. Then a single shell hit the wall on which they were standing. The blast was not a powerful one, and it did little damage, but the rain of falling debris did drop on the Four, and also Dunbar and his officers, who grabbed their hats and ducked. It was enough to convince the spectators that they were unquestionably at risk and a withdrawal to more effective cover was in order. The field telephone was gathered up, and the Albany High Command beat a pragmatic retreat to the blockhouse in the rear of the wall. Argo in no way questioned the courage of the field marshal and his people. During the past conflicts, Dunbar had proved his bravery enough times in the field, and a supreme commander is not expected to stand around and allow himself to be blown up just to prove a point. Argo simply saw no reason that he should do the same. He wanted to see it all in every facet of its terrible majesty. Cordelia and Jesamine also seemed ready to depart for a safer location, but Raphael looked to be of the same mind as him. The two boys were not only watching their first battle at first hand, but it was a battle that, whichever way it went, would be recorded as a turning point in history. Why should they leave on account of a little danger? What they really wanted was guns in their hands and parts of their own to play.

Then Yancey Slide was beside them, shouting above the racket. "What the hell do you two idiots think you're doing? Are you looking to get killed?"

Argo shook his head and gestured to the spectacle in front of them, hardly comprehending what Slide was saying. "Have you ever seen anything like it?"

"Unfortunately, I have. Many times, and considerably worse into the bargain. Now take cover. I didn't bring you all the way across occupied Virginia to have you blown apart by a stray shell."

Both Argo and Raphael stared at Slide in amazement. "We can't just run away."

Slide's eyes flashed angrily. "I'm not asking you to run away. I'm just telling you that you're no use here. You're needed as something other than cannon fodder, and I want you in one piece."

"We'll look like cowards."

"Right now you look like damn fools." Slide grabbed both boys roughly, one shoulder each, and propelled them after the girls, who were already making good their escape. "Get to safety right now, or I'll throw you off this damned wall myself."

JESAMINE

"Why the hell were you boys arguing with Slide? You wanted to stay out in all that?"

At least Raphael and Argo had the good grace to look shamefaced. "I guess we got a bit too caught up in the excitement."

Now Cordelia started. "You find all that killing exciting?"

Argo and Raphael attempted to explain the attraction of the moving men and the thunder of conflict but quickly realized that they were wasting their time. The Four were back in the house where they were quartered. In peacetime it had been the manor house of a village called Forest Heights, but, with the Mosul so close, the original owners had evacuated, and the army had taken it over and added extensive fortifications and a network of connecting bunkers to convert it into a command center and a lodging place, just in the rear of the Potomac defenses, for generals and distinguished visitors. A mile-long tunnel had been constructed that connected the manor with the main blockhouse, a dark and echoing cement tube with its own clanking system of rack and pinion subway cars, and that was how the Four had returned to the manor from the front when Slide had ordered them down from the wall. The village of Forest Heights had also grown beyond all prewar recognition. It had been made the railhead for the hastily constructed rail line that ran from the front all of the fifty miles to Baltimore, putting just two hours between the fighting and the supplies being shipped in through the road and river links of Albany's most southern and strategically crucial city. Locomotives hauling boxcars and passenger carriages arrived and departed all day and night, while men and munitions were shuttled the rest of the way to the river, both overland, by trucks that ran in constant convoy, and through the tunnel on the railcars, and since the Mosul assault had begun, previously idle ambulances and hospital trains were now worked to capacity bringing out the wounded.

Although the Four were away from the front line, the battle still made itself thoroughly felt. The floor constantly shook from the recoil of the rear artillery batteries, and sharper shocks followed the sound of any large explosion. Constant pandemonium was one factor of the battlefield that Jesamine should have anticipated but had not. Even though they were out of immediate sight of the conflict, there was no way that they could relax or put the reality of the nearby combat out of their minds. Slide might have brought them away from the fighting, but that did not mean that they were going to sit out the assault in the comfort of the rear. The boys had defended their wanting to stay on the wall by claiming it was a sense of duty that held them there. "I mean, how could we run away when men were dying out there?"

"We have another duty to perform, and that's to get our own end of things in order." Jesamine felt uncharacteristically unbending as she spoke, and something of a shrew, but she knew what she was saying had to be said. The Four had a power, but, as yet, they had been unable to focus their energy or direct it to a purpose. Jesamine had already communicated her feeling to Cordelia, and Cordelia seemed to agree that very little of any practical use was being done, and the boys were spending too much useless time swaggering around in their Ranger uniforms, although Jesamine privately considered that Cordelia did more than enough swaggering of her own. As a collective consciousness, or whatever they were supposed to be, they had only managed to keep returning to what they had started to call the Gold Rectangle. They could link hands and find their way to that first place of blazing light that they had accessed so briefly back in the Zhaithan Bunker, when the power had seemingly located them, but the imperative to escape had left them no time to explore. Now, with a little more time on their hands, they found they were unable to explore. They could enter the place of inexplicable geometry, linear energy, and black emptiness, but they could still find no perception or perspective to use for movement or location. The implacable right angles still stood at ninety degrees to each other, on and on to infinity, and refused to bend or make any accommodation for the Four. All keys eluded them, and no doors opened to permit them to advance into what they now all called the Other Place. Jesamine was certain that they had not completed the process that would make them truly operate as one, and she was equally certain that she was not alone in her belief.

"I think we have to talk about the problem right now."

Raphael attempted to play innocent. "What problem?"

"The one that we've all been thinking about, but no one has quite liked to mention."

Argo looked up from staring at his boot, something he had been doing since Jesamine had castigated him for supposedly enjoying the violence. "What no one is talking about is 'bonding in the old manner.'"

Cordelia raised an eyebrow. "'Bonding in the old manner'? Where did you hear that?"

"Something T'saya said to Slide. 'The two girls bonded last night in the old, old manner. They may not have known it at first, and they may be having trouble accepting it right now, but they're in the Place.'"

"That's what T'saya said?"

"As best I recall it. Then she asked Slide how he could expect better than that."

"And what did Slide say?"

"He seemed to agree."

Glances were exchanged between all four. They had been assigned two adjoining bedrooms in the manor house, in addition to use of the kitchen, and right there and then they were in the room shared by the two girls, which had almost immediately become more homely and inviting than the boys' room. Jesamine and Cordelia sat on their respective twin beds, and the boys sat cross-legged on the floor between them. Somewhere else in the building, amid all the rumblings of battle, someone was making a bad attempt to play the piano, murdering a song that Jesamine did not recognize. They all knew what T'saya had meant by "bonding in the old, old manner." Indeed, they had already laughed and joked about when the orgy was going to take place, but with Albany under full attack, it was no longer any laughing matter. "We have to face the blunt fact that the bonding required for us to make full use of our power may well be based in the four of us having some kind of sex together."

There, she had said it. It was out in the open. The matter could no longer be avoided. Argo shrugged. "Would that be so terrible?"

Raphael looked uncomfortable. "It does seem rather like sex as a means to an end. I mean, as people, we hardly know each other."

Cordelia smiled at him. "That's a quaintly old-fashioned attitude for a soldier. It's been my observation that sex is almost always a means to one end or another. Of course, it did help that Jesamine and I were extremely drunk when we bonded in the old, old way."

Jesamine smiled, part coy, part cunning, as she warmed to the idea. "T'saya has already covered that, after a fashion."

Cordelia looked surprised. "She left booze for us?"

Jesamine nodded. "In a manner of speaking." She stood up and opened a drawer in her and Cordelia's communal dressing table. She took out a bottle and a jar. "Herbs marinated in alcohol, and a kind of cream."

Cordelia blinked. "Damn."

Jesamine then moved around the room lighting candles with a box of lucifers. It was now twilight outside, although the guns still thundered, and the room was filled with a shadowy, dusty golden light. Argo had a little trouble finding his voice. "So what do we do?"

Jesamine sat down on the bed, smiling but with a set to her jaw.

"We make a move, don't we? Isn't that how the game is played?"

With the decisive swiftness of enough is enough, Cordelia stood up and slipped out of her RWA tunic. After only a slight pause, she pulled her light cotton undershirt over her head, so she was naked to the waist. ""I've done a lot of things for a lot of reasons, and I guess king and country's maybe a better excuse than most."

Argo half smiled. "Do we need an excuse?"

"No, but I need a drink. I'm not a total slut." Cordelia held out a hand, and Jesamine uncorked the bottle of green-brown liquid and passed it to her. Cordelia took a drink and grimaced, but quickly recovered and gave the bottle back to Jesamine. "Whew."

"You feel more of a slut now, my dear?"

Cordelia let out a slow sigh, let her head fall back, and her eyes lost their focus. "Wow." Deliberately and very carefully, she touched her own breasts. "Oh, wow." Then she grinned at the others. "I would suggest you see for yourself. In fact"—she sighed again—"you should all take a drink of that stuff before you start passing judgment."

Jesamine drank, and the brew was about as foul as Cordelia had indicated. She then handed the bottle to the boys, and Cordelia nodded. "Take a good swig each, my dears, and then get out of those damned uniforms."

Raphael was uncertain. "Isn't this all going a little fast?"

"Take a drink and find out."

Jesamine watched as the boys drank. Argo seemed to know what to expect, but Raphael was still hesitant. Right then, he seemed to be the weakest link in the forming conspiracy to orgy, and she wondered how much a Mosul boot camp might have messed up his head. Argo stood up, dropped his tunic, and then, with a considerable lack of shame, dropped his pants. Cordelia nodded. "Very good, Argo Weaver. Now come over here and take these britches off me."

Argo moved towards Cordelia. He still had the bottle in his hand, and he tried to kiss her, but she shook her head. "First you give the bottle back to Jesamine." Argo did as he was told. "Now you finish undressing me." He reached for the buckle on her belt, but again she shook her head. "No, no, no. Do it on your knees. Then, when you're finished, you can rub that cream all over my thighs."

Argo started to kneel, but Jesamine held up a hand. "Wait a moment."

"What?"

"Are we dividing ourselves according to skin tone here?"

Both Argo and Cordelia looked at Jesamine as though the idea had never occurred to them. Now Jesamine had become the instructress, and she gestured to Raphael. "Go to Cordelia."

Raphael's head dropped, and he looked at the floor. Then he reached for the bottle and took a long and somewhat desperate drink. The boy was all too obviously gripped by a sudden and inexplicable panic. Jesamine was instantly aware that some fairly profound problem had surfaced. How messed up was this young and plainly gorgeous Hispanian? Had the Mosul done things to him that he could not admit even to himself? Jesamine silently motioned for Argo to move away from Cordelia and come to her, and the Virginia farm boy was sharp enough to sense what was happening and comply without any fuss or comment. He left Cordelia and came and sat on Jesamine's bed, and Cordelia turned and looked at Raphael. Her voice changed from cocky and commanding to a tone of genuine concern. "What is it, Raphael? Is something wrong?"

"I . . ."

"Yes?"

Raphael avoided looking at three sets of eyes. "I've . . . never been with a woman. The Provincial Levies took me for a conscript before I ever . . ."

Cordelia almost ran to him and knelt down beside him. "Oh, baby, there's nothing to be afraid of. Your virginity is so easily remedied."

"I could make a complete fool of myself."

"We all make fools of ourselves. Some of us make fools of ourselves most of the time."

"It's not like this was just my first time. I mean, the Four . . . They brought us here because we were important, and I could so easily screw it all up."

Cordelia lowered her eyelids. "You leave the screwing to me, boy. I'll see you don't go wrong."

"I . . ."

"Stop agonizing and start both trusting and kissing me."

Right then, Jesamine grasped Argo by the hair. "Kiss me, too, Argo. Let's give them a little privacy by becoming totally involved in each other."

RAPHAEL

Raphael could not believe that the red-haired woman of his dreams was really naked in his arms and doing what she was doing. He had pretended and imagined for so long that the reality of passion was hard to accept now that it was upon him. His life had been so twisted out of shape by the Mosul and their rules of ugliness, he still saw beauty as an apparition from another world. As his earlier panic had mounted, he had started to believe that his callow ignorance would be the downfall of the Four. The fear had come at him as hard as any fear he had ever experienced, even perhaps the terror he had felt when he had walked into the Bunker with hardly a clue as to how he might free Jesamine and Cordelia. The options of failure— too fast, too soon, not at all—had danced all over whatever ragged self-respect and self-esteem had been left to him after the ministrations of Gunnery Instructor Y'assir, Underofficer Beg, not to mention all the spies and agents of the always-watching Zhaithan. The seeds they had planted had suddenly flourished to conspire against him, and his mind had been overtaken and choked by an all-too-vivid delineation of the other three standing over him and laughing at his inability, and then of Slide and T'saya and all those Albany officers staring with contempt at his failure. The anxiety had almost been self-fulfilling, but then the Lady Cordelia had taken him in her hands and led him gently and easily into her personal garden of delight, and now that she was making soft kitten sounds in his ear, he knew that he was neither unable nor a failure.

"Oh, Goddess, yes, fuck, Raph-ael, you are really sooo . . . oooh. I was trying . . . oh, yes, dooo that, and harder. Oh . . . I was trying to make you . . . make you feel good about . . . yourself. Yeees. Oh, please. But . . . now . . . yes, now . . . Now! Now! I don't have to, because you are soo good. Come . . . into . . . my . . . mind, and feel . . . what . . . I'm feeling."

Cordelia had made him lie face down. Her instructions had been strict. He was to do nothing while she straddled him and kneaded the cream that T'saya had given them into his back and buttocks and down the insides of his thighs. The hallucinations and physical sensations had started almost immediately, and when she had rolled him over onto his back, she had suddenly grinned at him. "You really had nothing to worry about, now, did you?"

He had been so pleased both with her and himself that he had wanted to take her right then and there, but she had held him back. "My turn now. My turn."

He had taken the psychedelic cream from her, and with her flesh making rainbow undulations under his hands, he had massaged it into the muscles of her shoulders, the softness of her breasts, across the slight curve of her stomach and then down onto the smoothness of her thighs.

"What is this stuff? It is so . . ." Cordelia searched for the word. "Extreme."

And as the active ingredients took hold, it became impossible to tell which words were spoken and which were the gasping thoughts of their rapidly melding minds as they overlaid the cries, whispers, and whimpers of their first coupling. A brief return to reality had occurred when Jesamine had come to take the cream for herself and Argo. "Our turn now. Our turn."

They had clearly been overheard, but a minute or so later, all became equal as, on the other side of the room, Raphael and Cordelia heard Argo groan and Jesamine make a musical keening from deep in her throat. At the sound, Cordelia had giggled and pulled Raphael close to her and wrapped her legs tightly around him. "Fuck me, my darling. Fuck me very slowly, very surely, and then very hard, because you have nothing to worry about anymore."

Outside, the barrage still thundered, and the flashes of guns lit up the night.

They were linked pairs on a single axis, separate but joined, ecstatically revolving on the helix of infinity through a universe of vibrant color and sensation that came close at times to being unbearable. Hands, mouths, lips, eyes, spread legs, enfolding arms, flowing hair, cocks and cunts, all ceased to have logical form and were blending in the same spinning continuum of warmth and light, and fervor was transformed into a mutual circuit of golden electricity in sky blue space arcing through a shared nervous system. Two and two, and four and three, and all soon to be one, their wildly rising spirits were transported by rolling waves of pleasure. The ringed moons and double and triple stars that Cordelia and Jesamine had seen before again left trails of light in their wake, and the same conical towers, the spheres and the cylinders, rose from the undergrowth of up-pointing crystal fingers. The complexity of time distortion had also returned, and they were both a fraction of a second ahead, and an equal fraction behind, the world as they knew it, and insubstantial impressions of what might be the future or the present were being superimposed on afterimages and echoes of the past. The primary difference from the time when Cordelia and Jesamine had bonded was that no third parties intruded on their joy and searing elation. This time no blue-black clouds roiled and reared, and no hunchbacked djinn-figures rode them down on vortices of dust. With nothing to threaten them, the supreme temptation was to want to remain forever, to never stop, never stop, but even in total exultation, entropy had ultimately to ground them.

"Oh, my lady!" Raphael pushed his hair out of his eyes and lay gasping for breath.

Cordelia hugged him tightly to her. "Oh, my Raphael."

"I did it, didn't I?"

"Indeed you did. We both did it. Simultaneously and together. Do you see what a fool you were to be afraid?"

Raphael sighed and nodded. "I was a fool."

"We are all fools sometimes, one way or another."

For a long time they lay in silence, listening to each other inhale and exhale, until they noticed that Jesamine and Argo were also silent. Thoughts of the other two came to Raphael as a complete intrusion. Beyond all doubt he was still recovering from the most profound experience of his life, and he did not want to share it with anyone but Cordelia. He wanted to hug the warm embers of the excitement just past and warm away a lifetime of cold. He wanted to laugh with her and cry with her and pretend that he was in love with her. Argo and Jesamine only served to remind Raphael that he was not in this room, or even this country, to be in love. He was here to fight a war, to cement the bonds that would make the Four into what everyone who knew hoped they would be: a formidable weapon on the side of Albany. He was more comfortable in Albany than among the Mosul, but the compulsion to relinquish his free will to what was perceived as the greater good still troubled him. Less than an hour ago, he was a virgin, and now he was about to swap partners like some degenerate libertine, and all in the name of the war effort and defeating Hassan IX and Quadaron-Ahrach.

Raphael let Cordelia slip from his arms, reached for the bottle, and look a long and grimly resigned drink. Jesamine was already disengaging and disentangling herself from Argo. He could not deny that she was beautiful and that, under more reasonable circumstances, he would have actively desired her, but it was too soon. It was all coming at him too fast. His only refuge was in the alcohol and the herbs that floated in and turned the liquor green. Already the hallucinations were starting to flicker in the periphery of his vision. Ideas of love and comfort were moved to one side, and a perverse, almost cruel desire for Jesamine replaced them. Cordelia must have sensed what was happening, because she rolled away from him and also sat up. "Give me the bottle and then go to her."

Her thoughts, previously open, were suddenly masked as he moved to leave her.

CORDELIA

"Just call me the whore of destiny."

Argo blinked. "Call you what?"

Cordelia petulantly rolled over. "A small and depressingly normal part of me refuses to believe any of this."

Argo put a hand on her arm. "It's a little strange for all of us."

Cordelia ignored his attempt to be comforting. "The small and depressingly normal part of me doesn't what to contemplate the fact that I have just fucked two men in quick succession, fast as any Grafton Street dollymop, and the bed on which I find myself is sticky."

The piano had started up again in another part of the manor house, or maybe it had been going all the time and they had not noticed. Cordelia snarled. "Why does that inept and tone-deaf moron insist on murdering Peter Townshend's best songs? How hard can it be to play 'The Good Has Gone'?"

She looked round at the others, but their blank faces showed that these refugees from the Mosul knew nothing of Albany popular songs.

The truth was that the experience had been intense, and all four of them were, each in his or her own way, still seeking a way to deal with the intensity. Cordelia reached for the bottle. She wanted a drink. In fact, she would have been more than happy to be mindlessly drunk, but she did not think she could handle any more hallucinations. "I wish we had some normal booze."

Argo was practical. "We could probably get some."

"Are you volunteering? You're ready for just about anything, aren't you?"

She knew it was wrong to be angry with Argo, but Cordelia was sick of doing what was right. She had felt a spark of jealous resentment when Raphael had gone from her to Jesamine. With Raphael there had been a sad tenderness, but circumstances had dictated that tenderness had no place in the ritual. As she had taken Argo in her arms and inside her, aware that he was still hot and damp from Jesamine's embrace, she had sought to lose herself in a cultivated deliciousness, a sense of wanton and lascivious wickedness, and not ask herself how could it be so wicked if it was what everyone wanted and it served the just cause. And in this she had been very successful. The drugged and hallucinatory sex with Argo had been spectacular, more spectacular even than with poor and strangely innocent Raphael, but perhaps it had been too spectacular. Although it had achieved the arcing and dizzy altitude of fireworks bursting in the dark of night, it had also seemed ritualist and transactional, a means to an end with a seething edge of violence and anger, a sense of sacrifice and jagged, breathless competition, that left her feeling soiled and used.

They had risen to the place of strangeness again, the power had come upon them, but somehow it had not been right. Instead of being passively carried by the vision, Cordelia had attempted to pilot and consciously manage their collective actions. It had seemed to be the most logical thing that she could do. According to everything that first Jesamine and then Yancey Slide and T'saya had told her, the Four were supposed to battle the paranormal forces of Quadaron-Ahrach and his velvet-gloved sister. The weird Other Place, where time seemed bent out of shape, and the stars warped in their courses, was not supposed to be some hallucinatory fairground ride over which they drifted as acquiescent spectators. The intention was surely that they should be able to navigate their way through the glowing, energy-generated landscape of cones and spheres, crystalline contortions, purple seas, and rolling, djinn-ridden dust clouds and ultimately engage their enemies in mortal combat. Instead of being able to steer a course, however, her efforts had sent her spinning out of all control, forced by what she could only describe as a blood red, flashing and all-consuming vortex, back to where Argo's bright energy thrust into hers.

Argo looked mystified. "What do you mean, I'm ready for anything?"

"Get high and have an orgy? And dress it up as our part in the fight against the Evil Empire?"

Raphael, who was lying prone and drained beside Jesamine, lifted his head and looked at Cordelia. "We all know that's not true."

Cordelia slowly uncurled like an angry cat and rose to her feet. "And what would you know, Raphael, late of the Provincial Levies and former virgin? You're over there with her? You've fucked both of us? That's all you really wanted out of this, wasn't it? To jump from my bed to her bed and make up for all the time you lost as a Mosul recruit."

Jesamine quickly sat up, raising a warning hand. "Wait."

"What?"

"Don't you see what's happening?"

"And what the fuck do *you* think is happening, Concubine Jesamine?"

"You're reacting, but the rest of us can feel it."

"What are you feeling, except maybe Raphael's cock?"

Jesamine's teeth clenched, her eyes narrowed, and she attempted to rise to her feet to confront Cordelia, but Raphael caught her by the arm. "Wait. This is all wrong."

Cordelia clenched her fists. "Damn right it's all wrong."

Argo did not move, but his voice took on an unprecedented authority. "We are dissatisfied because the bonding is not complete. Cordelia seems to feel it worse, and she's the first to get angry."

Raphael nodded but continued to hold on to Jesamine. "She's right. It hasn't worked. We were helpless in there. We couldn't move ourselves. We had no power and no direction."

Jesamine abruptly sat down with a faltering sigh. "Then we have to . . ."

Cordelia shook her head, cutting Jesamine off in midsentence. "No, no more. Not now. I already gave. How much fucking is a girl supposed to do in one afternoon?"

"It has to be finished."

"I said no. Which part of 'no' causes you a problem?"

"You're missing the point."

"I am? If we're flat-backing our way to victory, I think I just completed my shift."

"Girl, I have worked in a whorehouse, and that wasn't close to a *shift*."

"Well, I wouldn't know, would I, not being a runaway Mosul *tramp*."

Argo and Raphael jumped to their feet, ready to separate the two women, but, to everyone's total surprise, Jesamine suddenly burst into helpless laughter. She waved an unsteady hand in the direction of Argo and Raphael. "Will you look at those two? Bare-ass naked and ready to stop the catfight."

She stumbled towards a now-baffled Cordelia and placed a hand on her shoulder, as much to steady herself as a gesture of friendship. "This final act has nothing to do with either you or me. We have done what's expected of us."

Cordelia suddenly realized what Jesamine meant. Her jaw slowly dropped, and a truly wicked smile spread across her face. "Oh, yes, I see."

Jesamine pushed back her hair and looked at Argo and Raphael. "It's your turn, boys."

Cordelia nodded. "Drink the drink, rub in the cream. Then kiss each other nicely. Let the square be completed."

Cordelia and Jesamine became a triumphant double act. "We've already walked that path."

"We've already ploughed that furrow."

"Boys need to do what girls have already done."

Argo protested. "But it's different."

Raphael agreed. "It's unnatural."

Cordelia and Jesamine were smiling broadly, and the more the boys baulked, the broader their smiles became. "That's the point, though, isn't it? Everything's different."

"What's natural once T'saya's potions have done their work?"

Cordelia took Jesamine's hand. "Let the square be completed."

"While we girls watch the live show."

"And give encouragement."

THE FOUR

They rose as one. The bonding was complete. The links were forged. The exultation was under their command. The Four had a brand-new, multiple, and totally surprising sense of free will. At the same time, they acted as one and also as separate individuals that were part of that one. Each was a component, and yet each was free within confines of their common purpose. They did not have to agree; they simply knew what was to be done. They brought their own personalities with them, their own intelligence and their own memories, but they shared so much more. The commonality was greater than any one of them, greater perhaps than the sum of all four, but neither was it oppressive nor an imposition. Acting for the commonality was the same as acting in individual self-interest, and if ever it should seem confining, the freedom and power that came with it was more than sufficient compensation.

They were swimming fast and without effort, like exotic fish in a sea of light and color, delighting in their newly discovered abilities and feeling as though nothing was impossible. They flew like birds in a sky without clouds but filled with bright, mobile stars and planets. They shifted from one experimental formation to another, discovering that the rectilinear position in which they had started this first perfect voyage of discovery was merely an initial arrangement that could be changed at will. Very quickly, their personalities were revealed in the way that each of them related to this novelty of motion in the Other Place. Cordelia tended to surge ahead, while Argo followed like her wingman, ever watchful for unexpected danger. Jesamine could usually be found in a center position, and her inclination was to function as an anchor. Raphael was pragmatic and cautious; he brought up the rear and was constantly sensitive to what might suddenly appear behind them. Without the presence of the commonality reminding her of the presence of the others, and her need to remain linked with them, Cordelia might have streaked ahead and been lost on her own, but she instinctively knew that, without them, she would not have the speed and maneuverability that she so relished, and, even so, the linkage between them could be stretched so the parts of the Four were positioned like the points of a radically extended trapezoid.

In the first, wild flush of freedom, the temptation to soar and dive and frolic was too strong to ignore, and the Four allowed themselves the brief luxury of testing their apparently limitless power and reveling in the heady excitement of the first outing, with all the parts in place and all the vitalities fully functioning. Unfortunately, a landscape rapidly appeared under them, and their vibrant sea bottomed out, according the metaphor that presently ruled, reminding them that the pressure of time, no matter how oddly configured, demanded that even this primary, beginner's delight be severely curtailed. This landscape was one of shocking and violent combat, a parallel representation of the battle already raging in the world they had left behind, that manifested itself as a flowing field of destructive crimson energy flecked with poisonous silver that flashed, cracked, and sparked, and hummed with small chain reactions and, at regular intervals, burst forth in concentrations of larger and more damaging flares that rose in mushroom clusters, dark with the negative energy of human death.

As the geography of the new complete world of this adjacent dimension unfolded, the Four knew rather than saw that they were not alone. Much later, and with much more experience, the saying would be coined, "If you see them, it's probably too late." On this initial excursion to the Other Place, they had sufficient prudence to maintain what Cordelia would come to call "dream-altitude," but, below them, close to what, for ease of communication, they thought of as the ground, winged entities fluttered and followed the explosions of destruction, feeding on the ghost-gust streams of ruined mortality.

"Mothmen."

Raphael communicated the name to the others.

"What are Mothmen?"

"They fly. They are fierce and savage and have edges that cut."

Energy spikes immediately formed around Cordelia as she armed herself. She was the first to discover how to do this, but, as she knew, the others knew, too. Raphael and Jesamine eased back the momentum of the Four, or, without them, Cordelia would have power-dived in exuberant plunging attack, bearing down on the Mothmen, screaming out of the stars, but she was curbed by Argo using the collective will.

"We do not engage."

Glitters of disappointment surrounded Cordelia, but the bonds of the Four were in no way strained. A star formation of five Mothmen rose and dipped as if building violence with their energy-dance in preparation for the climb to the dream-altitude of the Four.

"They prepare to engage us."

"We break and return."

"We return?"

"They are savage and have edges that cut."

"And we are novices."

A final flicker of thwarted fury. "We return?"

"We return."

JESAMINE

"Before it happened, we were almost ready to tear each other apart."

"I called her a Mosul tramp."

"And I was going to rip her stupid red hair out."

Argo nodded in agreement. "It was tense there for a moment."

Raphael grinned wryly. "As it was when Argo and I found we had to . . ."

Argo interrupted. "I don't think that needs to be discussed."

Slide raised an eyebrow. "But you're fine now?"

"We're fine now, but for how long? When are we going to discover some new imbalance?"

"You did it, didn't you?"

"Oh, yes, we did it."

"So don't look for fresh problems."

"You have achieved the linkage. You are the Four. You never have to go through that part again."

The Four were being debriefed by Slide and T'saya. Outside was night. A lull in the fighting seemed to have ensued, and the big guns only fired spasmodically. In the manor house kitchen, time had all but ceased to exist, and only the guttering candles indicated the passage of the day. T'saya, although she did her best to hide it behind a venerable and all-knowing sternness, was plainly fascinated with everything they had to say. The Other Place where the Four flew was clearly beyond her extensive knowledge. Slide, on the other hand, seemed to know it all in front, as though he was a regular visitor to such netherworlds.

"You did right not to engage the Mothmen. The things you face are neither intelligent nor overly sophisticated. They are death feeders. That's how Quadaron-Ahrach attracts them to do his bidding, but they are the best he can get."

Cordelia frowned. "So why didn't we take them if they're so pig stupid? I was ready, but the commonality held off."

"And you were disappointed?"

"I was."

"The commonality was right. The Mothmen and the Dark Things are low on the dimensional food chain, but never underestimate them. They are powerful, brutal, and always hungry. Had you attacked them, it might well have been the last thing that you four ever did."

Raphael nodded. "I was attacked by a Mothman in a dream, back in the camp. It all but cut me in half before I could wake up."

Slide had brought a bottle of whiskey to the debriefing, and glasses had been distributed. Now Cordelia stared thoughtfully into the amber liquid in her glass. "I don't get it. Why do we have to hold off? What use are we if we run from every fight?"

"My dear Lady Cordelia, you will have more than enough fights presented to you sooner than you think. Do not go looking for combat when it's not looking for you. Especially on your very first outing after you bonded. Let's face it, you really hardly know each other."

Jesamine, was who beginning to feel a little drunk, could not help herself. She burst out laughing. "I'm sorry, but you're wrong, Yancey Slide. After what we had to do to complete the bonding, I'd venture to say that we know each other damned well."

Slide swallowed his whiskey and refilled his glass. "In combat terms you're only just getting acquainted." He extended the bottle to Jesamine, offering her a refill. She nodded, and he poured. "From what you've told me, you're already getting a feel of each other. Cordelia is headstrong and spoiling for a fight. While at the other extreme, Raphael is protective of himself and the rest of you. Although I hate to admit it, the Mosul taught him well, particularly that squad leader. What was his name?"

Raphael helped himself to more whiskey. "Melchior."

Jesamine sipped hers. "And what about me? Where do I fit in this wonderful balancing act?"

Slide looked round at the others. "From what I've heard, you may be the actual balancing point."

"You're calling me a fulcrum?"

"That would seem to be how it is."

"And what about Argo?"

Slide looked at Argo. "Where do you think you figure in all this?"

Argo looked like he did not know what to say. He thought and finally shrugged. "I do my part. What else? You taught me. Back in the hills when the Mamalukes were coming."

"Are you saying you're dependable, Argo Weaver?"

"I guess I am."

Jesamine looked hard at Slide. She was now quite drunk, and that was probably how she found the courage to ask the question. "And what about you, Yancey Slide? What are you?"

Suddenly every eye around the manor house kitchen table was on Slide to see how he would react. He stared at Jesamine for a long time and then spread his hands. "I am the entity who is going to forge you four into a formidable weapon."

Jesamine shook her head. This wasn't the answer that she wanted. "No, what are you really?"

Slide's gaze was unwavering. "I am a creature with time."

"A creature with time?"

"I am a creature with plenty of time, my dear. I'm damned for eternity."

"Were you ever a living man?"

Yancey Slide made a gesture that was both ultimately smooth and, at the same time, totally inhuman. "Do I look like a living man?"

A series of explosions suggested that, outside, the fighting was heating up again.

ARGO

Argo woke to gunfire that sounded closer than where the line was being held on the north bank of the river. His first sense was one of unthinking, mindless alarm. The Four had made a half-dozen more practice runs into the Other Place the previous evening, and after that he had dropped into his bed and fallen into a deep and surprisingly dreamless sleep. On their final excursion, they had encountered three Mothmen, linked in triangular formation, way up in their dream-altitude, perhaps a patrol, if such things as patrols existed in that world. The commonality loosed the restraints on Cordelia, and, with the other three in line beside her, she had led them against the enemy. Cordelia's skill had proved nothing short of amazing. She conjured shining shards of sharp-edged energy out of nowhere and directed them at the target with unerring calculation and precise aim. The straggler of the three power-flamed for a moment and then vanished, and Cordelia had her first kill, if such a term could be used about a thing that might not have been alive in the first place. When asked later how she had been able to do such things, she had not given it a second thought, and, with wide-eyed, childlike innocence, she had told them, "I just knew."

With one gone, and a seemingly dangerous and efficient quadruple adversary bearing down on them, the other two Mothmen had fluttered and fled, diving for the crimson battlescape below. Cordelia had led the others in a hot and spiraling pursuit, but that had almost proved their undoing. Some kind of dark alarm must have been sounded, because suddenly an entire swarm of Mothmen, far too numerous to count, was rising to intercept them. Jesamine had swiftly spun the Four away and set them racing to lose themselves in the protective cover of a tumbling thunderhead of purple cloud, glowing from within, that Raphael had deftly created behind them, and which was large enough to hide them for enough time to return to the real world. When asked how he had managed to so effectively save their paranormal bacon, he had repeated Cordelia's nonexplanation almost word for word. "I somehow just knew."

Even though all the action took place outside their natural world and dimension, the transformation of the Four left Argo mentally drained and physically tired. He could only liken the result to that of having run a long way with a heavy rucksack while solving complex problems of mental arithmetic, and it took him a minute or so to be properly awake. Raphael was faster and was already dressing while Argo was still trying to focus his eyes. The rhythmic coughing of the largest model of Bergman started, and it seemed to be just outside the manor house, and someone was shouting. "The Mosul have broken through! The Mosul have broken through!"

"You think that's true?"

Raphael spoke with the brevity of a Mosul grunt. "Sure as shit sounds like it."

"What do you think we should do?"

"I think we should go out there and take a look."

Argo took a deep breath. From one kind of combat, they seemed about to be plunged into another. Argo quickly climbed into his uniform, then, realizing that if the Mosul really were through the river defenses, they would need weapons, he picked up the carbine that the Rangers had given him, the dead man's gun that he had managed to hang onto through all the adventures in the Mosul camp. As an afterthought, he stuffed the old two-barrel pistol that he had stolen from his stepfather into his belt, more as a talisman than any effective piece of firepower. Raphael had the revolver that he had taken from the Zhaithan in the bunker. "Shall we go?"

"What about the girls?"

"I guess we'd better wake them."

Argo nodded. "Yeah, wake them and let them get themselves together while we see what's really going on."

Through the connecting door to the girls' bedroom, they discovered that Jesamine and Cordelia required no waking. They were much more than together—they had already gone. Frowning at the fact that they had been left behind, Argo and Raphael headed for the corridor, where, after only a few paces in the direction of the stairs, they ran into the two women coming back the other way, looking flushed, excited, and also a little scared.

"Where the hell have you two been?"

"Outside. There's a fucking war going on. The Mosul broke through the line, right by the blockhouse."

"When?"

Jesamine paused for a moment to catch her breath. "Maybe an hour ago. There's Mamaluke cavalry and Mosul infantry units within plain sight of the house."

"Some of the men we saw said that Dark Things are trying to break into the tunnel from here to the front."

"Why didn't you wake us?"

Cordelia looked truculently at Argo. "We didn't think we needed to."

"Have you seen Slide or T'saya?"

"No."

Raphael knew exactly what they should do and cut in on the exchange between Argo and Cordelia. "We have to go to the tunnel. We can be of the most use helping to stop the Dark Things."

The other three all nodded, but no sooner had they turned and started for the stairs that would lead them to the concealed tunnel entrance in the cellars of the manor than a massive explosion rocked the house. A sound like the clap of doom left them temporarily deaf, the lights went out, dust and smoke billowed, and fragments of ceiling plaster rained down on them.

"What the fuck?"

"I think we can assume the house has been hit."

"Is everyone okay?"

Three strained voices confirmed that they were, and, feeling their way, the Four descended the stairs, which still held up despite some ominous creaking. At the time, they assumed that the manor house was under artillery bombardment, but later they discovered that it had only been a lucky hit from an enemy mortar. On reaching the ground floor, however, they found that the mortar shell had been more than sufficient to bring down the cellar steps and block all interior access to the tunnel.

"We'll have to go outside and see if we can get in by the entrance under the stables."

Jesamine frowned. "That's a long hundred-yard dash over ground that may well be coming under fire."

Argo cursed, and Raphael checked his revolver. "Can you think of a better idea?"

Both Jesamine and Cordelia shook their heads. "No."

"Then we have to at least give it a try. We have to see if it's possible."

RAPHAEL

As he crouched in the kitchen doorway of the manor house, scanning the ground between the house and the stables, he told himself this was the kind of situation for which he had been trained. The extended misery of the Mosul training camp had to be put to good use, and it fell to him to take responsibility for seeing that others at the very least made it to the tunnel without being shot down before they could even commence to fight their own strange fight. Cordelia might be the one who set the pace in the Other Place, but here in the damp-ground reality of bombs and bullets, elementary infantry tactics, and the craft of negotiating an open space under attack, did not come out of thin air, and he was the only one with even the most meager skills. He was going to have to care for the lives of the other three in the same way that Melchior had cared for the squad of Provincial Levies, but with only a tiny fraction of Melchior's experience.

"The stables are still standing."

The Mosul must have struck in an overcast and mist-shrouded dawn, hitting the near-exhausted defenders in heavy concentrations. If it was true that they'd broken through by the blockhouse, they must have pushed enormous numbers of men across the river and taken horrible casualties in the process. Raphael knew enough not to unquestioningly believe every battlefield rumor, but distant figures of men and horses were visible through the threads of the river fog that had yet to burn off as the unseen sun climbed above the horizon.

"The fog's going to help us. We need to keep low and use every bit of cover. Our objective is the tunnel, not to get caught up in some other poor bastard's firefight."

He started planning a possible route to the stables. A loud and sudden flurry of gunfire from the other side of the house, from the direction of the railhead, reminded him that this was a situation where nothing could be counted on to remain static. The Mosul could mount a rush on the house at any time. He gestured to the others and pointed. "Okay, here's how we should do it. You see that stone wall on the other side of the kitchen garden? That's our first piece of cover. If we can make it to the wall without being seen, or at least without being shot at, we're halfway there. After that, we move along the wall to the corner by the stables, and then across the stable yard, and we're there. The wall will be easy, but there's no easy way to get across the stable yard, so in the last stretch just run like hell. It's only about twenty yards, so we should be able to do it, if no one spots us and figures out what we're up to. Okay?"

The other three gave their assent. "Okay."

"Keep low and don't bunch up. We'll go one at a time at ten-yard intervals."

Cordelia moved forward. "I'll go first."

Raphael stopped her. "No. This isn't the dream-altitude."

"So?"

"Let Argo go first."

Cordelia scowled. "Are you saying that because I'm a girl? If you are, it's quaintly old-fashioned but hardly applicable."

"I don't want to see you killed."

"Then don't watch."

And with that she skipped around him and started for the wall in a low, crouching run. Raphael cursed and looked at the other two. "I'm going next. You two follow. Don't bunch up."

With this final instruction, he sprinted after Cordelia.

CORDELIA

Raphael seemed to have an ability to straddle a line between sweet and irritating. Trying to protect Cordelia in the middle of a firefight like she was a damsel in distress was the perfect example. She could only think that Mosul schools and military basic training must have really messed up his mind and made it impossible for him to enter the modern world. She certainly did not want to die, but whether she made the run first or last made precious little difference. She was sure that the odds were pretty much the same either way. She raced through the kitchen garden of the manor house, over rows of flowerpots, over autumn herbs and glass cucumber frames, and reached the wall unscathed. Raphael was coming after her, and she hoped the fact that she had taken his virginity was not going to cause him to start following her around like a puppy dog. They were locked into the Four together, with no appreciable way out, and she prayed that he would not start acting like a lovesick calf. It would be an intolerable way to fight a war.

Raphael made the cover of the wall and waved to Cordelia to start moving. She edged along in the direction of the stables, pressing her body as close to the brickwork as she could. The manor house had taken a serious hit. One wall was half caved in, and it looked little short of a miracle that the old building was still standing and that they had not been buried under several tons of beams and masonry. From her new vantage point, she could see that a skirmish line of Mosul infantry was moving up on the railhead behind the house, but then a heavy Bergman, turret mounted on one of the cars of an armored train, opened up. Four Mosul were hit in quick succession, and the rest of the line scattered and dived for cover. Almost immediately, an underofficer was screaming and kicking the men to their feet again, seemingly working on the principle that the grunts feared him more than death. His theory worked for maybe a half minute, and then the underofficer himself jerked round and fell as a heavy caliber

Albany bullet took him in the chest. Cordelia knew that she was now seeing war up close and in all its deadly and futile stupidity.

She was at the corner of the wall, and the stables were in front of her. Raphael had been right. The stable yard was an uncomfortably exposed space. She braced herself for the final dash. Argo, followed by Jesamine, was running through the kitchen garden, heading for the cover of the wall. Some Mosul that Cordelia could not see must have spotted them, because musket shots rang out and lead balls kicked up dirt around their feet and smashed a large earthenware pot. Mercifully, neither of them were hit, and they fell against the wall, breathing heavily, and paused for a moment to catch their breath. Raphael was edging along the wall towards her, and she knew that she could not delay the dash across the stable yard any longer. She took a deep breath, focused on the open double doors of the stable and the refuge that she would find inside, and ran. She heard shots but did not falter or look back. Every moment she was in the open she expected a musket ball to slam into her back and pitch her forward, mortally injured, but then the stables were in front of her and she dived forward into the safety of the darkness.

JESAMINE

When they entered the tunnel, down the spiral stairs in the shaft that had been dug out under the floor of the stables, they found Yancey Slide already there. A number of the small trolley cars that normally shuttled between the manor house and the front had been overturned, and a combined squad of Rangers and men from the 3rd Infantry crouched behind it, weapons at the ready. The lights were on at the manor end of the tunnel, but they only remained that way for about fifty yards, and then all was darkness. Water dripped from the brickwork overhead, and a strange booming came from the far end, as though a giant hammer was beating on an iron door a long way away. The soldiers were tense, obviously waiting for an attack they knew was certain to come, and Jesamine noticed that they had rubber gas masks hanging from their belts, presumably to be used if the Dark Things released the black gas. Slide had risen slowly and nodded as the Four reached the foot of the iron stairs. "I guess I should have known that you four would figure it out and come down here."

"Are the Dark Things coming?"

"That's what we're expecting." They moved to where the armed men waited behind the makeshift barricades, and Slide made a warning gesture toward the other end of the tunnel. "Keep your heads down. There's been sniper fire. We've lost two men already."

He directed them to a sheltered spot behind the men who crouched over their rifles. "How are things up top?"

Raphael answered for the Four. With his military training, he seemed to be assuming the leadership role now that they were involved in the war in the real world. "There's fighting around the railhead, a lot of shooting and skirmishing, and we saw some cavalry in the distance."

"Mamalukes?"

"I think so."

Slide nodded. "The 17th Hussars are supposed to be moving up to counter them. All the reserves are being moved in to contain this."

"So can this breakthrough be contained?"

"That remains to be seen, doesn't it? The Mosul have been high-plains nomads for twelve centuries. They excel at fighting in open spaces."

Jesamine found a place beside Raphael and Slide. "A shell or something hit the manor."

Slide frowned. "Is it still standing?"

"Yes, just about, but almost an entire wall is gone. This isn't good, is it?"

Slide shook his head. "No, my dear, this isn't good at all."

"How did the Mosul break through the line?"

"The way we always thought they would. They switched from the broad attack and concentrated on two points. Then they threw in everything they had. They forced a breach by the blockhouse and started streaming through. It would have been a whole lot worse, except one of their battle tanks blew its boiler in the narrowest part of the breach, and our boys were able to finish it with flamethrowers. It created a bottleneck so no more of their mechanized armor could get through."

Cordelia had been listening intently, and finally she spoke. "Everyone always said if the Mosul broke through to open country north of the river, that would be the end of Albany."

Slide looked sadly at her. "Everyone could well be right."

Jesamine felt fear grip her. After being free of the Mosul, even for so short a time, she had no intention of falling back into their clutches. "So is it the end for Albany?"

"Not quite, but the odds have definitely shifted in favor of Hassan. We might shorten them a bit if we can keep the railhead and this tunnel open."

Argo now joined the urgent conversation. "What makes the tunnel so important?"

"It's a route to bring reinforcements up to the river right under the Mosul breakout. If we can clear the tunnel, we have a good chance of closing the gap and cutting off those who have come through already. If we can plug up the breach so no reinforcements get through, we have the firepower to destroy all of the enemy who are left north of the river."

"But the Dark Things are in the tunnel?"

Slide nodded gravely. "That's what I sense. I figure you must have sensed it, too, otherwise you wouldn't have been so motivated to come here."

Jesamine turned to the others. "We should find out for sure."

Argo sighed. "I think it's my turn to walk the point."

"You want to go into the Other Place and see if there are Dark Things at the other end?"

Argo nodded, obviously less than happy with the situation. "Yeah, I'll go in and see. I've the most experience of this sort of thing. I was scouting the Other Place when I was riding with Slide, only I didn't know it at the time."

Cordelia voiced what the others were thinking. "Are you sure about this?"

Argo shrugged. "You see any other way to play it?"

They shook their heads. "No."

"So let's get to it."

"What do you want us to do?"

Argo quickly became businesslike. "I want to go in fast, see what I can see, and get out fast. If Jesamine could stand behind me, half here and half in the Other Place, and Cordelia and Raphael remain in the real world as an anchor, we could probably pull it off."

Jesamine raised an eyebrow. "We've never tried anything even close to this. We've never attempted to be in two places at once."

Argo's jaw was set. "We don't have the time to go away and rehearse. We're going to have to make this one up as we go along."

ARGO

Had anyone been with him to listen, Argo would have freely admitted that he was scared. The experience was like nothing he had encountered before. He felt like a ghost between two worlds, and found a disconnected part of himself wondering if this was how death felt. The physical world existed like a shadow, grey and unsubstantial, but still there. The tunnel was still damp and claustrophobic, and the Rangers and infantrymen still crouched behind the overturned trolley cars waiting for the coming attack. The real difference was that he could see—or, maybe more accurately, sense—what was going on farther afield. He could cast outward for fleeting impressions of the fighting around the railhead, and he could perceive the desperation of the Albany forces in among the freight cars and locomotives at the manor house railhead. On the flat meadowland to west of the tracks, the Albany hussars wheeled to face the Mamaluke lancers, no longer in their flamboyant plumes and breastplates but now hunched over the shafts of their leveled weapons in drab camouflage and flat-peaked caps. Again the breathlessness, the combination of excitement and fear, was interwoven with the filmy vision, the pulsing emotions of men not only fighting for their own survival, but for the survival of their country, their world, and their way of life.

"Focus, Argo. You're not there to see the sights!"

Yes, focus, Argo. Jesamine was reminding him that he was not where he was to merely observe, but to search out the enemy and report its actions. She stood next to him, more in the real world than in the Other Place, but closer to him and more solid than any of his other surroundings, and linked to him by a thick lifeline of energy that then went on back to Cordelia and Raphael. It was a totally untried configuration for the Four, and Argo had no idea how it might work out, but he still had to focus. He sent his perception into the darkness of the tunnel and all but wished he hadn't. Mosul soldiers were edging forward, muskets and breechloaders at the ready, and behind them, Dark Things, what looked like dozens of them, were massing. Argo had expected that the Dark Things, if they were there, would be coming from above, descending the real-world stairs from the blockhouse, but these were spontaneously forming out of nowhere. They began as small globes, no larger than a child's ball, but then rapidly grew and expanded like inflating balloons to their normal size of between four and five feet in diameter. They kept on coming until they were packed one on top of the other, filling the tunnel space with their reeking malevolence.

"Can you see anything?"

"Yes, and it's not good."

"Should we pull you back?"

"Wait. Let me see one more thing."

Argo again looked at the far end of the tunnel. The mass of Dark Things was closer. As he had feared, they were moving forward, following the lead of the human cannon fodder.

"Okay, get me back. They're coming. They're coming slow, but there's a hell of a lot of them. They're coming."

THE FOUR

The Four braced for the coming of the Dark Things. Slide issued his final instructions in a low voice. "Don't go all out. Be circumspect with your energy. Do what Argo did. Be here and there at the same time. That particularly means you, Cordelia. No showboating."

Cordelia looked bleakly at Slide. "After being shot at in the stable yard, I have no intention of taking any risks, or showboating, as you call it."

Argo faced the other three. "We need to make quick jumps. In and out. It'll be strange at first, but don't be distracted. There are regular Mosul humans up front. I think they're intended as a diversion. There'll be shooting, but let Slide and his soldiers deal with them. We need to go up and over and destroy as many of the Dark Things as we can and get out. Everything indicates that they are very stupid, particularly if they don't have the Mothmen telling them what to do. So we may be able to repeat the process a number of times before they figure out what we're up to. Remember, though, bullets will be flying, so take care of your physical selves. Keep your bodies well under cover."

The Four jumped for the first time, and the tunnel became a spiral. They were farther into the Other Place than Argo had been during his reconnaissance, and they rolled with the curves. The Dark Things were now in their Other Place forms, the unnameably impossible entities that Raphael had seen all the way back on the Continental Highway, with angular, disgusting limbs, slime-coated and seemingly without bones, and huge, revoltingly distorted vulture heads that pulsed with dimly obscene energy. In front of them were the shadow shapes of the advancing Mosul, but they would be the concern of Slide and the men in the real world. The gross mass of Dark Things was the target for the Four, and, as on the previous occasion that the Four had gone on the offensive, it was Cordelia who had conjured the weapons. A stream of flat, sharp-sided rectangles flew from her Other World form and sliced viciously into the creatures of the enemy, and a terrible nonhuman screaming started. The others followed suit, and for a moment it seemed like a massacre was taking place. The Dark Things took a few subjective moments to respond, but without doubt the dark red globes that suddenly streamed from the screaming mess would have done terrible damage if any of the Four had been touched by one.

Jesamine read the situation unerringly. "Out! Out now!"

They dropped back into the real world to find themselves buffeted by a cacophony of gunfire. Bullets and musket balls ricocheted from the brickwork, and billows of black gas made the air almost unbreathable. The defenders all had their gas masks in place, and some of them could only have been firing blind, in a blurred confusion, as sweat fogged the glass eyepieces. Slide yelled quickly to Argo. "What did you do out there?"

"As much damage as we could, and then we got out."

"At least a dozen of the damned things burst like huge, ugly bubbles."

"Then we must be doing something right." He looked to the other three. "Back in?"

They nodded. Their adrenaline was pumping. "Back in."

Back in. The Dark Things were ready for them this time. They came into the Other Place and were met by streams of red globes, a hail of Other Place fire that they already knew was lethal to them in the form of the Four. The red globes were augmented by spinning spiky pale blue stars that could only be equally as murderous, but suddenly they had an added advantage. Maneuverable shields were around them with which they could deflect both the globes and stars and at the same time continue their own attack with the razor-sharp rectangles.

"Who made these things?"

The thought-voice of Jesamine supplied the answer. "I think I did. I realized we needed something, and it came to me, just like the weapons have come to Cordelia."

The globes and stars smashed into the shields with a noise like the pounding of heavy rain on a hollow roof, but the new protection held, even though each impact came with a completely out-of-proportion countershock. It took a few subjective moments for the Four to adapt themselves to these rewritten laws of Other Place physics, and in the course of this learning process, Raphael would have been brought down by a slashing vulture beak had not the Dark Thing in question suddenly let out a hideous violet scream as it cringed away from the impact of a slow-moving yellow particle, and then vanished.

"Who did that? What was that yellow thing?"

More of the yellow particles drifted lazily down the length of the spiral that represented the tunnel, and each time one collided with a Dark Thing, the creature screamed color and then disappeared.

"It's Slide. Those yellow things are bullets from his guns."

"We must be in a highly accelerated time stream if his bullets are moving so slowly."

"But so are the Dark Things. They just keep coming."

"We have to locate the source."

"The Dark Thing Mother." It was the voice of Jesamine again.

"What?"

The thought traffic between the Four was thick and fast and tended to jumble and distort when they all reacted at once. "I don't know. It was another of those ideas that just came to me."

"Has a way to destroy it come to anyone?"

Argo's thought felt profoundly unhappy. "I think I know a way."

"You do?"

"Use the weapons and shields to push forward to the other end of the tunnel. I believe we'll see the source."

It took all of their collective strength to move forward at the same time as manipulating the shields and maintaining the streams of destructive, cutting rectangles, and twice the Four almost came to a common grief when the shields slipped out of alignment and claws or beaks attempted to slash through the gap these errors created. They pushed on down the tunnel for what seemed like an eternity but was prob-

ably only a fraction of a second in the real world and were approaching the threshold of exhaustion when a thought flashed from Argo, who seemed to have adopted the role of scout.

"There!"

A monstrous nonform of slime, black light, and raw plasma was exuding shapeless quasilife that immediately grew beaks and talons, expanded into full-grown Dark Things behind the slashing and cutting appendages, and then moved down the tunnel to augment the attack.

"That's it."

The Four instantly launched a quadruple stream of cutting rectangles at the Dark Thing Mother but were shocked to see their previously effective Other Place projectiles harmlessly deflected by some kind of invisible barrier that could only be detected by a faint shimmer each time it was struck by one of the rectangles.

"Cordelia, do you have anything else?"

"Nothing comes to hand or mind."

Under attack, the Dark Thing Mother retaliated. Clouds of tiny red globes, no larger than pinheads, like blasts from a real-world shotgun, and quite as deadly as their bigger counterparts, screamed at high speed at the Four, who struggled to deflect them.

Jesamine's thought took on an aura of alarm. "We have to pull back."

"No!" *It was Argo.* "I believe I know what to do. I have to drop back into the real world."

"You're crazy. You'll be right in among them."

"You'll have to shield me."

Jesamine picked up on the thought. "It'll be the same as when Argo scouted the tunnel, only in reverse. He'll be in the real world, and we'll be here covering for him. We'll have the advantage, because we're moving on a much faster time scale."

Jesamine, Cordelia, and Raphael positioned themselves. "Okay, go."

Argo went.

He dropped into the real world with a bone-jarring jolt. Somehow, in the Other Place he had been maybe eighteen inches off the physical floor. Dead Mosul were under his feet, bullets flew around him, and Argo was hard-pressed to think of a more perilous environment. He was in the middle of a black mass of Dark Things that immediately snapped and leaped to consume him, but no sooner did they move than they exploded. The others had him shielded, and the worst that happened was that he was splattered with foul-smelling pulp. A part of him wanted to vomit, but he sublimated his urge to gag. He looked up and saw his objective. A sagging sack of leathery skin, almost three times the size of any of its offspring, sweating an oddly discolored fluid, clung to the roof of the tunnel. On the underside of the atrocious monstrosity, an orifice in the dead flesh spat out globules of black puss that dripped squelching to the floor and then proceeded to grow into the spheres he knew and loathed. He swung his real-world carbine, the dead man's gun, from his shoulder. He knew it would not have the same magick as Slide's extradimensional pistols, but surely the Rangers must have endowed the carbine with something, or otherwise why would the thought have come to him that the weapon would be of use against the abomination hanging over him? Argo raised it and fired. The skin of the Dark Thing Mother puckered under the impact, and it let out a banshee wail that came close to damaging eardrums in the confined space of the tunnel and must have been heard in the Other Place, because alarmed thoughts from the commonality crowded his mind.

"Argo, are you alright?"

"Argo, get out of there!"

Argo ignored them and pumped the trigger, firing again and again, until the clip was spent. The screams of the Dark Thing Mother rose in pitch, and the part of him still linked to the Four knew that the soldiers at the other end of the tunnel were reeling backwards, hands clapped to their ears. The monster's skin was punctured in a number of places, but it was far from dead. Indeed, he could sense it was preparing to retaliate. In what seemed like slow motion, it was detaching itself from the tunnel roof. He knew it was going to drop on him, to smother and absorb him. He tossed aside the empty carbine and pulled the only weapon he had left from his belt. As the monster freed itself from the brickwork with a gross sucking sound, he held the double-barreled pistol vertical so it was directly under the horror's reproductive orifice. He quickly cocked both hammers on the "cuckold's special," the one made by George and James Bolton of Jamestown, and waited for the thing to fall. Then, in the moment that it did, and without knowing what good it might do, he pulled the twin triggers and discharged both barrels with his hand actually inside the ghastly opening.

And the Dark Thing Mother burst apart. Argo was showered with unholy and sickening filth. He felt himself losing consciousness, and, as he spiraled into merciful oblivion, the last thing he saw was a vision of the face of Quadaron-Ahrach twisted in thwarted and cursing fury, silently vowing the most hideous revenge he could conceive.

EIGHT

CORDELIA

"Leave me the hell alone."

Cordelia had been in the furthest depths of a deep and dreamless sleep and saw no reason to awaken. She had trouble grasping why T'saya should be shaking her by the shoulder. They had fought the Dark Things and triumphed, although Argo had almost died or worse. What more did they want from her?

A voice was speaking to her, but what it said made little sense. "The Mosul are pulling back."

She opened her eyes, wholly unfocused and disoriented. "What?"

"The Old Guard has broken. They've been turned. There are reports that some of them shot their officers so they could retreat."

"I don't understand."

"The Battle of the Potomac is over. We've won."

"We've won?"

Finally she could see. T'saya had a tray on which reposed a cup of black coffee and a balloon glass of cognac. "Brandy for breakfast? Isn't that a little extreme?"

"You've slept for fourteen hours."

"Even so."

"Who alive today ever saw the Mosul in full retreat?"

Cordelia sat up and took the coffee. Now that the manor house was largely uninhabitable, she was in a railroad sleeping car parked on a siding by the railhead. "They're retreating to Savannah?"

T'saya shook her head. "No. That's too much to hope for, but they're pulling back to Richmond."

Cordelia sipped her coffee, took a deep breath to clear her head, and the immediate past suddenly came back to her. "How's Argo?"

"He's sleeping."

"I wish I was."

"He screamed for a long time."

Cordelia nodded. "He was screaming after we brought him out of the tunnel."

"He screamed for another three hours. Finally, I was able to give him some morphia."

"You don't have anything of your own better than morphia?"

"When it comes to pain, there's nothing better than morphia."

"But he's okay?"

"He's okay."

"And sane?"

"We'll see how sane he is when he wakes. He's strong."

Cordelia reached for the cognac. "I really hope so. Should I go to him?"

"Let him sleep. Jesamine's with him."

For a minute or so they were silent. Then Cordelia flexed her shoulders, wincing at the stiffness and laying aside her concern for Argo. "So are we going after the Mosul?"

T'saya shook her head. "Not yet."

"Why the hell not if we've got them on the run?"

"We have a few wounds of our own to lick."

"What turned the tables?"

"Taking back the tunnel was crucial. Without it, Dunbar could never have moved in the reserves to plug the gap. You four are heroes."

Cordelia looked at T'saya dubiously. "I hardly think we saved Albany on our own."

"The rocket bombs also helped."

"Rocket bombs? The Norse rocket bombs? They were finally used?"

T'saya looked at Cordelia in disbelief. "I thought you knew. You were on the NU98."

Now Cordelia was completely confused. "I don't understand."

"That was why the NU98 was diverted to Baltimore to meet the *Cromwell*. It was to pick up the Norse specialists who were going to make the rockets operational. The airship was supposed to take them to Brooklyn."

RAPHAEL

The vapor trail of a rocket bomb arced across the clear sky like a soaring symbol of victory and freedom. First Raphael had heard the elongated boom as the chemical propellants ignited and the projectile roared up its railed ramp some five miles to the north, then the hissing wail underlaid with a rhythmic coughing as it climbed steeply into the sky. Finally, at the peak of its upward journey, all sound ceased with a final cough. The tiny silver speck continued to ascend for a minute or so longer and then abruptly curved downwards, gathering speed as it fell like a falcon on its prey. With nothing to relate it to, it was hard to see, way up in the air, where the rocket might ultimately land, until the explosion, the flower of orange flame, and the eruption of dirt and smoke in among the retreating Mosul. Field Marshal Virgil Dunbar shook his head as the rocket exploded a mile or more beyond the Potomac, to the south, where the last of the Mosul horde was straggling away in the direction of Richmond. "Poor bastards."

After all that he had been through, Raphael was no longer in awe of any rank, no matter how elevated, and he looked at the field marshal with a puzzled frown. "They are your enemy, sir. I thought you hated them."

"Hate them, boy? Hatred is the fine line that every soldier walks, from private to general. Of course I hate them. I hate them for what they've done, and I hate bloody Hassan and all that he stands for, but the men on the ground? Are they that different from our own? We kill them, but can we really hate them? They bitch and complain, and they bleed and die, just the same as our own. You should know, young Captain Vega. You were one of them until a little while ago."

Raphael stood on the roof of the charred and shell-shattered blockhouse, looking across the river. He was again in the company of Slide,

Dunbar, and Dunbar's retinue of officers, in the identical location from which they had watched the start of the Mosul assault, except now they were seeing the Mosul evacuation. If, as little as a month earlier, anyone had told Raphael that he would be doing such a thing, he would have doubted their sanity and doubted it even more if they had told him that he would hold the honorary rank of captain in the Royal Albany Rangers and be considered something of celebrity, and maybe even a hero, but such seemed to be the case. He had woken from his long sleep to find that a new tunic had been placed beside his bed; one that carried the full insignia of a Ranger captain, but even though he had supposedly been fully accepted and even commissioned into the fold of Albany, he could not help but look with shock and considerable awe at the scene in front of him.

Where the massed lines of tents and bivouacs had once stood, where cannon had been arranged in neat lines and drab green legions had scurried about their regimented business, in the places where cavalry with titles from legend had pranced and paraded, and Raphael had seen men flogged and hanged, nothing remained but scorched and scarred earth and the sad and hideous debris of retreat. Gaping and still-smoking craters dotted the land to the south of the Potomac: the huge earth-wounds where the terrible rocket bombs had fallen, and the smaller shell holes gouged by the near-perpetual artillery barrage, while networks of abandoned, half-caved-in trenches disfigured what had for so long been the Mosul side of the river with an empty tracery of rout. Torn tent canvas flapped forlornly, like abandoned ensigns, and the charred uprights of burned barrack huts and supply sheds stood like black grave markers for the thousands of unburied dead who lay contorted and bloating amid the shattered guns, the now-silent fighting machines, the collapsed watchtowers, the broken wheels of overturned caissons, and all the other less-identifiable litter of a failed conquest. In the middle of it all, the blockhouse, although soot-stained and damaged, still stood.

Dunbar caught Raphael's stunned survey of the monstrously blighted landscape. "The field of victory can be far more daunting than the field of defeat, boy. When the end comes, the vanquished have either died or removed themselves. The victor is left with the blasted earth, the shattered trees, the counting of the dead, and the contemplation of the enormity of what he's done."

In Raphael's view, the dead seemed too numerous to even count. They not only occupied the land but seemed to cover the surface of the river. The corpses of men and horses still choked all but the deep water, caught like rotting logjams by the snags of half-submersed pontoons, sunken barges, destroyed landing craft, and still-floating but empty rafts. Telegraphs had come from the Norse cruiser *Cromwell* telling of a continuous stream of bodies and smashed and burning boats that had flowed past the ship since the start of the assault. The *Cromwell* had been stationed at the mouth of the Potomac, where it flowed out into the Chesapeake Bay, taking no part in the hostilities but ensuring that the Mosul had not been able to bring up maritime reinforcements.

Dunbar faced Raphael as the pillar of smoke from the latest explosion dispersed in the upper air. "You know, boy. If you and your friends hadn't given us back that tunnel, we might never have been able to do this. We would never have been able to move the men and guns in underground to plug the gap, and the Mosul would have reached the launching ramps before we ever got a single rocket into the air." At that point, however, a look of sadness had passed over the field marshal's weather-beaten face. "I fear, though, that these creations of science, just like the magick that you and Slide have brought to us, will be the end of warfare as my generation, and those who went before us, have always known it. In the future, wars will be fought at great distances and in places and ways that I cannot even imagine, and the old concepts of honor and chivalry will be anachronisms."

Raphael could see no way in which the scene on the other side of the river could be related to high-flown ideas like honor and chivalry. Maybe Dunbar knew better, but Raphael had learned enough in the ranks to believe that such things were delusions of officer vanity. Melchior, maybe marching with the Mosul army but more likely dead, had never talked of honor and chivalry. Raphael could see no way in which they could apply honor and chivalry to the walking wounded who still stumbled, lost and probably demented, in among the ruins and the stinking dead. Or the prisoners with their Albany guards, who were excavating the long trenches that would be the mass graves, or the Virginian scavengers who searched through the wreckage of battle for small valuables, hardly bothering the ghoulishly well-fed buzzards and ravens. A single Dark Thing flopped a few times, then flagged and deflated. The corner of Raphael's mind twitched.

The Other Place was still there. A victory had been won, but not the war, and sooner or later they would need him to go back there. Slide must have noticed his instant of revulsion, because he put a hand on Raphael's shoulder and started to steer him away from Dunbar. The field marshal noticed the move and smiled wryly. "That's right, Yancey. Take the boy away. Let the old soldier ruminate in peace on the changing times. They tell me the king is coming, and the boy needs to be ready. I hear he and his companions are to be decorated."

Directly they were out of earshot, Raphael glanced at Slide. "After all that's happened, he still calls me 'boy'?"

Slide smiled. "When you've been around as long as Dunbar, you call almost everyone 'boy.'"

Overhead, another rocket bomb climbed noisily to heavens in order to fall silent and then drop on the decamping Mosul.

JESAMINE

"So how are you feeling, Argo Weaver?"

Argo's voice was weak, and, although he struggled to sit up, he failed to manage it without Jesamine's help. He grinned lopsidedly as she plumped the field hospital pillows and tucked them more firmly behind his head. "I'm alive, but I'm not sure that's the good news."

"You're missing all the celebrations, boy. They say the temple bells in Albany have been ringing for four days nonstop, and no one in the city has drawn a sober breath in as long."

"I think the bells in my head have been ringing for about the same period."

"What do you expect? You were unconscious for two whole days."

She poured him a glass of apple juice from a jug that stood on the locker beside the bed. "Here, drink this. It'll make you feel better."

Argo took the class but only sniffed it. "The nurses keep telling me how it'll do me good. I'm getting to hate the goddamned smell of apple juice."

"You must be on the mend. You're starting to curse and complain."

Argo sighed. "Maybe it's like you said. I'm missing all the celebrations."

The field hospital had been set up in a schoolhouse a quarter of a mile or so from the manor and the railhead that had been specifically converted for the purpose. Argo shared a ward in what had once been a schoolroom with nine other officers. The room still sported a blackboard on one wall, on which the more ambulatory patients scrawled lewd comments on the supposed sexual proclivities of the better-looking nurses. Each bed was surrounded by optional screens, which, right then, were drawn shut to give Argo and Jesamine at least an illusion of privacy, although when Jesamine had drawn the screens soon after she had arrived for her visit with the fallen, it had drawn a good deal of shouted ribaldry from the other officers, which she found herself thoroughly enjoying. To be desired and courted was refreshing after a lifetime of enforced availability.

"If you reach inside the bottom of the locker, you'll find a little additive for this apple juice."

Slightly surprised, Jesamine did as instructed, and, just as Argo had predicted, she found a glass fruit jar behind a small pile of books. " 'Shine? You're laying in a hospital bed crocked on 'shine?"

Argo poured a stiff shot into his apple juice. "Makes it easier."

"How do you expect to get better if you're swilling that rotgut?"

"I took a hit to the brain, not a bullet in the chest. Besides, I'm still sleeping most of the time."

Jesamine still thought it sounded like craziness, and shook her head. "Where do you get the stuff anyway?"

Argo laughed. "You think a field hospital doesn't have its fixers and its black market? You ought to see what some of these boys get hold of."

"I don't want to think about it."

Argo proffered the fruit jar. "You want a belt, partner?"

Partner? Was that what they were? Since the battle in the tunnel there had been no chance to talk with Argo about what had gone before. She glanced round like she thought a nurse might come in and catch them drinking, but then shrugged. Argo certainly seemed stronger and more animated than when she had first walked in, as though laughter and companionship were actually speeding his recovery. "Ah, what the hell. Why not? We're heroes, aren't we?"

Argo winked. "So I hear."

As Jesamine mixed herself a moonshine and apple juice, she noticed Argo looking her up and down. He was definitely on the mend from his hit to the brain. Caught, he smiled sheepishly. "I like the uniform." Jesamine smiled and posed. "They made me an honorary captain in the RWA. Can you imagine that? Concubine girl is now an officer and lady."

"Does that mean you outrank Cordelia?"

Jesamine shook her head. "Cordelia was made a captain, too. In fact, she found a way to get a dressmaker to come down from Baltimore and fix up our uniforms just right."

Jesamine turned, displaying the quality of the tailoring, and Argo nodded. "It shows you off very nicely."

Cordelia laughed. "It shows off my ass is what it does."

Argo patted the bed. "Come and sit beside me."

"I'm not sure I can sit in this skirt."

"You'll find a way."

Jesamine perched on the edge of the bed and crossed her legs. Again she was conscious of Argo watching her moves. On the other hand, he was still very pale, and Jesamine hoped he was not putting on an act for her benefit. Jesamine was very fond of Argo Weaver, she had decided. More important than that, though, she trusted him. He was solid, and she felt a kinship with that solidity. She and Argo were the solid central axis of the Four, the midpoint between Cordelia's flamboyant and intuitive showboating and Raphael's concerned caution. "Seriously, Argo. Are you okay? I mean for real?"

Argo sighed and slowly nodded. He reached out a slow hand and rested it reassuringly on her knee. "I'm fine. I mean, I nearly burned out back there, but the strength is coming back. Right now I feel a hundred percent better for seeing you."

"Do you want to talk about what happened back there in the tunnel?"

"When that thing from hell fell on me?"

"When that thing from hell fell on you."

Argo looked away. "No."

"No because you don't want to remember, or no because you're not ready?"

Argo closed his eyes. "I don't want to talk about it because I don't even have the words to describe it." He abruptly opened them again. "We still know next to damn all nothing about the Other Place, Jesamine. We have to invent an entire new language to so much as talk about it."

"I know that."

"In fact, even though we've been through so much, we know damn all nothing about each other."

She was suddenly very aware that Argo's hand was still resting on her leg, pale white over honey gold. She covered it with her own. "We have a great deal to learn on both counts."

Argo gently stroked her leg. "You think it would be wrong . . ."

Jesamine shook her head. "No."

". . . to indulge in a little mutual education?"

Jesamine leaned forward and kissed him on the forehead. "I already told you. No, I don't think it would be wrong. It might even be therapeutic for both of us."

She straightened up and unbuttoned her tunic. She found herself charmed and amused by the way in which Argo's eyes widened. The white silk slip that Cordelia had given her scarcely hid her breasts. "Do you really think you're strong enough for the excitement I have in mind?"

Argo smiled a smile that was openly indecent. "Just be gentle with me, captain."

"I'm still concubine girl, baby. Only now I'm the one who decides who tastes the sweeties."

CORDELIA

Over the past two days, mountain men and partisans had begun mixing with the uniformed officers in the command tents as they came in from a fight on another front that neither Cordelia nor any of the Four had even known about. As it had been explained to her, on the second day of the assault, a Mosul flanking force of cavalry, infantry, and a dozen battle tanks had moved west, along the south side of the river, far enough inland to be concealed from Albany scouts. The plan had been for them to move some ten miles upriver, where the Potomac was comparatively narrow, with thick forest on either side, and way beyond the concentration of Albany defenses. The Mosul force was to make a crossing, advertising the fact as little as possible, and then circle back to attack the defenders from the rear. Fortunately, Dunbar and Kennedy had anticipated exactly such a tactic well in advance. The woods had been mined, pits dug on all the logical trails, and a force held in reserve ready to meet the Mosul before they even made it across the river. Unable to spare regulars from the main Potomac wall, the units to counter any flanking attack were specially recruited mountain men and partisans, companies of irregulars who had moved in from the Blue Ridge, the Shenandoah Valley, and the Appalachians, reinforced with Rangers and a large war band from the Montreal Nations led by Naxat himself. The force had been small in number but big on firepower and deadly ingenuity, and with the Mosul cavalry hemmed in by trees and undergrowth, and the fighting machines "about as useful as tits on a bull in that country," as one grizzled hillbilly had put it, the enemy had been turned and sent back downriver in time for the rocket bomb attack and to join the general rout as bearers of more bad news.

Cordelia had heard that, in the city of Albany, they were dancing in the streets, but here at the front, in the big tents that housed the mess and the map room, the atmosphere was more one of concern. Albany had saved itself, but in so doing had also sustained a terrible beating. The natural inclination of everyone present, from Dunbar on down to the Rangers guarding the entrance to the tents, was to go after the retreating Mosul horde and complete the process of destruction, exacting a terrible retribution for the Mosul's two centuries of fire and conquest. Even Cordelia knew, however, that this was simply not possible. Even after their bloody losses beside the Potomac, the Mosul still had an enormous army that could be augmented at any time with the dozens of town garrisons that were spread strategically across the countryside of Virginia and the Carolinas. Albany had thrown everything it had into holding the line at the river and, in the holding, had close to exhausted itself.

The general prediction, as reflected by the small blocks and flags on the big map table, was that the Mosul would pull back, probably no farther than Richmond, and laboriously regroup. Winter was mercifully on its way, and the Mosul did not operate well in the cold. If their supply lines could be disrupted, they could be kept freezing and hungry in occupied territory where food was already scarce. The civilians in Virginia would be starving, too, but such was the price of war. Already stories were coming in of uprisings in occupied Virginia, and also of terrible reprisals when those uprisings failed. Against such a background of disruption and unrest, Hassan would be slow to regather his strength, and if the main Mosul concentrations could be harried by hit-and-run raids and weakened by aerial rocket attacks, no action would be needed until the spring. In the spring, though, Albany would have to ride out on the offensive. They would have to cross the river and take the fight south to the enemy.

As far as Cordelia was concerned, spring was a long way away, and right there and then all manner of strange and exotic allies were moving into the weary but victorious Albany camp, and as a captain with no designated duties, and also a bona-fide heroine of the Battle of the Potomac, Cordelia was able to see and mingle with them in all their unkempt glory. Cordelia rather enjoyed being a heroine. She had no idea how long it was going to last, and she had resolved to make the most of it while she could. She was aware that stories were already circulating of how she, of all the Four, was the risk-taking daredevil, and she had privately begun to think of herself as Captain the Lady Cordelia Blakeney, Girl Ace of the Other Place. To make her joy of self-importance and celebrity complete, she had been told in confidence by a major on Dunbar's staff that the king, who was already in Baltimore and on his way to the front, would be decorating, her, Argo, Jesamine, and Raphael. Seemingly they were to receive the Golden Order of the Bear, and she rather fancied herself as a GOB. The medal was gold, with a very elegant purple-and-gold-striped ribbon, and she knew it would look just fabulous on her new captain's uniform. By an extremely deft combination of flattery, bribery, and deceit, she had caused a dressmaker to be spirited down from Baltimore to create a selection of uniforms and battledress for her and Jesamine. The designs had been entirely Cordelia's. Jesamine really did not have a clue beyond sheer veils and ankle bracelets. She had totally thrown away the RWA dress code to the point of styling the tunics of both the ceremonial and formal wear in the sharp, wide-lapeled style of the Rangers. That was what Argo and Raphael were wearing, and the Four should at least resemble each other. Especially when they came before the king.

Cordelia was well aware that she was using frivolity as a retreat of her own. It provided a refuge from thinking too much about all that had happened to her since she had boarded the NU98 for a day trip to Manhattan. During the fight in the tunnel, she had surprised and more than marginally frightened herself. She had never suspected she was possessed of such a wild and exulting ferocity, or that she was capable of enjoying the tactile feel of victory with such unseemly wantonness. Previously such teeth-grinding gratification had been reserved for the bedroom (and the backseats of some High Command staff cars), and she could not help but wonder if the exuberant delight she had enjoyed, since the dawn of puberty, in copulation and all of its possible refinements was maybe just a sublimating outlet for the warrior rage she was now discovering in herself. After much private reflection, she concluded that this was not the case. The joy of sex and the joy of destruction were two completely different emotions. Maybe linked, intertwined, and far from separate, but originally coming from two different places in the new and previously undiscovered depths of her psyche. The clincher in this internal argument was that, since the fight in the tunnel, she had walked around in an overheated condition of nearly constant desire. If sex was merely a substitute for the thrill of the kill in the Other Place, surely she should have been in a state of high satiation, and that was certainly not the case.

And, the Goddess only knew, more than enough objects of desire were crowding the Albany camp by the Potomac now the battle had been won, and Cordelia found herself one of the very few women amid a plethora, and seemingly infinite variety, of men, although she had heard that girls from the small sector of newly liberated Virginia were coming over the river by the boatload. Cordelia only had to look around the map tent to observe a cross section of the Albany male and his allies. Gentleman adventurers and tattooed Montreals rubbed shoulders with hussars from good families and bearded frontiersman from the interior, throwbacks to berserker Viking ancestry, with maybe the genes of a grizzly bear added to the pool some cold night. Not only was the selection of men exciting and varied, but it was spiced by the presence of an almost unbelievable selection of living legends. In addition to Yancey Slide, who, despite a growing familiarity, still caused strange things to move deep inside Cordelia, strange, unnatural stirrings that left her undecided as to whether they were nice or unpleasant, names from legend seemed to be all over the command post and the officers' mess. Bearclaw Manson was still around, having remained to see the outcome of the battle instead of vanishing back into the unknown. Cordelia knew Manson by sight, just as she knew Naxat and Chanchootok. With others, she needed names to be put to the hard, scarred, and weather-beaten faces. Members of English John's gang had been pointed out to her, although English John himself had refused to set foot in Albany until Carlyle II granted him a pardon for an alleged piracy and kidnaping from some ten years earlier. The Presley Brothers had been identified for her, along with Tommy McTurk, the absurdly overdressed Cassius Marcellus and his highlanders, and the Grisham boys, with their ivory-handled pistols and blue sunglasses.

Cordelia found herself basking in the admiration of leaders, heroes, and household names. She had been propositioned by the mighty and ogled by backwoods pathfinders in furs and buckskins, men who refused to be separated from their long rifles and looked like they had neither bathed nor seen a woman in at least six months. To a man, they had all been too close to death and needed her gift of life, and she entertained them all in her fleeting fantasies, imagining herself being wined, dined, and creatively debauched in a general's private railcar or having a reeking, bearded hulk bending her forward over the barrel of a cannon while she kicked and cursed and he rammed her like a beast from behind under a starlit sky with rocket bombs screaming overhead and bursting in the distance. The only blemish on this perfect world of temptation and attention was that Cordelia could not quite bring herself to succumb. At the most crucial of moments, she hesitated or made her excuses. The last time she had engaged in sex had been in consummation of the Four, and the return to it being for nothing more elevated than her own chills and thrills of idle excitement was a step that daunted her. She did not believe that the Four were locked in any kind of quadrilateral marriage. They had not gone into combat in the Other Place forsaking all others. She also did not think the bonds that secured the commonality of the Four would be shattered by any healthy knickers-ripped howling in a railcar or over a hard iron cannon barrel. But somehow Cordelia still hesitated.

Jesamine had proved no help and set no example. She had taken the easy way out by apparently falling for Argo, at least on a temporary basis, and Argo, who was of course the hero of the hour, and also still confined to a hospital bed, had little choice in the matter. He must have been well on the way to recovery, however, because, if the stories of stifled cries from behind the screens, and Jesamine's missing undergarments, were to be believed, his confinement was no impediment to their romance. The elementary answer would have been for Jesamine to take up with Raphael, but Raphael had resisted all attempts at being taken up with and looked to be suffering from a bad attack of combat aftermath. Where he had once seemed to be falling in love with Cordelia, he now avoided her and everyone else. With Argo in the field hospital, Raphael had their quarters to himself, and he spent most of his time on his own. Either reading behind a closed door or pacing the battlements like Hamlet of Denmark in the old book. He also spent a lot of time sketching the wreckage of war, and if Cordelia recalled the book correctly, Hamlet had not been an artist, so maybe there was a difference. Raphael's Mosul programming had to be breaking up like the ice on an April river, and he probably did not know if he was coming or going. He seemed to have attached himself to the periphery of Dunbar's staff, as though looking for the ultimate father figure. While he was in that kind of mood, he was of no practical use to Cordelia, and although he would ultimately come out of it, she did not see any signs that it would be soon enough for her to bother to wait.

The answer to Cordelia's dilemma did not come until later that night in the officer's mess, when, after three martinis, she found herself seated beside a young lieutenant of artillery who was in much worse shape than Argo. His ashen and horrified face had once been boyish and sensitive, but now it was glazed, with hollow cheeks and dark rings under wide, unfocused eyes. He was drinking gin hard enough to have had the bar steward leave the bottle, and his thousand-yard stare was down to five hundred or less. Right there and then, Cordelia decided that her duty was to fuck some humanity back into this young man before he went raving mad. An act of charity, therapy, and hope was clearly the delicate way to reenter the world of casual hedonism while still upholding her allegiances to the Four.

"Are you having trouble there, soldier?"

The boy looked up, devoid of comprehension. "What happened? Was I talking to myself?"

"You looked like you were about to start, so I decided I'd cover your back by speaking first. Now it looks to everyone like you're talking to me."

The young lieutenant squinted. "Are you real?"

Cordelia nodded. "Oh, yes. I'm real. In fact, I'm not only real, but I'm a captain."

"A lady captain?"

"You had better believe it."

"I'm being decorated by the king tomorrow for what I did."

"Me, too."

"I don't think I want a medal for what I did." Getting no response from Cordelia, the boy poured himself another shot. "I decided."

"What did you decide, Lieutenant?"

"I decided there were too many fucking bayonets, Captain."

"There's been plenty of horror to go round."

His hands were starting to shake. "We blew them to pieces at point-blank range, Captain."

"Let go of it, Lieutenant. And call me Cordelia."

"They kept on coming, Cordelia. When we ran out of ammunition, we fought them off with ramrods and shell cases. And you know something, Captain Cordelia?"

"What's that, Lieutenant?"

He stared horrified into his gin as though the liquor held a vision. "I'm afraid I enjoyed it far too much."

"Do you happen to know a cold and out-of-the-way cannon that you might bend me over?"

The boy blinked, stopped dead in his shell shock. "What?"

"I think I have to take you and your bottle out of here, because you seem to have forgotten what you were fighting for."

The lieutenant looked wary. "I'm not sure . . ."

Cordelia took him by the arm. "But I am. Bring your gin."

ARGO

Argo walked unsteadily in his immaculate new uniform. He was still a little weak, but he was determined to reach the platform at the rear of the royal train, where the investitures were to be made, without help. The sun was bright, making for a perfect autumn day, and he was all but overtaken by a sense of complete unreality. A voice that sounded a lot like that of Bonnie Appleford questioned him from inside his head. *"How the hell did you get here, Argo Weaver? How did you get to be walking up to the King of Albany to have a medal hung round your neck?"* A voice like that of his stepfather wanted to know how long he thought he could keep up the charade. *"You may have them fooled now, boy, but how long do think it's going be before they find out you're a shit-for-brains country turd out of Thakenham, Virginia?"* But they would not, and he was not. He had been given a strange and dangerous gift that had come out of nowhere, but he had used it to the fullest, and, in so doing, he had rendered such service to the kingdom that he could in no way be made to doubt his right to be where he was, even by the whispers of old ghosts. The only regret the ghosts could bring with them was that Bonnie Appleford was not there in person, in the flesh, brave and bawdy, to collect a medal of her own for her role in the adventure.

The Four moved forward to be honored side by side. Cordelia seemed hungover and heavy-lidded from dissipation. By all accounts, she had been celebrating the retreat of the Mosul in her own high style, but that did not stop her from being in an exceedingly good mood and turned out to stun in her outrageously styled uniform, with the clear intention of making every male at the battlefield investiture sick with desire. She was not, however, without competition. Jesamine's identical outfit clung to her with the same overt suggestion, and she walked with the pride of her new freedom and, in the unfamiliar and still-foreign clothes, a gliding and sinuous sensuality that openly challenged Cordelia as the focus of attention. In that moment, Argo felt a pride of his own in that Jesamine had, at least for the present, chosen to give herself to him. Only Raphael did not seem to welcome so much honor and attention. He moved with a rigid military precision and seemed to be maintaining an inexplicable emotional distance from his companions.

An honor guard of Rangers, some still with bandaged wounds but nonetheless at full salute, flanked the path that led to the platform at the rear of the royal train, while troops of the Household Regiment were lined up on both sides. The Crowned Bear banner of Albany and the royal coat of arms fluttered overhead. Although it was a ceremonial occasion, the victory was so recent, and the memories of combat so vivid to the men guarding the king, that they were alert and tensely watchful, scanning the sky and the surrounding terrain for any hint of a threat. Although the Mosul had gone, no one would put it past them to leave hidden suicide squads, waiting for a chance like the investiture to wreak sudden and deadly havoc. Raphael was the first to climb the four steps to receive his medal. The slim figure of the king, in a plain, understated uniform, had only the blue sash of the Companions of the Goddess to set him apart from the officers who surrounded him. Raphael and the king exchanged a few words, and then the Hispanian inclined his head and Carlyle placed the ribbon of the Golden Order of the Bear around his neck. Argo was too far away to hear what had been said, but he could easily see the slow smile spread over Raphael's face as he about-faced, away from the king, as though some pall of gloom had lifted in his mind. But then, as he stepped down from platform to make way for Jesamine, who was next in line, the Mothmen attacked.

THE FOUR

To say where they came from was impossible. The Mothmen just seemed to materialize from out of the sun in a batter of highspeed wings and slashing mandibles. At first it was hard to count their number, but later the survivors would all know there were seven in the first wave, and they attacked en masse and with a supernatural speed and fury. One of the Ranger honor guard was sliced almost in two, and the men beside and behind him were sprayed with blood and shredded flesh. Slide came from behind the last carriage with a pistol in each hand, firing as fast as he could pull the two triggers. The hail of bullets gave the creatures a moment's pause, and they rose defensively into the air.

Slide's wild gunfire gave Cordelia and Jesamine the chance to jump to the Other Place. Argo was a little slower getting there, and Raphael extended a helping handhold of energy as he made the transition. Cordelia and Jesamine had come in dream-high, but Argo and Raphael, probably because of Argo's weakness, entered low, close to the spill-through of the furor on the ground. Three Mothmen were closing on the king, a suddenly vibrant and targeted figure amid the grey, unfocused ghost images of the real world. With no time to be any more precise, Cordelia, with Jesamine at her side, loosed a searing sheet of primal white heat, and the wings of the nearest Mothman burned.

A Mothman crashed to the ground with a sound like falling liquid, smoke trailing from the charred remains of its wings. It tried to rise, but, all round it, the pump shotguns of the Rangers roared, reducing the thing to a cringing and unholy pulp. Guards from the Household Regiment attempted to hustle the king back inside the train, but Carlyle stood his ground with a drawn revolver and an expression of grim determination. "To me, boys. We'll not run from these hellspawned things."

Raphael's being was stretched into a screen of light particles that extended in all the multiple directions. He had defocused himself and let go of coherent form to become a living, asymmetric screen around the king, and, when the first Mothman attempted to batter its way through, it was thrown back by massive and momentarily crippling shocks, jerking it out entirely into the real world and the fire from the shotguns of the Rangers and the carbines of the Household Guard.

Following the example of the Rangers and the Household Guards, the rest of the parade quickly formed themselves into tight-knit, crouching squads. Down on one knee, weapons at the ready, all facing outward, one from the other, they covered the sky and the ground around their king. They had no notion of what the Four might be doing, and most would not have cared to have one. A potential clusterfuck had been turned into a fast, ad hoc, but workable deployment, and anything that emerged in an approximation of flesh from the flashing aurora above and around them would be brought down with a withering fire. An old-timer called out to the men in his squad. "We're in a shitstorm of magick here, boys. Just do your business and try to ignore it."

The railroad tracks leading away to Baltimore and the north, the ones down which the king had come, sang metallic. A close formation of five Mothmen, who must have been hiding somewhere up-country, were coming in low and at speed. Raphael maintained his shield, and Argo, who found that just entering the Other Place had used up most of his strength, remained static and provided a link with Jesamine and Cordelia, who, having transformed into deadly blue faceted teardrops of furious aggression, hurled themselves at this fresh quintet of enemies.

A young Ranger with a well-developed sense of theatre had grabbed a Crowned Bear banner and moved to stand beside Carlyle. His name was Hancock Pitt, and he would later be romantically immortalized in the painting by Gibbons. The real life tableau was said to have presented as heroic a composition as the painting, with the king under attack, standing in the middle of his kneeling riflemen, and the Bear banner flying bravely against a supernaturally burning sky. The only problem with this legend was that no one present had the time to look for spectacle.

With Cordelia beside her, Jesamine flew at the fresh formation of Mothmen with fire streaming from the heart of her being. How dare they go after her new-found king? The monsters would burn!

"Yes, my dear, these monsters will burn. But how many more will there be?" The

too-familiar voice whispered sickeningly, too clearly inside her own head. It had even maintained the hollow ring of the torture chamber. "How long will you be able to fight? How long before you are exhausted, and I come to take you?"

Jesamine must not be distracted. The voice of Jeakqual-Ahrach was just another weapon, a countermeasure, and her fury lashed the particle beams like a bull-whip as rage generated energy and a Mothman exploded.

"GET AWAY FROM ME, YOU OLD AND TWISTED BITCH!"

The scream seemed to work. The voice of Jeakqual-Ahrach became distant, as though being left behind in the speed of the confrontation. "I have a million more of those and others besides, concubine. You may win this skirmish, you might even save your king, but you will be mine. You escaped my pain and my technicians once, my dear, but they will have you again. That is both my promise and my prophecy."

The day darkened as an unnameable pall of something that was not smoke obscured the sun, and, in the gathering gloom, the steel of the railroad tracks sparked with strings of arcing electricity. The old-timer had told his comrades to ignore the magick, but now the magick was closing in on them. Rifles were clutched tighter, eyes rolled, and even the boy Pitt, holding high the royal standard, looked round apprehensively. When pulsing green light crackled silently along the armored surfaces of the railcars of the royal train like a poisonous Elmo's fire, no one cut and ran, although many secretly wanted to do just that.

Argo, with nothing to do but hold his position, perceive, observe, and remember, could detect faintly luminescent lines of control running southward to where the hordes of Hassan were beyond the horizon. He knew beyond any doubt that it may have been the sister who had attempted to disrupt Jesamine's concentration, but it was Quadaron-Ahrach who was the puppet master behind the attack by the Mothmen. Argo could also sense a distinct uncertainty on the part of both Quadaron-Ahrach and the Mothmen themselves. They were faced with a choice of making either the Four or the king the primary target of their attack. The death of Carlyle II would be a devastating symbolic disaster, but the Four represented a clear, present, and very active danger. Then, running through the system of control like a tremor, a decision was made. The king was to die, and all else was secondary. The remaining Mothmen sideslipped away from the relentless onslaught of Cordelia and Jesamine, and, massing as one, they hurled themselves in the direction of Carlyle II.

A pack of four Mothmen appeared out of the dark and lowering sky. Two were already burning from magick, and a third was brought down by the massed fire of men who were relieved to again have a part to play when it had looked as though they were fated to do nothing but wait and watch as the world they knew went insane. The fourth Mothman, however, came through all the defenses unscathed. The fourth Mothman had open access to the king.

Raphael's screen, having exhausted all the power he could muster, went down before the concerted attack. Cordelia acted entirely on her own initiative, half in the real world and half in the Other Place, and, bending time beyond what she had previously accepted as reasonable limits, she had enough solidity to push the king to one side and spear the fluttering horror with a shaft of light that was, quite literally, an extension of her arm, just as every fencing master had told her the good sword should be. The Mothman glowed and burned and was gone, and Cordelia collapsed.

Cordelia found herself lying on top of King Carlyle II in a way that would not have been seemly anywhere but in the aftermath of a life-and-death fight. Guards surrounded the two of them and solicitously assisted her to her feet, at the same time helping the king to stand and discreetly checking both of them for possible injuries. As they were disentangled from each other, Carlyle leaned forward and, under the guise of shaking her hand and thanking her for saving his life, smiled mischievously at Cordelia. "This might have been better if we'd been formally introduced and were in a place a little more private."

ARGO

Argo placed the box containing his Golden Order of the Bear on top of the folded clothes in the leather portmanteau that had been a gift from Prime Minister Kennedy. Then he closed the bag and buckled the straps. Everything was done. He was packed and ready to leave. In just under two hours he would be aboard the special and heavily guarded train that would take the Four north, first to Baltimore and then on to Brooklyn, Manhattan, and finally to the capital of Albany. Although both Manhattan and Albany promised more sophistication and urbane excitement than Argo had ever known, he was not leaving the front without a certain sadness. He could easily imagine that feeling was the same for the survivors of any battle, at least among the victors. When a unit formed up and marched away from the field, they were leaving the place where they had been tested and emerged intact, and they were leaving the place where they had achieved their moments of glory. The hard-won kinship with those around them was sundered, and both the elation and the horror were consigned to memory and increasingly fanciful barrack room tales, and, in Argo's case, as he was going to the rear, he would, in future, qualify for the contempt reserved by fighting men for the rear echelons.

The other three were also closing up their luggage in preparation for departure from their makeshift quarters, and, needless to say, the women were carrying far more than either Argo or Raphael, even though they had all started with nothing. They were taking a final look around when T'saya and Slide appeared in the doorway. They would be following the Four to Albany in a few days, after they had both completed some mysterious missions of their own. "You all ready to move out?"

The Four all nodded. "We're ready for the train."

"They've got that train better guarded than the one the king came in."

Cordelia moved a small trunk so it was beside the door. "This is what we heard."

Slide raised an eyebrow at the quantity of stuff that Cordelia had amassed. "Gifts?"

"From a grateful nation."

"You're out in the open now. The Four are no longer a secret."

Raphael sat down on the bed beside his single bag. "It would have been a lot better if we'd stayed one."

T'saya shrugged. "What could be done after the business with the king and the Mothmen?"

Slide moved aside as two privates, in fatigue overalls, started to carry out Cordelia's baggage. She instantly became the Lady Blakeney. "Be careful, you hear? Don't drop anything, or you'll be in fatigues for the rest of your military career."

"The High Command has managed to keep you out of the Albany newspapers so far, but most of Albany seems to know about you and wants to see you."

Again T'saya agreed. "You no longer have any element of surprise."

Cordelia glanced at Slide and T'saya as though she completely failed to understand their concern. "So? What do we have to lose? The enemy knows all about us anyway, so what's so wrong with a few parades? We've earned them, haven't we?" She turned to Jesamine. "You wouldn't mind being famous, would you?"

Jesamine seemed less certain and moved beside Argo. "Perhaps. I've never been famous, so it's hard to tell."

T'saya gestured warningly. "It brings its own pressures."

Cordelia appeared to completely forget to whom she was talking. "How would you know?"

T'saya regarded her coldly. "I was Jack Kennedy's lover once, girl. I've seen your high society."

Cordelia immediately regretted what she had said. "Oh . . . yes, right. I'm sorry."

Slide stepped in before the confusion could plough any deeper. "Your only option now is to become as good as you can get."

Cordelia pouted. "And I suppose that means a lot of boring training sessions?"

"It'll take work."

"But everyone's saying nothing's going to happen until the spring. We have plenty of time."

"I doubt the Ahrach siblings will leave you alone until spring."

A short silence ensued as each of the Four considered this. Slide had to be right. Quadaron-Ahrach and Jeakqual-Ahrach had been thwarted and humiliated, and they would be looking for any and every chance for vindication and revenge. They were not going to wait until spring. Finally Cordelia looked round questioningly. "There is one thing that I don't understand."

"What's that?"

"How is anyone going to actually train us? Who can teach us? Archbishop Belfast? Rabbi Stern? Shaman Grey Wolf? The Lady Gretchen? I don't think so. No one seems to know exactly what we are or what we can do. There's no one to teach us."

Slide laughed and made a unique and inhuman movement of his hand. "Don't forget me, Lady Blakeney. Don't forget Yancey Slide. I'm going to be with you, parade or no parade, every step of the way."

Cordelia's eyes narrowed. "You really don't see us as anything but a weapon, do you, Yancey Slide?"

A slow and less-than-pleasant smile spread across Slide's cadaverous face. "In that, my sweet Cordelia, you are, for once, absolutely correct. To me you are just a sword to be sharpened, an edge to be razor-honed and ground on the wheel."

Argo quickly stood up and reached for his bag before Cordelia could compose a retort. It was time this conversation came to an end, at least for the present. "Let's not keep our heavily guarded train waiting, shall we? Even heroes have to respect a timetable."

TO BE CONTINUED